THE POISON SEASON

**Books by Mara Rutherford
available from Inkyard Press**

The Poison Season
Luminous

Crown of Coral and Pearl Series

Crown of Coral and Pearl
Kingdom of Sea and Stone

MARA RUTHERFORD

THE POISON SEASON

inkyard
PRESS

ISBN-13: 978-1-335-91580-1

The Poison Season

For questions and comments about the quality of this book, please contact us at CustomerService@Harlequin.com.

Inkyard Press
22 Adelaide St. West, 41st Floor
Toronto, Ontario M5H 4E3, Canada
www.InkyardPress.com

Printed in U.S.A.

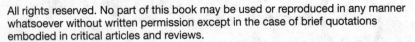

For Jack, my number one fan from the beginning.

I love you and everything is going to be okay.

Prologue

The wolf was not thinking of hunger as it chased its quarry through the dark woods, having feasted earlier that day on a large roe deer. It was driven by a sense of purpose, one that had infected its brain late last winter, when it had picked its way carefully across the ice to the wooded island that seemed so still and peaceful—and likely full of prey.

The wolf was not from this mountain. It had been born on another, not so far from here. The alpha had driven it from the pack, already aware that it would be competition some-day. But the wolf hadn't known that; it had only known that it was alone for the first time in its life. Alone, and hungry, and wanting…

There were no other wolves on this mountain. It had searched everywhere, but something about this Forest was not welcoming to wolves, or any other large predators, for that matter. It wasn't a lack of prey; it was something in the Forest itself. A warning of some kind, that this place wasn't for the likes of the wolf. But it was tired and hungry and search-ing, and so it had found itself on the island, padding about on silent feet, past the sleeping cottages and their unwitting inhabitants, which would have made a lovely meal. But the Forest told it, "No, they're not for you, either." And it had found itself in a pine grove in the island's center.

The wolf had snuffled at the base of the trees, picking up the scent of old blood and new growth, deep below the Forest floor. The roots of the trees, which had been replenished in a ceremony not long before the first snowfall, were always alive, even when the rest of the island slept. Feeling safe and quiet for the first time in many months, the wolf lay down amid the roots and slept a long, dreamless sleep.

When the wolf awoke the next morning, it felt *changed*. It was no longer hungry or tired or lonely. It was as if the Forest itself had sustained the wolf in the night, and now the Forest bid it farewell, told it to go away from the island, before the lake thawed and it would be trapped. The Forest only asked one thing in return: that the wolf nourish the Forest the way it had nourished the wolf. And now the wolf, which was still young and still learning, would finally fulfill its duty.

As the island came into view, the wolf released a long, doleful howl and drove its quarry onward.

Chapter One

The Watchers stood on the lakeshore, peering through the heavy mist that hung low on the water this time of year, when winter was just thawing into spring. Across the lake, the outsiders' voices were as hollow and mournful as a loon's cry.

Sound had always traveled strangely on Endla.

"What do you think they're doing?" Sage whispered against Leelo's ear, sending a chill down her spine.

Leelo shook her head. It was impossible to tell through the fog. They'd only been Watchers for a few weeks, and so far they'd had no interaction with the villagers across the water. They shouldn't even be here. They *wouldn't* be here if it were spring. Winter had made them complacent.

She stretched and looked out at the few remaining ice floes, scattered like the reflections of clouds on the water's glassy surface. The majority of the lake was too deep to freeze, and only the rare fool was bold enough to attempt the crossing. The carcasses of young migratory birds served as the occasional reminder—should anyone need it—of the lake's magic. They washed up on the shore with their feathers and flesh eaten away by a poison so strong it could sink a wooden boat long before it would ever make it across.

"Maybe we'll be lucky this year," Leelo murmured, more to herself than Sage. "Maybe no one will come."

Sage snorted. "They *always* come, cousin." She tugged on Leelo's blond braid and rose. "Come on. Our shift is over, and they're not going anywhere for now. Let's find Isola."

They hadn't seen their friend much over the winter, but Isola, who was a year older, had been finishing up her own mandatory year as Watcher. Now that Leelo had done it herself, she wouldn't blame Isola if she spent an entire month hibernating. Watching was both boring and exhausting all at once.

Leelo followed Sage into the trees, the soles of her shearling-lined boots quickly becoming mired in the mud and dead leaves left behind by the melting snow. She hated this time of year. Everything was dirty and drab, even their clothing. She wouldn't wear the bright, beautiful dresses her mother made until the spring festival.

Sage stopped to pluck a branch of red holly berries from a bush, quietly murmuring a prayer of thanks to the woods that provided so bountifully for Endla. As Watchers, it was their duty to protect their home from the merciless outsiders who had destroyed all but this, the last of the Wandering Forests. "We have to finish making our crowns. You haven't even chosen a theme yet."

Leelo sighed. "I still have time."

She had always loved the spring festival, but now she clung

to the days like a child at her mother's skirt. The sooner it was spring, the sooner her little brother, Tate, would be leaving, unless by some miracle his magic emerged before then. Whenever she thought of Tate out there among the outsiders, she wanted to cry. Because if she wouldn't be there to care for him, who would?

They left the main trail and made their way to Isola's cottage, where Sage knocked briskly on the door. Nearly a minute passed before it opened a few inches, revealing Isola's sleep-swollen face and tangled hair.

"What is it?" Her words came out as a croak, clearly the first she'd spoken this morning.

"We're sorry." Leelo ducked her head, already retreating. "We didn't realize how early it was."

"It isn't early," Sage said. "Isola is just lazy."

Leelo nudged her cousin with her elbow, though Sage had never been known for her tact.

The girl blinked a few times, trying to rouse herself. "I didn't sleep well, that's all. What are you doing here? Shouldn't you be Watching?"

Sage shrugged. "Our shift ended. Nothing was happening, anyway."

A shadow passed over Isola's gaze. "Nothing ever happens, until it does."

It was such a strange thing to say that Leelo wondered if something had occurred on Isola's Watch, something she and Sage had never heard about. It was entirely possible an outsider had attempted the crossing without all the younger islanders knowing. But any successful breach would have been announced. Outsiders caught by Watchers were always given a choice: the Forest or the lake. Either way, they were never heard from again.

A low voice called Isola's name from inside the cottage before Leelo could ask what she meant.

"Sorry, that's my father. I should go."

Sage rolled her eyes and turned back to the woods, not even bothering with a goodbye. Isola shrugged an apology at Leelo, and she smiled in sympathy, having borne the brunt of Sage's short temper for seventeen years.

Every rose has its thorn, her mother would remind Leelo after Sage had said or done something cruel. Her cousin *was* prickly, but she was also strong, intelligent, and fiercely loyal. If Leelo were ever in trouble, she knew Sage would come to her rescue, no questions asked.

They were almost back at their own cottage when movement in the bushes caught Leelo's eye. A flash of dark hair and pale skin. She stopped and looked around as if she'd just had an idea.

"You're right, I should get to work on my crown. Take my bow and tell Mama I'll be home soon?" Sage and her mother had moved in with Leelo's family when both of their fathers died in a hunting accident, when Tate was still a toddler. It wasn't unusual for several generations of one family to live together on Endla, but it was rare that two women would be widowed so young, especially sisters.

Fortunately, Leelo's mother, Fiona, and her aunt, Ketty, were resourceful women. Ketty had taken over tending to her family's small flock of sheep, which produced the wool Leelo's mother wove into clothing. Endlans traded for most of their possessions and food, so it was important to have a skill, something that few other people could provide. They weren't the only shepherds, but Leelo's mother made the finest woolen goods on the island. Together, the sisters were able to provide for their family, but winters were always lean.

"I can help," Sage offered, but Leelo shook her head.

"No, no. Aunt Ketty will be expecting you. I won't be long."

"Suit yourself." Sage hefted both bows and went into the house, the little string of bells they kept on the doorframe tinkling as she let the door fall shut behind her. It was several more minutes before Tate dared reveal himself, afraid he'd be caught shirking his duties by his strict aunt.

He had grown so much in the last year Leelo almost didn't recognize him as the same raven-haired baby she'd helped raise. He was so beautiful he was often mistaken for a girl, at least until he was old enough to walk and people saw him clad in trousers, not skirts.

Ketty had given him his name, calling him *as ugly as a potato* when he was born. She said it so often that "Tate" stuck, even though everyone knew it wasn't true. But sometimes, when Leelo's mother was nursing him to sleep in the middle of the night, Leelo heard her call him Ilu, "precious one," with a faraway look in her eyes that Leelo had never seen before.

"Come on, then," Leelo said, waving her brother closer. "You can help me make a crown for the festival."

He grinned, happy to be involved however he could. Islanders like Tate—*incantu*, they were called, or "voiceless"—weren't allowed to attend the festival, even though he wasn't quite old enough to be affected by the magic yet. Once an islander reached adolescence, generally around age twelve, they were susceptible. But even though she understood the reasoning behind it, Leelo hated the rule. As if the incantu didn't feel like outcasts already.

They walked in silence for a while, until the trail faded into the undergrowth and they were forced to forge their own path. "What should I choose for my crown?" Leelo asked Tate. It was tradition for each young adult to decorate a crown honoring Endla's flora or fauna, a way of symbolizing that they were all an important part of its ecosystem. Sage had decided on a deer. Mostly, Leelo surmised, as an excuse to wear something sharp.

Tate chewed on his lower lip for a moment, eager to come up with the right answer. "What about a fox?"

"Hmm… A bit too cunning for me, perhaps."

He stared at his feet, thinking. "A squirrel?"

Leelo grinned and twitched her nose. "I was thinking of something a little less whiskery." They had wandered close to the lake, but they weren't in danger of encountering an outsider here, where the far shore was barely visible.

"A swan!" Tate said suddenly.

"Now, where would I get…" Leelo's voice trailed off as she saw the cygnet floundering in the shallows. She glanced around, making sure they were alone, before picking up a muddy stick and hurrying toward the water.

"Careful!" Tate called, shrinking back. They were taught from the time they could walk to never go near the water, but the poison was always weaker at this time of year. Leelo suspected it had something to do with the ice melting, diluting the poison somehow, but she didn't know for sure. All she knew was that the swan would die if she didn't help it.

"Foolish fellow," she said, trying to reach it with the stick. It had stopped struggling, its heart and lungs probably already damaged beyond repair. Finally, she managed to nudge the swan close enough that she could reach it.

Wrapping her hand in her cloak, she took a hold of the swan's long, graceful neck. It was so weak it didn't even struggle.

"Is it dead?" Tate asked, peering over her shoulder.

"Not yet, but I'm afraid it's too late to save it." Leelo's fingers itched to stroke the gray down giving way to snowy white feathers. The creature was so beautiful she felt her eyes fill with tears. "The poor thing. It didn't deserve to die this way."

Every year, young birds made the mistake of landing on what appeared to be a pristine mountain lake, not realizing no fish lived in its waters, no plants grew in its shallows. Within a day, the birds were reduced to nothing but their hollow bones. Given long enough, even those would eventually dissolve. Leelo had never encountered a bird that was still alive before.

Feeling the creature's life slip away in her hands was somehow worse than hunting, because this death was senseless. They couldn't eat the meat, as it was already tainted by the poison.

After a few minutes, Tate placed his hand gently on his sister's shoulder. "It's not suffering anymore, Lo."

She sniffed and dried her cheek on her shoulder. "I know."

"Maybe you can wash the feathers and use them for your crown. Then a small piece of it will live on, in a way."

Leelo turned to look into her brother's brown eyes, her

heart swelling at his gentle earnestness. She rose and pulled him into an embrace. "That's a lovely idea," she whispered against his soft hair. "Will you help me?"

He nodded. "Of course."

Together, they rinsed the lifeless cygnet with fresh water from Leelo's waterskin, then wrapped it in Leelo's cloak before heading back toward the house. On the way, Tate gathered a few thin branches from the Forest floor, supple enough to bend into a crown. Leelo pointed out some brilliant blue berries that would make the perfect adornment. Tate plucked half a dozen, whispered a prayer, and placed them in his pocket for safekeeping.

When they were nearly at the house, Tate stopped to tie his bootlace and motioned for Leelo to kneel down next to him.

"What is it?" she asked.

He kept his voice low, though they were still alone. "Aunt Ketty is watching from the window." Leelo knew well enough not to look up. "She hates me."

"She doesn't hate you," Leelo assured him. "She's just Ketty."

He frowned. "She's going to wonder what we were doing."

"I'll tell her I asked for your help. Don't worry, little brother."

"I'm scared."

Leelo knew he wasn't talking about their aunt anymore. She reached out and cupped the dwindling roundness of his cheek for just a moment. "If it's any consolation, so am I."

They shared a small, sad smile before straightening. "I'll wash and pluck the swan," Tate said. "You should go and finish your chores."

"Be careful. Wear gloves."

He raised his chin as he took the bundled creature from her hands. "We look out for each other, don't we?"

Her chest ached with love, and with guilt for the lie she was about to tell. "Always."

Late that night, when everyone else in her house was asleep, Leelo sneaked out, taking a knife from the kitchen on her way. Guided by nothing but moonlight and her own sense of purpose, she made her way to the center of the island, to the heart of the Wandering Forest.

The trees here were special. Each belonged to one of Endla's families, serving as a kind of patron saint to which the family prayed and left offerings. But winter was the one season that the islanders kept away from the grove. Offerings required a song, and Endlans didn't sing in the winter. It was the only way to ensure outsiders didn't come across the ice inadvertently. After all, it was one thing for a Watcher to stop an outsider intent on attacking the Forest or its inhabitants; accidentally luring an innocent with song, however, was against their code.

But tonight, Leelo was prepared to violate the code. Prayers hadn't worked, which could only mean the Forest wanted a sacrifice. And while she wouldn't kill an animal—the killing song, which lulled prey into a trancelike state, was too powerful to perform on her own, and there was too much of a risk someone would hear—a small blood sacrifice might be enough to wake Tate's dormant magic.

She hunched down below her family's tree, a tall, stately pine that was hundreds of years old, as ancient as the Wandering Forest itself, according to Aunt Ketty. Even before she dragged the knife across her palm, Leelo could feel the music pressing at her throat, so eager to be released after months of silence.

As the blade bit into her skin, the music poured out of her along with the blood, and she almost believed she could hear the trees sighing, though that was probably just the wind. And the way the blood seeped into the ground so quickly, like the roots were drinking it up, was probably just the moonlight playing tricks on her.

And if somewhere across the water, an unwitting young traveler was tossing in his sleep, unaware that the lake whose shore he slept on was full of poison, or that the Forest on the island in its center was just awakening after a long, hungry winter…

Well, then, he should have camped somewhere else tonight.

Chapter Two

"Where have you been?" Stepan demanded, closing the door behind Jaren. He did a cursory inspection to make sure his son was unharmed, then let out a sigh of relief. "We thought the forest spirits had taken you."

Jaren cast a sheepish glance at his father as he walked to the washbasin. "I wish I could blame my tardiness on sprites or will-o'-the-wisps, Father. But—"

Before he could go on, his entire family finished for him. "You got lost."

He nodded. "I got lost." He'd never spent a night in these woods before, and he was grateful he'd managed to find his way home when he woke with the dawn.

"Of course you did." His oldest sister, Summer, smiled at him from where she sat whittling by the fire. She was as warm as her name implied, the gentlest of his three sisters. "You were daydreaming again, weren't you?"

"Head in the clouds, feet in the mud," his middle sister

sang, tutting at his filthy boots. As twins, Story and Jaren were closest in both age and bond, though Story had been born first and liked to lord those eleven minutes over him whenever possible.

Their youngest sister, Sofia, was still the baby of the family at fifteen. They called her Tadpole, mostly because she'd been as wriggly as frog spawn from the time she could move, but also because she pretended to hate it. Currently, she sat on their sofa, braiding her long red hair. "You didn't find any early spring flowers for me, did you? I'm so tired of all this." She waved her hand vaguely toward the front door.

"You *could* look for flowers yourself," Summer said.

"No flowers." Jaren held up his basket. "But I did find some wild onions."

Tadpole folded her arms across her chest, pouting. "I hate onions."

Story yanked on her little sister's braid, just hard enough to let her know she was being rude. "Then learn to cook your own food. It's time you did something useful around here."

Their father tapped a wooden spoon against the pot, his way of telling his children to settle down. Since their mother died, he had bravely taken over the cooking, and they'd all been surprised to find he was a much better chef than his late wife. None of them mentioned it, however. Stepan wouldn't have wanted anyone insulting his darling Sylvie's cooking, no matter how inedible.

"Leave Tad alone," he called over his shoulder. "She's tired."

"From what?" Story asked, her brown eyes wide with incredulity. "Sitting?"

Jaren left his sisters bickering in the family room and

climbed up to his loft to change. His sisters shared the sole bedroom, while their father slept on a pallet by the fire. The girls fought constantly, but Jaren sometimes envied their closeness. He knew he was excluded from their most intimate conversations because he was a boy, not because they didn't love him, but it made him feel separate from them. The fact that he was a dreamer and easily distracted didn't help.

He still couldn't believe he'd missed one of the trail markers yesterday, taking him miles in the wrong direction. By the time he'd realized his mistake, it was twilight, and while he didn't believe in fables and folktales like his father, he also wasn't foolish enough to try to navigate a rocky trail in the dark. With his luck, he'd twist his ankle and be stranded until another passerby happened upon him. Which, considering he hadn't seen anyone yesterday, could have been ages.

"Come eat!" Story called up the ladder. "The soup's getting cold."

Jaren pulled a clean shirt over his head and climbed down. He mumbled an apology, but the rest of the family was already dipping chunks of bread into their soup.

"Tell us," Stepan said, curiosity replacing his concern now that Jaren was home. "Did you see anything of interest in your wanderings? You must truly have gotten yourself lost this time."

"I found a beautiful lake," Jaren replied. "By the time I settled down for the night it was too dark to see anything. But this morning, I was amazed at how perfectly clear it was. I've never seen that color blue before."

Stepan raised his head from his bowl, leveling Jaren with a stern gaze. "What was the lake called?"

Jaren shook his head and fumbled a scalding piece of potato around in his mouth. "I have no idea. It wasn't marked."

"Closest town, then?"

"I was lost, Father. I honestly couldn't tell you if I was still
in this kingdom."

Stepan's expression remained stony. "You didn't drink from
the lake, did you?"

Jaren shook his head. "No, I filled my waterskin in a stream.
Why? Do you know something about this lake?"

Stepan glanced at his daughters. "Klaus told me there is a
lake in these parts, one that looks pristine but is actually full
of poison."

Jaren laughed, but his twin sister touched his hand. "I've
heard of it, too. From the townspeople."

Jaren was certain this was just another bit of local superstition. They had moved to the small village of Bricklebury a
little over a month ago, after their mother died and Klaus, an
old friend, invited them to rent his house for a good price.
Jaren knew his father was too haunted by memories of Sylvie to stay in their old home, and Bricklebury was a perfectly
nice town. But Jaren had never seen such a gullible, gossipy
group of people in his life.

Considering his mind was always wandering in fanciful
directions, Jaren himself might have been prone to believing in tall tales. But the stories Jaren told himself while he
walked and worked weren't fairy tales. They were stories of
what might be or what could have been, conversations he
wished he'd had or hoped to have one day. Maybe he only
felt lost because he was surrounded by three headstrong girls

who knew exactly what they wanted. But at eighteen, Jaren still had no idea where he was going.

He was tempted to tell his father just what he thought of this "magic lake." But he also knew if he didn't acknowledge his father's fears, he'd likely send his sisters to do the gathering next time. Jaren hated chopping wood and hunting, the two other duties he might be tasked with.

"I won't go back," he said, and he meant it. There was no reason to go so far afield, and besides, he'd slept horribly last night. He vastly preferred his own bed to stones and snow-melt. "But you don't need to worry, Father. I never saw so much as a squirrel out there. Spring is late this year."

"It always comes late this far up the mountain," Summer said, with the air of someone who knew something the rest of the family didn't.

Sofia shoved a hunk of bread into her mouth. "Says who?"

"Don't talk with your mouth full, Tadpole," Story said, elbowing her little sister.

Summer avoided their eyes. "I heard someone say it at the market."

"It's that carpenter, isn't it?" Story grinned, her eyes glinting in the firelight. "I *knew* you liked him!"

While his sisters teased each other and their father tried to quiet them, Jaren's mind was filled with a strange, mournful song he couldn't place. He had no musical ability to speak of, so it wasn't likely he'd made it up himself. And his mother, though she'd loved to sing, wouldn't have chosen something so sorrowful.

"Yoo-hoo," Story called, waving a hand in front of Jaren's face. "Where did you go?"

He realized his spoon was dangling in front of him, forgotten. "Sorry."

"You're clearly exhausted," their father said. "Get some rest. Your sisters and I will take over your chores for the rest of the day."

Jaren nodded and mumbled an apology. But, though he did feel exhausted in every fiber of his body, he lay awake for hours, trying to tease out the melody of the strange song in his head.

Chapter Three

Several days later, Sage and Leelo were sent to visit Isola. Her mother, Rosalie, had complained to Fiona and Ketty that Isola had been acting strangely all winter, sullen and tired for no good reason.

"Maybe she's ill," Sage suggested as they made their way to Isola's cottage. "She did look terrible when we saw her last."

"Or perhaps being a Watcher was too hard on her. Winter duty is exhausting."

Leelo had once asked her mother why they didn't start their year as Watchers in the spring or summer, giving them more time to learn before the lake froze.

Because the winter is long and takes a toll on even the more experienced Watchers, her mother had explained. *Going through it all at once is too much, so we split it up, make it a little easier.* Everyone, no matter their size or physical ability, was required to spend a year on duty, guarding the island. Leelo was still recovering from the night she'd spent in the woods, followed immediately by an entire day patrolling the shore.

Sage was about to respond when they heard a commotion from inside Isola's house.

"I don't want him to go!" she screamed. "You can't make him!"

The shrill desperation in Isola's voice made Leelo's skin crawl. "We should leave," she whispered, turning back to the trail.

But Sage shook her head and pulled Leelo along after her. "And miss this? I don't think so."

"Sage," Leelo hissed, but they were already crouched behind a tree, listening.

A moment later, the door to Isola's house burst open. A young man, half-undressed, was being shoved over the threshold by Isola's mother, who was beating at his head with a wooden spoon.

"Fool!" Rosalie yelled. "The ice is gone! Tell me if it was worth it when the lake takes you!"

The young man raised his arms over his head to protect himself, the muscles of his torso rippling with the movement. Leelo and Sage stared slack-jawed as Isola ran out of the house after her mother, clad in nothing but her shift.

"Please, Mother!" the girl wailed, but the young man was already tugging his shirt over his head and running through the woods toward the lake.

Rosalie snatched at her daughter's sleeve. "Stop this nonsense, Isola! You know he can't stay. What were you thinking?"

But Isola pulled free and ran after him, stumbling barefoot in the mud. "Pieter! Come back!"

Pieter. Now Leelo recognized him, though he'd been only a little older than Tate the last time she'd seen him. His father was a painter, and his mother sometimes bought Ketty's wool to make the warm felted boots they wore in winter. But beyond that, Leelo couldn't remember much about the boy, other than that he was incantu. What was he doing back on Endla?

"Come on," Sage said, yanking Leelo behind her.

Rosalie was following her daughter at a rapid clip, but she didn't run. She had to know Pieter would only make it so far. "Get your family," she called to Leelo and Sage over her shoulder. "There's going to be a drowning."

Leelo gasped, but Sage's expression was strangely intent as they ran back to the house. What *had* Isola been thinking? Leelo knew she would want to see Tate after he left, but she would never allow him to risk his life by coming back to Endla. And Pieter wasn't family, just a former friend who had somehow become something more.

When they reached the house, the girls pulled off their muddy boots before going inside. Sage paused to warm her hands by the stove for a moment as she hollered for her mother. "Hurry up!" she shouted. "There's going to be a drowning!"

Leelo's stomach twisted at the echoed phrase. She had always been too sensitive, according to Aunt Ketty. Whenever a lamb was slaughtered for their summer festival, Leelo didn't have the heart to eat it. It wasn't the sight of blood that made her vision tunnel and her knees grow weak; it was the thought of anything enduring that much fear and pain. And while she knew a drowning wasn't a slaughter, exactly, that Pieter had chosen his own fate, he was nevertheless going to suffer greatly.

Ketty came in from the yard, where she'd been chopping

firewood. She had the same auburn hair and hazel eyes as Leelo's mother and Sage, while Leelo had her father's silvery blond hair and blue eyes. Tate didn't look like any of them. Her mother said he resembled their grandfather, who had died before Leelo was born.

"A drowning?" Ketty asked, hanging her apron on a hook near the door. "Are you sure?"

Sage nodded. "It's Pieter Thomason. He was in Isola's house. He must have come across the ice and hidden all winter. Isola's mother chased him into the woods."

Ketty sucked in a breath. "Poor Rosalie. This will be a lasting shame on her family."

Leelo had never heard of an incantu returning to Endla, and she wondered how this differed from an outsider trespassing. But unlike her aunt, Leelo wasn't thinking of Rosalie. She was thinking of Isola and, more importantly, Pieter.

Ketty shook her head, muttering to herself. "Best get Fiona. She's upstairs resting."

"I'm awake." Leelo's mother came down the stairs on unsteady legs, leaning heavily on the wooden banister. She had been weak and tired often lately, though she promised she was fine. Leelo had helped her with the weaving and embroidery before she became a Watcher, but now Fiona had to do all that work herself. "Pieter Thomason, you say?"

Leelo took her mother's arm and helped her into a chair by the fire. "We can stay here, if you're not feeling well enough."

"Everyone has to attend," Ketty said. "You know that."

"Mama?" Leelo crouched down next to her mother. "I don't mind staying."

"I don't think I have the strength for it," Fiona said to Ketty.

"Exactly why you should come, sister. The singing will help bolster you."

Fiona frowned and rubbed her temples. "My head is pounding. I'll try to follow, but you should go ahead, Leelo." Her mother's voice was soft with compassion, though she looked troubled. "That poor boy. And his parents. I wonder if they know."

Leelo bit at the jagged edge of a fingernail. Her mother understood how much Leelo hated the drownings, but she had missed the last one, when a man who claimed to be lost in a snowstorm was found by a pair of Watchers on their first day of duty. He had been given the same choice as everyone else, and Leelo had been surprised when he chose the Forest. In the winter, there was at least a chance of making it across the ice. But the Forest would no sooner tolerate an outsider than a dog would a flea. The man had been crushed by a falling tree within minutes of his release.

Leelo's repeated absence would be noticed. Besides, drownings were important to Endla. They were a reminder of how precious this place was and how vital it was they protect it at all costs. Only the incantu were spared from these occasions, as they weren't considered true Endlans.

Despite the food and shelter the Wandering Forest provided, outsiders believed it was evil, as Aunt Ketty had explained a hundred times. *That's how outsiders are. If they don't understand something, like the Forest, they have to destroy it. Anything that doesn't function the way they decide it should doesn't deserve to live in their eyes.*

That was why all the other Wandering Forests had been chopped down or burned by outsiders and why it was so vital no harm should come to Endla. Pieter wasn't an outsider, of course, and he likely had no intention of harming the Wandering Forest. But if he could come across the frozen lake so easily and remain hidden, what was to stop an outsider from doing the same?

"All right, Mama," Leelo said finally. "We'll be back soon." With a pit forming in her stomach, she donned her muddy boots and trudged back into the woods with her aunt and cousin.

Sage linked her arm through Leelo's, and she could feel Sage's—she didn't want to say *excitement*, though that was what it felt like—buzzing inside of her. "I know you hate it, Lo. But it's necessary. He can't stay here. You must understand that by now."

"I do," Leelo said because it was easier than arguing with Sage. But surely Pieter didn't *have* to die. She thought of him stumbling out of Isola's cottage half-naked, how vulnerable humans were when it came to the violence of nature. A flash of memory—the way the roots of her family tree had so eagerly absorbed the blood sacrifice—made the wound on her hand pulse with pain. She had seen birds fly into trees and never fly out again, had even watched an entire deer disappear into a sinkhole once. She knew all too well what the Forest was capable of.

As they reached the water's edge, Leelo saw that a crowd had gathered near the shore, spread out in a half-moon shape. Sage pushed her way through to the front, dragging Leelo along with her.

Pieter stood with his heels nearly touching the water, brandishing a stick as though it could protect him. He bared his teeth, reminding Leelo of a badger she'd once caught in a snare. She didn't know if an incantu was given the same choice as an outsider, but it seemed Pieter had chosen for himself.

"Stay back!" he shouted, waving the stick at a woman who had come close to jeer at him. "I mean it."

"Pieter, please!" Isola was screaming again, but her mother and two other islanders restrained her. "Stay with me!"

"Hush," her mother said, trying to calm her daughter. "You know that's impossible."

Pieter glanced behind him. There were a few small ice floes left. The nearest was only a couple meters offshore, but there was no way to reach it without touching the water. Leelo scanned the crowd for Pieter's parents and found them standing stoically near the end of the line of islanders. Aside from a few tears on his mother's cheeks, you would never know their son was about to die. *Why didn't they do something?* Leelo wondered. How could they just stand there and let this happen?

Suddenly, Pieter spun and hurtled through the shallows, somehow reaching the nearest ice floe. He stood there, his legs spread in a wide stance for balance, searching frantically for his next move. The islanders watched as he made a leap, landing half on the ice and half off.

"Look!" someone shouted. A group of outsiders had gathered on the far shore.

"Hurry, Pieter," one of them called. "You can make it!"

Pieter was almost halfway across the lake, but the ice was even more sparse on the far side. There was no way he could reach it without swimming. The outsiders were hauling a boat through the mud toward the water, but they seemed hesitant to risk it. Leelo couldn't blame them.

"Help!" Pieter screamed as the ice beneath him cracked. One moment he was standing, and the next he was gone with only a small splash and a strangled cry.

"Pieter!" For one moment, Isola burst free, but the others managed to grab her again before she reached the water. It was clear to Leelo she would have gone in if they hadn't stopped her.

"This is awful," Leelo sobbed, turning her head away, but Aunt Ketty was right beside her.

She grabbed Leelo's jaw and forced her to look at the water. "You must bear witness to their foolishness," she insisted. "See what happens when we don't put the island above all else?"

Pieter resurfaced for a moment, but Leelo knew it was hopeless. Once the lake took hold of its victims, there was no turning back. As he disappeared again, the islanders spread out along the bank, linking arms with each other. Leelo found herself between her aunt and cousin, who had already closed their eyes and bowed their heads.

It was still winter, but every sacrifice deserved a song. This one didn't lure creatures like the hunting song, or pacify them like the killing song. Her mother said it was for the lake, to ask it to be gentle with its victims. Though not truly a part of the Forest—the lake had been here before the Wandering Forest and would remain should it ever leave—it was nevertheless their protector. *But there is nothing gentle about this death*, Leelo thought as she remembered the swan. She only hoped it was swift.

The first note was so low that Leelo barely heard it. One by one, the others joined in, the mournful dirge echoing in her ears as her own lips formed the notes of the drowning song.

As much as she hated the drownings, feared the poison of the lake and the hunger of the woods around her, she couldn't stop her magic any more than she could stop the changing of the seasons. Once again, she felt that insistent press against her throat: the music and the magic, desperate to be free.

Across the lake, the villagers thrust their hands over their ears and fled like a herd of deer.

Leelo watched the spot where Pieter had disappeared, wondering if his bones would wash up on this shore or the other, if they ever made it out of the water at all. She wondered if his parents were singing, if they had known he'd returned, or if he'd kept the secret from everyone but Isola.

It seemed so unfair, to be first punished by being born without magic, and then again by being forced to leave. But the incantu weren't safe on Endla. Because the islanders would sing again, and those without magic would no sooner be able to resist it than a moth could resist a flame.

Leelo knew then that the only thing worse than her brother leaving would be to find herself here, standing on the lakeshore, singing the drowning song for Tate.

Chapter Four

That night, Fiona gently brushed Leelo's long hair while Ketty pulled Sage's auburn strands into something resembling a plait. Tate was already asleep, and the living room was silent save for Sage's muttered protests and the crackling of the fire.

All day, Leelo had been trying to make sense of what they had witnessed. She'd always believed there would be no contact with Tate once he was gone and that anyone who knew what the Forest was capable of would run as far from it as possible so they would never be tempted to return.

As a child, Leelo had doted on her little brother, before she understood that he would be leaving by his twelfth birthday—only weeks away now—if his magic didn't come. It was generally assumed that if it hadn't appeared by then, an Endlan was well and truly incantu, and while they may not immediately fall prey to Endla's music, they would eventually. It was a far better fate to leave early than to stay until it was too late.

Around his tenth birthday, Tate gave up on singing his

prayers to the Forest and began speaking them instead, knowing there was no magic in his voice. Leelo did her best to distance herself from him then, but it quickly became clear that the separation would be as painful as severing a limb, whether they did it now or when it came time for him to leave. He still tried to crawl into her side of the bed on cold nights, and sometimes she didn't have the heart to kick him out. Sleeping next to him, his face still bearing the slightest traces of baby fat, she couldn't imagine him alone in the world.

"Why do we send them away?" Leelo whispered, even though she knew the answer.

"Those without magic aren't strong enough to resist it," Fiona said, her voice so soft it made Leelo's eyelids heavy. "That's why we can't allow them to stay on Endla."

Leelo sighed. "But surely we could protect them somehow."

"You know that's impossible. They would run straight into our traps the moment we sang the hunting song," Ketty answered, her voice as sharp as her gaze in the firelight.

Sage scrambled away from her mother's rough hands and picked up a set of small antlers, still covered in soft velvet. The young buck she'd taken them from had died of natural causes; hunting wouldn't resume on the island until after the festival. Sage had strung holly berries on a thread earlier and now proceeded to wind them around the antlers, fashioning her crown for the spring festival.

"So what if a few incantu are caught," she said. "At least the Forest would be sated."

Leelo frowned at her cousin. "How can you say that? Just because someone doesn't have magic doesn't mean they deserve to die."

"Which is precisely why we send them away," Ketty said. "It's a kindness, not a punishment. Pieter knew the consequences of coming back."

"What about the consequences of harboring an incantu?" Sage asked.

Ketty cleaned her daughter's hair out of the comb and tossed it into the fire, where it was quickly reduced to ash. "Isola's family will be shunned. For a time, anyhow. I'll speak with the council on Rosalie and Gant's behalf. They are too much a part of this community to be outcasts forever, and it doesn't seem as if they knew about Pieter until today."

"And Isola herself?" Sage pressed.

"That poor girl will be dealing with the consequences for the rest of her life," Fiona said quietly.

Sage rolled her eyes, unsatisfied with this response. "No one will marry her now, I bet."

"Isola is ruined," Ketty agreed. "If her parents are smart, they'll turn her out sooner rather than later. There's no reason they have to be pulled down by her mistake."

Leelo's heart ached for Isola. She couldn't imagine being turned out by her own family. "But Pieter was one of us, and he wasn't harming anyone. We didn't even know he was here until today."

Ketty scowled. "Once an incantu leaves, they're an outsider, and outsiders are forbidden on Endla. Why must we go over this a thousand times, Leelo?"

"Not all outsiders are evil, Ketty."

Leelo turned to look at her mother. She rarely spoke, and when she did, it was usually to agree with her sister. But tonight, it seemed, she wasn't in the mood to placate.

Ketty responded to her sister's comment with a look that could cut flesh.

"I'm tired," Fiona sighed, rising from her chair. "I think I'll go to bed."

Taking their cue from Fiona, Leelo and Sage headed upstairs to their shared room, leaving Ketty to smolder in the dark along with the embers.

Sage and Leelo prepared for bed in silence, but Fiona's words played over and over in Leelo's mind as she climbed into bed, toying with one of the balls of bright felted wool she had made and strung into garlands. They hung from the headboard, the windowsill, the little bookcase they shared. The only other decoration was a pink-and-red circular woven rug that took up most of the floor. Their grandmother had woven it, before she died. It told Endla's story, if you knew how to read the colors and patterns.

When she was younger, Leelo had asked her mother about it. "I know we came here to protect the Forest and ourselves," she'd said. "But what happened out there in the world that was so terrible we had to leave?"

Fiona had sighed, as if she'd known this moment was coming. "Our ancestors once lived in a small walled city on the mainland, cut off from the rest of the world. But one day a little girl from a nearby village was lured away from her home by our singing, and she was never seen again. The villagers attacked the city, trapping many of our people inside the walls and setting fire to everything within. But some escaped, and they fled up the mountain, desperate for shelter.

"When they came to Lake Luma, they say the island called to them. One of our people had snuck into a nearby town to get supplies, and she heard the locals talking about the Wandering Forest, how it was evil, devouring anyone who traveled to the island. Many had gone there to try to put an end to the Forest—or at least to drive it somewhere else, where it could no longer harm humans. But those people never returned. Our ancestors decided to risk the Forest."

"How did we cross the lake?"

"It wasn't poisonous back then," Fiona had explained. "When all our ancestors made the voyage safely and the villagers could see that they were still alive on Endla, they decided to cross and burn everything down, including our people. They made an assault on the island a few weeks later. But before they could reach the far shore, their boats began to disintegrate. Dozens of outsiders drowned. They tried again, several weeks later, and the same thing happened. The lake had become poisonous, and it could never be crossed safely again.

"The Wandering Forest had found people who would protect it, and so it, in turn, protected us."

Chapter Five

Days passed, and no one spoke of the drowning. It bothered Leelo that people could simply pretend a man hadn't died, or worse, that he had never lived. She tried not to think about Pieter, but she worried for Isola. She hadn't seen her friend since that morning, and she doubted she'd be coming to the spring festival tonight.

Fiona straightened the hem of Leelo's new dress and looked up, her eyes wet with tears.

"What is it?" Leelo asked, staring down at her mother with concern.

"I was just thinking how beautiful you look."

"And that made you cry?" Leelo teased.

Fiona smiled and rose to her feet, wobbling slightly. "I know you're becoming a grown woman, but it's hard to believe I was only a few years older than you are now when I gave birth to you."

According to their culture, the children of Endla became

adults during their year as Watchers. But Leelo didn't feel grown-up, and she certainly didn't feel ready to have children. She frowned and turned to look in the mirror. The swan crown, which her mother had helped make, started at the front of Leelo's hairline and swept down like two wings to the back of her head, just above her plait. The berries were clustered like blue jewels at the front of the crown.

Her new dress had been made to flatter her complexion, the wool dyed in soft tones from the pale sky of her eyes to the wintergreen of snow-covered pines. A pattern of snow-flakes, winter-white foxes, and silver pinecones decorated the skirt; the collar, cuff, and hem were trimmed in soft white rabbit fur.

"You look like the Snow Maiden," Sage said from the doorway. Her own dress was woven in autumnal shades, with tawny deer, russet squirrels holding hazel acorns, and golden oak leaves decorating the fabric. A small capelet made of deer hide was tied over her shoulders. She had already donned her antler crown, the red berries bright against the tines.

Leelo smiled and took Sage's hand, leading her downstairs. They were both too anxious to eat much, so Aunt Ketty gave them a breakfast of toasted bread and blackberry jam.

"Careful not to stain your dresses," she said. "Our mother wasn't nearly as good at sewing as Fiona, and you'll want to save those for your own daughters."

Sage rolled her eyes. Her maternal instincts, if she had any, had yet to surface. Both girls had been there for Tate's birth, but while Leelo had been in awe of her mother's strength and the quiet assuredness of the midwife, Sage had seen only blood and pain.

"Yes, Aunt Ketty," Leelo said. The truth was, she didn't know if she wanted children. But Endlans had a responsibility to maintain their population, not only to keep their magic alive, but as protectors of the last Wandering Forest. At least she had a few more years before she would be expected to marry.

"Come on," Sage said, shoving aside her half-eaten breakfast. "We don't want to be late."

Tate peered at Leelo from behind the door to his little room below the stairs and gave a shy wave. Leelo waved back, feigning cheerfulness. She had often fantasized about keeping him on the island, even if his magic didn't come. They would build a little house on the far side, where few islanders went, and Leelo would visit him every day.

But she knew now that was no kind of life for Tate. He would be miserable all by himself. The best she could hope for was that he would find other exiled Endlans to live with so he wouldn't lose touch with his home completely.

"We'll be back in a few hours," Leelo assured him.

"Stay here," Ketty said, as if he didn't know. "And whatever you do, don't go near the lake." The spring festival always marked the day when Endlans could sing again.

Tate nodded and retreated into his room.

"You don't have to be so stern with him." Fiona knelt down to help Leelo with the laces of her knee-high boots. "He's a good boy."

Ketty didn't reply.

Outside, Leelo was surprised to see Isola trudging down the trail ahead of them. She had assumed Isola wouldn't come today, given the fact that her family was being shunned, as her aunt foretold. Ketty had forbidden the girls from going to visit their friend, but Isola was here now, and Leelo wasn't going to ignore her. She noticed with a start that Isola's long, dark hair had been cut almost to her chin.

"Isola," Leelo called, trotting to catch up to her.

The girl gazed at her with empty eyes. "Leelo."

"Are you… How are you?"

Isola turned back to the trail ahead. "I'm fine."

Leelo thought of offering some kind of condolence for what had happened to Pieter, but what could she possibly say? He was gone, and Isola must feel partially responsible.

Sage strode up next to them, oblivious. "I can't believe it's finally our turn," she said, twirling as she skipped along the trail. "Seventeen years spent watching other people partici-pate in the ceremony, and now we get to do it."

"Congratulations," Isola muttered. "You both look nice."

Leelo glanced down at Isola's dress, a simple cream-colored wool embroidered with flowers. Her mother had made it for her, but it wasn't nearly as fine as Fiona's work.

"What happened to your hair?" Sage asked. Leelo shot her an admonishing glance, but Sage didn't notice.

"My mother cut it."

Sage frowned. "Why?"

"Because I stopped brushing it."

Leelo could feel the sadness coming off the girl in waves. Hesitantly, she put her arm around Isola's waist and drew her against her side, and Isola let her head fall on Leelo's shoulder.

Leelo bit her lip and glanced behind her. Rosalie and Fiona were walking together, talking in hushed tones, no doubt about Pieter and how badly Isola was taking his death. Ketty tried to urge her sister on ahead, but Fiona ignored her.

Leelo realized her shoulder was wet, that Isola was crying. "Why did you come today?" she asked gently.

Isola sniffed and wiped her face on her sleeve. "The council said we had to, that it was important to make an example of me to the new Watchers. But I'll understand if you don't want to talk to me. You could get in trouble."

Sage winced and trotted ahead to join some of the other villagers, and a part of Leelo—the part that followed rules, that would never betray Endla, especially if it meant bringing shame on her family—longed to join her. But instead she let herself feel the dampness on her shoulder, the tangible reminder of Isola's suffering, and stayed.

They had finally reached the far side of the island from where Pieter had died. They came here for the spring ceremony and little else. The opposite shore was clearly visible from here, but there was no nearby village on the mainland this side of the island, so the threat of outsiders observing them was lower. The Watchers were sometimes told to patrol this area, but Leelo and Sage hadn't been here since last year's ceremony, when one of their distant cousins had been celebrating. It wasn't mandatory for Endlans to attend, but as one of the island's ten elected council members, Ketty went every year.

This year, twelve adolescents had become Watchers, and most had already arrived with their families. They greeted each other with barely contained excitement, the six boys gathered in their own cluster. Leelo knew them all, of course. They'd played with each other growing up, and on an island this small, there were no strangers. But the Watchers were always teams of two, and with so much of their time spent on duty, they rarely saw each other anymore.

"Your dresses are so beautiful," a girl named Vance breathed, touching the soft trim on Leelo's sleeve and nodding toward Sage. Vance was wearing a crown of owl feathers, adorned with dried thistles and dark purple berries. "You're blessed to have such a skilled seamstress in the family."

Leelo smiled and glanced behind her at Mama, who had joined the other parents at Rosalie's insistence. Isola's mother didn't want the stain on her family to bleed onto Fiona's. Vance had an older sister without magic, but Leelo could barely remember her. She'd left when the girls were still small. Leelo wondered if Fiona and Vance's mother were talking about what it was like to say goodbye to a child.

"How is Isola?" Vance asked, gesturing to the girl. She had wandered off and was standing at the lake's edge, staring blankly into the water, her muddy hem nearly touching it.

"Not well."

Vance pursed her lips, and the expression, paired with her large yellow-green eyes, made her look very much like an owl. "I just can't understand what she was thinking. Risking everything for some boy. An *incantu* boy."

The words rankled Leelo. She loved Tate just as much as she loved Sage; magic had nothing to do with it. "She must have really cared about him."

"If she had, she wouldn't have let him come back," Sage said.

Leelo waited with her mother after that, until everyone who was coming had assembled. Ketty had been speaking with the other council members, each of whom represented roughly thirty islanders, but she approached the girls now.

"The ceremony is about to start," she said to Sage and Leelo, squeezing their shoulders. "You should go down by the water."

Leelo obeyed her aunt, treading carefully to keep her boots clean. The banks here were muddy from snowmelt, though shoots of green grass were valiantly poking their way through. Soon, the entire island would be verdant with spring. Leelo would still be a Watcher, and, unless a miracle occurred, Tate would be leaving.

"Watchers," one of the council members said, clapping her hands. "The ceremony is beginning. Please take your lily from Councilwoman Ketty."

Ketty was standing in front of a metal basin filled with water. Floating along the top were twelve white water lilies, one for each Watcher. They were grown by the council in a pond that Endlans were forbidden to visit before their year as Watchers was over.

Ketty smiled proudly at Leelo and Sage as they took their flowers. When they had all gathered at the shore, the rest of the islanders began to sing, a beautiful melody that was as uplifting as the drowning song was mournful. For the first time that day, Leelo felt some of the excitement she imagined the other Watchers must be feeling. She would be an adult by the time this year was over. She would be able to make her own decisions.

But of course, she couldn't really. She couldn't give Tate magic or make her mother well again. And she couldn't keep her own heart from breaking. She remembered how her mother had told her once that heartache and grief are their own strange kind of gift because they remind you that you still have a heart to break.

When you stop caring, when you stop grieving, that's when you know you're really lost, Fiona said. Leelo understood even then that she was talking about Aunt Ketty, who never once spoke of loss. Hers or Fiona's.

The Watchers knelt down and set their lilies in the water, where they floated like tiny ice floes on the surface. Slowly, the lilies drifted out into the lake. They would eventually take root, until finally the poison in the lake dissolved them. They lasted longer than birds or people or anything else that went into the water. But eventually the magic consumed everything it touched, like a beast that devoured every scrap of its prey, leaving nothing behind.

Not even bones.

Chapter Six

Jaren sat on a tree stump on the shore, directly across the lake from where the islanders had released what appeared to be flowers into the water. He had promised his father he wouldn't wander, and he hadn't intended to. But every time he went gathering, the mournful memory-song rose up in him, and he felt the strangest urge to come back here. The first time, the island had been quiet, with no visible signs of life. There was no reason to return.

But as soon as he'd set out this morning to forage for net-tles and dandelions, the only edible plants available this early in the spring, he found himself on the trail again, the one leading to the lake. He had still been more than a mile away when he heard the singing. In that moment, he finally un-derstood where he'd heard the song that had haunted him for days. He had rushed through the woods to get here, ignoring his father's warning. The eerie, distant tune had been real, as real as the person who sang it.

This song, however, was nothing like that. It was joyful, making his foot tap against the mossy roots despite himself. Despite the fact that he was beginning to wonder if the stories of Endla were true.

Last night, he had met some of the other villagers at Bricklebury's only pub for a drink. He was still considered an outsider, but he was an outsider with three pretty, eligible sisters, and that was apparently enough to earn him an invitation.

Casually, Jaren had asked one of the other young men about the lake. Lake Luma, they called it. The empty lake.

"It's not *exactly* empty," one of the villagers said. His name was Lars, and he was tall and lanky, with a shock of red hair that seemed to have a personality of its own. "It's full of poison." He lowered his voice an octave. "*Magic* poison."

"Magic," Jaren repeated, hiding his chuckle behind his pint.

"Laugh all you want," a young woman with unruly eyebrows spat. "It won't make it any less true."

Jaren ducked his head. "I'm sorry. I don't mean to laugh. I just don't believe in magic."

The woman's brows dipped into two angry slashes and she stormed off, in search of better company. Jaren grimaced at Lars. "Whoops."

Lars leaned closer, cupping his mouth behind his hand, though he had to shout to be heard above the boisterous conversation filling the small pub. His red hair tipped toward Jaren, as if it, too, were in on the secret. "Maggie's father was killed by the lake."

"But if everyone knows it's poisonous, why would he go in?"

Lars had explained that the islanders were like the sirens

of old pirate shanties, calling to the villagers late at night in voices too beautiful to resist. But though the song seemed to haunt him, Jaren didn't think anything could tempt him into that water. Not after Lars had described Maggie's father's death in gruesome detail.

Now he watched as the Endlans danced together, their haunting voices their only instrument. They wove through the trees, flashing horns and antlers, feathers and fur, as if they had become creatures of the Forest instead of people.

He straightened as one of the girls detached herself from the group. From here, she was little more than a pale smudge against the trees. She wasn't wearing horns like some of the other girls, but there was something on her head, whiter even than her hair.

She walked to the edge of the lakeshore, and for a moment Jaren was afraid *she* might actually walk into the water. But she paused at the edge, bending down to release something she held in her cupped hands.

He rose from the stump and made his own way to the water's edge. He was directly across the lake from her, and it was easy to pretend that this clear blue water wasn't full of poison, that the girl on the other shore was just an ordinary girl, like his sisters. She watched the object she'd released float for a few moments before it sank beneath the surface. She stood, smoothing her dress, and looked up.

Too late, Jaren realized he had left the safety of the trees. He was as exposed as the girl; there was no chance she didn't see him. For a moment, the superstitions of the villagers pricked at his conscience. What if she started to sing? Would he be strong enough to resist?

He shook off the idea almost as fast as it struck him. Even if he wanted to go to Endla—and he truly had no desire to—there was no boat available for him to cross.

Besides, the girl wasn't singing. She wasn't doing anything but staring back. He couldn't make out her features from this distance, and he doubted she could see his. They were just two ageless, faceless people, watching each other over a lake full of poison.

So when the girl raised her hand in a wave, Jaren figured there could be no harm in waving back.

Chapter Seven

Leelo left the festival before Sage. She had hoped after the ceremony she would feel different somehow, altered. That participating in these rites of passage would help her understand why things on Endla had to be this way. But she still felt like the same girl she'd always been. And she still couldn't accept the fact that Tate was leaving.

She spotted a small white crocus that had fallen from a Watcher's crown and saved it from being trampled by the dancers. Singing a quiet prayer for the first time in weeks, she carried it with reverence to the water's edge, releasing it as she had the lily, this time as a symbol of her brother. But unlike the lilies, the crocus bud sank almost instantly, like a bad omen.

Leelo rose, wiping tears from her cheeks, and saw the man. He stood directly across the lake, watching her.

She thought about running. The closest village was across the lake on the other side of the island, so it was strange that he was here at all, and there was something about the idea of an outsider watching the ceremony that made her stomach turn. It was sacred to Endla.

But for some reason, she hesitated. He was younger than she'd first thought, perhaps a year or two older than Leelo, and beardless. She had keen eyesight, which Ketty had said would make her a good Watcher, but she couldn't make out much of his features from here, other than his hair, which was a chestnut brown.

She didn't realize she was waving to him until she saw his arm go up. She dropped her own instantly, a warm rush of blood flooding her cheeks, but she didn't turn away. It wasn't like he could hurt the Forest from there, anyway.

The man lowered his arm abruptly when something fell into the water close to his side of the shore. He looked up into the branches overarching the water, his mouth forming an O of surprise. Leelo wondered if a pinecone had dropped. But then she saw him peering into the water and realized a bird must have fallen from its nest.

She gasped and put her hand over her mouth, but the young man had already found a muddy branch on the shore and was attempting to rescue the creature, just as she had done with the swan.

He removed his coat and wrapped one hand in it before fishing the tiny chick from the water with the stick. He brought it to his face, probably examining it for signs of life, and looked up at her.

She knew it wasn't possible from this distance, but she felt for one trembling moment that their eyes were meeting.

Unconsciously, she had taken a step forward, until her boots were dangerously close to the water. He shouted something and she stopped. He shook his head. The bird wouldn't have survived the fall, let alone the water, and she certainly couldn't help from here. The young man walked a little way into the woods and knelt in the dirt. It took her a moment to realize he was burying the hatchling.

"There you are!"

Leelo startled at the sound of Sage's voice directly behind her.

"What are you doing?" her cousin asked, coming to stand next to her and squinting into the distance. Her brow was beaded with sweat from dancing. Leelo could feel the heat radiating from her body. "Is that an outsider?"

Leelo blushed again, this time in shame. "Yes."

"What is he doing?" Sage started to turn. "We should tell our mothers."

"No," Leelo blurted, grabbing her cousin's arm. "Don't."

Sage's expression warped from curiosity to suspicion. "Why not?"

Leelo found herself scrambling for an excuse before she could even ask herself why. "What's the point of disturbing the festivities? He hasn't done anything wrong."

"He shouldn't be watching us, Lo."

Her initial, bitter thought was, *No, that's what we do.* "He wasn't," she said instead. "Not really."

Sage still looked suspicious, her hazel eyes sharp beneath her crown. "He could have seen the ritual. He could tell someone. This is what Watchers are for, Leelo. We should sing the hunting song and get rid of him before he tells anyone what he's seen."

Leelo's stomach twisted at the idea of luring this hapless stranger into the lake. "He hasn't done anything. And he didn't see the ceremony. I'm sure of it."

"Why are you protecting him?" Sage asked, arms folded across her chest. "We protect *Endla*, above all else."

And Endla protects us, Leelo finished silently. "I just… I really don't think he's here to harm the Forest." For some reason, she didn't want to tell Sage about the hatchling. It felt like a secret, a good one, and Sage would find a way to twist it. "Let's go back." She didn't feel like celebrating anymore, but she wanted to leave before Sage insisted they do something about the outsider.

Sage followed Leelo away from the lake, but her expression hadn't changed. Leelo wished she could tell Sage what she was thinking, tell her all the thoughts that had sprung up when she saw the man save the bird. She wanted to understand how broken Isola was over Pieter, and why he'd had to die, and why Tate had to leave.

But they had rejoined the others, and Leelo decided to check on Isola, who stood staring out at the horizon, her eyes as empty as the waters of Lake Luma.

That night, Leelo lay awake for hours, watching shadows move across her ceiling in the moonlight. She could tell from Sage's breathing that she was also having a hard time falling asleep. They had to be up early for Watcher duty, and they should be exhausted. But for some reason, sleep refused to come.

"I'm not sure I ever want to fall in love," Sage said suddenly.

Leelo gave a tiny, involuntary gasp. "Why?"

"Because I don't want to give up a part of myself for some-one. Look what it did to Isola," she added.

Leelo's eyes widened, but she didn't respond; she was afraid any reaction would frighten Sage back into her shell. This was the first time she'd ever revealed something so personal, and Leelo held her breath, hoping she'd say more.

"Isola was fine before him," Sage continued. "She was free and happy, just like us. And now it's like part of her died along with Pieter."

"But maybe it's worth it," Leelo ventured after a moment. "To feel a love like that."

Sage stiffened beside her, and Leelo was afraid she'd pushed her too far. "How can it be love, if it kills you?"

Leelo thought of her mother, of her quiet resolve and stead-fastness. Of Tate, who only wanted to love and be loved in return. If the knowledge that she had people like that in her life made Leelo less afraid, then *more* love could only be a good thing. "I don't think love kills you. Not often, anyway. Love makes people stronger."

"I don't think my mother ever really loved my father, and she's the strongest woman I know," Sage said defensively.

Leelo was quiet for a long time, but finally, she worked up the nerve to roll toward her cousin. "I want to tell you some-thing, but I'm afraid you'll be angry."

Sage softened and reached out, placing her hand on Leelo's shoulder. "You're my best friend, Lo. You can tell me any-thing. Even if it's about that man by the shore."

Leelo rolled onto her back again. Sage was too perceptive sometimes. "I saw him save a bird that fell into the lake. He tried to, anyway. But it was already dead. He buried it."

"So?"

Leelo sat up and looked down at Sage. "If outsiders are so terrible, if all they want is to destroy our Forest, why would he make the effort to bury a hatchling?"

"Don't tell me you were protecting that boy just because of a stupid bird," Sage moaned. "Do I think that some outsiders are better than others? Of course. Saints know that some islanders are better than others."

"But your mother hates all of them."

Now Sage sat up, her voice hardening. "You don't know anything about my mother."

"Then tell me," Leelo said. "Why does she hate the outsiders so much?"

Sage stared at her for a moment, as if she might have something to say, but instead she lay back down and rolled away from Leelo. "Just go to sleep. We're on the early shift tomorrow."

Leelo could tell that Sage wasn't anywhere close to sleeping; her breathing was fast and angry. She waited a few minutes and then left the room, padding quietly down the stairs. She opened the door to Tate's room and slipped into the dark space, crouching to avoid hitting her head on the sloped ceiling. Tate slept on a mattress on the floor, and it was easy to kneel onto it, lift the blanket, and crawl in next to her brother.

"Hello," he murmured sleepily.

"I'm sorry I woke you."

He turned toward her, his eyes shiny in the dark. "Are you all right? Mama said the ceremony went well."

"I'm fine. I just wanted to see you."

"We don't have much time left," he whispered.

She swallowed the lump in her throat. "We'll make the most of it."

Tate was quiet for long enough that Leelo thought he must be on the edge of sleep, but then he spoke again. "Is it true that we can really never see each other again once I leave?"

Leelo bit her lip to stifle a sob. Her prayers hadn't worked, and neither had her sacrifice. What would it take, she wondered, to appease the Forest? A flock of birds? An entire caribou?

"Maybe you can send me some sign that you're all right," she said. "In the winter, when you won't have to worry about the singing."

"What kind of sign?" he asked, brightening.

"A fire, near the lake's edge? No one ever camps there, so I'll know it's you."

"But how will you see it?"

"I'll come to the shore, starting the first night of winter. An hour after sunset, so I can see the flames." Most islanders hated the winter; they couldn't sing, and they didn't have the lake to protect them from the outsiders. But while Leelo might miss the greens and pinks of spring and summer and the flame-bright foliage of autumn, she was starting to think winter had its own quiet beauty. The dormant Forest was soft and still beneath its snowy mantle, the animals tucked safely away in their dens. Winter was the only season on Endla that wasn't corroded by poison.

She squeezed her brother's hand. "Knowing you're safe will bring me so much peace, Tate."

He was quiet for a long time. But then he said, "I still wish you could come to visit."

Endlans didn't leave Endla. Everyone knew that. They said the island grew roots around your feet so you couldn't leave, even if you wanted to.

But why would they? Other places faced war, famine, cruel rulers, and wild beasts. Here, life was peaceful. No one was impoverished or oppressed. The lake protected them better than any sovereign could. The Forest provided for them. And if the cost was that they could never leave, so be it. That's what Aunt Ketty would say, anyhow.

Leelo kissed her brother's forehead and closed her eyes. Sage had said her mother was strong, but Leelo didn't think of her aunt that way. She was hard and brittle as bird bones, as kindling. And Leelo knew all too well that brittle things didn't bend under pressure.

They broke.

Chapter Eight

"What's that song you keep humming?" Story asked Jaren as they headed to the market. His oldest sister, Summer, had been desperate to go, probably hoping to see her carpenter, but Tadpole was sick, and someone had to cater to her every whim. Father would have done it himself, but he was out hunting spring hares and wild turkey today. Tad wouldn't listen to a word Story said, and, given his distractedness, Jaren made a terrible nurse.

His eyes darted to his twin. He hadn't even realized he'd been humming. Weeks had passed since he went to the lake and saw the girl, and it had taken a disconcerting amount of resolve not to go back. When he'd fished the hatchling from the lake, a part of him was still skeptical about the poison. But after just a few moments in the water, the tiny corpse was already beginning to skeletonize, and any lingering doubts vanished. Still, that didn't make it *magic*. There were plenty of poisonous things in nature: berries, mushrooms, insects, plants… Why not a lake?

"Sorry. Just a tune I can't get out of my head."

Story raised a hand and pressed her palm to Jaren's forehead. "Hmm, no fever. I thought perhaps you were coming down with the same thing as Tad."

"Tad's not even sick," Jaren said, brushing her hand away. "She's just angry because Father says she's too young to do the shopping, so she's punishing Summer."

"I know all her tactics, Jay. But you *never* sing."

"What can I say, the fresh spring air is getting to me." He glanced at Story to see if she would accept the lie or push him further.

She shrugged. "Well, it's pretty, whatever it is. A little sad, but pretty."

They had reached the market. It was held every Sunday in Bricklebury, the perfect excuse for all of the locals to congregate and peddle stories along with their wares.

"I saw it. Big as a cow, it was." The man who was speaking, an old, grizzled fellow, was gesticulating wildly at the gathering crowd. "Must have descended from the giant wolves who roamed these mountains when our grandfathers were young."

An elderly woman selling knit booties nodded sagely. "I've heard the tales. None have been spotted in decades, mind."

Story rolled her eyes at Jaren and pressed through the throngs of people to a small stand. The woman here sold medicine, some genuine, some more likely to kill the patient than cure them. Story picked up a small green bottle that said Fever Tonic on the label.

"What's in this?" she asked the shopkeeper, tipping the bottle back and forth to study the viscosity of the fluid inside.

As the woman rattled off the ingredients, Jaren let his eyes wander around the market. He spotted Lars easily enough. The young man and his bright hair waved in greeting before he returned to his conversation with the butcher. And there was Maggie, the woman with the formidable brows. She glared at Jaren, clearly still upset about what he'd said regarding magic.

"Who are you looking for?" Story asked, handing a coin to the shopkeeper and tucking a brown bottle with no label into her satchel.

"Oh, no one in particular," Jaren replied. The truth was, he realized now, he'd been looking for a girl with pale blond hair, which was foolish. He knew Endlans didn't leave their island, magic lake or no.

Story twisted her lips like she had more to say.

"I was hoping to buy honey today," he added. "But I can't find the stand."

The diversion worked. There was a pretty, young woman who sold the honey, and Story would make her own assumptions from there. "She only comes every other week," Story said, linking her arm through Jaren's.

"Why do you think the people here are so obsessed with magic?" he asked in a low voice as they strolled the market. "Is it the thin mountain air? Too much time on their hands?"

She shook her head. "I don't know. I can sort of feel it myself, when I'm in the forest. It feels different from the forest back home."

They had moved from a city more than two weeks away by horseback when Klaus, who had known Jaren's mother as a girl, had written to Stepan, describing the bountiful forests, clean air, and welcoming community. So far, it had all proven to be true, for the most part.

But Jaren still didn't understand what everyone was talking about, not even his sister, who wasn't prone to superstition. The forest just felt like a forest, albeit a quiet one.

They had made their way back to where the old man was still spinning his yarn about the wolf, which had now grown to the size of a cottage. Quite a crowd had gathered by this point, and Story tugged Jaren over to listen.

"My dog went after it," the old man said. "I kept trying to call him back, but he wouldn't listen."

"Are you sure you weren't drinking again, Thom?" a younger man asked. "Your stories tend to get more fanciful the more ale you've consumed."

"It was a troll the last time," someone else said.

"Fairies, the time before that!"

Jaren found himself nodding in agreement. It seemed there were at least a few people in this village with some sense.

But the old man ignored their jibes and reached into his pocket. He pulled out a massive fang, bigger than any Jaren had ever seen. "I yanked this out of my poor Alfie, once the wolf abandoned his body. And don't tell me you've ever seen the likes of it, unless you're all drunk yourselves!"

Jaren and Story shared a wide-eyed look and slowly backed out of the crowd.

Once they were on the trail back to their house, Story turned to Jaren. "That was…"

"Strange? Bizarre? Disturbing?"

Story nodded emphatically. "Yes."

"Even I have to admit that was an impressive fang."

"Starting to believe in magic now, are you?" she asked, bumping him with her shoulder.

Jaren scoffed. "Hardly. But I am starting to believe the people in this village are even nuttier than I thought." He gestured to Story's satchel. "What did you buy for Tadpole?"

"Oh, just some cod liver oil. I'm going to tell her it's a fever remedy. Hopefully it tastes so terrible she won't be tempted to fake an illness again anytime soon."

Chapter Nine

Time is going by too quickly, Leelo thought as she and Sage made their way across the island to their patrolling spot for the day. She had continued to sleep in Tate's room since the night of the festival, and Ketty even managed to refrain from scolding him when he burned the supper. But though Fiona had seemed better for a little while after the spring festival, her condition had worsened since. She was hardly able to get out of bed most days, and Leelo suspected it was at least partly from the knowledge that her only son was leaving. Tate managed to keep a brave face for his family, but at night he cried in his sleep.

Spring was finally here, at least, and the island was blanketed in green, with more flowers bursting through the soil every day. There was to be a slaughter tonight, a ritual killing of an animal by each family to thank the Forest for its abundance and protection from the outsiders. After this, the Forest would be fully awake. Leelo was dreading it, the smell of the blood, the harsh, angry notes of the killing song. But she knew she would have to go, and there was no point fighting it.

Sage nudged Leelo with her elbow as they sat on a log, watching the opposite shore. "He's going to be fine, you know."

Leelo twirled a piece of grass between her fingers. "But I *don't* know that, Sage. I'll never know." She thought of the fire Tate had promised to make for her, but she had no idea if he would be able to manage it. He was still so young, and if outsiders were half as bad as Ketty said, he could be in great danger.

"He's a smart boy," Sage said. "He's more resourceful than you give him credit for."

"He's not even twelve. What were we doing at his age? Playing with the lambs and gathering mushrooms? He's never been on his own. We might as well be throwing him to the wolves."

Sage was quiet for a moment. "You're right. I'm sorry. I don't know how to make this easier for you."

Leelo wiped her damp cheeks on her sleeve. "You can't make it easier. No one can."

"Then what can I do?"

Leelo looked her cousin in the eyes, relieved to find there was genuine concern there. "*Try* to understand what this is like for me. And if you can't, then just be kind."

"I think I can manage that." Sage slung her arm around Leelo's shoulders. "Will you come back to our room, after he's gone? It's been lonely."

Leelo nodded. "I will. I just… I wanted to have as much time with him as I could."

They were both startled by a splash on the far side of the lake. They rose and peered into the distance. A group of villagers stood on the shore, throwing rocks into the water and singing a made-up rhyme in high, irritating voices. This wasn't uncommon. The younger villagers would sometimes dare each other to come to the lakeshore, just to prove they were brave enough to face the islanders, that they weren't afraid of the Endlans' songs.

Leelo thought again of the ritual tonight and wished these fools would leave. They had no idea what they were dealing with.

"Should we report them?" Leelo asked.

Sage stared at the villagers for a moment, then shook her head. "No. Our shift is over, and they're harmless." She picked up her bow and linked her arm through Leelo's. "Come on. Mother needs help with the lambs today. There were twins born just last night."

Leelo smiled as they left the villagers to their rude words and name-calling, happy to have something else to think about. "Can Tate come? He loves the lambs."

"Oh, I suppose it can't hurt. We just have to make sure Mother doesn't see."

Leelo squeaked in delight, which made Sage laugh, and for a moment Leelo felt a surge of hope. Even Fiona seemed a little better today. When they got home, she was in the rocking chair by the fire, knitting. She smiled when the girls entered, still wearing their boots.

"And where are you headed now, my love?" she asked Leelo.

"To see the lambs. One of the ewes had twins last night."

"I hope you'll take Tate with you. He's been moping all day long."

"We will," Leelo said, kissing her mother's forehead, which was blessedly cool and dry.

"You should stop at Isola's house and see if she'd like to come. Rosalie said she hasn't left the house in days. Some sunshine would do her good."

Sage looked appalled. "We're not supposed to talk to her. Mother said the council forbid it."

"The council doesn't need to know," Fiona replied curtly. "Go on now. I'll tell Tate to meet you at the pasture."

Sage complained the entire way to Isola's cottage, trying to convince Leelo to change her mind. "We're going to get in trouble. And why should we risk our reputations for her? She did a terrible thing, Leelo."

"She made one mistake, Sage. How long should she suffer for it?"

"I'm not saying she has to be punished forever. I'm just saying I don't think *we* should be the ones to stick our necks out for her."

"Then who should?"

Sage rolled her eyes. "You sound like Aunt Fiona."

"We're at least going to ask her." Leelo knocked on the cottage door while Sage tapped her foot impatiently as they waited for Rosalie. When she finally answered the door, she looked exhausted, but she let Leelo in.

"It's good of you to come. Perhaps you'll have better luck than I have," she said, closing the door behind them.

Isola was sitting by the window, staring into the woods

with a faraway look in her eyes. Leelo knew without asking that she was thinking about Pieter.

"We're going to see the lambs, Isola," she said gently. "We thought you might like to join us. Some fresh air might help."

Isola dragged her glassy eyes from the window up to Leelo's. "I doubt it."

"Well, at least the lambs will. It's impossible not to smile when a lamb is frolicking for the first time."

For a long moment, Leelo was sure Isola would refuse. But then she rose to her feet and nodded. "All right."

As they made their way to the pasture where the sheep were kept, Leelo breathed in the scents of spring: worm-turned soil, new grass, sun-warmed stone, and damp moss. In the shadows, the ground was spongy from spring rains, but the trail was dry, and there were patches of flowers growing in every clearing: lily of the valley, daffodils, and hyacinth. Leelo had exchanged her Watcher leggings and tunic for one of her mother's spring dresses. To ward off any lingering chill, she'd added her favorite sweater today, a soft cardigan with bright knit stripes.

There were five ewes nursing lambs, all creamy fleece and knobby knees. The ewe with twins was the most docile. Tate was already at the fence, trying to tempt her with a handful of grass. She made her way over eagerly, her babies tripping along as they attempted to walk and nurse at the same time, a skill they had not yet mastered.

"She's such a good mother," Tate said, patting the ewe on her woolly head.

Sage nudged him out of the way. "It's her nature."

Tate and Leelo shared a glance; they knew that not all

mothers were as kind and loving as theirs, that not every woman took to motherhood so readily. *Perhaps it's different with sheep*, Leelo thought.

"What are their names?" Isola asked, lifting her chin at the babies.

Sage rolled her eyes. "Names? They're not pets, you know. We'll keep the female for breeding and wool. The male will likely be eaten at some point. You don't name your dinner, do you?"

Leelo frowned at Sage. Isola was showing interest in something, and her cousin was doing her best to squash it.

"I think we should call that one Fleecy," Tate said, pointing to the little male.

Leelo smiled when she saw Isola's eyes light up just a bit. "And what about the other one?" Isola asked Tate.

He thought for a moment. "Weecy."

Sage snorted. "That's not even a name."

Tate ignored her and held out some more grass for the mother. "And I'll call you Clover."

Leelo's heart felt like it might burst in her chest from how much she loved her little brother, and that surge of hope she'd felt earlier vanished. Tate was too good for the outside world, too pure. He would never survive among those horrible villagers. He'd need to go farther away. Far enough where the people wouldn't know anything about Endla or its inhabitants. Which meant he'd probably be too far away to come back this winter.

The barn door opened so violently it hit the outside wall with a bang, startling the lambs. Ketty emerged, her face contorted in a scowl.

Leelo tried to hide Tate behind her and cast a worried glance at Isola. But Ketty's anger was directed elsewhere. She stormed past the four of them, heading back toward the house.

"What's wrong, Mother?" Sage asked, hurrying after Ketty.

"One of the ewes won't nurse her lamb," she said over her shoulder. "I have to fetch a bottle."

"I can do it," Tate offered, but Ketty only cast him a withering glance and disappeared into the house.

"It's all right," Leelo said to him. "Let's go look for tadpoles in the stream instead."

"You're wrong," he said gruffly, shrugging off Leelo's hand. "She does hate me. She'd get rid of me herself, if she could."

That evening, Ketty led a sheep by a rope around its neck into the woods. Fiona had insisted on staying home with Tate, despite Ketty's protests, and Leelo wished she was back there with them, cozy by the fire instead of tromping through the Forest to the slaughter.

"At least try not to look miserable," Sage said to Leelo as they gathered in the pine grove. Leelo hadn't been back since she made the blood sacrifice for Tate's magic. She'd never liked this place. How could she, when it contained the memories of so much suffering? Each family stood at the base of their tree with their offering, a motley assembly of animals, ranging from chickens to a lowing calf.

When they were children, Ketty had insisted that the girls each sacrifice an animal themselves, to fully appreciate their responsibilities as Endlans. In the end, Leelo hadn't been able to do it, and Sage had been forced to kill both of their rabbits.

Later that night, Leelo had been crying in bed when Sage asked her what was wrong.

"Aunt Ketty said I was too soft for this world, that it would always find a way to break my heart," Leelo said through her tears. "Do you think that's true?"

"Of course not," Sage had assured her. "Mother just doesn't know you like I do."

But even now, a part of Leelo knew that Ketty was right. One of the council members led them all in the killing song, and one by one, the head of each household ran a knife along the throat of their sacrifice. Terrified bleats and lows split the night, and Leelo stifled a gag as the iron tang of blood filled the air, pooling at the base of each tree before disappearing into the soil. Once again, Leelo thought she heard the wind rustle through the highest branches, like the sigh of a man satisfied with his meal, and she shuddered before glancing at Sage.

"Which one did Aunt Ketty choose this time?" Leelo asked, watching as the life drained out of the poor sheep.

Sage's gaze was fierce in the lantern light. "The one that wouldn't nurse her baby."

Leelo felt bile rise in her throat. "Why?"

"She wouldn't even care for her own offspring," Sage said. "I might not know much about being a mother, but even I can see how wrong that is."

Leelo swallowed down the bitter taste in her mouth. She couldn't help thinking of Fiona and Tate, how Ketty wouldn't stand for a sheep that refused to nurse its baby but was perfectly willing to let Tate be sent away, as innocent as a lamb himself.

The animals were all silent now, and so were the island-ers. As they turned to go, Leelo glanced once more at the sheep, its dead eyes seeming to stare right through her. For a brief flash, almost like a vision, she saw her own mother lying there instead, and the thought made Leelo shiver the entire way home.

Chapter Ten

Jaren wiped his mouth as he stumbled down the trail in the moonlight, wondering if he was going to be sick again. He should have listened to Lars and Maggie, she of the eyebrows. Because even if the villagers had been wrong about the songs luring people into the lake—he was running *away* from the lake, as fast as his legs could carry him—they were still evil. He knew that now for a fact.

It had all been a stupid bet, one he'd agreed to in part because he wanted an excuse to come back here. But as he quickened his pace through the woods, the notes of that horrible song, some almost as high and piercing as the sounds of the dying animals, echoed in his head. He didn't know how it was possible that the same people who had made such joyful music the last time he was here, or songs as beautiful as the one he still heard in his dreams, could produce anything so discordant. And while he was certainly no stranger to animal slaughter, the sound of so many animals dying at once, paired with that awful music, had turned it into something cruel and ritualistic, rather than necessary.

Stupid, stupid bet.

He had only gone back to the pub because Tadpole begged him to take her. She had retaliated for Story's cod liver oil trick by cutting off a hunk of Story's hair in her sleep, which had resulted in Tad being punished severely by Father (although perhaps not as severely as she should have been—Father simply couldn't hang on to anger toward his children since his wife died). Story, who was attempting to cover up a not insignificant bald spot at the back of her head with some creative styling and a rotation of hats, had vowed to get her own revenge soon enough.

Eventually, Story either forgot about Tadpole's betrayal, or she was playing a very long game. But his little sister watched sadly from the window every time her older siblings went to the pub, until finally, after an hour of desperate pleading, Jaren had buckled under the pressure and agreed to take her.

Summer and Story had gone to a dance in a neighboring village, and Father was visiting with his friend Klaus, the one who had invited the family to Bricklebury. Tadpole, who was giddy with excitement at finally breaking free of her prison, gripped Jaren's arm tightly as they walked into the village. She wouldn't be the youngest person at the pub, he knew. But he also knew that she had the energy and common sense of a chipmunk. He would have to keep a close eye on her the whole night.

Sure enough, Tadpole had quickly set her sights on an older boy, one Jaren already knew by reputation was something of a bully. While he drank his pint, he kept one eye on his sister, the other on Lars, who claimed he, too, had spotted the massive wolf.

"You saw it yourself?" Jaren asked, not sure if he should be impressed or concerned.

"Well, I didn't see the wolf so much as its tracks. But they were gargantuan. As big as my plow horse's hooves."

"Maybe it's not a wolf," Jaren said. "Maybe it's some kind of bear."

Lars shook his head, and Jaren had the distinct impression his hair was waggling like an accusatory finger. "I know bear tracks. These *weren't* bear tracks."

Before Jaren could apologize, he heard a squeak and turned to see the bully, Merritt, attempting to pull Tadpole in for a kiss. He set his pint down, ignoring the ale that sloshed onto his hand, and pushed through the crowd. He should never have left her to her own devices, but he found himself drawn in by Lars's stories, the so-called wolf and the poison lake, in a way he couldn't explain.

"Get your hands off my sister," he shouted, but she had already managed to knee Merritt in the unmentionables. Tears streaked her face, and Jaren tucked her under his arm. "What are you thinking?" he demanded. "She's fifteen!"

Merritt finally managed to straighten to his full height, which was a good six inches taller than Jaren's. "*She* flirted with *me*."

"She's fifteen!" Jaren repeated, because surely that was all the explanation necessary.

"She's a tease," Merritt spat. "She shouldn't be here."

Tadpole shrugged out from under her brother's arm. "I

have every right to be here. Maybe *you* shouldn't be here, if you can't handle your drink!"

A few other villagers chuckled, and Merritt's already ruddy face turned a darker shade of mauve. "Get out! Now, before I thrash the both of you."

Jaren knew his own limits, and there was no way he was fighting Merritt. "Come on," he said to Tadpole. "Let's go home."

She started to protest, but he gripped her firmly by the arm and led her through the parted crowd. They were almost to the door when she turned.

"My brother could thrash you with his arms tied behind his back!" she called over her shoulder.

Merritt had grinned in a way that made Jaren's stomach do a clumsy somersault. "Is that so?"

"Erm, no," Jaren said, not about to put pride before his own mortality. "You know how little sisters are," he said with a forced chuckle. "Think their big brothers are capable of anything."

"Jaren," Tad whined, embarrassed by his cowardice. "Everyone is looking."

Jaren truly didn't care what the other townspeople thought of him, but the expression of utter disappointment on his little sister's face made his stomach twist with disappointment in himself. With a sigh, he started to raise his fists. Merritt's grin widened.

And just when Jaren thought he was about to be pummeled to death by a red-faced oaf with fists the size of ham hocks, Maggie had stepped forward and whispered something into Merritt's ear.

Merritt had chuckled darkly and nodded. "Maggie here has an idea. Personally, I'd rather kick your ass into next Tuesday. But judging by the state of you, it won't be much of a fight."

Jaren swallowed audibly.

"I'll tell you what," Merritt said. "I'll give you a choice."

"And since you don't believe in magic," Maggie sneered, "it should be an easy one."

Merritt raised his voice so everyone in the pub could hear him. "Go to Lake Luma and bring back a vial of water."

The crowd gasped in unison. It might have been comical under other circumstances.

"Tonight. Alone," Maggie added, and Jaren knew he'd made an enemy for life.

"Or stay and fight me now," Merritt said. "The choice is yours."

At the time, it had seemed like Jaren was getting off easy. Back home, the very worst dare was jumping off of Dead Man's Ridge into the river below, which had earned its moniker more than once over the years. But Lars had assured Jaren that a glass vial with just an ounce or two of lake water was transportable. At least, he thought it was. In theory. Jaren had decided it was worth trying, if only to buy him some time before he had to face Merritt.

Now that very vial, carefully collected from the lakeshore in the moonlight, jostled in Jaren's pocket. He pressed his hand over it, afraid if he fell, it would break and spill poisonous water all over *his* unmentionables.

Stupid, stupid bet! Jaren thought, and ran as fast as he could away from that cursed lake.

Chapter Eleven

Five days. Five short days until Tate would board the boat used to send incantu children away before their twelfth birthdays. Five precious days before Leelo would never see her brother again.

Leelo held a branch aside as she and Tate made their way through the underbrush. They were practicing his hunting skills the old-fashioned way, since he wouldn't be able to lure animals with song the way the Endlans did.

Incantu could sing, of course. They weren't truly voiceless. But their songs held no magic, and the shame that came with their inadequacy meant most incantu children wouldn't even attempt to sing in front of others.

Tate had a small wooden bow and arrow that he'd fashioned himself over the winter, and as he quietly followed the rabbit he'd chosen, Leelo tried to reassure herself that he would be all right. The rabbit seemed to sense Tate's presence, but it continued to munch on the clover in the little clearing it had found. At least Tate knew how to hunt. He wouldn't starve out there.

Yesterday, she and Sage had done their own hunting after their shift as Watchers. There were very strict rules about how many animals Endlans could take for themselves and how many they needed to give to the island. While the Forest was capable of taking its own food, as Leelo had witnessed, it was perfectly content to let the humans help. After all, if it got too greedy, the animals would cross the ice to the mainland in the winter and never return. Everything on Endla was a careful balance of give and take.

Sage had set the snare, and Leelo had done the singing. While every Endlan had a beautiful voice, Leelo had an especially wide vocal range and unique tone. Besides, she far preferred the singing to the killing, and it was always a relief to let the notes out, even if it had only been a few days since she'd last sung.

They were a good team; they'd caught two squirrels and a fat hare. The Forest had gotten the squirrels, since they didn't have as much meat on them and Fiona could use the hare's pelt for clothing. Sage had volunteered to take the carcasses back to the pine grove, which had given Leelo enough time to finish all her chores yesterday so she could spend this afternoon with her brother. Sage might not be able to understand what Leelo was going through, but at least she was trying.

For several minutes, Tate sat with his bow poised and an arrow notched, until finally, he released it. The arrow struck the rabbit in its haunches, immobilizing it, and Tate made quick work of slitting its throat, letting the blood run into the soil as he murmured a prayer of thanks to the island.

"Well done," Leelo said, trying not to look at the rabbit. One of the other good things about hunting with Sage was that she was always willing to do the dirty work, knowing how sensitive Leelo was when it came to death. But she had to get over this squeamishness somehow. If there was one thing she had learned from her aunt Ketty, it was that survival was a bloody business.

Tate smiled at her over his shoulder and cleaned his blade on the grass. "I know you're worried about me," he said. "But I really will be okay."

There was an assuredness to his tone that Leelo hadn't heard before, and she was grateful he was managing to be so brave. "It's not you I worry about," Leelo said, looking off toward the village on the other side of the lake. "It's them."

"That's what I mean. Mama told me something… I'm not supposed to tell you. But it's a good thing. Something that will keep me safe. So you don't have to worry anymore."

"What something?" As far as Leelo knew, her mother had never kept a secret from her before. Certainly not with Tate. He was terrible at keeping secrets, like the time he'd overheard Leelo confide to Sage she had a crush on a boy and Tate had immediately told. Of course, that had been years ago. She looked back at her brother, marveling at how much he'd grown.

Tate kept his lips pressed together and shook his head. "Mm-m. I'm not telling."

If their mother had told Tate a secret, especially one that could keep him safe, then she wasn't going to pry. She just hoped it wasn't a lie Fiona had concocted to make him feel better. He deserved to go out into the world with his eyes wide-open. She remembered the villagers with their taunts and stones all too well.

And then she remembered the boy who buried the hatchling. She hadn't seen him again, and none of the other Watchers had reported a sighting. She wondered what had brought him here that day and what he thought of Endlans. He had waved when he could just as easily have thrown rocks. Perhaps Tate could find someone like *him*. Even Sage said some outsiders were better than others.

There were two more incantu leaving in five days with Tate. Another boy and one girl. Only three islanders out of more than three hundred. *Why did Tate have to be one of them?* Leelo wondered. *Why couldn't it have been some other family?* But she knew deep down that those other families would grieve the loss just as much, that her desire was selfish.

At home, Tate skinned his rabbit while Leelo helped her mother sort wool for knitting. Fiona was making Tate another sweater—he already had plenty, but it was Fiona's way of working out her feelings—and Ketty was pulling a savory pie out of the oven.

"What's the occasion?" Leelo asked, inhaling the smell of butter crust and roasting meat.

"Didn't Sage tell you? We're going to the Hardings' for dinner."

Leelo shot Sage a look. Hollis Harding was the boy Leelo had once had a crush on. She'd liked him for months, until one day he made fun of Tate for not having magic. After that, she'd considered him an enemy, and she hated it when her Watcher duty overlapped with Hollis's. "Why?" she asked.

"Because their daughter is also leaving." Ketty shooed Sage

away from the pie. "Now wash up. We're expected in an hour."

Sage went upstairs with Leelo following. "Why didn't you tell me we were going to the Hardings'?" she asked when they reached their room.

"I forgot. What difference does it make? At least it's something to do."

Leelo couldn't ignore the sting of Sage's words. "Something to do? We're about to send Tate away. I have plenty of other things I'd rather be doing." She changed out of her tunic and leggings and grabbed the first pieces of clothing she found in the wardrobe, a black skirt embroidered with red flowers and a white blouse. "I didn't realize Hollis's sister was incantu."

Why would he make fun of Tate if his own sister lacked magic? Unless that *was* the reason. Sometimes sadness made people lash out at the very people who could understand their hurt the most.

To Leelo's surprise, her mother was dressed and waiting when Leelo and Sage came downstairs. She was pale from the effort of standing, but she was there, clearly trying for Tate's sake.

Leelo looped her arm through her mother's, and all of them, including Tate, left the house together. Leelo told herself to be grateful for this time and not to dwell on the future. Ketty had given Tate the pie to carry, a generous gesture from their aunt, who usually never entrusted her baked goods to others.

Sage was on the other side of Fiona, helping to steady her, wearing her dress from the spring festival. It was a bit special for a dinner at the neighbors', but she looked very pretty in it.

"Oh!" she said in realization.

"What is it?" Fiona asked with an amused smile. "Did something bite you?"

"It's nothing," Leelo replied, scrambling for an explanation. "I just remembered something I want to pack for Tate."

She looked at her cousin again, who was using her free hand to smooth her hair. Was it possible this was what had prompted Sage to say she never wanted to fall in love? Could she have feelings for Hollis Harding? Sage's expression was as serious as always, but Leelo had never known her to dress up for dinner at a neighbor's house.

The Hardings' cottage was in a different sector of the island, about an hour's walk from their home. Some families kept wooden carts and ponies to travel from one end of the island to another, a two-hour journey by foot. As much as Leelo liked walking, she hoped Mr. Harding would offer them a ride home. Fiona was making an effort to appear comfortable, but it was just that: an effort. Her breathing was labored and her face was pale except for two bright circles of color high in her cheeks. Aunt Ketty strode ahead at her usual brisk pace, oblivious to her sister's struggle.

"We can rest, Mama," Leelo said, but Fiona shook her head, as Leelo had known she would.

"I'm fine, dear. I suppose this is what comes from spending so much time in bed." She managed a smile, and Leelo returned it, because she knew that was what her mother wanted.

"If you would sing more, you wouldn't be so weak," Ketty said over her shoulder. "There are consequences to missing so many rituals."

Fortunately, they reached the house not much later, and

Leelo made sure Fiona was comfortably seated before she left the adults to find the other children in the yard.

Mrs. Harding had a wonderfully green thumb, and her garden was a riot of colorful flowers and the loud buzzing of various pollinators. She traded her flowers with the islanders, some dried for teas and tinctures, others fresh simply because they were beautiful. Sage and Hollis were sitting on a bench underneath an arch dripping with wisteria, while Tate and Hollis's little sister, Violet, played with a litter of kittens near a hydrangea bush.

Leelo managed a tight smile as she approached Sage and Hollis. She didn't know if he remembered her crush, but she couldn't look at him now without thinking about how humiliated she'd been when Tate confessed that he'd revealed her secret. Needless to say, Hollis had not returned her feelings, calling her pale and scrawny.

Since then, he'd grown into a hulking brute of a boy, with golden curls Leelo had once been so desperate to touch that she found any excuse to be near him. One day, a leaf had fallen in his hair, and she'd been elated at the prospect of removing it for him. She chuckled to herself at the memory, finding it hard to believe she'd ever acted that foolish over a boy.

"What's so funny?" Sage asked. Her hands were fisted in her skirt, and when she saw Leelo looking at them, she quickly released the fabric and attempted to smooth it out.

"Nothing," Leelo said, taking a seat on the grass. It was still late afternoon, and the ground felt warm and alive beneath her. "How are you, Hollis?"

He shrugged. "All right. I'm getting tired of Watcher duty. Kris can't seem to stop talking."

"I'm sorry about your sister." Leelo ran her fingers through the grass, only vaguely aware of the earth vibrating beneath her touch. "I didn't realize she was leaving until today."

Sage's gaze snapped to Leelo, as if she'd done something wrong by mentioning Violet.

But Hollis only shrugged again. "She's kind of a pain anyway."

Leelo visibly flinched, but Sage's lips twitched in a grin. "I know what you mean."

Angry and hurt, Leelo rose and went to where Tate and Violet were playing. The litter of kittens was probably around ten weeks old, ready to be weaned. Tate was holding a brown-and-white kitten with tufted ears and a pink nose.

"This one's my favorite," Tate said, holding her out for Leelo to admire. "I wish I could keep her."

Leelo stroked the kitten's fur and smiled. "I wish you could, too." They played with the kittens for a while, laughing at their antics, until Mrs. Harding yelled, "Time to eat!" from the house. Leelo helped put the kitten back into its basket, but it promptly climbed out and followed Tate to the house, where Mrs. Harding gently nudged it away from the threshold with her foot and closed the door behind them.

Mr. Harding was a big man, which explained Hollis's size. He was seated at the head of the table, with Hollis at the other end. Leelo couldn't help but notice how different it was to be in a household with men. Ten years had passed since her father died alongside Sage's, and she'd forgotten how much space men could take up. At home, their table was round, with no one's position more favorable than anyone else's.

Violet, a small girl with her brown hair in twin pigtails,

was wide-eyed but silent as everyone passed around the food and ate. Leelo wondered how someone so shy would manage out there. It would be hard enough for Tate, but Violet was half his size, and as far as Leelo knew, no one had ever taught her to hunt.

"Leelo?"

She glanced up to see the others looking at her. "I'm sorry, did you say something?"

"I was just asking how Isola has been doing." It was Mrs. Harding who spoke, but everyone was looking at Leelo intently. "Your mother said you've been spending time with her."

Leelo glanced at Aunt Ketty, who was scowling, but Fiona nodded in encouragement. She must have decided this was a safe space to discuss Isola and her family. Leelo had been busy with her Watcher duties and trying to spend time with Tate, but she made a point of walking at least an hour every day with Isola, just to ensure she got outside.

"She's still sad, obviously. But I think she's doing a little better."

"What was Rosalie thinking?" Mrs. Harding whispered to Fiona. "Allowing her daughter to ruin their family like that?"

"I don't think Rosalie knew," Fiona said.

"Really, now. We would know if our daughters were…" She trailed off as her eyes met Leelo's. "You know."

"It's Pieter's parents I feel sorry for," Mr. Harding said. His voice was a deep rumble, reminding Leelo of distant thunder. "They didn't even know their son was back on the island. Isola kept him well hidden somewhere, but she won't reveal the location."

Leelo's ears perked up at this news. She had wondered how Isola had managed to keep Pieter a secret in her own house. A flash of memory—Pieter's muscled torso, Isola's screams—swam up, and Leelo swallowed thickly. She glanced at Sage, who was busy watching Hollis. He was too busy eating his second slice of pie to notice.

Sage looked away from Hollis and turned her eyes on Leelo. "They put their feelings before Endla," she said in a flat voice. "They deserved their fates."

Mrs. Harding laughed uncomfortably, Fiona frowned, and Aunt Ketty, who hadn't touched a bite of her pie, nodded.

"The wolf is always at the doorstep," she said ominously. "That is why we Watch."

Chapter Twelve

Jaren would have just as soon forgotten about Endla altogether, but a bet was a bet, and he was forced to prove he'd been to Lake Luma with the vial of water. Lars did the honors of placing a rose into the vial, making a bit more of a show of it than seemed necessary.

For a moment, Jaren was afraid nothing would happen and he'd be humiliated in front of the entire village, but a few seconds later, the stem began to shrivel up and turn black. As the poison rose, the bottom of the stem started to disintegrate, and by the time the crimson petals had withered and blackened, the stem was gone. The flower head fell onto the table, where it crumbled to ash and blew away.

Even Merritt seemed impressed, though slightly disappointed he wouldn't have the opportunity to beat Jaren to a pulp. But at least he'd walked away to the bar, leaving Jaren with Lars, his body blessedly intact.

"I can't believe you went to Lake Luma," Lars said, eyeing

the vial of water where it sat on the table. Someone would have to dispose of it, and Jaren had no intention of volunteering. "Most of us have never gone near it, and we've lived here our entire lives."

Jaren flushed, embarrassed that his skepticism had nearly cost him his life. "I don't think I really understood how dangerous it was until now." It was still hard to fathom that such a beautiful, crystal-clear mountain lake could be so deadly. He imagined what could have happened if he'd tried to drink from it his first time there and shuddered. His family might never have found him.

Lars passed him a pint of ale. "Well, I don't think you'll have to worry about Merritt anymore. You've got boasting rights for life, friend."

"I don't want to boast. I'd just like to be left alone. And I won't make the mistake of bringing my little sister to the pub again."

"Probably a wise decision."

Jaren drained the pint and turned to Lars. "I know you said you've never been to the lake before, but what do you know about the people who live on the island? Aside from the nonsense about sirens, of course."

"What makes you so sure it's nonsense?"

Jaren hadn't told anyone about the Endlan singing he'd overheard on his second visit, because doing so would be admitting he'd visited the lake again despite his father's orders. But now that a pub full of people knew he'd gone to save his sister's honor, there was no point in keeping what he'd just witnessed a secret.

"When I was there, I heard what I think was some kind

of animal sacrifice. There must have been a dozen animals or more, and the islanders were singing while they did it. It was horrible."

"And you didn't feel the urge to cross the water?"

Jaren forcefully shook his head no. "I never want to go near that place again."

Lars absently patted his hair the way a man might stroke a dog's fur. "I'd say you were lucky, then."

Despite his insistence that he wanted nothing to do with the lake, Jaren still felt that strange, inexplicable fascination with Lars's tales. Maybe that was it: he needed an explanation. There had to be *something* rooted in reality that made it all make sense, if only he thought about it hard enough.

"Have you ever met anyone from Endla? I heard they banish all the islanders without…" He didn't want to give credence to what he still thought was superstition, but for the sake of conversation, he said the word. "Magic."

Lars nodded. "We have an Endlan in the village. She doesn't talk about Endla, though."

Jaren's eyebrows rose. "Someone in Bricklebury came from Endla? Who?"

"The young woman who sells honey. She left the island about six years ago now. A local family took her in, and she's been with them ever since."

For a moment Jaren was sure he'd mishcard. It wasn't that he'd expected Endlans to have horns sticking out of their foreheads, but the honey girl seemed so…normal.

Lars chuckled, as if he could tell what Jaren was thinking. "I know. It's strange to think someone like her came from such an awful place. But it's true."

"Why doesn't she speak about it?"

"I imagine it's too painful," Lars speculated. "She had a family there."

Jaren nodded, but inside he was thinking that the honey girl had been fortunate. She'd gotten out, unlike the girl he'd seen the day of that festival. He tried to imagine her slitting an animal's throat but couldn't.

Later that week, when the farmer's market returned, and with it, the honey girl, Jaren couldn't help but go to her stall for a closer look. Story was busy choosing fabric for new dresses for herself and her sisters, and if history was any guide, she would be occupied for hours.

Aimlessly perusing the jars of honey, Jaren waited for the girl to finish helping another customer. Finally, she turned her attention on him.

"Can I help you?" she asked, a lilt of amusement in her voice.

"Er, I was just wondering, where do you get your honey from?" It was a ridiculous question. He couldn't have cared less where it came from. And it was hardly a good way to learn about Endla. But he had never been good at making small talk, and he had to start somewhere.

"My parents keep bees in a meadow not far from here," she said as she packaged up a bottle for another customer. "Oh, here they are now."

A man and a woman materialized out of the crowd, back from doing their shopping, by the look of things. Both of them carried baskets full of food.

"My parents," the girl said. "Oskar and Marta Rebane."

"And who might you be?" the woman asked, sizing Jaren

up. He was tall for his age and not scrawny, but something about her made him feel rather small.

"My name is Jaren Kask," he said, holding out his hand.

"Not the same Jaren Kask who went to Lake Luma and brought back a vial of poisonous water?" she asked, but there was a teasing quality in her voice similar to her daughter's. "You're practically famous here in Bricklebury. Isn't he, Lupin?"

Jaren could feel the girl's eyes on him. "I'm afraid that's me, ma'am," he said.

Marta exchanged a glance with her husband and picked up a jar of honey. "Here you are, then. For your mother. She must have quite a job of keeping you safe."

Jaren was surprised by this stranger's generosity. A hold-over from spending most of his life in a city, he supposed. "My mother passed away. But I'm sure my father and sisters will appreciate it. Thank you."

"Oh, we're sorry to hear that, aren't we, Oskar?" She elbowed her husband, and he coughed, nodding.

"Indeed. Very sorry. What brought you to Bricklebury?"

As Jaren explained how Klaus had invited them to move here after his mother's death, he stole glances at Lupin, who had gone back to selling honey to other customers. He wondered if she'd figured out why he came to talk to her and felt ashamed for thinking of her as nothing more than a curiosity. Whoever she'd been before, it was clear Oskar and Marta were her parents now, and Endla was likely a part of her past she didn't care to dwell on.

As Oskar and Marta returned to their customers, Jaren thanked them again and started off to look for his sister. A moment later, he felt a hand on his arm and turned to find Lupin standing there.

"Did you really go to Lake Luma?" she asked, her green eyes searching his face.

He nodded. "It was a ridiculous bet to protect my sister." He decided it wasn't necessary to include the part about protecting himself. "I didn't mean anything by it."

"I suppose you heard I'm from Endla, then?"

There was no sense in lying now. "Lars told me."

She twisted her lips to the side, considering, and nodded. "Well, then. I suppose you have questions. Come with me."

Chapter Thirteen

The day of Tate's departure had finally arrived, and Leelo wasn't sure how she would survive it. Fiona hadn't moved from her bed since dinner with the Hardings, and Ketty and Sage had done all of the chores, leaving Leelo to care for her mother and Tate.

The boat would leave at dusk, which seemed unnecessarily cruel. Tate and the others would have to navigate an unfamiliar forest in the dark.

"Stay with Violet and Bizhan as long as you can," Leelo told him as she finished tying up his bundle. He had few possessions to take with him aside from clothing and his bow and arrows, but Leelo had packed him enough food to last a week, if he was sparing. "Violet is going to be terrified, and I imagine Bizhan is, too."

Tate nodded. "I will."

Leelo considered asking him again what their mother had told him. If she was so certain he would be safe out there, why was she unable to leave her bed? But Leelo wouldn't pry. If her mother wanted her to know, she'd have told her herself.

"I'm so sorry, Tate," Leelo said, trying not to cry.

"Why should you be sorry?" he asked. "This isn't your fault."

"I…" Leelo sighed. "I tried to bring out your magic. I even offered a blood sacrifice."

He looked up at her, his dark eyes questioning. "You did?"

She wiped her tears and nodded. "I did."

"But you know that's not how it works, Lo. The island doesn't give us magic. We're born with it, or we're not."

"I know. Of course I know. I just hoped…"

He nodded in understanding. "I know. So did I."

She didn't tell him how worried she was about their mother. Tate couldn't do anything to help her, and he had more than enough on his plate right now. Perhaps it would be a sad kind of relief once he was gone, and Fiona would slowly get better. There wouldn't be this constant dread looming over them, mingled with their dwindling hopes that Tate's magic would appear. For whatever reason, he hadn't been born with magic, and they had to accept that now. It was the only way to find peace moving forward.

"I have Watcher duty," Leelo said, rising from Tate's bed. "But I'll be back in plenty of time to say goodbye. Will you sit with Mama until I get back?"

"I will. And, Lo?"

She stopped in the doorway to his little room, which would soon be just a broom closet again. "Yes?"

"Promise me you'll be happy when I'm gone. I need to know you'll be happy."

She nodded, hoping he hadn't seen the tears coursing down her cheeks when she turned to go.

Of all days, Sage and Leelo were tasked with Watching on the far side of the island for the first time, a fact that annoyed Leelo, since the launch would occur clear on the other side of Endla. Getting back would take two hours, giving her no time to wash up or change in between.

Sage, sensing that Leelo's emotions were as taut as a bowstring, was silent for the first half hour of the walk. It wasn't until they were deep into the woods that she finally cleared her throat and spoke.

"Do you ever wonder what your father would have done, if he were still alive?"

The question was so out of the blue that Leelo stopped walking. "What?"

Sage glanced around at the Forest, and that was when Leelo realized where they were. This was the location of the accident that had killed both Hugo and Kellan.

The details had always been fuzzy to Leelo, but of course, she'd only been seven when her father died, and her mother never wanted to talk about it. All she knew was that somehow Uncle Hugo had shot Kellan, Leelo's father, by accident. And when Hugo had gone to help his brother-in-law, he'd stepped in his own trap, severing an artery. Both men bled out before they were found.

"I think my father would be devastated that Tate is leaving, if that's what you're asking," Leelo said coldly. "He loved us both equally."

Sage's lips flattened into a line, and Leelo felt her blood begin to rise.

"He did. My father wasn't prejudiced, like some people."

They had both resumed walking. "You mean people like Mother and me?" Sage asked.

"I was thinking of Hollis, but yes, people like you."

"You don't even know what you're talking about," Sage muttered.

"Then tell me!"

Sage rounded on Leelo, her hazel eyes burning with an intensity that frightened Leelo. "My mother gave up more than you'll ever understand for you and Aunt Fiona. Just remember that the next time you want to call us prejudiced."

Leelo spluttered, unable to form words, but Sage had already forged ahead into the brush, and Leelo was too tired to run after her cousin, spouting apologies she didn't mean. Whatever Sage thought Ketty had done, it didn't justify the way they treated Tate.

As Leelo stomped down the trail, a starling off to her left let out a short burst of song. Smaller birds weren't uncommon on Endla; they could generally escape the Forest, which preferred larger prey, though they never nested here. So it wasn't the presence of the bird that startled Leelo. It was the song itself: the prayer she'd sung the night she offered the island blood for Tate's magic, in a voice that sounded eerily like Leelo's.

If anyone found out she had been performing a blood offering on her own, before the spring festival no less, she'd be severely punished by the council. Endlans weren't supposed to use songs on their own before their year as Watchers was finished. The bird called again, and Leelo glanced around, her heart pounding, wondering if Sage had heard.

She knew she needed to catch up with Sage, that they were

probably already late for their shift by now, but she couldn't risk letting that bird fly around all of Endla, singing in her voice. She followed it off the trail a way, wincing every time the bird trilled again. She considered singing something else; perhaps the bird would pick *that* up instead. But there was no song without consequences, and for all she knew she'd end up creating a worse problem for herself.

The bird flitted from tree to tree, chirping merrily, and Leelo had the distinct impression it was mocking her. "Damn you," she shouted, shaking her fist as it disappeared into another tree. "You'd better hope I don't catch you!" She removed her bow from her shoulder, knowing the odds of hitting the bird up in a tree were slim to none. Perhaps she could scare it off, at least.

She wasn't even sure where she was now. Endla wasn't that large; she'd be able to orient herself soon enough. But Sage was probably wondering what had happened to her, and skipping out on Watcher duty was arguably as bad as singing without permission.

"Damn it!" she swore, turning to leave.

Leelo froze.

The cottage was so well hidden that she never would have seen it if she hadn't come face-to-face with it. In fact, *cottage* was too generous a word for what was little more than a hut, buried under branches and leaves, with no visible chimney. A grown man would barely be able to stand up inside, and it was clearly only big enough for one room. She glanced around, the starling forgotten, and approached the hut.

The little door swung open with a groan, the hinges rusty with disuse. There were two small windows, both so dirty that hardly any light filtered through the glass. Leelo no-

ticed a candle stump on a small table and lit it with one of the
matches she always carried on Watcher duty. At night, this
place would be nearly pitch-black, but it was small enough
that she could make out the pile of blankets in one corner,
along with a crooked stack of books, in the candlelight.

Was this where Pieter spent the entire winter? Leelo wondered.
If so, it was a miracle he hadn't frozen to death. Without a
fire, no number of blankets would be enough to stay warm.
Unless you were with another person, she thought, and blushed so
hard she looked around to make sure there were no witnesses.

The image of Pieter running from Isola's house came back to
her again. How were they brazen enough to bring him into her
house? Unless Rosalie did know, like Mrs. Harding had said.

No, she thought, extinguishing the candle and stepping back
out of the cottage. It was clear from the way Rosalie had beaten
Pieter from her house that she hadn't known before that. Otherwise she would have sent him on his way sooner, surely. She
closed the door and tried to block out the memory of Pieter falling into the lake, his last desperate cry for help, and Isola's screams.

She found the trail a minute later and shrieked when she
ran headlong into Sage.

"Where have you been?" Sage was angry, but it was the
anger of being abandoned on Watcher duty, not from their
argument before. "Our shift started half an hour ago!"

Leelo glanced around and was relieved she couldn't spot the
cottage from here. "I just needed time to think, and I got a
little disoriented. I'm really sorry." And without waiting for a
response, she hurried down the trail, away from Isola's hideout.

Chapter Fourteen

Jaren wasn't sure why Lupin decided to confide in him about her life on Endla, but he was grateful that someone was willing to talk about it. Someone who knew the truth, not a bunch of silly stories.

They strolled around the market once, with Lupin pointing out the best vendors of various items and who to be wary of. "Never buy from him," she said, gesturing to a man peddling what looked like ordinary copper pots and pans. "He's a crook. And a smelly one." Eventually she continued past the very last stall and guided Jaren into the forest.

"Don't you need to help your parents?" he asked, glancing over his shoulder at the market and making eye contact with Story for just long enough to see the look of amusement on her face before they disappeared behind a veil of trees.

Lupin strode confidently into the forest without looking back. Jaren had the impression she rarely did. "They'll be all right. To be honest, I needed a break. You're not the only person in Bricklebury to look at me funny, Jaren Kask."

THE POISON SEASON 103

"I'm sorry. I didn't mean to stare."

The corner of her mouth raised in a grin. "It's all right. I wouldn't have noticed if I hadn't been staring at you, too." She glanced at Jaren and barely managed to stifle a laugh. "Don't tell me the girls didn't like you back in... Where did you say you were from?"

He was grateful for the change in subject, though the truth was, he had never paid much attention to girls back home. He had been too busy helping his family to go to school, let alone to court anyone. "I'm from Tindervale."

"Ah, a city boy. No wonder you're so out of your element here. Us mountain folk are known for our strange ways."

Jaren studied Lupin from the corner of his eye. She had long, glossy hair the same color as the honey she sold, and her green eyes twinkled with what appeared to be good humor. But there was something about her sharp nose and high laugh that made her seem more than a little impish, like a woodland elf bent on mischief.

Not that he believed in elves.

They had come to the fork in the forest trail that led to other towns and eventually cities in one direction and deeper into the wood toward Lake Luma in the other. Lupin paused, as if she was waiting for Jaren to decide their direction.

He meant to choose the fork leading away from Endla. He already knew where the other fork led, and he had no desire to go back there. But somehow his feet decided otherwise. Lupin didn't argue, just continued to watch him from beneath her lashes.

"So, what did you want to know about Endla?" she asked after a few minutes. "Or were you just hoping to spend time alone with a pretty girl?"

At that, Jaren dropped Lupin's arm and took a sidestep away from her. "No, I'm sorry. I hope that's not the impression I gave. I would never presume…"

She had a high, tinkling laugh that he imagined some people would find charming, but the sound made him uneasy. "I enjoy making you blush," Lupin said. "Don't worry, I'm not going to bite." She reached for his arm again and he gave it reluctantly, wondering why he wasn't enjoying spending time with an attractive girl as much as he suspected he should.

"Go on, then," she said. "Ask me your questions about Endla."

Jaren resumed walking. "I suppose I was just wondering why you were sent away," he said, hoping he wasn't being rude. "Lars made it sound like you were forced to leave your family."

She arched an eyebrow. "Didn't you hear, city boy? I'm incantu. Without magic. Endlans send us all away before we reach our teen years."

"So it's true? There really is magic?" Jaren was grateful there was no one around to hear him. If he'd said something that asinine in Tindervale, he'd have been laughed out of town.

"You city folk and your skepticism. Of course there's magic."

Jaren didn't doubt that Lupin believed what she was saying, but he had direct proof that Endlan "magic" hadn't worked the way everyone said it did. "I heard the singing myself."

Lupin stopped abruptly and turned to face him. "What?"

He nodded. "Twice now." He thought of the night he'd camped by the lake and the strange music that had been stuck in his head after. "Three times, maybe."

She glanced around at the trees, as if she was listening for something. "And you didn't feel the urge to cross the lake?"

"No," he said. "Far from it."

"Interesting." She started walking again, but Jaren could feel the tension in her body. "I suppose it's possible that you didn't hear the right songs. Or you were too far away for the magic to work. Or perhaps your skepticism protected you somehow. Either way, you were lucky, Jaren Kask."

He knew the lake was poisonous. After seeing what happened to the bird and the rose, that couldn't be denied. But he didn't feel as though it were luck or skepticism keeping him safe. Certainly the songs had gotten in his head. They *had* affected him. Just not the way he'd imagined.

"How does an Endlan know if they have magic or not?"

"If their voices hold no power by their twelfth birthday, then they are incantu. And anyone without magic on Endla is vulnerable."

"To what?"

"To the Forest, of course."

Now Jaren was the one to stop. "What do you mean?"

"Haven't you heard of the Wandering Forest?" She clucked her tongue, but she was smiling again. "You silly, pretty thing. So much to learn."

He wasn't sure he liked being called silly *or* pretty, but he was curious despite himself. "What exactly is a Wandering Forest?"

"It's what it sounds like. A wooded area that appears where it wants, when it wants. In the old days, a traveler who happened upon one would likely never find it again, no matter how many times they returned to the spot."

"And what would they find there?"

"An ordinary forest. One that doesn't interfere in the natural order of things. A normal forest is a neutral party in the affairs of its inhabitants. It stands impassively by while life and death play out the way they always have. But not a Wandering Forest. Or at least, not this one. It is a bloodthirsty thing, killing so many of its own creatures that it needs the Endlans' songs to draw in more and their sacrifices to sate it."

Jaren shuddered. "And the Endlans? What do they get in return?"

"Ask any Endlan, and they'll tell you the Wandering Forest is there to protect them. As long as they sing, as long as they lure in prey and make their offerings, the Forest is happy enough."

"Happy?" Jaren asked, trying to sound genuinely interested and not condescending. "I don't understand."

Lupin tapped him playfully on the nose. "You don't have to. The Forest doesn't rely on the likes of you. It lives in a kind of symbiosis with the Endlans, and as long as no one disturbs the order of things, it works out well enough." A shadow passed over her face. "Except for the incantu, of course."

"But who do the Endlans need protection from?"

"From us, the mainlanders. Or outsiders, as they think of us. It was outsiders who drove the Endlans there and killed all but the last remaining Wandering Forest."

Jaren was trying desperately to follow Lupin's logic, but it still didn't make sense to him. "Why do the 'outsiders' hate the Endlans? Because of what happened to Maggie's father?"

"Him, and others like him. Whether they go by accident or by choice, outsiders are killed by the Forest, if the poison of the lake doesn't get to them first. But they were hated long before they went to the island, simply for being different. I imagine a few people were lured to their deaths by Endlans, and it was convenient to make them the scapegoats every time a child went missing or a husband didn't return to his family. They *are* safer on Endla, just so long as the Forest doesn't turn on them."

Jaren considered her words for a moment. "What about *this* forest?" He waved vaguely at the trees around them.

"Hmm? Oh, it's just a forest. But the animals here seem to be aware of what happens on Endla. I think they're always watching and waiting, to see what the Wandering Forest will do."

Jaren had never even considered that a forest could be watching him. He looked up into the branches that swayed slightly in the breeze, imagining that the trees were listening. He had always found this forest to be oddly quiet, and now he realized why: there was no birdsong or rustling in the underbrush. The only sound was the wind. "What about the poison in the lake? Is that part of the Forest's magic?"

"Perhaps. I don't know all of Endla's secrets. They're kept especially well from incantu, lest we leave and tell them to the outsiders. They say they send us away to protect us, but the truth is, we're dangerous to Endlans."

"How?"

"Because we don't need the Forest like they do. And if we knew Endla's vulnerabilities, we could share them with outsiders. Perhaps they think we have a vendetta against them."

"Sounds like you'd have good reason to."

"Some, maybe. I've made my peace."

"Have any Endlans left by choice?" he asked, thinking of her parents.

"I'm not sure," she admitted. "I heard of a woman who tried to cross the ice one winter, when I was just a baby. But the ice was too thin, or the island didn't want her to go, and she fell through a crack and disappeared."

"So the Endlans are prisoners, in a way."

"I suppose so. I know I'm glad to be clear of the place, even if I do miss my parents. I thought of trying to go back in the winter, but I don't trust the island or the other Endlans. They have people who guard the shoreline, just in case. Watchers, they're called. After they complete a year of duty, they attend a secret ceremony and become true citizens of Endla. And whatever happens to them there must be powerful, because after that, they don't question the way of things again."

Jaren had a final question, but it felt almost too personal.

Lupin arched an eyebrow. "You're wondering why they don't kill us outright."

Jaren flushed. He didn't like the way this girl seemed to read his thoughts. "It doesn't sound out of the realm of possibility, given what I've heard about Endlans."

"I'm sure some would like to, but our parents wouldn't allow it. And I've heard not all children are so lucky. Stray too far from the safety of home, and an elder might give you to the Forest. If it's hungry enough, the Forest might take you itself." She glanced at him and burst out laughing.

"What?"

"Your face. You look terrified."

He blushed, and she ruffled his hair affectionately, turning them around. And though Jaren was mostly grateful to be heading away from the lake and back to the relative safety of his sister and the marketplace, there was a part of him that felt as though they were heading in the wrong direction.

Chapter Fifteen

Tate stood on the lakeshore with the two other incantu children, all looking vulnerable and terrified. Everything about what they were doing felt wrong to Leelo, and while she wouldn't put up a fight, she also didn't try to hide the tears streaming down her cheeks. Fiona was beside her, sobbing openly, and even Sage looked a little wilted. Ketty's eyes were dry, however, as she helped the other council members drag the boat to the water.

Leelo didn't know what made this boat safe to cross the lake on; surely if it were something natural, the outsiders would have discovered it by now, too. But the boat was as much a secret as the lilies, at least until the year of Watching was over. Otherwise, people like Leelo might be tempted to use it to see their lost family members. She tried not to think about all the parents who knew how the magic worked and yet hadn't gone in search of their children. There had to be a good reason for it, but every reason she came up with just made her more afraid for Tate.

Like Leelo, Fiona had already said goodbye to him at the cottage, but she started forward as Tate climbed into the boat.

"No, Aunt Fiona," Sage said, pulling her back. "You know you can't."

Fiona shook her off with more force than Leelo thought she was capable of. "Don't tell me what I can and can't do." She managed to make her way down to the boat, and Leelo was relieved when no one else tried to stop her. She watched as her mother embraced her brother, whispering something in his ear, and Tate, though he was visibly trembling, managed a brave nod.

"All right now," one of the other council members said to Fiona, gesturing for her to rejoin her family. "You know how this works, Fiona."

The children were given oars to row themselves across the lake, though none of them had ever rowed before. A special rope tied to the rear of the boat would be used to drag it back across after the children disembarked. Long ago, there had been a more permanent ferry, but its existence meant killing any outsider who attempted to use it. The current method involved far less bloodshed.

Tate and the other boy, Bizhan, each took up an oar, with Violet, the smallest of the three, huddled between them. They each had a single knapsack of belongings and the clothes on their backs. Endlans operated on a barter system, so there had been no coin to send Tate with, but Fiona had placed some of her finest knitwear in the sack, hoping Tate would be able to trade for it. Leelo had a feeling her brother would sooner starve than part with any of his mother's things, though. They were all he'd have to remember her by, outside of memories.

As the children made their way across the lake, the other

families in attendance turned to leave. They didn't sing for this ceremony; it would only endanger the children, and while they may be deficient in the eyes of some Endlans, they were still innocent.

Suddenly a thunderclap sounded so loudly that Leelo jumped and covered her ears. There had been no warning signs of a storm, and yet there could be no disputing that one had just arrived. Some said the Wandering Forest affected the weather itself, though how that could be, Leelo didn't know, any more than she understood how the Forest affected the lake. But as the rain began to fall in fat, cold drops, she saw the poor children huddle closer together in the boat. Now they would be soaked through by the time they arrived on the far shore.

Fiona was still sobbing, and Leelo decided it wouldn't help to watch. She took her mother and turned her away from the lake. As the council members began to pass them, heading back into the Forest, Leelo called after Ketty.

"What about the boat?"

"We'll fetch it in the morning. No one will be out in this weather, and there's no sense making ourselves sick over it."

It was a terribly callous thing to say, even for Aunt Ketty.

By the time they reached the cottage, Sage and Ketty were already warming themselves by the fire. Leelo helped her mother remove her sodden clothing and change into a warm flannel nightgown, then tucked her into bed.

"You're such a dear girl," Fiona said, cupping Leelo's cheek. "I'm so fortunate to have you."

Leelo kissed her mother, trying her best not to cry, and went to her room. She shivered violently as she stripped out of her own soaked dress and stockings. Still naked, she climbed under the covers of her bed and pulled them up over her head, waiting for the tremors to pass. Most spring storms weren't this cold or this sudden, and Leelo was usually good at predicting the weather. It was almost as if the island were inflicting one final punishment on the incantu, its own way of saying, "And don't ever come back!"

Eventually, Leelo felt her hands and feet go tingly with blood, and the shaking that had wracked her entire body subsided. She had no desire to spend time with her aunt and cousin at the moment, so after getting out of bed and changing into dry clothing, she went out back to the covered porch. The sun had gone down, but at least the storm had passed, and the moon was nearly full. The children wouldn't have to navigate in complete darkness. The Endlans wouldn't sing again until tomorrow night at the earliest, which gave Tate and the others a chance to get well clear of the lake.

Leelo could hear Sage and Ketty in the kitchen, preparing supper. She should probably set aside her anger and sadness, eat dinner, and go to bed. That would be the sensible thing.

A shadow passed in front of the moon, swooping low on silent wings and coming to land in the wooden beams above her. It was a barn owl, Leelo realized. Birds of that size weren't common on Endla, so it always felt like a good omen when one appeared; for whatever reason, the Forest hadn't taken it yet. Its pale, heart-shaped face turned at some noise in the distance, and then it was off again, winging into the Forest to hunt.

Without thinking, Leelo stood up, crossed the yard, and headed into the woods. Despite the rain, the Forest floor wasn't too muddy, thanks to the spring foliage overhead, and she could see well enough in the moonlight. After a few minutes of what she'd thought was aimless walking, she realized where her feet were taking her.

It took longer than it should have to reach the pine grove. In her troubled state of mind, she had taken several wrong turns, and it didn't help that her eyes were blurry with tears. When she finally reached the grove, she felt the months of pent-up anxiety and fear and hope burning deep in her bones.

She looked up through the branches, to where the moon glowed overhead. The tops of the trees swayed in a wind that took a moment longer to reach Leelo's skin, and she forced herself to take a deep breath. This place was so peaceful and serene right now, it was almost impossible to believe that it was where they had killed countless animals, that the Forest itself was bloodthirsty.

She could hear Aunt Ketty's voice in her mind. *This place is not evil. It protects us. We would be lost without it.*

The knot of sadness that had been stuck in Leelo's throat was becoming unbearable. She wanted to sing, but she knew she couldn't. There was still a chance the children were within earshot, and regardless, she wasn't allowed to sing alone.

But there had to be some way to release all this…rage. It wasn't an emotion Leelo had a lot of experience with, but now that she'd identified it, there was no denying that's what it was. She was full of seething, burning rage. Tate was gone, her mother was going to die, and what would she have then? Her bitter aunt and her prickly cousin, who was being slowly poisoned by Ketty, just like the lake.

What had happened to Ketty? she wondered for the thousandth time. A loveless marriage was bad, but surely not so bad that it could permanently alter a woman's heart. After all, her husband was long dead. She was free to marry again if she wanted, or not; she could *choose* happiness. But Ketty didn't seem interested in being happy. It was almost as if she relished her spite. And Sage was following right in her mother's footsteps.

Fiona would tell Leelo to be calm, to let her anger pass like a storm, to sit removed and watch it dissipate into the ether until she found acceptance. Her rage was of no use to anyone, certainly not Tate. And it wasn't as if Leelo would be stuck with her aunt forever. Mama would make sure Leelo found a suitable husband, someone she liked, if not loved. Leelo could start her own household with Fiona. Let Ketty and Sage keep the house. It wasn't important where they lived, if they had each other. Perhaps if Fiona was away from Ketty and her constant criticism, her health would improve and she'd be able to weave again.

But the rage wasn't fading. If anything, it was building. The more she thought about Tate out there on his own, away from the loving arms of his mother and sister, the angrier she got. And the more she thought about Ketty's indifference to her sister's pain, never mind her nephew's, the more she wanted to hurt someone herself.

Once again, the song—Leelo wasn't sure what it was, not the hunting song or the drowning song, but something new and insistent—pressed against her throat. She felt almost mad with the need to release it. And so, without really thinking it through, but feeling that it was the only thing she could do to punish everyone and everything that had stolen her brother from her, she pulled her little knife out of her pocket. And, choking on her own music, she drove it into the pine tree she had fed her entire life, with sacrifices and prey and even her own blood. She drove it in again and again until her arm ached from the motion and the knife lodged so deep into the wood that she couldn't draw it out again.

As if coming out of some kind of scarlet-stained trance, Leelo sank to her knees, exhausted. For all her effort, the tree showed little wounding, just a few patches of pale wood exposed by the blade, an errant splinter or two.

Tate was gone, and she had to accept it. From now on, she would put her mother and herself first. Fiona's health would be her main priority, and while she would do her chores and her Watcher duty because Fiona would want her to, she wouldn't attend the ceremonies anymore. Even if it cost her everything else. Even if it cost her Sage.

And because she still couldn't release the song in her throat, Leelo threw back her head and screamed.

Chapter Sixteen

Jaren didn't see Lupin after their conversation, but once word got out about their private stroll in the woods—thanks to Story, he assumed, although she wouldn't admit it—the gossipmongers of Bricklebury made sure that Jaren and Lupin were associated regardless. Everywhere he walked, whispers and giggles followed in his wake. He hadn't shown his face at the pub in days, not since the last time he'd gone and Lars had waggled his eyebrows suggestively.

"I still don't understand why you don't like her," Story said as they worked side by side in the garden behind their house. "She's a very pretty girl. Too pretty for you, some might say."

Jaren flicked a clod of soil at his sister. "It has nothing to do with how pretty she is. She's just...odd."

"Why? Because she's from Endla?"

He shook his head in frustration. "It's not that at all. She said the Forest there is *evil*. That it eats people, like it's a wolf or a bear or a—"

"A monster?"

"Yes! And it was clear she wasn't trying to scare me." She had accomplished that by flirting with him. "It was like she really believed everything she was saying."

Story carefully placed two carrot seeds in each little well she'd dug. "Why would she lie about it?"

"She wasn't lying. That's what I'm saying. I think she may have lost her senses a bit when she was exiled. And I don't blame her for that. She was a child."

"Well, you don't have to court her. But it's not going to look good for her, or you, if you don't at least make a show of it for a little while. People think you two were doing more than strolling, if you know what I mean."

Jaren rose to his feet. "And whose fault is that? If you hadn't gone blabbing to everyone in earshot, no one would have even noticed!" He knew that wasn't entirely fair. People had seen them with their own eyes, and he should have known well enough not to go wandering off alone with a girl in a town full of busybodies. But then again, so should Lupin. Unless she *wanted* people to think something had happened between them.

He shook his head. Girls didn't make sense at all.

"Oh, calm down," Story said, grabbing his hand to yank him back to work. "Soon enough another scandal will come along, and everyone will forget all about you and the honey girl."

But later that day, when he let his sisters drag him to the pub because Father insisted they needed an escort after he heard about Merritt, it was evident that no one had forgotten. Especially not Lupin.

It was the first time he'd seen her at the pub, and her eyes found his the moment he walked in the door, like she'd been waiting for him.

She wound through the other patrons toward him, smiling. "Jaren Kask. It's been a while since I've seen you in town. I was starting to think you were avoiding me."

Jaren blushed and shook his head. "Of course not. I'm just not used to so many people being aware of where I go, or with whom. I don't like all that attention."

"Says the boy who fetched water from Lake Luma." There was a hint of resentment in her voice, but she gestured to a table in the corner and he felt like he had no choice but to follow. His sisters had abandoned him the moment they arrived.

"Don't worry about the townspeople," Lupin said once they were seated. "They only gossip because they are safe and worry-free up here on the mountain. There's little possibility of a plague ever reaching Bricklebury, considering how rare outsiders are, and there is plenty to eat, thanks to the mountain's fertile soil. They're bored, is what I'm saying. And bored people love nothing more than a scandal."

"But surely a walk in the woods together is hardly a scandal."

"Perhaps you haven't noticed, but people tend to avoid me, Jaren. So it wasn't the walk in the woods that got them talking. It was the girl."

"I'm sorry. I didn't know. I hope your reputation wasn't harmed."

She threw her head back and laughed, revealing all of her white teeth. "My reputation? I may as well be a witch, as far as these people are concerned."

Jaren glanced around the pub. Sure enough, people were staring at them.

"Why do you stay here?" Jaren asked. "I couldn't stand everyone judging me like that all the time."

"People will judge you anywhere you go. I know who I am. Why should I care what they think of me?"

Jaren wished he had that kind of confidence, the kind that only came with knowing who you were. "I'm sorry if I gave you the wrong impression, Lupin. I'm not looking to marry anytime soon. I haven't even chosen a trade yet."

She ran her finger around the edge of her pint glass and smiled. "Oh, silly boy. Who said anything about marriage?"

Jaren couldn't sleep. Every time he closed his eyes, he saw Lupin's wolfish grin. And every time he tried to find a comfortable position in his bed, a few notes of the first song he'd heard from Endla played in his mind. Jaren had never had the experience of getting a song caught in his mind before, and he thought it might be driving him a little mad. Maybe that explained Lupin and her strangeness.

Or maybe it was simply that he didn't know the whole song, just that one little strand of notes, and some part of his brain kept snagging on it, trying to fill in what came next. If he'd had any musical inclination, he could have played the notes out on an instrument and attempted to finish the song. But he didn't know anything about scales or melodies, and he certainly couldn't play an instrument. So he was stuck with those same notes replaying in his mind. Yes, a person could definitely go mad from that.

Around midnight, when he was not a whit closer to sleep

than he'd been when he first went to bed, Jaren threw back his covers, pulled on his trousers, and crept down the ladder as quietly as he could. As he tiptoed past his father, who generally slept so soundly that not even an earthquake could wake him, Jaren grabbed his boots from the hearth and slipped silently into the night.

An intense rainstorm had passed through this evening, leaving the air cool enough to help clear his head a bit. If he walked for a bit, he might be able to clear the song away altogether. It wasn't the most brilliant plan to wander alone in the woods at night, but anything was better than slowly going mad in his own bed.

Unfortunately, Jaren had a habit of finding a topic that troubled him and ruminating on it until his thoughts circled around and around, like a dog chasing its tail. And if he wasn't going to think about the music—and he wasn't going to think about the music, damn it—there was little to think about other than Lupin.

Lupin, with her honey hair and meadow-green eyes, with her hollow laugh and her relentless flirting. With her insinuation that she wasn't looking for marriage but was willing to do other things. Jaren knew if any of his sisters did those other things before marriage, they would be permanently ruined. But then, Lupin was already ruined in the eyes of the townspeople.

Despite the fact that he was surrounded by girls, Jaren found them predictable in one thing and one thing only: their unpredictability. One moment Story would be laughing and joking, and the next, she was angry about something. And worse still, she would refuse to acknowledge that she was angry. Tadpole's crushes were as fleeting as a summer storm, and Summer, arguably the most even-tempered of the three, was not immune to changes in mood that could leave a man reeling in confusion. And these were the girls he'd grown up with! How could he possibly be expected to understand the motivations of a near stranger?

His mother, on the other hand. His mother he had always understood. She would get angry, of course, but her reasons were never a mystery. He had left his muddy boots by the hearth again, or he'd burned the bread because he was day-dreaming, or he'd gone to market for apples and come home with potatoes instead. If she was upset about something, she would excuse herself to go for a walk or retreat to the bedroom she and Father had shared in their old, larger house, and when she came out she was herself again. She'd even offer an explanation of why she'd been upset, if Father couldn't figure it out on his own. And when Jaren's sisters were particularly volatile, Mother would tell the men to go make themselves useful, and by the time they returned, everything was right as rain again.

You're spinning, Jaren, he thought as he meandered down the forest trail. He was so distracted he wasn't even sure which trail he had taken, but he supposed it didn't matter, as long as he returned by it when he went back.

Something crossed his path, a low, stealthy creature, most likely a fox. A night bird called somewhere in the distance, and every now and then he would hear something small rustle in the bushes. All typical nighttime forest activity. Less than he'd expect, in fact.

Suddenly, a long, mournful howl raised the hairs on the

back of Jaren's neck. He couldn't help thinking of the monstrous wolf the townspeople spoke of. He hadn't even brought a knife with him, he realized. He was as defenseless out here as a loaf of bread.

Still, the howl had been far-off, and turning around wasn't necessarily the better choice, since he couldn't be sure which direction it had come from. He kept walking, though his thoughts were decidedly not on the whimsies of women anymore. The howl came again, and this time, it sounded closer. Jaren froze on the trail, listening. Somewhere above him, an owl hooted and took off from its perch, likely in search of prey of its own. He glanced around at his surroundings and recognized the split tree off to his left, the circle of toadstools to his right. He realized with a sinking sensation that he'd done it again.

He'd taken the trail to Endla.

Another howl, this time much closer than the last. Jaren spun around, attempting to tell which direction it was coming from, until he was dizzy and even more lost than before. He laughed, a little hysterically, and wondered if he truly was going mad, if the magic of Endla had indeed ensnared him like a siren's song. How else could he explain why his feet kept finding this same trail? How else could he defend the decision to go walking, alone, in the middle of the night?

The next sound Jaren heard wasn't a howl, and it was much, much closer. It was the low, rumbling snarl of a predator. He turned slowly, eyes frantically searching the darkness, until he saw the two glowing eyes staring back. And they were far too large to belong to anything other than a massive, hungry wolf.

He bolted. Instinctively, he knew this creature wasn't going to back down no matter how big Jaren made himself, no matter how much yelling and flapping and stick flailing he did. This animal was clearly the alpha of this forest, probably the entire mountain, and one measly, defenseless human was not going to scare it away.

By some miracle, Jaren didn't stumble as he sprinted down the trail. His feet, at least, seemed to know the way. He could hear the wolf behind him, not snarling now, just breathing as it ran, and something told him that the beast wasn't actually trying to catch him, because surely it was faster on its four legs and with its keen night vision than he could be. Was it trying to tire him? Or was it driving him exactly where it wanted him to go: into the waiting jaws of the rest of its pack?

Jaren didn't have the breath in his lungs to scream for help, and he knew that no one would come if he did. He was completely alone out here, by his own daft will, and he was going to die that way. He hoped there'd be enough left of him for his family to identify his remains, although the loss would be devastating regardless. The girls had just lost their beloved mother, after all. *I should have known better*, Jaren thought bitterly. Even if he didn't value his own life enough to stay away from this forest and that cursed island, he should have put his sisters' safety and comfort first.

As his feet beat down the trail, that inane, insidious song returned to his frantic mind, and to his surprise, it calmed him, in a way. He focused on the melody, rather than the fact that a beast that was all claws and fangs and hunger was just behind him, its breath hot on his back.

And with what little breath Jaren had left, he said a prayer to whoever was listening to spare his life.

Chapter Seventeen

Leelo was only halfway home when she heard the howl. She'd foolishly fallen asleep below the pine tree. Now, her entire body erupted in goose bumps, and she could feel every hair on her arms standing straight up, like a lightning storm had just passed through.

For a moment she stood stock-still, wondering if she'd imagined it. Wolves never came this far up the mountain, and this one had sounded so close it could be on Endla itself. But then it happened again and again, and Leelo felt the sound in every part of her, as if this were a song she'd known all her life.

"Tate," she breathed.

A sudden gust of wind blew past, making the trees around her creak like old, forgotten doors, and Leelo knew this time that she wasn't imagining things. The Forest was speaking.

And a wolf was at the doorstep.

Chapter Eighteen

At the time, the boat had seemed like the only option. Jaren had found himself between the wolf and a lake full of poison, and while the wolf hadn't advanced on him, it hadn't retreated, either. It sat there, staring with eyes made yellow in the moonlight, and let out three long, hair-raising howls.

Swimming was clearly not an option. Jaren thought of the rose turning to ash in its vial and shuddered. He liked his odds better with the wolf, even if the old man had been right when he said it was the size of a cow. Where had this monster come from, and why had it chased him here, of all places?

Even now, in what were inarguably very unlikely circumstances, he still wasn't convinced this was magic. The wolf was enormous, but not *impossibly* enormous. And if a wolf wanted to corner its prey, what better place to flush it than here? He had to admit, however, that the fact that the wolf wasn't trying to eat him was perplexing.

They stared at each other for a long while, before the wolf

rose and advanced with one large claw-tipped paw, then another, and Jaren found himself unconsciously backing toward the water. He wasn't sure he'd have caught himself in time if his foot hadn't met with something solid. He risked a glance over his shoulder and saw it, hidden among the rocks. A boat. The wolf must have seen it at the same moment Jaren did because it rushed forward suddenly, causing Jaren's body to make a choice his mind hadn't yet been willing to face.

The next thing he knew, he was in the boat, and the sudden movement had lurched it out into the open water. Into the poisonous lake.

Jaren didn't know enough about Lake Luma to be certain that a boat couldn't make it across, although he could deduce as much given what he'd seen with the rose. Still, he thought he must have at least a little while before the boat began to erode, and in the meantime, perhaps the wolf would tire of whatever game they were playing and leave. But the wolf only paced up and down the shore, as if to tell Jaren that it was pointless to come back, that they'd only end up right where they were now.

Jaren could just make out the island in the moonlight. It looked innocent enough from here, covered in what appeared to be ordinary trees, aside from a copse of tall pines peeking above the rest of the Forest in the center of the island.

A breeze traveled over the water, like a long, languorous sigh, and the bare skin at the nape of his neck prickled with fear. He remembered what Lupin had told him about Endlans and tried to take comfort in it.

"Are they a cruel people?" he had asked as they walked back toward the market.

"Not as a whole, no," she'd said. "My parents were wonderful, loving people, and I know it broke their hearts the day they sent me away. I was the only incantu that year, and the ride across the lake in the Endlan boat was particularly difficult for me, as I'd never rowed before."

This boat must have taken incantu children to the mainland. From what Lupin had told Jaren, the poison in the lake destroyed outsider vessels. Why this boat hadn't been pulled back to the other side of the lake, he couldn't say. He had drifted to the center of the lake now, and if there had been oars in the boat at some point, they were gone. He was entirely at the mercy of the wind, and it seemed to be nudging him toward Endla.

A sudden gust jostled the boat even more, and that was when he heard a sound that chilled him to his bones: sloshing. The boat must have scraped the rocks when he shoved it back into the water. And now it had sprung a leak.

Jaren peered through the waning darkness to the shore, wondering if someone was waiting for him even now. Would they spare him, if he somehow managed to make it across? He doubted it.

He glanced down to see the water level rising in the floor of the boat. He lifted his feet onto the bench where he sat, then looked back to the shore. He wasn't going to make it, he thought hopelessly. The water was rising faster than he was traveling. He tried not to think of the rose, of his sisters, of his poor father, and failed.

Chapter Nineteen

Leelo knew she should be sprinting toward home, not the shoreline, but her only coherent thought right now was of Tate. If there was a wolf across the lake in the woods where her brother and the other children had landed, he was as good as dead.

He has to be far away from here, she told herself as cold tears of terror streamed across her cheeks. Because what if this was her fault? What if her assault on the pine tree had somehow caused the Forest to retaliate?

She hadn't brought her bow and arrow with her; all she had was the knife, which she'd finally managed to dislodge from the tree by bracing her foot against it and pulling so hard she'd gone flying backward when it came loose. But just as it had been worthless against the tree, she knew it wouldn't help her fight a wolf. Still, she had to try.

When she finally reached the shore, she froze among the trees, listening. The wolf had howled intermittently as she ran, but it was silent now. The only sound was the wind whipping through the trees. It had picked up again, blowing from the mainland toward shore. She couldn't see the wolf from here. All she could see in the moonlight was the dark expanse of the lake.

There was no way to know if her brother was safe. Not from here. She glanced at the rock where the rope was tied. If she pulled the boat back, she could row over to him and check for herself. If she was fast enough, she could do it before dawn. How could she ever sleep again, not knowing if Tate was safe?

But when she went to the rope, prepared to do whatever it took to check on her brother, she noticed with a gasp that it was slack. She looked out at the water, her heart pounding. The boat was no longer on the shore. It was in the middle of the lake.

And there was someone in it.

For one heart-stopping moment she thought it was Tate, that her prayer had worked, that the Forest had listened and he was coming home.

But the person in the boat was far too large to be her brother, which could only mean it was an outsider. And he was headed straight for Endla.

If she ran to get help, the outsider would make land before she could return. As a Watcher, this was what she was supposed to do: find anyone who was trying to harm the island and kill them. But the thought of taking on a full-grown adult, alone, made her legs go numb underneath her. She was supposed to have a bow and arrow. She was supposed to have Sage.

While she'd run toward the shore, dawn had slowly been creeping up to the horizon, and the sky was light enough now that she could make out the figure more clearly as the boat continued to make its way to shore. She was fairly certain it was a man, judging by the silhouette, but she couldn't make anything else out.

She dropped into a crouch behind the rock, aware that if she could see the person in the boat, it was entirely possible he could see her. She knew what Sage would do; she'd hide here, behind this rock, and stab the man in the back when he passed her. But Leelo wasn't Sage. She couldn't even kill a rabbit. How was she supposed to kill a human being?

The boat was close enough now that she could make out two things clearly: it was definitely a man, and the boat was riding lower in the water than it had with the three children in it. Even given how small Violet had been, their combined weight had to have been more than one man. Which could only mean the boat was sinking.

She breathed a ragged sigh of relief. The lake would take care of him for her. She wouldn't have to do anything. Emboldened by the knowledge that he wouldn't make it, she rose to her feet.

And gasped.

In the growing light of day, she could see that this wasn't a man; not a full-grown one, anyway. He didn't look much older than her, in fact. He was perched on the bench in the middle of the boat, clinging to it to keep from being tossed out by the waves. Suddenly, he looked up, and their eyes met.

It was the young man from the day of the festival.

She wasn't sure how she knew. She hadn't been able to

make out his features that day, only his dark, tousled hair. But she could see his features clearly now, and he was terrified.

She looked around in vain, as if there were some adult nearby to help her. Why had he gotten in the boat? Why would he want to cross to Endla, knowing what he must about the island?

She walked to the water's edge without meaning to. He wasn't going to make it. Not at the rate he was going. He gesticulated at the stern of the boat, then at her, then back to the boat again.

She shook her head in confusion.

"The rope!" he screamed.

Of course. The rope. She could pull him to shore. It might not be enough, but she could try.

She could.

Her eyes darted to his face again. He wasn't far offshore now, but the boat was listing dangerously, thrown off-balance by the water pooling inside it. Any second it would tip, he would fall into the lake, and he would die.

She groaned in anguish. She couldn't kill an outsider, but she couldn't *help* an outsider, either. Every day of her life had been in preparation for this moment. So why was she hesitating? She reached for her knife, hefted it in her hand. Cut the rope, and he would die. She would have done her job. Would probably even be revered for it.

But then she saw the terror in his eyes and thought of her brother, of the dread he must be feeling as he fumbled his way through a dark, unfamiliar wood with a wolf on the prowl. She thought of Pieter and his last desperate cry for help. Somewhere, someone loved this boy, and if he died, their heart would break as surely as Isola's had. *Not all outsiders are evil*, her mother had said, and it hadn't been speculation. She had said it with as much quiet conviction as when she told her children she loved them.

The warring voices of her aunt and Sage echoed in her ears. *We protect Endla above all else.*

But Leelo wasn't Ketty, and she wasn't Sage. She couldn't save her brother, but she could save this man's life.

The knife slipped from Leelo's fingers, and the next thing she knew she was grabbing the rope with both hands and pulling with all her might.

The young man was shouting now, but she didn't look up. She didn't want to know how close it was going to be. She was doing everything she could. A few moments later, she heard the sound of the hull scraping against the rocks and sand. Dawn was only minutes away. Sage would be here soon, and how would Leelo possibly explain this?

Without looking back at the boat, she dropped the rope, grabbed her knife, and fled.

Chapter Twenty

Leelo was breathless as she sprinted through the Forest toward home. Sage would be arriving for Watcher duty any second, and the council members would be returning for the boat soon. They would find it back on this side of the shore, either containing the remnants of an outsider, or empty. Despite what she'd just done, she was praying for the former. They would think an outsider had attempted to cross and failed, and she couldn't be blamed for that.

If he wasn't dead, he was certainly injured. The rough landing on shore would have made it impossible not to get any water on himself. She could only hope he was injured badly enough he wouldn't remember that Leelo had helped him. It had only been for a minute or two, anyway. She wasn't even sure that she *had* helped him. He might have made it to shore all on his own.

I should have killed him, she thought bitterly, but she couldn't get the image of the young man's panicked face out of her mind. She resented him for putting her in this position. He must have heard tales of Endla wherever he came from. What reason could he possibly have for coming here, other than to cause harm?

Leelo sobbed as she ran, her lungs burning. She couldn't risk running into Sage in this state. She needed to calm down and come up with a plan.

She left the trail and headed into the Forest, which would at least help her avoid her cousin or a council member. She would skirt the pine grove and set a less direct course toward home. It would take longer, but it was her best option. When she was deep enough into the trees, she stopped to catch her breath and attempted to calm her racing thoughts.

The situation was bad; there was no denying that. But she had gone to the lake tonight for a reason: the wolf. Others must have heard it howling. And maybe it wasn't her attack on the pine that brought it. Maybe the Forest had used it to alert the Endlans that danger, in the form of an outsider, was nearby. She should have woken her mother then, not come out here on her own. But her intentions had been pure, at least.

She sighed. Deep down, she knew that reasoning would never hold up under Sage's and Ketty's scrutiny, and certainly not the council's. What kind of Endlan *saved* an outsider?

"Not an outsider," she said out loud, trying to drown out the voices in her head. "A human being."

After she'd collected herself, she resumed jogging at a more maintainable pace. She couldn't call attention to herself, and she couldn't be in a state of panic when she made it home. She would tell her family she'd heard the wolf, that she'd gone out to investigate and hadn't found anything. A rabbit darted across her path, making her gasp, but aside from that, she saw no living creatures in the Forest. Most of them knew to stay away from the pine grove, at least the ones that had survived long enough to learn.

A bird flapped from a tree suddenly. Leelo froze, and in the silence, she heard the faint sound of someone talking.

Two someones talking.

She dropped down behind a bramble bush, listening. She must have veered closer to the trail than she realized.

Leelo would know her cousin's voice anywhere, but it took her a moment longer to recognize the second voice.

Hollis.

"It's quieter without her there. I guess I should have expected that. Violet was always complaining about something. She was small for her age, you know, so she couldn't do what the other kids could. She was always falling behind and yelling for me to wait up."

"And did you?" Sage asked.

"Only if my parents made me…" His words faded as they disappeared farther into the woods, and Leelo realized she'd been holding her breath to hear him. She exhaled raggedly and sat down all the way. Hollis must have taken over her Watcher shift when Sage woke up and found her missing. Leelo had never lied to her cousin before, and now she could see the lies she'd have to carefully weave together multiplying.

What she really wanted to do right now was go home and climb back into her bed. Mama would come and look in on her, pressing her cool palm to Leelo's forehead to check for fever, the way she always did when Leelo was ill. She would bring warm honey-lemon water and a hot stone wrapped in a knit cover for her feet. She would sit by Leelo's bedside and stroke her hair and sing something soft and meaningless, not a true Endlan song, just something she'd made up to soothe Leelo as a baby.

Leelo longed for those early days, before Tate was born and her father was dead, before Aunt Ketty's meanness crystallized into amber, when she and Sage were two girls in pigtail braids with no cares in the world.

She couldn't do any of that, but she had nowhere else to go.

As she approached her cottage, Leelo felt a moment's relief. It looked peaceful and safe amid the greenery of late spring. Her mother had planted red geraniums in the window boxes, their color bright and cheerful against the blue-and-white trim. She pulled off her leather boots and left them by the front door, relieved that only Mama's were there. Ketty must be with the sheep.

Inside, Leelo found her mother sitting near the fire. Normally, they wouldn't heat the house at this time of year, but she was always chilled lately.

"Ketty?" Fiona called when she heard the door open. "Oh, it's you, dear." Worry flickered across her brow. "Did something happen on duty?"

Leelo desperately wanted to tell her mother everything. She of all people would understand why Leelo had been unable to kill the outsider.

But she also knew she would be making her mother complicit if she told her about the young man, and whatever happened from this moment, she wouldn't let her take any of the blame. Leelo wasn't sure Mama's heart could take it, and she couldn't bear the thought of being shunned like Isola.

"I never made it to my Watch this morning," Leelo said instead. "I missed Tate too much. I went into the woods, to be alone."

If Fiona didn't accept the lie, no one would, but she nodded and smiled gently. "I understand. Your aunt and Sage were already out when I came downstairs, but I suppose they noticed your absence."

Leelo twisted her braid between her fingers. "Do you think I'll be punished? I know it's terrible to miss my Watch."

Fiona patted the arm of her chair, inviting Leelo to sit. She wrapped her arms around Leelo's waist and kissed her shoulder. "We'll tell them I couldn't sleep last night and I sent you out early this morning for some foxglove on the far side of the island. Ketty will still be angry, but she'll forgive us."

Leelo breathed a sigh of relief, grateful for her mother's calm, reassuring presence. It was a good lie, since Leelo did often gather foxglove leaves for tea. It was supposed to help Mama with her heart troubles, though Leelo had been warned to be careful. The entire plant was extremely toxic.

"Thank you, Mama. How are you feeling today?"

"Oh, fine. I was just thinking of your brother."

"Are you worried about him?"

"No, no. He's a brave, strong boy. I was only missing him, selfishly. But he'll do just fine out in the world. I imagine it's a far more welcoming place than Endla."

As small and insular as her island was, Leelo had never considered leaving. She didn't even try to imagine what life on the mainland was like, because her elders made the rest of the world sound terrible and frightening. Endla's Forest was ruthless in some ways, but it was all she'd ever known, and as long as she played her part in its survival, she had nothing to fear from it. So it was strange to hear her mother say that Endla was less welcoming than the rest of the world. Hadn't the outsiders been the ones who drove the Endlans to this island in the first place?

"Go on," her mother said. "I'll be fine here."

Leelo kissed her cheek, drank some water from the pitcher, and headed back outside. She'd been up and walking for hours, and it was starting to take a toll on her. At least her mother had given her a plausible story. As long as the outsider was dead, everything would be fine.

Except that a person will be dead.

When she finally arrived at the beach, she found Hollis and Sage sitting on a log together, talking.

"I'm so sorry I'm late," Leelo breathed as she trotted up to them. "Mama was ill and I—"

"It's fine," Sage said abruptly. "Hollis was able to cover for you. But you'll have to take his shift this evening."

Leelo had expected Sage to be worried or frustrated. At worst, she'd expected Sage's anger. But she hadn't expected her cousin to side with Hollis over her. "We still have over half our shift left. I can take half of his tonight, if he wants."

"It's fine," Hollis said. "I can do a double shift."

"No," Sage said. "That's not fair. My mother will take care of Aunt Fiona. And Leelo can take the shift with Kris."

Leelo stared at her cousin, hurt despite the fact that she'd brought this on herself. Sage stared right back, as if daring Leelo to argue again.

Suddenly remembering the outsider, she glanced around the beach. The boat was gone, and there was no sign of him.

"What happened to the boat?" Leelo asked.

Hollis shaded his eyes against the sun and looked up at her. "The council members found it washed up on this side of the shore this morning. Huge hole in the hull. They took it away for repairs."

Where is the outsider? she wanted to scream, but she couldn't admit that she'd seen him.

Sage was still watching Leelo with an inscrutable expression. "Why do you care about the boat?"

"I don't," Leelo lied. "I just didn't realize they'd already taken it." She forced herself to take a breath. The young man must not have made it to land after all. Which meant no one had been there to sing for him. She hoped he'd died quickly, at least.

"You can go," Sage said when Leelo didn't move. "You still have time to rest before your shift starts."

Leelo glanced at Hollis to see what he made of all this, but he was just staring blankly across the shore. Sage seemed to be showing off for him, but Leelo couldn't fathom why. Sage was not the kind of girl to swoon at the sight of muscles, and Hollis wasn't anywhere close to an intellectual match for her.

Whatever the case, Sage wasn't going to budge, and Leelo was exhausted. "Thank you for covering for me, Hollis," she said.

He grunted in acknowledgment as she left the shore and headed back into the Forest. She would go home, sleep, and forget about the outsider, she told herself. But her mind kept snagging on Sage and Hollis. For someone who had all but sworn off marriage, he was an extremely odd choice for Sage. And for someone who had always been so loyal, she seemed rather quick to dismiss Leelo, especially for something as small as coming late to Watcher duty.

With a sick twisting in her stomach, Leelo started to wonder if Sage might know more than she was letting on.

And then she saw the trail of blood.

Chapter Twenty-One

Jaren stumbled through the Forest, dragging his injured leg behind him. After the girl had abandoned him on the beach, he had lain on the rocky shore for a few minutes, as far from the lapping water as he could get.

He hadn't even inspected his leg. He knew it was bad, and he couldn't risk staying out in the open, exposed. When the girl had grabbed the rope, he had been certain she was going to try to tip him or prevent him from coming ashore. Instead, she had hauled him toward the beach. But if she was trying to help Jaren, surely she would have checked on him. She had disappeared before he was even out of the boat, probably to get reinforcements, if he had to guess. His only hope right now was to hide somewhere and pray the wound wasn't fatal.

He had hardly gone far at all when he heard voices in the Forest ahead. Somehow, he managed to scramble up a tree and hide among the leaves. He held his breath and watched as a boy and girl passed below him. If one of them glanced up, they would spot him instantly.

Fortunately, they were too absorbed in their conversation to notice him. He exhaled as quietly as he could and slid out of the tree, doing his best to avoid scraping his damaged leg. He had no idea if the poison would work the way it had on the rose, traveling throughout the entire flower until it was dead. If that was the case, then hiding wasn't going to do him any good. But there was still a chance he might live, and if it meant getting back to his father and sisters, then he had to try.

When the pain and exhaustion proved too overwhelming, Jaren crawled through an opening in some dense hedges and sat down. He hoped he was hidden here. He needed water desperately, but he had no idea where there was a safe source on the island, so that would have to wait.

Gingerly, he peeled his trousers away from his damaged skin. The fact that he'd only been splashed on one leg was a miracle in itself. He took a deep breath, bit his lip, and looked down. It was worse than he'd feared. The poison had burned straight into his shin in several places, through the skin, muscle, and sinew, down to the bone. Fortunately, the bone itself appeared intact, although he'd have felt a lot better if he could have rinsed the wound with clean water, or better yet, alcohol. But he didn't have anything with him, not even a waterskin.

He tore off the part of his trousers that had been soaked, just in case any more poison made its way through the fabric. He used a strip of tunic to bind the wound, although the bleeding seemed to have stopped on its own. Lars had said that when Maggie's father died, it was because he had literally walked into the water on foot, drawn by the song coming from the island. He had been so entranced that he hadn't even flinched as the poison began to burn off his flesh, and he had ignored the screams and shouts from his friends on the shoreline. They had never recovered any of his body.

Jaren felt a stab of guilt for laughing at the idea of magic. He owed Maggie an apology, if he ever made it out of here alive.

He didn't realize he'd fallen asleep until he heard someone coming through the undergrowth. He sat up, feeling feverish and disoriented, the pain in his leg excruciating. He peeked through the bushes and saw something pale flash in the trees. He took a deep breath and willed his heartbeat to slow, though it pounded so loudly in his own ears he was sure he'd be discovered.

As the person drew nearer, he gasped. It was the girl with the silver-blond hair again. The girl he'd seen at the festival, and the girl who had hauled the boat to shore. He peered through the brush. She was clad in a tunic and trousers, just like he was. Her hair was braided, a few loose strands framing her heart-shaped face. She was looking at something on the ground, her brow furrowed in concern.

Blood. She'd been following his trail this entire time. He swallowed thickly, cold sweat breaking out on his forehead. She was still alone, but that didn't mean she wasn't here to harm him. Perhaps she'd come to finish the job, not wanting to risk the lake before. Lupin had said most Endlans were good people, and she had seemed harmless enough the day of the festival, waving when she could have raised a weapon or opened her mouth in song.

But he was exactly what the Endlans feared most: an outsider, likely bent on destruction, as it didn't seem anyone came to this island for sightseeing and a picnic. He glanced at his leg again. He had two choices: remain hidden, pray that his wound didn't kill him before dark, and attempt to repair the boat...or take a chance on this stranger. He winced, the effort of moving causing stars to dance in his vision. He would never make it back to the mainland on his own.

The girl crouched down and put her fingers to the blood. She raised her hand and sniffed. And then, like a hawk narrowing in on its prey, her head swiveled to his hiding place. Their eyes met through the screen of branches.

They rose at the same moment.

"Hello," he said, and fainted.

Chapter Twenty-Two

As she stared down at the unconscious outsider, Leelo couldn't help studying him. It wasn't that his clothing or appearance were so different from an islander's; it was the realization that she had never seen a face like his before, and she knew all of Endla's faces. In a place like this, you came to recognize the cut of a jaw as quintessential Stone, or the arch of a brow as undeniably Johansson. Even if she hadn't watched him cross from the mainland with her own eyes, Leelo would know him for an outsider. She hadn't seen this jaw, or this brow, in her life.

The man's eyelashes started to flutter, and she moved into shooting stance, an arrow notched so fast even Sage would be impressed. He was badly injured; he likely wasn't a danger to her in his current state. But she wasn't taking any chances.

As his eyes blinked open, Leelo noticed that his irises were the gray of storm clouds. His chestnut hair was thick and tousled, full of leaf litter from the Forest floor.

His fingers scrabbled in the dirt next to him, like he was trying to gain purchase on an object.

"Stop moving, or I'll shoot."

The man looked up at her and held something out. It was a feather, long and striped in shades of brown.

"You dropped this," he rasped. It was one of the hawk tail-feathers she collected for arrow fletching. It must have slipped from the buttonhole she had tucked it into earlier.

Leelo hesitated, unsure how she was supposed to proceed. This outsider—this man, or young man, she supposed—didn't *seem* to mean her any harm. *He's an outsider!* Sage's voice hissed in her ear. But he seemed as confused as she was.

When she didn't take the feather, he lowered it to his side and managed to sit up, running his free hand through his hair and ruffling it further.

"What's your name?" the man asked her.

Leelo had been staring. She blinked and glanced around, sure that someone must be watching them and waiting for her to do the right thing, to sound the alarm and turn him over to the council. But she was still paralyzed with indecision. She'd heard once that the human body reacted one of three ways in an emergency: fight, flight, or freeze. And she was firmly in the third category.

"I'm Jaren Kask," he said when she didn't respond. She had the distinct impression he was trying to calm her, like one might a spooked animal, but it was just as likely he was distracting her, buying himself time to attack. "I recognize you, from the day of the… I suppose it was a festival of some sort. You waved to me?"

Leelo's breath caught. He recognized her. She pulled the arrow back a fraction more.

He hurried to fill the silence. "Don't worry. I won't tell anyone. I know I'm not supposed to be here. This wolf…"

As the man rambled on, explaining how he'd managed to get here in the first place, Leelo was scrambling for a solution to what was turning out to be an even larger problem than she could have possibly imagined. If Sage had also seen the blood, if she knew there was an outsider on Endla and that Leelo was partially responsible…

She had to get rid of him. It was the only option. But ending his life here seemed impossible. If she hadn't done it back when he was still on the boat, when she didn't know his name, how could she possibly kill him now? Jaren didn't look menacing, lying on the ground at her feet with his pupils blown wide.

He looked terrified.

Do it, Sage's voice said in her mind. *Kill him and be done with it.*

If Leelo did, she'd be lauded as a hero. Even Aunt Ketty would have to respect her for taking down an outsider all on her own. The man was only a few feet from her. One shot through the throat, and he'd be finished. He was already injured; he might die anyway. She'd be doing him a favor.

Jaren Kask probably wasn't even his real name.

Leelo glanced at his leg again and saw something pearly white flash beneath the wound. Saints, it was down to the bone. "Can you stand?"

He nodded. "I think so? I might need some help."

Help. As in, he needed her to provide him more aid than

she'd already given. Leelo didn't know what the consequences for helping an outsider were. Isola was ruined for life just for sheltering an incantu, someone who had been born here. Pieter clearly hadn't meant Endla harm. But though this man claimed to have been driven here by accident—by the very wolf she'd heard, in fact—how could she trust him? Of course he would try to convince her he meant no harm; she was his only hope for getting off Endla.

Jaren's hand was out, waiting for Leelo to help him to his feet. If she refused, he might not be able to move, and she needed to get him away from the shore, away from Sage and Hollis. Sage was shrewd; if she found the outsider, she'd put together Leelo's absence this morning and her question about the boat and know this was her fault. She wouldn't be a hero. She'd be a traitor.

Confused, frightened, and more unsure of herself than she'd ever been, Leelo reached for him. The sight of her small hand wrapped in a large, male hand was so strange that she couldn't stop looking at it, even as she pulled him to his feet.

As soon as he was upright, she yanked her hand free of his. "Come on," she said, plowing into the undergrowth in the opposite direction of home. She wasn't sure she could find the hut again. It had been an accident the first time, and she had never planned to go back. But she had to hide him until she could cobble together a way out of this mess, and Isola's secret hideaway was the only place she could think of right now.

For all his bewilderment, Jaren must have sensed she wasn't trying to kill him, because he followed.

After a few minutes, she glanced over her shoulder. "I'm

Leelo." She added, "You really shouldn't be here," in case it wasn't obvious.

He gave a low, ironic chuckle, doing his best to limp along behind her. "Believe me, I know."

"You said the wolf chased you here? That doesn't make sense. Wolves don't come to Endla."

He paused to rest against a tree, his brow beaded with sweat. "I can't explain it. I found the lake by accident, months ago now, and ever since then, since the singing, it's like a part of me has been trying to come back."

She had been rummaging in the undergrowth for something that would work as a walking stick, but she froze at his words.

Jaren was tall, at least a head taller than she was. She swallowed, grateful that he wasn't big the way Hollis Harding was, in the way that felt menacing even when he was just standing there. "You heard us sing?"

She saw his throat bob as he, too, swallowed down his apprehension, as if *her* presence unnerved *him*. Then she remembered the bow slung over her shoulder, the knife at her waist. He was gravely injured, and she was supposed to kill him. He had good reason to be scared.

"That can't be right. You would have gone into the lake, if you had."

"That's what everyone in Bricklebury said. But I heard it. Once at the festival, and once when you were… Well, I didn't see anything, but it sounded like you were slaughtering animals."

He'd heard the killing song? While some of Endla's songs were more powerful than others, anyone who listened long enough would be drawn to the sound, some part of their brain searching for the source. Her mother had told her of foolish outsiders who'd been lured into the water by accident, simply because they wouldn't stay away from Lake Luma's shores. The killing song was one of their strongest; it should have spelled his doom. None of this made any sense.

Suddenly she heard the call of the starling, the same damn bird that had stolen her voice before. At least she knew she was close to the cottage.

"That," Jaren said. "That song. That's the first one I heard, the one I can't get out of my head."

The blood drained from Leelo's face as she realized what he was saying. "You know this song?"

He started to hum the tune, and she slapped her hand over his mouth so quickly he startled and grabbed her arm. For one long, strange moment, they were connected, and Leelo wondered if Jaren's arm was humming with a current the way hers was, emanating from the point where her hand touched his lips.

Stunned into something between wonder and horror, her hand slipped free of his mouth just as his released her arm.

"Be quiet," Leelo said. "No one can know you're here. If they find you, you're as good as dead."

He nodded, and she could only hope he hadn't noticed that the voice coming from the bird's throat was hers.

Chapter Twenty-Three

As the girl—Leelo—led him farther into the woods, Jaren couldn't help but wonder what the odds were that of all the people on this island, he'd found *her*, the same girl he'd seen at the lake's edge. Lupin had told him that outsiders would die in the Forest if they made it past the lake. He assumed she'd meant because of the Watchers. And now here he was, following one of them into that very Forest, with no idea what her intentions were.

Jaren knew he should be questioning Leelo and where she was taking him, but he also knew that she was his best hope for getting off this island, assuming he could convince her not to kill him herself. His mind had been so full of fear and confusion since he first encountered the wolf that it was a relief to follow someone else for a few minutes, to give his brain a moment to process where he was. Besides, Leelo seemed to have a destination in mind, and that was better than what he'd had when he ran into her.

As he limped behind her, his stomach roiled with nausea from the pain in his leg. He studied the pale braid snaking between her slim but square shoulders, the bow across her back, the soft falls of her feet. He tried to picture Story in her place, to give himself something other than the pain to focus on, but his mind could only conjure an image of her cursing as she tried to tear her skirt free from the undergrowth. She wouldn't know how to walk quietly in the woods if her life depended on it.

Finally, Leelo came to a stop, peering into the undergrowth as if she was looking for something. "There," she said after a moment. It took him a little longer than her to see what she'd found: a small, crooked shack hidden among the trees.

He followed her through the slanted door into the cramped space, where he was forced to bend his knees to avoid hitting his head.

"What is this place?" he asked as she struck a match and lit a candle.

"Just a cottage."

The word seemed far too generous for whatever this was.

"My friend used it to… Well, it doesn't matter. No one else knows about it. You should be safe here."

He collapsed onto a blanket on the floor, wincing as the pain in his leg intensified. "Thank you. For helping me."

She reeled a little, like he'd struck her. "I'm not helping *you*," she said, her voice suddenly cold. A silence followed that begged to be filled, and he knew there was more she wasn't saying.

"Right, of course."

She dropped her gaze. "Your leg. It's bad, isn't it?"

He glanced down at the makeshift bandage. It was only

spotted with blood, which was strange given the depth of the wounds, but perhaps the poison had cauterized the blood vessels somehow. Or maybe it was spreading through his body and he was dying right now.

"It's bad," he said.

She bit her lip, considering. "If there's an antidote to the poison, I don't know about it. The best we can do is treat the wounds. I'll get supplies. But I won't be able to make it back before dark."

Dark was hours away. If he made it that long, there was a good chance he'd survive. But it might be a slow, painful death in the meantime. "I understand."

"Just promise me you won't go anywhere. The fact that you're here, that I hel—that I haven't killed you…" She swallowed and raised her chin. "Yet," she added, a reminder of how precarious his situation was.

"I won't go anywhere," he said, gesturing to his bad leg. "I promise."

She nodded, looking a little relieved.

When she'd said she wasn't helping *him*, he'd had the distinct impression she'd meant she was helping herself. If she really was one of the Watchers Lupin had told him about, then it was her duty to kill him. For whatever reason, she hadn't, but the fact that he benefited was merely incidental. He wondered what would happen to her if someone found out. Judging by her expression, nothing good.

She handed him her box of matches. "You must be hungry. I don't have any food on me, unfortunately."

He shook his head, even though he hadn't eaten since yesterday. He didn't want to push her generosity any further. "I'll be fine."

She stared at him with eyes the color of the faded blue velvet in his mother's little glass jewelry box, the one all of his sisters coveted and took turns secretly smuggling into hiding places, hoping the others wouldn't notice. "I suppose you'll have to be."

And with that, she turned and closed the door behind her.

For a while, Jaren sat on the floor, thinking. Perhaps waiting here wasn't the best idea. He sensed that Leelo's actions had far more to do with her than with him, and she could change her mind at any moment, or tell someone else and let them do the dirty work for her.

Unfortunately, running didn't really seem like an option right now. The wound on his leg was throbbing, pulsating in time to his heartbeat. His body temperature was fluctuating between hot and cold, and his mouth felt as dry as his mother's meatloaf.

He fell back, too weak to even sit, and thought of his father and sisters. They would have noticed he was missing when the sun rose, and they would have absolutely no idea where he went. They might find his footprints leading into the forest, and if they followed them long enough, they would surely see the paw prints of that blasted wolf. They might even follow them all the way to the lake.

But they wouldn't know that he'd gotten into a boat and *crossed* the lake. They'd assume he was eaten or drowned. They'd never imagine he was here, on Endla. And even if they knew, they had no way to get to him. He had to make it off this island.

He glanced around the cottage, desperately hoping that the last inhabitant had perhaps left a pitcher of water, because he was getting thirstier by the second. All he found was another candle stump—in itself a blessing, since he wasn't keen on the idea of spending all day and evening in the dark—and a stack of books.

He picked up the first one and dusted off the leather cover. It was a poetry collection, he realized with disappointment, written by a well-known poet who'd lived two hundred years ago. Children were forced to study her work in school. He tossed it aside and sifted through the remaining books. They were all similarly boring, novels he'd already read or texts that were so obscure he had no interest in the subject matter—and he doubted very much that the hovel's previous occupant had found them riveting, either.

He was about to close his eyes when he noticed one last tome tucked under the wooden crate that served as a makeshift table. As soon as he pulled the book free, he realized it was being used to steady the crate, and the lit candle nearly slid off onto the blankets. He managed to shove the poetry collection under the crate just in time, sighing in relief that death by fire hadn't just been added to his list of possible ends.

This book was different from the others. It was crudely made, with a spine sewn with catgut. There was nothing written on the wooden cover. Carefully, he opened to the first page.

It appeared to be a handwritten book of Endlan songs. Unfortunately, he had no idea how to read music. These songs, like the ones he'd heard in the past few weeks, didn't have lyrics. They were just a series of notes to be hummed or chanted. Or perhaps the notes had meaning he simply didn't understand. But it was the sounds themselves that made the music so haunting. He hadn't realized before that a voice could be so full of sorrow or hunger or mourning without any words at all. Combine that into dozens of voices, and the effect was almost overpowering.

Or *was* overpowering, at least for some.

He set the book aside and did a cursory exploration of the hut, but there was nothing to eat and nothing else to distract himself with. He settled down on the blanket, willing his mind to still, to ignore the dull throbbing in his leg and the hunger in his stomach.

For an hour or so, he was on the edge of sleep, his lucid thoughts mingling with almost-dreams. Until the call of a bird in the trees outside the shack woke him fully.

It was the same bird they'd heard earlier, the one singing the song from his dreams. He wondered if that song was in the book, but without the ability to read the music, it was impossible to know. Instead he listened intently to the bird, humming along with the call until he matched it note for note. Unfortunately, it was the same few notes he already knew, and he was left still searching for the rest of the song.

Restless and suddenly desperate for air, he crawled to the door of the cottage and nudged it open. The shriek of the hinges caused him to wince and duck back inside, but after a few moments, the bird called again, and he took that as a good sign that no one was coming.

He crept outside, taking greater care to keep the door from squeaking, and slowly straightened to his full height, testing out his bad leg. The pain wasn't as intense as it had been, but that was mostly because the leg had started to go numb. That didn't seem like a good sign at all.

Judging by the sun's position, it was midafternoon, which

meant he had at least a few more hours before the girl returned. He had promised her he would stay put, and he had
no desire to get himself lost, or worse, run into another islander. Instead, he found a tree stump just a few feet from the
hut and sat down on it, letting his head tip back so the sunlight could shine on his face.

He heard the bird call again, this time a little farther away,
and hummed the tune to himself. A moment later, the bird
responded. Closer, now.

This went on for several minutes, and the idea that he was
somehow communicating with a wild creature made Jaren forget just how much danger he was in. Before long, the bird
landed on a branch in a tree a few yards from where he was sitting. It was an ordinary-looking blackbird at first glance, but
when the sun shone on its feathers, they took on an iridescent
sheen.

Jaren hummed the tune again, and the bird hopped to a
lower branch, then closer, and closer, until it had landed on a
fallen log just feet from where he sat. The bird cocked its head
at Jaren, studying him, and this time when he hummed the
tune, he remembered a few more notes than he'd sung before.

But his elation was short-lived. One moment the bird was
there, innocently watching him, and the next, it was gone.
Jaren hadn't seen the long, snaking root rise up from the
ground and wrap silently around the bird's leg until it was
too late. He stood, horrified, but the only sign that the bird
had ever been there at all was a few shiny feathers, drifting
slowly to the Forest floor.

Jaren backed up to the shack and crawled inside, closing
the door firmly behind him.

Chapter Twenty-Four

Leelo tried to take a nap when she got home, but it was impossible. She was too wound up from the events of the day, and the idea that Sage might know about the outsider—Jaren—was driving her mad.

And, truth be told, she was wound up about the very fact that she'd spent time alone with an outsider. She knew his name. She'd promised to help him, when she should be gathering up the courage to kill him. And yet when she imagined wrapping her hands around his neck while he slept, ending his life as she was expected to, all she saw were gray eyes rimmed in thick black lashes, the kind Leelo, with her fair complexion, could only dream of. She wasn't sure what she'd expected of an outsider, but it hadn't been this. Even his leaf-strewn hair had looked soft and inviting.

Get a hold of yourself, she said to her reflection in the mirror. He was clearly using his wily outsider charms to trick her into helping him.

But she had tricks of her own. She'd already let slip that she should have killed him, so he knew his best chance of survival was doing as she said. He didn't need to know how much her own survival depended on him.

Fiona had fallen asleep while knitting, so Leelo quietly gathered anything she thought Jaren might need: plum brandy—the only alcohol she could find—to disinfect the wound; a full waterskin; dried meat and fruit as well as a few slices of bread (anything more would be missed); and some warmer clothing, in case the night got chilly.

And then, with only a few hours until her Watcher shift with Kris started, she went to see Isola.

As usual, her friend refused to go for a walk the first three times Leelo asked, but finally, whether out of annoyance or boredom, she agreed. She didn't question Leelo when she led them off the main trail into the Forest. Isola never asked where they were going; she never asked any questions at all. And even though by the end of their walks Isola seemed a little less sorrowful, she was always just as sad the next day.

"The lambs are getting big," Leelo said. "You should come see them again sometime."

"Perhaps." Isola's hair had grown a bit, and Leelo was re- lieved to see she was back to brushing it. But she had grown pale from so many days spent indoors, and she was thinner than Leelo had ever seen her.

"I'm helping my mother with a new dress," Leelo pressed on, desperate for some inroad into the real purpose of this visit. "Would you like to learn? You could make your own dress for the summer solstice."

Isola, who generally kept her eyes downcast or on the trail

ahead, stopped and turned toward Leelo. "I'm not allowed at the summer solstice."

"Saints, Isola. I'm sorry. I forgot."

"Why are you being so nice to me, Leelo? You're not supposed to visit me. I'm not even good company. I never have anything to contribute to our conversations, and I never will."

Leelo shook her head. "But you *will*, Isola. If you find ways to distract yourself, you'll be a little less sad every day. I know it's painful, but it will get less painful, with time."

"How do you know?" Isola asked, but there was no venom in it, only genuine fear. "How can you be so sure?"

Leelo gestured to a fallen tree, where they sat down next to each other. "I was young when my father died, but I was old enough that his death left a big hole in my life, and an even bigger hole in my mother's. But she had two young children to care for, and she had to keep going for our sake. I know at the beginning she was just going through the motions of living, making us our meals and sewing our clothes, but eventually she started to come back to us. She'd smile when Tate made a silly face, or laugh when she spilled flour on the floor instead of crying. She wasn't the same, maybe, but she was okay."

Isola plucked a wildflower from near her feet and began pulling off the petals one by one. "Your mother had something to live for, though. What do I have?"

"You have your parents. And Sage and me. Aunt Ketty said she'd talk to the council on your family's behalf." She left out the part about Isola being ruined forever. It wouldn't help anything, and besides, Leelo was hopeful that people would forgive her in time. "Someday you might even meet some-one else you can love the way you loved Pieter."

She dropped the ruined flower and crushed it with her foot. "No, I won't."

"Perhaps not," Leelo said. "But you won't know unless you try."

They sat in silence for a long while, until finally Leelo couldn't bear it anymore. She'd come here today for a reason, and though she knew Isola wasn't going to be spreading gossip anytime soon, she needed to approach this delicately. "Isola, I need to ask you something."

"If it's about why I helped Pieter, don't bother. I know no one understands, and I'm tired of trying to explain."

Leelo wanted to tell Isola that she *did* understand, better than her friend could imagine, but she knew Isola wouldn't believe her. "It isn't that."

Isola waved her hand absently. "Go on."

"I found the little cottage. The one you kept Pieter in."

Isola stiffened beside her. "What are you talking about?"

"You don't need to worry," Leelo said quickly. "I won't tell anyone. But I was wondering how you kept him safe all winter."

"Leelo, if you think Tate can come back here—"

"I don't, I swear. This isn't about Tate."

"Then what is it about? If you hadn't noticed, I *didn't* keep Pieter safe. It got too cold in the cottage. Eventually I had to sneak him into the house. That's when my mother found him."

Of course. That explained why Isola had taken such a big risk by bringing him inside. Fortunately for Jaren, freezing temperatures wouldn't be an issue. "Did you build it?" Leelo asked.

"Pieter and I found it, when we were children. We were best friends, you see. Before he left, we made a pact that he would return to Endla someday, and we would live in the cottage together. Back then, it seemed possible. We were children. We didn't know."

Leelo placed a hand over Isola's. "Of course not."

She looked up, eyes brimming with tears. "I didn't think he'd actually go through with it, Leelo." Her voice cracked as she began to cry. "I felt so awful, making him stay in there all alone. It was so cold. If we'd been able to build a fire, maybe he would have been all right. But we couldn't risk the smoke."

"I'm so sorry, Isola."

She nodded, wiping her eyes with her thumbs.

"Does anyone else know about the cottage?"

She shook her head. "No. Like I said, we were careful not to even light a small fire."

Leelo hated to make Isola relive her pain, but she had to understand. "I don't mean this as an accusation. I'm genuinely curious. Why didn't you send him back before the ice melted?"

"I tried. He didn't want to go. He said he had nothing to go back to."

Leelo had assumed it was his love for Isola that had made him reckless. "But the villagers across the water knew his name. He must have had a life there."

Isola scoffed. "What do you think it's like out there for incantu, Leelo? Do you think they all lead merry little lives like we have here on Endla? They're *children* when we send them away. If they don't find someone to take them in, they're forced to live as thieves. Or worse. Pieter may have known some of those villagers, but he didn't have a family. He didn't have anyone who loved him like I did."

Leelo shuddered at the phrase "or worse." What could possibly be worse than being entirely alone in the world? Her heart ached at the thought of Tate having to steal food or sleep in the cold, but he had said he would be all right. Whatever her mother had told him, Leelo had to believe it would keep him safe.

"But the other incantu don't return," Leelo said feebly. "So some of them must make it." *Unless they all died.* She shoved the thought away. It was too horrible to consider.

Isola softened, just a little. "I'm sorry. I know you're scared for Tate. And I'm sure some of them do find nice families or learn a trade and live an honest life. But Pieter was not the same when he came back. He was so broken, Leelo. Like a bird kicked from its nest too soon who never learned to fly. I couldn't help but love him. I couldn't help but promise he could stay with me. Even if I knew it wouldn't last forever, that eventually I'd have to say goodbye."

Leelo held Isola while she sobbed against her, still so brittle and raw after all these weeks.

Leelo didn't love Jaren. She didn't even know him. Whether he lived or died should mean nothing to her.

But deep down she knew that his being here was her fault. She had sung the prayer for Tate when she shouldn't have, and Jaren had heard her, as improbable as it seemed. If he was discovered, it would all lead back to her. For the sake of her mother, she needed to get him safely off the island before anyone knew what she'd done.

When Isola's tears had subsided, Leelo asked gently, "Do you know where they keep the boat? The one the incantu children use?"

Isola's reddened eyes narrowed in suspicion. "Haven't you heard anything I've said? You can't bring Tate back here. Did you know that half the council voted to exile me for helping Pieter?"

Leelo felt as though her entire body had been doused in ice water. "What?"

Isola's mouth twisted in a bitter smile. "That's right. They thought I should be thrown out like an incantu. Only worse, because if outsiders discovered what I was, they'd kill me."

Leelo didn't know what to say. Having the entire island shun her the way it had Isola was unthinkable. If they had almost *exiled* her for helping an incantu, then Leelo was in even more danger than she'd thought.

"They only let me stay because I already know—" Isola cut herself off. "It doesn't matter. Just leave this alone, Leelo. Tate isn't coming back." She blinked. "Unless you're thinking of leaving yourself."

Leelo shook her head vehemently. "No. No, of course not. There are just so many secrets on this island. Before, when it didn't affect me, it was easy to ignore them. But losing Tate has made me question so many things."

Isola rose and turned to face Leelo. "You're right. This place has many secrets. And some of them are not so pleasant. But we keep them for a reason. Forget the boat. Forget the cottage. Forget about Tate, if you can."

"I can't," Leelo whispered.

Isola had started to walk away, but she spun around a second later, fixing Leelo with a look that could rival Ketty's. "Endla may be the safest place for us, Leelo, but never forget. The Wandering Forest cares about one thing and one thing only. Survival. And if pushed far enough, this island will eat its own."

Chapter Twenty-Five

Jaren was startled awake by the strangled screech of a door opening. For a moment, he sat blinking in the pitch darkness, trying to remember where he was. And then it all came back to him in a rush: he was on Endla, wrapped in a musty blanket in a shack, waiting for a girl who might want to kill him.

The rasp of a match striking, followed by the hiss of a flaring flame, brought him fully awake.

Leelo was crouched just a few feet from him, her pale eyes bright in the candlelight. One of her hands was at her waist, where she kept her knife.

He attempted to smooth his mussed hair and sat up. He noticed with a growing sense of dread that his left leg was completely numb. A rainstorm had started in the night, and the air in the cottage was surprisingly cold. "Is everything all right?"

She shook her head and sat down fully with her back against the door, but he noticed that her hand remained on the hilt of her blade. Her hair and clothing were soaked through, clinging to her skin. She reached into a satchel near her feet and handed him something small wrapped in parchment. "I brought you food. There's water in here, too. Plus a sweater. It can get cold at night."

She passed him the satchel and he pulled out the water-skin and the sweater, woven in forest green wool. It was finer than any clothing he'd ever owned, and his eyes darted up to hers, questioning.

"It was my father's," she said. "It won't be missed."

From the way she said it, Jaren assumed he was either dead or estranged. "Thank you. That's very kind." He was about to set the sweater on the floor next to him, taking care not to undo the neat folds, when he noticed that she was shivering.

"Maybe you should put it on," he said, holding it out.

She shook her head, still trembling. "I'm fine."

He wasn't going to push her. He knew from experience with his sisters that if a woman was being stubborn, there was little he could do about it. "I don't suppose there's another boat available?"

"There's only one as far as I know. I don't even know where the boat you crossed over in went, and I don't know how long it's going to take me to find it. And once I do, I don't know if I'll be able to fix it. Even if I can, I don't know how we're going to get you out of here without anyone seeing."

"You're thinking of turning me in, aren't you?" He tried to keep his eyes on hers, but they darted involuntarily to her blade. He didn't ask if she was thinking of killing him, too. He wasn't sure he wanted to know the answer.

She was silent for a moment, and when she did speak, her tone was grave. "I just want you to understand the reality of your situation. There's a good possibility that you'll have to stay here on Endla. At least until the lake freezes over, and that won't be for a good six or seven months."

Jaren swore under his breath. His family would have long since given up on him by then. They might not even stay in Bricklebury. "I can't wait that long. I have to get back."

They sat in silence for a few minutes until Leelo said, "I can bring you food and water. You won't go hungry out here."

"My leg…" He trailed off. There wasn't anything to say, really.

"That I can help with." Leelo produced a bottle of some kind of liquor, fresh bandages, and a jar. "If you'll let me."

Jaren studied her for a moment. There was none of the flirting he experienced with Lupin, and none of the teasing he was used to from his sisters. This girl was quiet and serious, her eyes wary even when her posture was relaxed. She didn't trust him—why would she?—but he sensed that deep down, she didn't want to hurt him. "I would be forever in your debt, if you would help me, Leelo."

She glanced up at him, their eyes meeting for a moment.

"I am, however, going to have to insist you take the blanket."

"I'm fine—"

"Please," he said. "Your hands are shaking like leaves. And I'd really like to keep my leg, if possible."

She rolled her eyes but finally took the blanket from him, draping it over her shoulders like a shawl. And then she set to work.

Jaren had never experienced a more exquisite, blinding pain than the alcohol being poured onto his wounds. It was so horrific that for a moment he thought he might faint again. But just as his vision started to tunnel, she was applying the cooling ointment to the wound, and he felt his pulse slowly return to normal.

"Can I ask you something?" he said when he'd found his voice.

Her eyes flicked up to his and then immediately back to his leg. She didn't like maintaining eye contact, that was clear. "What?"

"That song I heard. The one the bird was singing. What was that?"

She bit her lip, worrying it with her two front teeth. He noticed there was a tiny gap between them.

"You don't have to tell me. I was just curious. I've had it in my head for so long, and it's been a bit maddening to not know the rest of it." He hummed the little bit he knew.

Her eyes went wide, just for a moment, and she cleared her throat. "It's a prayer."

He winced as she tightened the bandage around his leg. "I think I must have heard it in my sleep, that night I camped by the lake. What kind of prayer is it?"

She blinked, her eyelashes suddenly damp. "It's a prayer for lost things," she said in a ragged voice. "A prayer for them to be found."

Gently, he asked, "What did you lose?"

Leelo gasped and sat back, her hand once again flying to her waist. He hadn't even meant to say "you." But her reaction confirmed what he suspected: that she was the one he'd heard singing that night. For the first time, he admitted to himself that he had been wrong about magic. It was as if an invisible string had been connecting them ever since he camped on the shore, and it had slowly, inevitably, reeled him in.

"I'm sorry," he said, holding his palms out as if she were a cornered animal. "I'm sorry I put you in this position. And believe me, I want to get home as badly as you want me to leave. If you have any idea where the boat is, I can look for it myself. There's no reason for you to get dragged down by my foolishness."

She shook her head a fraction. "You're not the only fool here."

"What do you mean?"

She ignored him, tidying up her belongings with clipped, precise movements. She removed the blanket and laid it over him, though he could see that her hair and clothing were still damp. "I'll get you out of here. Just promise me you'll stay in the cottage, no matter what happens. If another Endlan sees you, I won't be able to help you."

"Am I safe here?" he asked, glancing at the windows as if the trees might reach through and snatch him any minute, the way the roots had done to that poor bird.

The fact that she didn't answer immediately frightened him. "You're an outsider on Endlan ground," she said finally. "I don't know if you're safe anywhere on the island. But I do know you're safer here than anywhere out there."

It was hardly reassuring, but he knew it was the best she could do. And for now, he was trapped on enemy territory with no other allies. His family would be worried sick about him. He couldn't help imagining his sisters and father, glancing at the door every time it rattled in the wind, wondering if it was Jaren, coming home from another one of his wanders.

He could feel his thoughts beginning to spiral, and he knew if she left now he'd never fall asleep. It was late, and she was probably expected back at her house, but he didn't want to be alone.

"I have sisters," he blurted.

She was so caught off guard she laughed a little. "What?"

He blushed and hoped she wouldn't notice in the dim light. "I meant to ask if you have any siblings. I have three sisters."

She was silent so long Jaren was sure she wouldn't answer. "I have one brother," she said finally, and then immediately pressed her lips together in a flat line.

Saints, was her brother dead along with her father? He was about to change the subject when she finally sat back down again. Before she could stop him, he moved the blanket so that it was covering her legs, too.

She cast him a look he couldn't read. "I have one brother and a cousin who's like a sister to me. Sage. She can be..." She was quiet for a moment, choosing her words carefully. "Well, she can be prickly. But she's family."

Jaren smiled. "My youngest sister, Sofia, isn't so much prickly as sticky, like one of those burrs that gets caught in your hair. She's always getting into trouble and dragging you along with her." As he talked about Tadpole, then Story and Summer, Leelo seemed to relax, even smiling from time to time. She kept her hand near her knife, but she wasn't coiled like a snake anymore. If he could just get her to look at him as a person, not a threat from the outside, maybe he really could get back to his family.

Eventually, he couldn't help but yawn, even though he'd napped through most of the evening.

"I should go," Leelo said, removing the blanket from her legs and tucking it around him with surprising care. "My shift ended, and I'll be expected at home."

"When will you be back?" He hadn't meant it to sound so needy, but her mouth quirked in the smallest grin.

"When I can," she said, and slipped out into the darkness.

Chapter Twenty-Six

By the time Leelo slid into bed next to Sage, it was well past midnight. She'd have to be up in five hours for her shift. She would search for the boat on her next day off. Based on Isola's reaction, she didn't think anyone would offer up its location freely.

Leelo rested her head on her pillow and closed her eyes. After talking to Isola, Leelo had determined to put an end to her problem. She couldn't risk being caught and exiled. Her mother wouldn't survive it. She had sharpened her knife before she went to the little hut, steeling herself for the spray of blood when she slit Jaren's throat. That had seemed like the quickest way of taking his life, though the thought of all that blood made her woozy.

She had knelt down next to him for several minutes, listening to his breathing to make sure he was truly asleep and not pretending. She could feel the heat from his body, and it reminded her of Tate, how he always seemed to burn hot-

ter than she did, so that even on the coldest nights she didn't
need a warm stone in her bed if he was with her.

Thinking of Tate had made her throat thick with tears, and
she'd had to take several deep breaths to regain her compo-
sure. She had gone so far as to set the blade against the delicate skin of Jaren's neck. And then he'd hummed a few bars
of the prayer in his sleep.

The sound was unexpectedly beautiful. His voice wasn't
smooth and practiced like the Endlans'; it was ragged and a
little off-key. But he had gotten the emotion of the prayer
exactly, and her nerve fell away like autumn leaves. He was
just a boy, and she'd brought him here.

With a heavy sigh, she had gone back to the door and
opened it loudly on purpose, waking him.

Sage rolled over next to her, sighing in her sleep. A part
of Leelo wanted to wake her cousin and tell her everything.
If she already suspected what Leelo had done, then waiting
would only increase Sage's sense of betrayal. She was better off
confessing now, explaining that she hadn't known what she
was doing, that she was sorry she hadn't told Sage right away.

If Sage didn't know and Leelo confessed, she might be
able to help. She wouldn't want to get Leelo in trouble, not
real trouble. She was just angry with Leelo for being so upset
over Tate.

At least, she hoped that was all it was. But then she remembered the way Sage had looked at her when she asked about
the boat. How Sage had said Pieter deserved his fate. And if
she could be that callous about an incantu, what would she
do to a true outsider? The image of Ketty slitting the sheep's
throat came back to her, and Leelo covered her eyes with her

hands, pressing the heels of her palms into the sockets until she saw stars.

Jaren didn't seem like he would deliberately cause her any trouble. He was bigger and older than her, but he was also scared. She couldn't blame him. He'd been chased here by an enormous wolf, and he was alone and friendless in a tiny hut in the middle of nowhere. She remembered how affectionately he'd spoken of his sisters and his father, how devastating the loss of their mother had been.

Leelo had felt so much empathy that for a moment she'd considered telling Jaren about Tate, but though she wanted to trust him, she couldn't undo all the years of warnings she'd received about outsiders.

They say when the Wandering Forests were cut down by the outsiders, the trees screamed in agony, Ketty would say, when she told stories at night around the fire. *When their roots were torn from the soil, they wept sap as red as blood. And when the animals of the Forest lost their shelter, they also lost their minds, turning into ferocious, bloodthirsty creatures who had to be destroyed.*

Leelo had imagined such carnage when Ketty told her tales, fields full of bloody stumps and crazed animals with red glowing eyes. She'd had nightmares every night for years. Sometimes she overheard her mother pleading with Ketty to stop scaring the children, but Ketty would call her sister a traitor, a fool, and Fiona would eventually back down as she always did.

If Leelo confided in Sage and she "solved" this problem for her, Leelo would be indebted to her forever, just like her mother and Aunt Ketty. She could envision them years from now, Sage making all their decisions for them, constantly reminding Leelo of her foolishness, and the guilt would drag on her like an anchor. She couldn't imagine her mother ever getting into a mess as bad as this one, but whatever Ketty had done for Fiona, she would never let her sister forget it.

No, Leelo thought as she adjusted her pillow for the hundredth time. She wouldn't let Sage hold this one mistake over her for the rest of her life. She would simply have to solve this problem all on her own.

When Leelo woke in the morning, she was stiff from shivering. She rolled over to find that Sage had stolen all the blankets.

With a sigh, she pulled them back to cover herself, but a second later, Sage yanked on them again, leaving Leelo more exposed than before.

So that's how it is, Leelo thought. Sage was doing this on purpose, probably to punish her for missing her Watcher shift. Annoyed, she ripped the covers back over herself, starting a far-too-intense-for-early-morning bout of tug-of-war with Sage.

"Sage," Leelo said through gritted teeth. "Just give...me... the...blanket!" Leelo pulled so hard she almost fell off the bed. "What's the matter with you, anyway?"

"What's the matter with *me*? What's the matter with you!" Sage's auburn hair was tangled from sleep, and her yellow-green eyes were so wide Leelo could see the whites all around.

"There's nothing the matter with me, except for the fact that I'm freezing because you're hogging the blanket!"

"Girls!"

They both turned to the door without releasing their fistfuls of quilt. Aunt Ketty stood with her hands on her hips, watching them with disgust. "What in the name of all that is sacred has gotten into the two of you?"

Leelo and Sage began yelling to defend themselves at the same moment.

"Enough!" Ketty shouted. "Leelo, your mother is trying to rest. And, Sage, *your* mother is trying to start breakfast. Whatever has happened between the two of you, work it out. Your shift starts in half an hour, and no one wants to listen to you bicker."

As Ketty stormed out, Leelo scrambled out of bed and yanked on her tunic and trousers, her back turned on her cousin.

A second later, a pillow hit her square between the shoulder blades.

Leelo whirled, her own braid whipping her in the face. "I can't believe you just did that."

Sage stared at her, chest heaving in rage, her hazel eyes filled with tears. "And I can't believe you missed our shift yesterday!"

Leelo had to close her eyes to keep from rolling them. "I said I was sorry. Mama was ill. Why are you so upset?"

"I woke up and you were just *gone*. I…" As Sage trailed off, her tears spilled over. Leelo couldn't remember the last time she'd seen her cousin cry. "I thought you'd left."

Leelo shook her head, trying to understand what could unravel Sage like this. "I was just getting herbs for Mama."

"No, I mean I thought you *left*. Forever."

Leelo's breath hitched as she realized what Sage was saying. Her cousin hadn't seemed worried at all yesterday. She'd just seemed angry, and that was something Leelo expected from her. But Sage had learned how to deal with being hurt the same way her mother did: with anger and resentment, instead of honesty. Leelo should have known better than to assume Sage was siding with a boy she barely knew over her best friend, just because she was late to a shift.

"I'm sorry," she said, approaching Sage. "I really was gathering herbs. I would never just leave you. You have to know that."

Sage swiped her tears away bitterly. "I know you love him more than you love me."

Leelo looked away because while she knew it *shouldn't* be true, it was. She did love her cousin, the way you were supposed to love family: despite their flaws. But unlike Tate, Sage didn't know how to be vulnerable. She'd sooner die than admit she'd been wrong about something, and Leelo couldn't remember ever hearing Sage apologize.

Still, she'd always told herself they complemented each other. Together, an optimist and a pessimist could find something like the truth when they met in the middle. "It's just different with Tate," she said. "He's younger than us, and softer. He *needed* me, Sage."

"And I'm so hard and tough that I couldn't possibly need anyone? Is that what you think?"

"I don't think that at all," Leelo said, pulling Sage's stiff body into her arms for a hug. "I'm truly sorry. I won't disappear again." Silently, she prayed the words were true. She would have to somehow search for the boat without drawing Sage's suspicion. Which meant she was probably not going to be getting much sleep until she did.

Sage eventually softened, turning her face so her lips were

against Leelo's ear. "Did you put the hole in the boat?" she whispered.

Leelo leaned back. "What?"

"I won't tell, I swear it. I just... I saw the way you looked when the boat was gone. Like you thought maybe something had happened to it. Like maybe you *wanted* something to happen to it."

She shook her head and pulled Sage into her arms again so she wouldn't see the fear in Leelo's eyes. "Of course not. I love Endla. It's our home."

Sage sniffed and nodded. "Exactly, Lo. It's *our* home. *Ours.* And nothing is going to change that."

Chapter Twenty-Seven

When Jaren woke the next morning, he was relieved to discover he could feel his left leg again, even if what he felt was excruciating pain. Leelo's remedies must have helped. He sat up and reached for the waterskin, rinsing out the sour taste in his mouth, and ate a little of the food she'd brought him. The sweater had kept him warm and the Forest hadn't tried to eat him while he slept. If he did end up having to stay here for a few days, at least he knew he could survive it.

At midday, Leelo arrived at the cottage. He'd dreamed last night that she had come to kill him, slicing his throat from ear to ear while he slept. He'd woken up in a cold sweat, sure Leelo was in the hut with him, but then the door had opened and it was really her, coming to his aid. The dream had felt so real, but he told himself it was just his fever breaking.

Now, though he wanted to trust her, he peered out the small window for a moment after she arrived, to be sure she was alone. It didn't make sense for her to heal his leg only to kill him, but maybe this was some part of an Endlan honor code: make sure your prey stands a fighting chance before hunting him down, or something.

"Hello," he said, opening the door for her.

She propped her bow and arrows against the front of the cottage and nodded. It was a warm day, and her hairline was damp with sweat. "You're alive. Good."

He barked a laugh, some of the tension leaving his body. "I'm glad you think so. Is everything all right?"

"I came straight from duty. I can't stay long. Sage thinks I went to visit a friend, but I don't like lying to her."

"I understand."

"How is your leg feeling?" she asked as she scooted inside the cottage next to him. "Better?"

"I can feel it, which is a vast improvement. Thank you again, for helping me." He'd thanked her a hundred times already, but he figured she'd be less likely to kill him if he was gracious. He still remembered the way she'd kept her blade close the last time she visited and how it had sliced through his flesh like butter in his dream. Fortunately, her hands were otherwise engaged at the moment, as she rummaged through her pack.

She pulled a full waterskin and some more food out and gave them to him. "I'll take the empty waterskins and fill them before I go."

"Is there a water source close to here?" Jaren couldn't rely solely on Leelo, and having access to water would be reassuring.

She nodded. "There are spring-fed pools nearby."

"So the poison in the lake doesn't get into your drinking water?"

Leelo's eyes flicked up to his. "I suppose it doesn't."

"Right. Or you'd all be dead," he said, then immediately regretted it. "Any luck on finding the boat?"

She shook her head. "No. The day after tomorrow is my day off. I'll be able to search then."

Jaren drummed his fingers on the floor. He knew he couldn't offer to help. He doubted he could keep up, and there was too much of a risk of his being seen. But he also didn't just want to sit in this hut for days, doing nothing.

"This might be a strange question, but do you think you could teach me how to read music?" he asked.

Leelo blinked, clearly caught off guard by the request. "Why would you want to do that?"

He fished the little songbook out of the pile and handed it to her. "I found this. I'd like to learn the songs. Just as a way to pass the time."

She snatched the book out of his hands as if he'd stolen it. "You shouldn't have this."

"I'm sorry. I didn't know."

He watched in dismay as she tucked it into her satchel. "This is an Endlan songbook. It's not for outsiders."

Leelo was clearly angry. She was looking at Jaren the way she had when they first met: with suspicion. "I'm not from Bricklebury," he said, desperate for a change in subject.

"So?"

"So, I mean, yes. I am an outsider. But I'm an outsider to Bricklebury, too. I don't know a lot about Endla."

"You know about our music, though. You know how dangerous it can be. Why would you want to read it?"

He realized now that saying he wanted to simply as a way to pass the time was insulting and ignorant. And he knew deep down there was more to it than that. Endla was a mystery, and his involuntary reaction to it, even more so. And while he had tacitly accepted that there was "magic" in the world, all that word meant to Jaren was something people didn't understand yet. But perhaps there was a way to understand it. Everything had an explanation, in the end.

"Curiosity, I suppose," he said finally. "To be honest, I've never been much of a singer."

She arched a pale brow. "Much?"

He grimaced. "Okay, I've never sung anything before."

"Never?" she asked, the other eyebrow joining the first.

He shook his head. "Not really. The occasional folk tune, I guess. My mother was the musical one in the family, and even that's a bit of a stretch. She would sing to us at bedtime or while she was working. But we've never had an instrument."

"What do you mean, an instrument?"

Was it possible she'd never seen a musical instrument? That the only instruments Endlans knew about were their voices? "A flute," he said. "Or a guitar?"

She looked at him like he was speaking another language.

"I suppose you must not have them here. They're objects that produce music, with the help of a person. A flute is a long tube that you blow through. A guitar is wooden, with strings over a hole..." He trailed off when he saw that she still didn't understand. "If you bring me some parchment and charcoal the next time you come, I'll draw them for you," he said. "But you'll just have to take my word for it that they make beautiful music."

"You said you're not from Brickle…"

"Bricklebury. A nearby village."

"Right."

"I'm from a city called Tindervale. It's far away from here, far from the mountains. Things were very different there. In Bricklebury, everyone knows everyone. And everyone talks about everyone else's business. Back in Tindervale, I didn't even know our closest neighbors. There were so many people, it was almost like they all decided that since it would be impossible to know everyone, there was no point in knowing anyone."

"I can't imagine that," Leelo said, her voice quiet. She fiddled with a loose string on his blanket for a moment, like she was embarrassed by her inexperience.

"I couldn't imagine a place like Bricklebury, before I got there. I went for a walk with a girl, and the entire town was talking about it."

Leelo blushed, her eyes still downcast. "Imagine if they saw us in this cottage."

He smiled. "I think their heads would explode. Too much gossip for them to handle."

"Are you going to marry her?" Leelo asked, still not meeting his eyes.

Jaren laughed, which made her blush harder.

"I'm sorry," she said. "That's probably too personal."

"It's not that. I hardly know her. She sells honey at the market. She's from Endla, actually. I'm not sure why I didn't think of that before. You must have known her. Her name is Lupin."

Leelo cocked her head. "The only Lupin I know is elderly. Are you sure she's from Endla?"

"I'm sure. But I suppose she could have changed her name. She has long blond hair. Darker than yours. And green eyes."

She shook her head. "There are lots of girls on Endla that look like that. When did she leave?"

"She's my age. Eighteen. So six or seven years ago, I suppose."

Leelo thought for a moment. "I didn't pay as much attention to who was leaving when I was younger. I'd already been singing for years by that point. But my mother would probably remember."

"It's not important. As I said, I hardly know her."

Leelo brightened suddenly. "So this girl. She found a home in Bricklebury? Who does she live with? Is she healthy?"

Jaren told her everything he knew about Lupin, and there was something about the way Leelo hung on every word that made him think she knew one of these incantu, quite well, perhaps.

When he was finished, Leelo looked happy, relieved. He wanted to ask her about it, but he was afraid he'd inadvertently misstep again, and he liked seeing her smile.

They sat in silence for a while, until it began to feel awkward. Jaren shifted, and Leelo blinked, like she'd been far away in her mind.

"I should go," she said, all business once again. "As I said, I have the day after tomorrow free, so I'll be able to look for the boat. I'll come when I can. Will you be all right until then?"

He nodded. "I think so. I just don't like not helping. I'm the one who shouldn't be here. I should be doing something to make it right."

"I understand not wanting to sit still. But believe me, that's the most helpful thing you can do right now."

"All right, then. I'll be here."

She moved toward the door, then paused and reached into her satchel. She pulled out the songbook and stared at it for a moment before handing it to Jaren.

"Are you sure?" he asked, taking it gently.

"No," she said with a crooked smile. Her eyes met his for longer than they ever had before. They were such a particular shade of blue, crystalline against her fair skin. Finally, she looked away. "I'm not sure about anything anymore," she said, before closing the door behind her.

Chapter Twenty-Eight

The next morning, Sage and Leelo sat on the shore, Watching near the spot where Pieter had died. Sage seemed to have forgiven Leelo, and they passed the time by talking about the solstice, what they would wear and who they thought would get engaged. It was a beautiful morning, the surface of the lake as smooth as glass, but Leelo kept thinking about her brother. It was possible that Tate really had found a nice family in a nearby village to live with, that he was safe and sound. She had wanted to believe Jaren so much it made her chest ache with hope.

But it was also possible he was telling her these things so she wouldn't kill him. If he humanized outsiders, maybe she would come to believe they weren't as bad as she'd always thought. Jaren didn't seem like a bad person, but he could be acting. Saints knew *she* wasn't really a battle-scarred Watcher who could slit his throat in his sleep if she chose to.

She needed to be more like Sage, she thought, watching

her cousin from the corner of her eye. She was whittling something, her hazel eyes flicking up every thirty seconds to scan the horizon.

"What are you making?"

"This? It's a fox. Can't you tell?" She held up the wood and grinned. So far, it was just a shapeless lump.

Leelo smiled. Here she was thinking she should be more like Sage, and Sage was whittling the craftiest creature on the island. Endlan foxes were the bane of families like Isola's, who raised chickens. Dirty, disease-ridden scavengers, to most.

"Why a fox?" Leelo asked.

Sage dropped her hands to her lap and turned her attention on Leelo. "Foxes," she said, "are brilliant. Do you realize that in all our years of hunting, we've never once caught a fox in our snares? We've never even found a carcass. When they raid Rosalie's henhouse, they leave nothing behind but feathers. They're like shadows, silent and stealthy."

"And you admire that?"

"Sure I do. When you didn't show up for duty, I was almost looking forward to doing our shift alone. To really test myself, you know? A fox doesn't need a pack to hunt. They don't need anything but their own wit." She frowned and picked up the wood again. "It was my mother's idea to ask Hollis."

"But we have each other, Sage."

She shrugged. "We do for now. But we won't always be together. And if I ever come across an outsider, I want to be ready."

A chill ran down Leelo's spine. "Ready?"

"I swear, when we arrived for our Watch and the boat was

there, I was praying an outsider had come. Praying for my chance to protect Endla."

"Wouldn't you be scared to meet an outsider?"

Sage laughed and nodded toward the far shore. "Scared? Of one of those pathetic villagers? I'd welcome it."

Leelo swallowed, her mouth dry. "What if they snuck up on you? What if they caught you by surprise?"

She shook her head. "Impossible. How can I be surprised, when I'm the one doing all the sneaking?"

Leelo was quiet for a moment. "What if…what if they weren't a monster, like you thought? What if they were good?"

Sage looked at Leelo like she'd grown an extra pair of hands. "Good? Don't be a fool, Leelo. Your mother has put some ridiculous notions into your head, but that one is just plain dangerous." She shook her head again, this time in disgust. "You're lucky you have me, you know. Left to your own devices, you'd probably bring an outsider home for dinner."

Leelo paced near the hidden cottage, wasting precious time as the sun sank below the treetops. Her conversation with Sage had renewed her fear of Jaren, or at least of being caught. Saints, if Sage knew the mess she'd gotten herself into, she'd never let Leelo out of the house again.

But every time she thought about telling her mother, or worse, leaving Jaren to starve, she kept coming back to this: it wasn't his fault. She'd been singing when she shouldn't have been. She knew there were consequences, and though she'd told herself it was worth the cost if it meant Tate could stay, she had been wrong. Whatever other outsiders were like, she didn't sense that this one was dangerous, even if that did make her a fool. Even if it was simply because she wanted to believe that Tate stood a chance among people like Jaren, not the monsters Sage and Ketty said they were.

Finally, she knocked on the door and entered. Jaren was lying on his blanket, staring up at the ceiling, his head resting on her father's sweater. He scrambled upright at the sight of her, straightening his mussed hair with a sheepish grin.

"Are you busy?" Leelo asked with mock concern. "I can come back another time…"

"No!" he shouted, so loud she glanced around to be sure no one had heard. He lowered his voice to a whisper. "Sorry. I'm just bored to tears. I always thought I'd enjoy a break from my noisy family, but it turns out, I need human interaction as much as I need water."

"Speaking of which." Leelo entered the cottage and closed the door, taking her usual seat with her back against it. She pulled out fresh waterskins and food. "Here you go. Oh, I almost forgot." She reached deeper into her pack and pulled out a piece of parchment and a bit of charcoal. "So you can draw those instruments for me."

"Thank you. I wasn't sure if you were coming today."

"Neither was I."

Worry flickered over his brow as he drained a waterskin. "Oh?"

She took a deep breath, releasing it slowly. She had thought she could keep up the charade that Jaren was entirely dependent on her, without telling him the truth about her own vulnerability. But she needed him to know that there were stakes for her as well. That coming to see him wasn't simply a matter of inconvenience.

It was a matter of life or death.

"What's wrong?" Jaren asked, with what sounded like genuine concern. "Anything I can help with?"

She puffed out a rueful laugh. "Not unless you can turn back time and stay far away from Endla."

"Sadly, I haven't figured that out just yet."

"Pity." She took a deep breath, praying she wasn't about to make a huge mistake. "The thing is, Jaren, I was supposed to kill you."

"I surmised that when you mentioned not killing me *yet* the other day."

She pushed her hair out of her face. "It's not just that I was supposed to kill you. It was my sworn duty to kill you, to protect Endla from outsiders. That's the whole purpose of the Watchers."

"And I take it not killing me means you could get into a lot of trouble."

"Not just trouble. I could be exiled."

"Leelo—"

She cut him off, wanting to get this out and be done with it. "I know Endla must seem like a frightening place to you, but you have to understand that it's your world that is frightening to me. We have good reason to distrust outsiders, and I could be sent away from Endla forever for helping you. The villagers across the water would kill me the moment I stepped foot on the mainland. Not that you would care, but—"

He shook his head. "That's not true, Leelo."

"My mother is ill, Jaren. And if I can't take care of her, she could die. It was bad enough when my brother left, but if I went, too—"

"Your brother is incantu, isn't he?"

Leelo's breath caught. She hadn't meant to bring Tate into this. She wasn't sure she was ready to lay her soul that bare. But it was too late to turn back now. She nodded, and the next thing she knew, she was sobbing.

All she could see was Tate in that boat, rowing in the rain, possibly being eaten by the same wolf that had brought Jaren here. The idea of living the rest of her life without knowing his fate seemed impossible. She wrapped her arms around herself to keep from falling apart entirely, though how could she not, when her baby brother was gone?

She opened her eyes at the sensation of a hand settling lightly on her shoulder. She froze, and for a moment, she thought he might remove his hand. But he kept it there.

"Leelo, I'm not going to endanger you, or your mother."

She raised her head a little and whispered, "I'm scared." It was the first time she'd admitted it out loud. She wasn't just scared of Jaren and being caught. She was scared of what had happened to her brother, of her mother's illness, of growing up. She was even scared of Sage sometimes. This island was supposed to be the one safe place for Endlans, but it didn't feel safe anymore. It seemed as though one false step had landed her in a snare, and the more she tried to fight her way free, the more entangled she became.

"Leelo," Jaren said, and she finally looked at him. He shrugged and gave a small, sad smile. "If it's any consolation, I'm scared, too."

Before Leelo went into her house, she washed her face with the remaining water from her skin, rinsing away any lingering dried tears. She still couldn't believe she'd cried in front of Jaren.

She stepped inside to find her cousin setting the table.

"Dinner's ready," Sage said. With her hair pulled up into a messy knot and an embroidered apron tied around her waist, Sage was far less threatening than she'd been on the shore. As tough as she claimed to be, she'd never had to look a person in the eyes with the intent of ending their life.

They sat down to eat, and if Sage was suspicious about where Leelo had gone, she didn't mention it. Aunt Ketty even told her she looked pretty with a little color in her cheeks. Fiona joined them for dinner, and no one argued or complained. Aside from the fact that Tate wasn't there, it felt almost normal.

"What are you planning to do with your day off tomorrow?" Mama asked as Leelo helped wash the dishes. Ketty and Sage had gone to check on the lambs before nightfall.

"I have chores," Leelo said. "And I promised Isola I'd visit her." Isola had become a convenient excuse for sneaking off, but Leelo wasn't sure how long she could keep it up. If anyone asked Isola about it, the girl would have no idea what they were talking about. Fortunately for Leelo, no one visited with Isola except for her. But she felt guilty for using Isola as a cover, and besides, it was going to take more than an hour or two to search for the boat.

"I can take over your chores," Fiona said. "If you'd like."

Leelo dried off the bowl her mother handed her. "You should be resting."

"I'm feeling much better. Really. It's time I start pulling

my weight around here again. You're seventeen. You should have some freedom on your day off."

Leelo didn't meet her mother's eyes. She was too afraid there would be suspicion there. "What would I do with freedom?" she asked.

"I don't know. There must be someone you like. I've never heard you talk about anyone in particular."

For some reason, her mind automatically went to Jaren, even though that clearly wasn't what her mother meant. She meant an Endlan, a future partner. "How do you know if you like someone that way? Or if they like you?"

Fiona smiled, her eyes lighting up in the way they did when she sang to Tate as a baby. "Well, generally they take a special interest in you, and you take one in them. It's an attraction, but not one based solely on appearance. Perhaps it's the way they sing or laugh. Maybe they go out of their way to be kind to others. And of course, there's something more…intangible about the person. Something that makes you think about them all the time, that makes your heart race when your eyes meet or you know you'll be seeing them."

Leelo had never seen her mother blush before. She was staring out the window above the sink, her eyes clearly seeing something besides the Forest. "You felt all of that when you met Father?"

Her mother blinked and glanced at Leelo. "Um, yes, of course. Well, we'd always known each other. But one day it was just…different."

Fiona's tone had changed entirely. She went back to the dishes, the light gone from her eyes. What had Leelo said? Had the reminder of Father upset her?

"I think Sage likes Hollis Harding," she said, hoping to recover the conversation.

"Oh?"

"She got all dressed up when we went to dinner that night."

Fiona nodded. "I think that might have been Ketty's idea, truth be told. She thinks the Hardings would be a good connection for our family. Hollis and his father are strong, hard workers."

"Is that all Aunt Ketty cares about?"

Fiona sighed. "I know it might seem that way. But she cares deeply about the safety and well-being of everyone in this family."

Leelo bit her tongue to keep from saying, "Except for Tate." She finished drying the last dish and wiped her hands on a towel. "Have you thought of a husband for me?"

Mama turned to her and took her hands, smiling. "I haven't met anyone yet who I think is worthy of you, Leelo. When I was your age, all the boys seemed so young and immature. Hardly ready to be husbands. You're such an intelligent girl. I can't see you with any of the boys your age."

Leelo thought about the men in their twenties around the island. She didn't know any of them personally. And besides, most of them were already married. But she did know what her mother meant. Perhaps because she'd known all of the boys their whole lives, it was hard to see them as anyone other than who they'd been as children, even if their voices were deeper and they could grow a beard.

Jaren was different, though. She hardly knew him, and that made him…interesting. Try as she might to keep her guard up in his presence, his candor and warmth continued to disarm her. She'd never met a boy who talked with such regard for his sisters, or one who seemed to take a genuine interest in her life. She avoided meeting his eyes because every time she did, a little jolt went through her. When she left today, she'd forced herself not to look away from him, testing her resolve. It had been almost physically painful, but in an oddly pleasant way.

"*Is* there someone?" Fiona pressed, apparently seeing something on Leelo's face.

She laughed and shook her head. "No. Of course not. I just can't imagine myself with any of those boys, either."

"Well, not to worry. You've time yet. And there is someone for everyone out there."

"Even Ketty," Leelo said with a conspiratorial grin.

"You shouldn't joke about that." Once again, the tone in her mother's voice had changed suddenly and completely.

"I—I'm sorry, Mama. I didn't mean anything by it. I know she and Uncle Hugo loved each other. She can just be so… contentious." Leelo took her mother's wrist, but Fiona didn't meet her eyes. "Mama, what is it? Did something happen to Aunt Ketty? Sage mentioned something, about her sacrificing for you."

Finally, Fiona glanced over. "She did?"

"Yes. She was angry with me. She didn't say what it was. But it's always been obvious that something happened between you two."

Fiona sighed and leaned back against the sink. "Has it?"

She suddenly looked old and weary to Leelo, who had never noticed the strands of silver threaded through her auburn hair before. Fine lines had begun to appear around her lips and eyes. She had to look closely to see them, but they were there.

"Relationships between sisters are always complicated," Fiona said. "Much the way your relationship with Sage is."

"But something *did* happen, didn't it?"

Fiona nodded. "Your aunt's husband was not a nice man, Leelo."

"Uncle Hugo?" Leelo's memories of him were vague. They hadn't shared a home then, but she remembered him as tall and bearded, with sandy blond hair and a loud laugh. He had never been cruel to Leelo, and if he was cruel to Ketty and Sage, Leelo had never witnessed it.

"Yes. He was jovial and loving around others, but alone, he could be very different. He yelled at my sister and sometimes at Sage. He even hit Ketty from time to time."

Leelo gasped. She couldn't imagine anyone striking Aunt Ketty. She was the fiercest woman Leelo knew. "Why?"

"There was never a reason for it. Of course, what reason could there have been? He had a temper, and he never learned to control it. Some men on Endla think a woman should be obedient to their husband."

Leelo's stomach soured. "Was Father like that?"

"No, of course not. Your father was a good man. A bit too agreeable, some would say. He listened to your uncle more than anyone. They were friends, you see, long before your aunt and I married them. Kellan and Hugo had Watcher duty together, during a particularly challenging year. A group of outsiders decided to cross the ice the winter they had just started duty. They came bearing axes and hatchets, determined to chop down the Wandering Forest."

Leelo hung on her mother's words. A group of outsiders? A planned assault on the island? Why had she never heard of this before? "What happened?"

"Your father and uncle were the first men—well, boys, really—to discover the outsiders. They managed to take a couple down with their arrows, but they were vastly outnumbered and made a run for it. The Forest helped in its way. One man was crushed by a tree he himself had felled; another plummeted into a pit and broke his neck. More Watchers joined the fight, and eventually three outsiders were captured."

Leelo stared wide-eyed at her mother. "And then? The lake or the Forest?"

Fiona sighed. "It was something else, something we don't need to speak of. All you need to know is that they died."

Leelo steadied herself on the counter next to her mother. "And Father and Uncle?"

"They became inseparable after that. And when Ketty and Hugo married, it seemed inevitable that your father and I would do the same."

Leelo couldn't help but notice that Fiona hadn't said anything about love. "What did Aunt Ketty sacrifice for you, Mama?"

Fiona's hazel eyes were damp with tears when she turned to her daughter and said, "Everything."

Chapter Twenty-Nine

Leelo had been tromping around the middle of the island for what felt like hours, and she'd found nothing resembling a boat. She had never seen the pond where the flowers for the ceremony were grown, and she had no idea where the council members even met once a month. It didn't make sense. It was a small island, and she knew it like the back of her hand.

She tried to think of anywhere the adults had discouraged Endla's children from visiting. The only place she could think of was a small grotto northwest of the pine grove.

From a geographical perspective, it was a completely illogical place to keep a boat. It was at the bottom of a chasm, and the children were told to avoid it because it was not only dangerous to reach—it was supposedly full of disease-infested bats. But now that she thought about it, Leelo had never seen a bat on Endla. She wasn't even entirely sure what a bat was.

She'd gone to visit Isola first, so that if anyone asked if Leelo had visited her, Isola would say yes. Leelo had planned to account for the rest of her time with foraging for berries, which were just starting to ripen. She had a basket with her and had filled it as quickly as possible, which also lent credence to her story.

Still, if she tried to make it to the cave and back, she would have very little time to check on Jaren before nightfall. And Sage, who had quickly lost interest in spending the day with Leelo once Isola's name was mentioned, would wonder where she had gone. Berry picking didn't take all day.

But Leelo had no other plan, and she had to get Jaren off the island as soon as possible. The summer solstice festival was coming up in a few weeks, and it was the one time of year when every single islander joined, since the incantu were gone and there was no safe way for the outsiders to cross. They knew what happened on the solstice; if they chose to be out on festival night and got lured into the lake, that was their own fault.

The festival was always full of drinking and dancing around a large bonfire. Many proposals took place on the summer solstice. And Leelo didn't know how she'd keep Jaren safe from the singing if he was still here.

She hid her berry basket in a bush at the top of the chasm leading down to the grotto. It was already noon, and she was sweating despite the fact that she was only wearing a light-weight linen dress. Scanning the surroundings to be sure she was alone, Leelo started to make her way down the steep slope.

It was slower going than it had seemed from above. There was no path or trail, and the closer she got to the bottom, the steeper her descent became. From above, the grotto was hardly visible among the trees and ferns along the floor of the chasm, which must have held a creek at some point. She'd never had any interest in exploring here, though she knew sometimes children dared each other to brave the possibility of a fall, poison ivy, or an encounter with a rabid bat to snatch one of the colorful stones supposedly found in the cave.

But as she skidded and slid her way down, Leelo saw no poison ivy, and when she finally reached the mouth of the grotto, she was a little disappointed to find there were no special rocks here, either. It was just a shallow recess swathed in shadow, with dust and pebbles along the ground.

Leelo paused and took a long drag from her waterskin, then poured some on her neck beneath her braid. It was humid down here, and her dress was already soaked through at the back. Fortunately, it was not one of her nicer garments, just a simple dress that wouldn't be missed if it disappeared at the end of this excursion.

Leelo ducked her head and entered the cave, wishing she'd brought a lantern with her. Or better yet, that her brother was here to help. Tate was a quiet, sensitive boy, but he was always brave when it came to Leelo. She hoped that wherever he was now, he was being brave for himself.

The cave was only about twenty feet deep, and she didn't see any sign of bat droppings or bats themselves. Her hope dwindling, Leelo left the cave and sat on a log, draining the last of her water. If the boat wasn't here, where else could it be? She kicked at a rock near her foot and was surprised to hear a crack.

Leelo's hand flew to her mouth when she realized it was a bone. A human mandible. She rose and spun. Among the ferns and saplings struggling to grow in the filtered light, the ground was littered with bones, all disturbingly human. Was this what had happened to the outsiders Mama told her about last night?

Leelo looked at the cave again and gritted her teeth. This time, she went straight for the back, feeling around with her hands instead of relying solely on her eyesight. There. A gap in the stone, just large enough for a person to squeeze through...

Leelo emerged in a much larger cave. Light streamed in from above; there must be holes in the Forest floor, another good reason to tell the children to avoid this area. If anyone fell through, the drop was at least twenty feet, and the water on the cave floor didn't look more than a few feet deep. The boat was propped against the cave wall, the hole at the bottom still unrepaired. There were ropes and a pulley nearby. That must be how they got the boat into the cave.

"Damn it," she swore. She didn't know how to repair a boat, and she had no idea where the substance was that the council members used to protect the hull and the rope from the lake water. She walked closer to the water and peered through the dim light. Something was floating on the surface.

Lilies. Dozens of them, the buds tightly closed. This must be where they were grown. At least Leelo had answered two of the mysteries of Endla. But none of this was any use to her. Even if she and Jaren could pull the boat out of here on their own, it wasn't usable. She would have to wait until the council members repaired the boat themselves.

As she huffed and puffed her way out of the ravine, Leelo thought about what she would say to Jaren. They'd have to find some way to keep him safe during the festival. Perhaps stuffing wool into his ears and locking him inside the cottage would be enough. Or maybe, since he didn't seem to have been harmed by the other songs he'd heard, he'd be safe anyway.

By the time she made it to the cottage, Leelo's braid was unraveled, her hands and knees were bloodied from slipping so many times on her way out of the gorge, and her dress was filthy. She couldn't go home like this, not without some sort of explanation for where she'd been.

She entered the cottage without knocking, her thoughts on all the different conundrums she found herself in.

Jaren glanced up from the book in his lap. The songbook, she saw as he closed it and set it aside. "Hello, Leelo," he said. "You look like you've been on quite an adventure." His smile faded when he noticed the blood on her. "Saints, are you hurt?"

She snorted and sat down on the floor. "No, just frustrated." She explained about the cave and the boat, though she left out the part about the lilies, since that had nothing to do with him. She had betrayed Endla enough as it was. She didn't need to add this to the list.

When she was finished, she waited for Jaren to digest everything. He managed to keep the disappointment he had to be feeling off his face, mostly. "I might be able to repair the boat, if I could get to it. But I'd still need an opportunity to move it to the shore."

"The council members would wonder how it had gotten fixed, anyway." Leelo absently untied the ribbon holding what was left of her braid, combing out her hair with her fingers. "I'm sorry. I was hoping to have better news." She looked up to find Jaren watching her, and she dropped her hands to her lap, suddenly self-conscious.

He cleared his throat and looked away. "It's not your fault," he said. "We'll think of something."

It was kind of him to say "we" when Leelo knew it was all dependent on her. He couldn't do anything from here.

"Oh, by the way." Jaren pulled a piece of parchment off the makeshift table. "It turns out I'm not an artist *or* a musician. But here." He handed her the parchment.

"These are instruments?" she asked, turning the paper this way and that because she wasn't sure what was supposed to be the top.

"You have to imagine them made of wood and metal. And in three dimensions. And properly proportioned."

She continued to stare at the drawing until he pulled it away from her.

"Okay, so this didn't help at all. At least it gave me something to do."

"Keep working on it," Leelo said with a nod of encouragement.

Jaren brushed an invisible speck of dust off the drawing. "I was thinking—because aside from this masterpiece, I haven't had anything else to do—about your brother."

"Tate?" Leelo hadn't mentioned him to Mama recently because it only seemed to make her sad. But it was nice to have someone to talk about him with. Even if it was an outsider.

"Maybe, if I get off of Endla, I could check on him for you? I could tell him that you're okay, and I could make sure he's doing well. I'd have to find him, of course, but it's entirely possible he ended up in Bricklebury."

Leelo's heart stuttered in her chest. "You would do that for me?"

Jaren's flush reached all the way to the tips of his ears. "Well, sure. It would be the least I could do, considering you saved my life."

The last time he'd mentioned what she did, she insisted she wasn't helping him for his sake, that she'd only done it for herself. But she couldn't claim that was true anymore. She could have brought him supplies and left them outside his door. She didn't need to bring him drawing supplies, of all things. Spending time with Jaren right now was a choice, not a necessity.

Guilt replaced the hope that had bloomed in her chest just moments ago.

"I should go. I need to clean myself up before I go home."

"Could I… I don't mean this to sound untoward, but could I go with you? I haven't bathed in days and while I've become somewhat immune to my own aroma, I can't imagine it's particularly pleasant for you."

Leelo smiled. She couldn't smell him over her own odor. "Are you sure? I don't think we'll encounter anyone, but it could be dangerous."

"I understand. But if I'm going to die anyway, I'd prefer to do it clean."

Chapter Thirty

Jaren followed Leelo through the woods as quietly as he could, which was still nowhere near as quietly as Leelo. He was overjoyed at the prospect of washing up, even more so at the notion of cleaning his wound. His leg still hurt, but he'd checked the bandage earlier and hadn't seen any redness creeping around the edges. That had to be a good sign.

The pond was more of a series of small spring-fed pools, the largest of which was only big enough for two or three people. Jaren walked to it as quickly as he could, already tearing off his filthy tunic and boots. It wasn't until he was starting to pull off his breeches that he remembered Leelo was behind him. He turned to find her cheeks flaming, her eyes fixed firmly to the ground.

"I'm so sorry," Jaren said. "I didn't really think this through."

She managed to drag her eyes up to his, though he noticed they lingered on his bare torso for just a moment. "I didn't, either."

"We can take turns," Jaren said. "I won't look. You have my word."

"I need to wash my dress. And you should probably wash your clothing, too."

"Right."

She bit her lip, revealing that tiny gap again. "But I'm not sure what we'll do while we wait for it to dry."

"We'll just have to stay in the water," Jaren said. "I'll take this pool, and you can take that one."

Leelo nodded, but the furrow between her brows remained. She went to her pool and Jaren jumped into his, still wearing his trousers. The water was cold but he adjusted to it quickly, grateful to be clean again for the first time in days.

"Thank you for bringing me here. I didn't realize how badly I needed this." He stripped out of his trousers and laid them on the rocky edge of the pool next to his tunic, which he'd already scrubbed and wrung out.

"I'll bring soap for next time," Leelo said behind him. "I'm sorry I didn't think of it sooner."

"You read my mind," he said, sniffing his clothing with a wince. "Water alone isn't enough, I'm afraid." Finally, he unwound the bandage on his leg, wincing as the scabs pulled against the fabric.

"How is the wound?" Leelo asked.

"Better." Jaren still had one large hole in his shin, along with a few smaller ones, but they were clean and appeared to be healing. "Thank you."

"I think it's all right if we turn around," Leelo said. "As long as we're both under water."

"Are you sure?"

There was a short pause. "Yes."

Slowly, Jaren turned to face Leelo. Her pool was slightly below his, but the rocks between them hid her body from view. All he could see was her sleek head, her fair hair made silver by the water. Her eyelashes were usually so pale they were hard to see, but now they were darker and clumped together into little spikes.

He was staring. He swallowed and shook his head to break the tension, sending water droplets spraying. She held a hand out in front of her face, laughing.

"I feel so much better," he said, slicking his hair away from his forehead. "You?"

She nodded. Her dress was splayed out on the rocks like his clothing. It had to be getting closer to evening, but the sun was still bright. The days were long now, with the summer solstice approaching.

"Have you made any progress with the songbook?" she asked. "I saw you were reading it when I came in."

"Alas, no progress. I almost resorted to reading the poetry book, but I couldn't stomach it."

"What's wrong with poetry?"

He shrugged. "Nothing, I suppose. It's like singing without the music."

She raised a brow in question.

"Right. You don't sing words when you sing, do you?"

She shook her head. "No. Do you?"

Jaren didn't love the idea of singing in front of someone who clearly had a far better voice than he did, especially when he'd never practiced. But he remembered the tune and words of one of the songs his mother had crooned to him as a baby, and he sang it quickly.

Leelo's eyes lit up. "That's wonderful!"

"Is it?" He chuckled. "My mother used to sing it to us when we were little. I'm surprised I still know the words."

She smiled to herself. "I would never have thought to sing about a little filly in a meadow. But I liked it. Especially the part about the butterfly."

Jaren sighed and crossed his arms on the rocks between them. "I wish we had something to eat. I'm starving."

"I left the berries back in the cottage. I'm sure there are more nearby, though."

"What kind of berries?"

"Blueberries. Maybe some lingonberries, but I don't know if they're ripe yet."

"Right. Turn around. I'll go find us some." He waited until she was looking away, pushed out of the pool, and pulled on his still-damp trousers. It only took him a few minutes to find the blueberry bushes, and he picked them as quickly as he could, using his tunic as a makeshift basket.

He moved a little farther into the Forest and was just about to reach for a branch when he realized this wasn't a blueberry bush; it was nightshade. Poisonous, even fatal, the small, blue-black berries looked similar to blueberries to the untrained eye. He glanced around him and noticed a patch of amanita toadstools growing nearby, their red-and-white-spotted caps bright against the grass. Fairy houses, Tadpole called them. But they were toxic, too.

Jaren was surrounded by danger, from the bright purple foxglove quivering in the breeze to the diamond-backed snake winding silently through them. He decided he had collected enough and made his way quickly out of the Forest to the clearing, then froze.

Leelo was standing with her back to him, still submerged below the waist. Her hair was so long it was nearly touching the water. She was doing something with her clothing, humming to herself as she worked.

She had the most beautiful voice Jaren had ever heard. Whatever she was singing now was nothing like the Endlan songs he'd heard before. It was, he realized, the song he'd sung for her, but in her wordless, haunting voice, it sounded otherworldly. He took a step forward without realizing it, until he stepped on a branch and froze just as her head whipped around.

She dropped below the surface of the water quickly, but not before he'd caught a glimpse of her face, her blue eyes wide with fright. Her hair had covered her chest, so he'd only caught a flash of bare skin. But saints, it looked like he'd been spying on her.

"I'm sorry," he said, already turned around and facing away. "I have the blueberries."

"Just a second." He heard the water ripple, followed by the rustling of fabric. "All right."

When he turned back around, she was wearing her still-damp dress. Her hair hung in long, loose waves. They would both need a little more time to dry.

"Here." He laid his tunic out on the rock next to her and she thanked him, eagerly popping a blueberry into her mouth. He was still shirtless, but she wasn't blushing, at least.

They ate in silence for a few minutes. Jaren stared out at

the Forest, wanting to ask her something, anything, but not knowing where to begin. They had nothing in common, no shared experiences. Her life was confined to this small island, to people who all behaved and thought the way she did.

They reached for the last blueberry at the same time, their fingers brushing. When he looked up at her, her lips were stained purple, in stark contrast to her pale skin. *She looks*, he thought with a blush of his own, *like she's just been kissed*.

"You take it," Leelo said. "I have plenty more."

With the blueberries finished and their clothing fairly dry, there was no reason not to go back to the cottage, though Jaren was dreading more time alone in the cramped space. He wished he could go home, where Father would undoubtedly be cooking something delicious and his sisters would tease him for getting lost again. But really, they would all be relieved that he was back.

"Are you okay?" Leelo asked as they walked. She was braiding her hair over one shoulder, and he almost asked her to keep it loose, though that would be wholly inappropriate and frankly rude. He'd once told his twin she should curl her hair like Summer did, and she'd thrown a shoe at him.

He glanced over at Leelo with a shrug instead. "I'm fine. Just homesick, I suppose."

"I've never had the chance to be homes—" Suddenly, Leelo froze.

"What's wrong?" he whispered.

"I heard something." She pulled him behind a tree next to her, so focused on listening she probably didn't realize she was still holding his hand.

Their bodies were pressed close together. The scent of her

damp hair made him a little dizzy. After a minute passed, he shifted his weight off his bad leg. When Leelo pressed her hand to his chest to still him, he was sure she'd be able to feel his heart hammering beneath it.

Something moved in the undergrowth, this time loud enough for Jaren to hear. His stomach twisted when he remembered how precarious his situation was. If someone found him, they would kill him, and Leelo would be exiled. He held his breath and closed his eyes.

And opened them at the sound of Leelo laughing.

A porcupine waddled past them, oblivious to their terror.

"Saints," Jaren breathed. "I thought we'd been caught for sure."

"So did I." Leelo seemed to realize she was not only holding Jaren's hand but also had her other hand pressed to his chest and stepped quickly aside. "Sorry."

He mumbled something that was supposed to be "no apology necessary" but came out as utter nonsense. Fortunately, she was moving again and didn't seem to notice.

They stopped outside the cottage. Jaren had hoped she might come in, but the sun was setting now. She bent down and took up the full basket of berries she'd picked earlier.

"You're all dry now, at least," he said.

"Thank goodness. Oh, I almost forgot." She lifted the cloth inside the basket and poked around underneath, removing a little parcel. "It's not much, but it should last you until I can bring more food again."

"Thank you. For everything."

She nodded and glanced over her shoulder. He could tell she needed to go, but something was stopping her.

"What is it?" he asked.

"I was wondering if you'd teach me that song. The one you sang before."

Jaren laughed in surprise. "The lullaby? Are you sure? It's only a silly nursery rhyme."

"Right. Of course. I just—"

Why was he arguing with her when what he wanted was for her to stay as long as possible? Before he could overthink it, he held out his hand.

She only hesitated a moment before taking it, and he led her over to the stump he'd used as a seat before. She sat down next to him, placing the basket near her feet but not letting go of his hand. He wondered if she knew how beautiful she was, or if she was truly as unaware as she seemed.

He sang the song for her three times, and on the last time, she joined him. He didn't think she meant to do it. Her eyes were closed, and she sang so softly that the words drifted over his skin like snowflakes, chilling him.

When she'd finished, she opened her eyes and looked over at him, her face lit up with wonder, like that silly little nursery rhyme was the most brilliant thing she'd ever heard. And he had done that. He wanted to do it again.

"Did I get it right?" she asked.

He wasn't sure anything he said would be coherent, so he nodded instead.

Leelo looked around, as if she was waiting for something to happen, but the Forest was as it always was, full of distant birdsong and rustling in the undergrowth. There were no roots snaking up out of the soil toward them. No storm clouds loomed overhead. "I keep expecting the Forest to respond," she said, so quietly it was little more than a whisper.

"They must not like my song choice," Jaren said with a smile, but all he could think about was the fact that her hand was still cradled in his. Any second now, she would realize and pull away. But even when he ran his thumb along the ridges of her knuckles, she didn't move. When he glanced at her out of the corner of his eye, it looked like she was holding her breath.

Her berry-stained lower lip was caught between her front teeth again. Before he knew what he was doing, his hand came up, and he gently tugged her lip free with his thumb.

"Your lips are stained," he said softly.

"So are yours." She released his hand, but it was only so she could run her fingers over his mouth, as delicate as butterfly wings. "I should go."

His mouth quirked in a crooked grin. "I don't want you to."

She rose anyway. "I'll come back tomorrow."

He stood up next to her. He wanted to kiss her. He knew it was a terrible idea.

She picked up her basket once again. "Good night, Jaren."

"Good night, Leelo."

He watched her go, wiping the stain from his mouth with the back of his hand and wishing she had kissed it away instead.

Chapter Thirty-One

That night, Leelo lay awake for hours, trying to come to some sort of solution to her predicament and failing.

One thing was certain: she had to get Jaren off the island. Eventually, he would be caught like Pieter, and it would end the same horrific way. She hardly knew Jaren, but the thought of any harm coming to him was almost unbearable. It didn't make sense, to care so much about the fate of a stranger.

But he wasn't a stranger anymore, she reminded herself. She knew about his father and his three sisters, who Leelo thought she would like very much. She knew the song his late mother sang to him when he was a baby. She knew that whatever other outsiders might be like, this one, at least, had no intention of harming Endla. And if that was the case, wasn't it also possible that other outsiders didn't want to harm it, either?

Unconsciously, she remembered the way the muscles of Jaren's torso had rippled when he lifted his hand to brush the hair from his face, how she'd caught him watching her, and how for a split second she had considered letting him watch, had wanted him to see her. She tugged at her lower lip, but it didn't elicit the same curling warmth in her stomach as his touch had. She wasn't sure what to make of any of these feelings, but at the same time, she thought she knew exactly what they meant.

Sage would tell her to get ahold of herself and stop acting so ridiculous and moony. But Leelo couldn't help it. As wrong as she knew it was to get close to Jaren, she also didn't want to stop.

The next morning, Sage was quiet as they patrolled their stretch of beach, close to the spot where the boat had come ashore with Jaren. The blood trail had washed away in the summer storms so common at this time of year, but keeping a secret was almost as difficult as keeping a song in her throat. Leelo wanted to tell her cousin about everything that had happened the past few days. She wanted to whisper how Jaren's trousers had been slung so low on his hips it was a wonder they hadn't fallen off, to giggle and cover her face in embarrassment until Sage told her she knew exactly how she felt.

But there was no possibility of her telling Sage about Jaren. Leelo knew Sage would tell Ketty immediately, and Ketty would tell the council, if she didn't kill him herself.

"What's gotten into you?" Sage said instead, a suspicious glimmer in her eye.

"What do you mean?" Leelo pretended to be fascinated with her arrows so she could avoid Sage's gaze. She still had the hawk feather that Jaren had rescued for her. For some reason, she hadn't wanted to cut it for fletching.

"Your cheeks are bright pink. Did you get a sunburn on

your day off? Where were you, anyway? I feel like you keep disappearing."

"I've just needed time to think, that's all."

"About Tate?"

"Yes, about Tate." The lie was bitter on her tongue. It didn't stop her from deflecting, however. "Mama said she thinks Aunt Ketty is trying to get close to the Harding family. Are you interested in marrying Hollis?"

Sage scowled, and Leelo couldn't help but smile. Sage never hid her feelings. Leelo doubted she could even if she tried. "My mother thinks it would be good for our family. She doesn't seem to care that Hollis is a hulking brute who has no interest in me whatsoever."

"Are you sure? He didn't seem to mind sharing Watcher duty with you."

"Tolerating me and wanting to marry me are two very different things, Leelo." Sage sighed and tugged off her boots, followed by her stockings. She winced as she touched a painful-looking blister on her big toe. Sage had a way of wearing through her boots twice as quickly as Leelo did. It looked like Ketty would be trading for another pair soon. "I don't know. I thought I could like him, maybe. At least for the sake of the family."

"And you don't?" Leelo asked.

"I hardly know him. I guess I just thought my mother wouldn't make me marry someone I don't love. Not after…"

She trailed off, but Leelo wanted this secret, at least, to be out in the open. "Not after the way your father treated her?"

Sage looked up. "How do you know about that?"

"My mother told me. Don't be angry. It's good that I know. It explains some things."

Sage bristled, ready to defend her mother, but Leelo shook her head. "I just mean I understand Aunt Ketty a little better now."

Sage raised her eyebrows. "You do?"

"Yes. If my husband beat me, I wouldn't love him, either. And I would probably be distrusting of other men."

"Is that all your mother told you?" Sage asked, her tone wary.

Leelo had thought she finally knew the truth, but now she wondered if she had only scratched the surface. "Why? Is there more?"

Sage was quiet for a long moment. She put her socks and boots back on and rose. "Come on. If we hurry, we can be home in time for lunch."

Leelo caught her hand. "Wait, Sage. Tell me the truth. Is there more?"

Sage's expression shifted as she glanced down at Leelo's hand. Then she reached into her pocket and pulled something out. "I made you this."

It was a crude carving of a long-necked bird. Leelo took it, a bemused smile on her lips. "What's this for?"

"It's to go with the fox I made. So we each have one. It's supposed to be a swan."

"Why a swan?" Leelo asked. "Why not a matching fox?"

Sage released a soft puff of laughter. "Because you're nothing like a fox, Lo. Foxes are sly, resourceful, alert." She brought her hand up to Leelo's face, tucking a strand of her corn silk hair behind her ear with calloused fingers. "You're like a swan, rare and beautiful. You have so much magic in you, Leelo."

Leelo began to smile, but Sage's fingers slid lower, wrapping loosely around Leelo's neck.

"But you're so fragile, cousin. Anyone could break you. I know you think I'm too hard to feel like you do. But if I told you everything, if you knew the truth, it would shatter you like glass."

"Sage—"

Sage's hand slid away. "You might be as naive as those swans that land on a lake full of poison, but you're still mine. And I'll protect you, like I always have."

Leelo's confusion quickly turned to anger. "What aren't you telling me, Sage?"

Her cousin's hazel eyes were just like Aunt Ketty's, giving nothing away. "Forget I said anything. Come on, I'm hungry."

"Sage!" Leelo called after her, but she'd already disappeared into the Forest.

Leelo was certain now that she wasn't the only one with secrets. And something told her that Sage's were sinister. The kind that best stayed buried.

Chapter Thirty-Two

In the days that followed, Jaren's entire world became sleeping and waiting for Leelo's visits. Sleeping at least made the time go faster; the waiting was excruciating. He had only gone to bathe one more time, alone, and all it did was make him think of Leelo and her lips and her hair and her bare skin. He knew it was dangerous to start to care about a girl he'd almost certainly never see again, but it was also a welcome distraction from worrying about how he'd get off the island and what his family was doing in his absence. And, if he was being honest, a distraction from the way the trees surrounding him seemed to press a little closer at night, how the wind through the branches sounded like whispering voices, and when rain fell, it had a strange cadence, like a song.

But when Leelo came, Jaren forgot about all of that. He was able to coax a little more out of her each time, and he gathered those facts like a bird adding trinkets to its nest. He spent hours thinking of questions to ask her, so soon he knew her favorite color (blue), her favorite food (cake), and her least favorite chore (anything to do with hunting—they had that in common). And every time she left, he felt like she trusted him a bit more, and his odds of dying were lower.

One night, when she'd come to visit him after a late Watcher shift, she had actually collapsed next to him on the blanket instead of sitting with her back to the door.

"Sorry," she'd said when she saw him looking down at her with a bemused grin. "I forgot this was your bed."

"What's mine is yours," he'd said with a laugh. "Literally."

If their eyes met for too long, she would grow shy and reserved, like she was remembering that she was supposed to hate him. So he never stared at her too long, though saints knew he wanted to.

Unlike his sisters, Leelo didn't think Jaren was too brooding or boring. On the contrary, she seemed to find him interesting. He knew that was likely because he was the first person she'd ever met who didn't live on Endla, but seeing himself through her eyes made him feel like maybe what he had to say *was* interesting. After all, he'd lived in two different places. He had a large, boisterous family, and he spent enough time gathering in the woods that he could identify hundreds of plant species.

Leelo was particularly curious about life in Tindervale versus life in Bricklebury. "What's a pub?" she'd asked when he told her about the bet he'd made with Merritt.

"A place where people gather to eat and drink," he explained.

"Like a festival?"

"I suppose a very small one. Indoors. With ale."

She'd considered this for a while, chewing her lip, and then said, "I think I'd like to go to one. As long as there are no boys like Merritt around."

"I'd say I'd protect you, but I think we both know it would be the other way around."

She had blushed with pleasure, and Jaren had felt like he finally understood how Summer felt around her carpenter, and how Story must have expected him to feel with Lupin.

But with Leelo, things were so much simpler. He didn't have to worry about what any of this meant. It was forbidden, which he knew added at least some element of excitement to it, but it was also pure. They both knew they could never marry, that this relationship wasn't advantageous to either of them or their families. They were not supposed to want anything to do with each other, just two strangers brought together by dire circumstances. But instead, Jaren wanted *everything* to do with Leelo. There was attraction, yes, but it was also something else. Jaren admired Leelo, her determination, her bravery. She was unlike anyone he'd ever met. He had a feeling that even on Endla, Leelo was special.

She arrived late one blisteringly hot afternoon. It was hard to believe an entire month had passed, with the days being so long and dull, yet also so similar that they bled into each other, distorting time. He lived for the moment she knocked lightly on the door, entering without waiting for an answer. And every time she left, he knew he would be counting the hours until she returned.

"Here," she said, tossing him a parcel of food the moment she entered. He wondered how she was managing to sneak food without anyone in her house realizing, and he hoped she wasn't using her own rations on him.

He opened the wrapping and tore the sandwich in half, offering it to her, and was a little relieved when she shook her head no. He was famished.

"Thank you," he said before tearing into the sandwich like an animal.

"Slow down," Leelo cautioned. "You'll make yourself sick."

He drained the first waterskin she brought him. "I'm sorry. You'd think with me lazing about all day I wouldn't have much appetite."

"My mother says young men are always hungry." Their eyes met, and she blushed. She was wearing a dress again today, a soft gray linen embroidered with little pale blue stars that matched her eyes. "She says it's because they're still growing," she clarified.

Jaren glanced down and patted his now full belly. "Up and out, as Story says."

Playfully, she pinched his arm. "You could stand to have some more meat on your bones."

"Is that so?" He was tempted to pinch her own slender shoulder, but he knew it was very different for her to touch him than for him to touch her. If anything physical were to happen between them, it would only be if she initiated it.

"The winters on Endla are harsh," she said. "We can't hunt, so we generally eat more in the warmer months."

"Why can't you hunt?"

"Because the ice freezes. Our songs might lure the animals out of their dens, but they could also bring an outsider across the lake. If we're lucky enough to come across a deer or a rabbit, we can try to kill it, but our odds of success are much lower."

"So Endlans don't deliberately try to bring outsiders over?"

Her brow immediately furrowed. He'd offended her. He wished he could take back the words, but it was too late. "Why would we do such a thing? We're not monsters."

"I know that," he said quickly. "Now. But some of the people in Bricklebury tell stories. One girl's father was killed entering the lake. From the way I heard it, his death wasn't an accident."

She shook her head. "That person was wrong. We live on Endla for our own protection. We aren't the ones indiscriminately killing people. What could we possibly stand to gain from that?"

They sat in silence for a few minutes, Jaren still regretting that he had ever mentioned Maggie's father. But eventually, his curiosity got the better of him.

"Leelo, why do you think I was able to hear the singing and not cross?"

Her brow furrowed again, but this time he could see she was thinking. "Honestly, I have no idea."

"Have you ever heard of that happening before?"

"No. But that doesn't mean it never has. Which reminds me. The summer solstice festival is tomorrow night. There will be a lot of singing. It won't be near here, but it's important you don't leave the cottage." She reached into her bag and pulled out a little tuft of wool. "I thought you could put this in your ears, just in case."

"Thank you. I won't leave."

She smiled, but there was a strain to it. "I don't know when

the boat will be repaired. I have another day off after the festival. I'll check then."

"It's all right. I know you're doing everything you can.
And I truly am grateful."

She fiddled with the wool in her fingers, stretching it out
and then rubbing it between her palms back into a ball. "What
were you doing that night you heard me singing?"

Jaren explained about how he got lost often, beginning
when he was just a child. "I was only five the first time. We
were visiting friends at their country home. My oldest sister
was supposed to be watching Story and me, but she got distracted. I went outside, presumably just to explore near the
cottage. But there was a frog hopping about in the grass, and
I started following it. The next thing I knew, it was nearly
dark."

"Your poor parents. They must have been so frightened."

"Terrified. Fortunately, I stayed put once I realized I was
lost, and they found me a little while later. But despite how
scared I'd been, I continued to do it. I don't know why. It's
like I've always been searching for something, even subcon-
sciously." He hesitated, wanting to choose his words carefully.
"I guess I don't feel like I fit in, even though my family loves
me and has always been supportive of me."

Leelo had been sitting cross-legged, but she stretched her
legs out now, so they were side by side with Jaren's. As much
as he hated how small the shack was most of the time, he
was always grateful for the closeness whenever Leelo came.
"I sometimes feel that way, too."

"Really?"

She nodded. "The very fact that I helped you when I should

have turned you in makes me unlike any other Endlan I know."

"I understand how much you risked in helping me, Leelo. And I'm very grateful you did."

They were quiet for a few minutes again, the air thick with unsaid words. It was taking all of Jaren's strength not to ask if he could kiss her. He didn't know what the conventions were on Endla, but Leelo had already told him she was expected to marry young. She could already be promised to someone else, for all he knew.

"How's your leg?" Leelo asked suddenly, breaking the tension.

"It's fine. Much better, in fact. The good news is that when we do get that boat repaired, I'll be able to pull my weight. Not that you couldn't handle it on your own."

She laughed. "I'm strong, but I know my limits. I can't get a boat to the shore on my own." She pulled her legs up to her chest. "I should go. I won't see you tomorrow, because of the festival. Do you think you'll be all right until the day after?"

He wanted to tell her no. He wanted her to stay. He wanted to tell her that going even a few hours without seeing her was too long. He wanted her to slip away from the festival and spend that time with him instead. But he nodded because what he wanted was irrelevant. "Of course."

He was waiting for her to leave, but she didn't move. "Jaren, I…" She ran her hands over her braid, clearly anxious about something.

"What is it?"

"I like you. More than I should. I shouldn't even say that. I'm not a good Endlan."

He couldn't stand to see her look so ashamed, not when she'd done nothing wrong. He leaned forward and held out his hand. This time, she took it without hesitating. "I don't know what makes a good Endlan, Leelo. But I do know you're a good person."

She shook her head. "You don't understand."

He wouldn't contradict her. Maybe he didn't understand, but he knew without a doubt that she was good. "Leelo."

She slowly dragged her eyes up to his.

"I like you, too." One side of his mouth tugged up in a grin. "A lot."

Chapter Thirty-Three

"You girls both look beautiful."

Leelo smiled at her mother, who watched as she and Sage fluttered around the house in preparation for the solstice festival. Despite her concerns for Jaren, Leelo had somehow gotten caught up in the excitement once it was time to get ready. Even Sage seemed eager, to Leelo's surprise.

"Is my hair all right?" Leelo asked, twisting to get a glimpse of herself in the mirror.

"It's perfect." Her mother tugged on one of the long blond waves that she'd woven through with daisies from the Forest. She'd presented Leelo with her new dress that morning, made of fine white cotton embroidered with bright flowers and trimmed in the most delicate handmade lace. Sage was wearing a similar dress in her namesake color.

"You've matured over the last few months, you know. Both of you."

Sage wrapped her arm around Leelo's waist and squeezed. "Imagine what we'll be like when the year is over."

Fiona sighed. "I wish I could freeze time and keep you as you are now."

Sage laughed and released Leelo. "You know that's impossible, Aunt Fiona." She skipped out of the room, but Leelo stayed with her mother.

"And how are we now, Mama?" she asked.

Her mother looked wistful when she spoke. "A little harder around the edges, perhaps, but still soft enough to be hopeful."

"Hopeful about what?"

Her mother sighed. "Everything, my darling."

Something about Mama's tone worried Leelo. "You're coming, aren't you? Are you feeling well enough?"

"Of course I'm coming. I'll change, and we can go." She kissed Leelo's forehead, now nearly even with hers.

Together, they left the cottage, falling silent as they passed by Isola's house. Her family wasn't allowed to attend such a celebratory occasion. Still, by the time they'd reached the meadow where the festival was held, they were nearly twenty people in all, the majority of the families Aunt Ketty oversaw as council member. Despite how small Endla was, it wasn't often that everyone gathered on the island. It was a time to catch up with people they rarely saw, for the adults to comment on how big the children had grown, for friends to share gossip and elderberry wine, and for the young people to dance until their feet ached.

Leelo's thoughts turned to Jaren once again when she saw the sheer number of people who had gathered, but she knew the songs they sang tonight would be harmless, mostly. Even her mother seemed pleased to be there, and she avoided most of Endla's ceremonies. She said they took too much out of her, which Leelo had always chalked up to her mother's introverted, quiet manner.

But as the sun went down, Fiona seemed quite satisfied with the elderberry wine and various dishes Aunt Ketty continued to bring to her, where she sat in the shade of an oak tree. Content that her mother was being well looked after, Leelo chatted with some of the people she hadn't seen since the ceremony. Vance admired Leelo's dress, just as she had last time. Sage stood with Hollis, talking animatedly about saints knew what, but certainly not looking for Leelo. She passed a table full of perfect miniature cupcakes dusted with icing sugar and topped with fresh strawberries. She only meant to take one for herself, but then she took a second.

She knew Jaren would love it.

She knew she would love watching him eat it.

It had taken a lot for her to admit to Jaren that she liked him, though she assumed he already knew. Partly she had wanted to get this secret off her chest, and partly she had wanted—had hoped, desperately—to hear him say he liked her, too. When he did, she felt both relieved and alive in a way she'd never felt before. She didn't know if this was what would be considered courting; she'd never spent enough time with a boy to learn much beyond their peculiar habits and, as they got older, their even more peculiar smells. All she knew was that she went to the cottage feeling nervous or tired or guilty, and she left feeling… She wasn't sure she could describe it.

But she wanted that feeling now.

Perhaps it was the two small cups of elderberry wine that

were making her feel so reckless. She noted that her head seemed pleasantly disconnected from her body and her lips were a little numb. She had made Jaren promise to stay as far away from the festival as possible. Going to him now could compromise his safety—not to mention her own—all for the sake of watching him eat a strawberry. And, if she was being honest, so he could see her in this dress. It almost seemed a waste *not* to go to him.

If anyone noticed she was gone, they would attribute it to the wine, or the darkness, or how all the children looked the same in the firelight. And by then, it would be too late to stop her.

Leelo might have changed her mind at any point on her way to the cottage, but before she knew it, she had arrived. She stood among the trees for a moment, straightening her hair with her free hand, then slapping her cheeks lightly to clear her head.

She glanced up a moment later to see Jaren standing in the open door of the cottage. It was twilight, and he hadn't lit his candle yet. The thought of him sitting alone in the dark sent an ache through her, and she was glad she'd come, that at least for a little while, he wouldn't be alone.

Far away, she could hear the faint singing from the festival. And if she could hear it... Without thinking, she rushed forward, shoving him back into the cottage so hard he tripped over the threshold and landed on his backside in the nest of blankets.

Leelo slammed the door shut behind her and dropped to her knees, grabbing Jaren roughly by the face and turning his head from side to side.

She sighed in relief when she saw the creamy tufts of wool in his ears. Jaren's mouth quirked in a grin. Suddenly, she realized she was practically on top of him. Flushing furiously, she started to lean back, but Jaren's hand caught her waist, stopping her.

"What are you doing here?" he asked, a little too loudly because of the wool.

Leelo strained to listen, but she couldn't hear the singing inside the cottage. Hesitantly, with tingling fingers, she plucked the wool from his ears. With his face so close to hers and his body heat warming her through the thin fabric of her dress, it took a moment to remember why she'd come in the first place.

She lifted the little cake in her left hand, frowning when she saw that in her haste, she had squished it against his tunic. "I'm sorry. I don't know what I was thinking."

But Jaren wasn't looking at the cake. He was looking at her mouth. Her head spun a little, and she wasn't sure if it was the wine or Jaren. Probably both. She thought of the islanders who would get engaged tonight, of the look on her mother's face when she'd spoken about how you knew when you liked someone. *You think about them all the time…your heart races when your eyes meet…*

She didn't just like Jaren, though. She *wanted* him. She wanted him to want her. The next thing she knew she was leaning forward, pressing her mouth to his.

When his hand slid beneath her hair to cup the nape of her neck, she let the crumbled cake fall, freeing her hand so she could touch his own soft waves, her fingers tangling in the silken strands. He smiled against her lips, and she would have laughed if she wasn't too busy kissing him. This, she decided, was far better than any cake.

He eased his lips free of hers after a moment. "Leelo," he said, his gray eyes a little hooded. "As much as I enjoyed this greeting, I feel it is my duty to point out that you've been drinking."

She sat back, self-conscious that he'd smelled the wine on her breath. But he didn't look angry or disgusted, just mildly amused. "I'm sorry," she said, shaking her head a little to clear it. "I don't know what came over me."

He handed her his waterskin. "Elderberry wine, by the taste of things."

Her face went scarlet as she clamped a hand over her mouth, but he pulled it away gently. "Leelo, I like the way you taste."

Now her face was truly on fire. She drank so much water she nearly choked, and he patted her on the back.

"Easy, there."

At least the room had stopped spinning. She sat back on the floor and waited for his face to come into focus. "I really am sorry. I didn't think. I just wanted to see you. And I thought you'd like the cake." She gestured feebly to the heap of crumbs on the blanket.

"I'm extremely happy you came to see me," Jaren said, and truth be told, he looked a little tipsy himself.

"You drank some of the plum brandy, didn't you?" she asked.

He colored and looked down. "Guilty. I was feeling bad for myself that you were at a festival with your friends while I was stuck alone in this shack."

Leelo laughed, a little less embarrassed now. "I thought you might be feeling that way."

"And you weren't having fun?" He pinched some of the crumbs between his fingers and tossed them into his mouth. "The food was clearly excellent."

Leelo sighed, tugging a daisy free of her hair and spinning it between her fingers, just to give them something to do. "I don't know. Everyone was dancing, but my heart wasn't in it." *It was here, with you,* she thought, and then wondered what was happening to her. She'd known Jaren just a few weeks. She couldn't be falling for him. That was ridiculous.

He tossed a few more crumbs into his mouth and leaned back. "I feel like this is a dream, and any moment I'm going to wake up."

"Why does it feel like a dream?" she asked shyly.

"Because I wished you would come here. And I wished I could kiss you. So, you see, I've had two wishes come true in a row, and that never happens. Clearly, I must be dreaming."

"Technically," Leelo said, scooting closer to Jaren, "*I* kissed *you.*"

He reached up, twisting a lock of her hair around his finger. "That is a fair point."

Her voice dropped almost to a whisper. "So only one of your wishes came true."

He smiled, his thick lashes falling against his cheeks as he sat up and closed the space between them. His lips were soft but firm, his entire body radiating warmth that she wanted to curl up in like a blanket. She pressed as close to him as she dared, and when he wrapped his arms around her, bringing her even closer, any trepidation she'd felt before coming here melted away. She felt the farthest from scared she could imagine. In fact, it was the safest she could remember feeling, as if the rest of the world didn't matter when they were here together in this tiny cottage in the woods that no one else knew about. As if nothing else existed at all.

When he finally pulled away, he cupped her face in his hands, looking into her eyes with such earnestness she felt something swell in her chest. "Two wishes," he whispered, and leaned in to kiss her again.

Chapter Thirty-Four

By the time Leelo returned to the festival, it was full dark. The sky was awash with stars, the familiar constellations her father had taught her before he died so clear and close she felt like she could touch them. Most of the elders and children had already returned to their homes, leaving the young adults dancing and singing in small clusters, their voices a little off-key, occasionally breaking off into fits of laughter.

Leelo was still feeling warm and light, though she could no longer attribute it to the wine. It was the lingering effect of kissing Jaren, of knowing that he liked her as much as she liked him. Of knowing that tomorrow was her day off and they would spend it together.

She found her mother where she'd left her, leaned up against the base of an oak tree, sound asleep. Leelo smiled and pulled Fiona's light summer shawl closed to keep her warm and went in search of Sage. But it was her aunt who found her.

"Where have you been?" Ketty asked, her cold voice a

harsh juxtaposition to the night. *She* hadn't been enjoying herself, clearly.

"I've been here," Leelo said, and for once, she didn't feel bad for lying.

Ketty's eyes narrowed, the dying firelight dancing in her irises. "Who were you with?"

Leelo felt all the warmth rush out of her. She couldn't claim she'd been with Sage. That would be too easily disproven, and Leelo didn't trust Sage to cover for her. Vance was a risk, too. Leelo didn't even know how long she'd stayed.

She swallowed, trying to get some moisture back into her suddenly dry mouth. "No one in particular. I was just dancing." She dropped her eyes to her feet. "I might have had too much wine and lost track of time."

Before Ketty could respond, Leelo felt a hand close over her shoulder.

She turned to see Sage standing behind her. Her cousin's eyes were as dull as her aunt's were sharp. "What's wrong?" Leelo asked.

"Nothing is wrong," Ketty said. "Hollis proposed to Sage. She has accepted his offer."

Leelo whirled back to her cousin. "What?"

Sage nodded, but her mouth stayed closed in a firm line.

Leelo found herself at a loss for words. She had known that Ketty intended for this to happen eventually, but tonight? Sage hadn't even finished her year of Watcher duty. Her eighteenth birthday wasn't for another six months. Surely it was too soon.

Fiona walked up to them, still blinking away her drowsiness. "What's this I hear? A proposal?" She was smiling, but in the darkness, Leelo couldn't tell if it was genuine.

"That's right." Ketty lifted her chin, almost as if she were challenging her sister. "My girl will be married on her eighteenth birthday. Mr. Harding has already begun drawing up the plans for their cottage."

Leelo felt as if the ground was shifting beneath her, and she had to hold on to her mother for support. "You're moving out?" she asked Sage.

Sage's eyes flicked to her mother, then back to Leelo. "Yes."

It was all too much to make sense of. Couldn't Ketty see that Sage wasn't happy about this? And if Ketty's bitterness was the result of marrying a man she didn't love, how could she possibly want the same thing for her own daughter?

"It's late," Fiona said. "We should get home."

Leelo allowed her mother to take her hand and begin leading her back to the house. The voices of the still-carousing Endlans were drowned by the roar of blood in Leelo's head, and she realized almost too late that she was going to be sick.

She retched so violently she fell to her knees, her mother pulling her hair back just in time.

"It seems you really did have too much wine." Ketty's voice was loud and grating. By the time Leelo wiped her mouth and sat back on her haunches, her aunt and Sage were gone. Fiona helped her to her feet.

"Are you all right?" she asked.

"I think so," Leelo said. "I'm sorry."

"Don't be sorry. We've all had a little too much wine on a summer solstice night." Mama smiled and linked her arm through Leelo's. "Where were you tonight, darling?"

Leelo glanced at her mother from the corner of her eye. She should have known she would notice her absence, no matter how much wine she'd had. "I needed to get away for a little while, that's all."

Her mother arched a brow. "*Is* that all?"

"What do you mean?"

Her tone was soft and coaxing when she said, "You met someone, didn't you?"

For a moment, Leelo wondered if she was going to be sick again.

"It's all right, Leelo. You can tell me. I promise I won't expect you to marry them, just because you like them."

Leelo knew she couldn't continue lying to her mother, but she also couldn't tell her about Jaren. It wasn't that she thought her mother would be angry with her. But she would be worried. She would do whatever it took to keep Leelo safe, even if that meant killing Jaren. And Leelo couldn't bear to think of that now.

"I do like someone," she admitted finally. "But I'm not ready to talk about who it is yet."

Fiona rested her head on Leelo's shoulder. "That's fine, my darling. You don't have to tell me. I just hope you'll be careful."

"What do you mean?" Leelo didn't think her mother could possibly know about Jaren, but she was intuitive. She observed more than Ketty gave her credit for.

"I don't want you getting hurt. That's all."

Leelo relaxed a little. "I won't, Mama."

Fiona lifted her head, and Leelo shivered at the sudden absence. "Just remember, my girl. It's not the falling that breaks you."

Leelo didn't ask her what she meant. After tonight, she

thought she understood. They walked on for several moments before Fiona sighed.

"It's not the falling," she said in a soft voice that sent chills over Leelo's bare arms. "It's the landing."

By the time Leelo had changed for bed, Sage was asleep. Leelo crawled under the covers, her head pounding with the latent effects of the wine and the news of Sage's engagement. While she had never relished the idea of living with her cousin for the rest of her life, she wasn't ready for Sage to move out. She wasn't ready for Sage to move on.

Leelo rolled onto her side, away from her cousin. A few moments later, she felt Sage's fingertips on her shoulder. They were ice-cold.

Leelo turned to find Sage's eyes glimmering in the dark. "What's wrong?"

Her voice was flat and detached. "Nothing."

Leelo didn't want to assume that Sage was unhappy about the engagement. She had seemed resigned to it before, and knowing Sage, she wasn't going to talk about how she truly felt. When Leelo attempted to console her, it usually backfired. "Were you expecting it tonight?" she asked instead.

Sage sighed and rolled onto her back. "I don't know. Maybe."

"What did he say? Does he love you?"

Sage snorted dryly. "What do you think, Leelo? That Hollis poured his heart out on bended knee?"

"No, I suppose not."

"We were dancing, and somehow we ended up in the trees by ourselves. Out of nowhere he said, 'You're going to be my wife.' And I asked him what he was talking about. That's when he told me we were getting married in six months, that our house was already planned. He wants children. Soon."

So that was it. Hollis had informed Sage he was marrying her with as much emotion as if he was telling her about the weather. No wonder Sage seemed so numb. "You don't have to marry him. I know Aunt Ketty wants it, but that doesn't mean you don't have a say."

When Sage turned her head toward Leelo, for a moment she felt like she was looking at her aunt instead of her cousin. "Of course I don't have a say. Maybe, if you were the one getting married, I could have put it off for a while. But your mother would never expect you to marry someone like Hollis. She's as impractical as you are, only thinking about feelings." She swallowed thickly. "I was never hoping for love. But respect, admiration. Even attraction. I had hoped…" She broke off, and for the first time Leelo could remember, Sage began to openly weep. Full, hiccuping sobs that wracked her entire body. The sight of her cousin coming undone was unbearable.

Leelo curled up next to Sage, holding her tight, trying to keep her from falling apart, as if Sage might actually crumble from sorrow. And a part of Leelo wished that it *was* her getting married instead, that she could spare Sage from this fate somehow. That there really was some Endlan boy she had fallen for instead of an outsider.

Instead of the one boy she could never have.

Chapter Thirty-Five

Jaren waited the entire day after the festival—the evening that Leelo had kissed him, as he would always think of it, touching his fingers to his lips and wishing they were hers—for Leelo to come to him. She had mentioned having that day off from Watcher duty and, considering how clear she'd made her feelings for him, he had no reason to think she wouldn't visit.

The hours in the cottage always passed slowly, but that day they dragged on interminably. No matter how hard he tried not to think of Leelo, tried not to think of her berry-sweet mouth and the feel of her body against his, he couldn't seem to help himself. He'd hardly slept that night after she left, his mind spinning in a thousand directions, every nerve in his body aware and humming in a way he'd never experienced.

It wasn't that he'd never been attracted to someone before. He was a young man; sometimes it felt like he was attracted to everything and everyone, whether he wanted to be or not. And yes, he had imagined what it would be like to someday be married to someone he loved, like his mother and father. But it had all been theoretical before.

Now it was thrillingly, dangerously real. And he didn't know how he would make it another minute, another hour, another day without her.

As the daylight slanted through the windows of the cottage, moving with agonizing slowness across the floor until it had faded entirely, Jaren finally accepted that Leelo wasn't coming. He told himself it had nothing to do with him; she'd had more chores than she realized, or, like him, she hadn't slept last night and had overslept this morning. There were plenty of perfectly reasonable explanations for why Leelo hadn't come. But his anxious mind insisted on conjuring more and more *un*reasonable explanations, mostly centered around her not liking him as much as he liked her.

By the morning of the third day, Jaren's concerns had turned more practical. He'd been out of food since the first day, and now he was completely out of water, too. The interior of the cottage had grown musty in the humid summer heat, and Jaren knew he couldn't put off bathing one more day. He couldn't stomach his own stench, let alone imagine subjecting Leelo to it, if she ever returned.

He'd stripped down to his britches at some point yesterday. Redonning his reeking pants and tunic was a visceral experience he didn't care to repeat. He grabbed the small knife Leelo had left for him and his empty waterskins, then headed into the woods.

Finally, Jaren admitted to himself that he was angry. Leelo knew he was completely dependent on her. It wasn't his fault he was trapped on this island, that he had no way of finding the boat or fixing it. He liked being helpless as much as he liked being trapped in a hovel for days on end. Even if Leelo was mad at him for one of the thousand reasons his brain had conjured—the one he kept coming back to being that he was a terrible kisser—it was no excuse to leave him to starve to death.

He stewed the entire way to the pools, having imaginary conversations with Leelo, crafting the perfect thing to say when she finally did show up. He already knew he'd forgive her the moment he saw her. And deep down, he still believed there was a perfectly good explanation for this. He was being selfish, expecting too much of her. But anger was a more comfortable emotion than fear. Better to believe she was punishing him than that something bad had happened to her.

He was already stripped out of his filthy clothing when he reached the pools. With a quick glance around to make sure he was alone, he dropped into the water, relishing the feel of it on his sticky skin. Almost immediately, he began to feel less irritable.

He allowed himself a few minutes to soak, but he knew he couldn't linger, even if Leelo was right and people rarely came here. Rarely wasn't never. Naked, he climbed out of the pool and took his clothes downstream a way, not wanting to wash his clothes in water that might be used for bathing or drinking. Leelo had brought him a little chunk of soap to use on his body and clothing, and he gave himself a cursory sudsing before thoroughly scrubbing his tunic and pants and rinsing away the soap in the stream.

When he'd finished, he wrung the clothing out and laid it out on the rocks to dry, then filled his waterskins and glanced around for something to eat. He'd gotten so desperate yesterday that he'd picked a few petrified crumbs from the smashed strawberry cake off the blanket and sucked on them until they disintegrated. There were more berries now than the last time he'd been here, but he ate them as fast as he picked them, leaving himself with nothing for later.

He looked up into the trees and spotted a red squirrel with impressive ear tufts, blithely grooming its bushy tail and chittering away as if it knew he had no way to catch it. A deer who had been watching from the trees eventually established he wasn't a threat and made her careful way to the pond to drink. He knew that even if he'd had a bow with him, he wouldn't have the heart to kill her.

With a sigh, Jaren settled for some wild asparagus and chanterelle mushrooms that he would have been far more excited about if he'd had a means of cooking them. With his clothes mostly dry, he headed back to the cottage, trying not to think of the long, hot night awaiting him.

When he reached the cottage, he froze. The front door was wide-open.

He knew he had closed it when he left. He remembered it distinctly because he'd had an argument with himself about whether or not he should leave it open to let the place air out. In the end, he'd decided that he didn't want to risk any snakes or insects finding their way into the cottage while he was gone, or worse, one of those bird-eating roots, though he hadn't seen anything like that happen since he first arrived.

So if the door was open, it could only mean that Leelo had finally come back.

Looking back on his mood of just an hour ago, he couldn't

believe how ridiculous he had been. He hadn't known Leelo long, but she'd already put her own safety on the line for him multiple times. She wasn't someone who would just abandon him for no good reason (and no, he told himself, a lackluster kiss was not a good reason). He had needed food and water. Cleaning his clothing and himself had washed away any lingering worry. All he wanted now was to kiss her and forget about the last three miserable days. If she wanted to kiss him, that was.

With his heart somewhere in his throat, Jaren hurried the rest of the way and ducked into the cottage.

It was empty.

Jaren's heart plummeted to his stomach. Not only was Leelo not here, but he must have missed her by mere minutes. Was it possible she'd gone to the pools to look for him on a different trail? He set his food on the table and backed out of the cottage, fully prepared to return to the pools if it meant seeing her.

But when he turned around, there was a different girl staring at him. She cocked her head and placed her hands on her hips, her eyes narrowed with clear suspicion, and asked, "Who the hell are you?"

Chapter Thirty-Six

Leelo's heart ached for her little brother with every beat. She worried about her mother whether she was gone for one hour or five. But not being able to go to Jaren, knowing that he was waiting for her, was driving Leelo mad.

It wasn't her fault. After the festival, with Sage so clearly miserable and their mothers in a silent battle no one would explain, she'd had no chance to escape. She spent her entire day off doing Sage's chores in addition to her own, watching in misery as the sun sank lower and lower behind the tree-tops, dragging her hope down with it.

All day, her stomach had been roiling, either with butter-flies at the memory of kissing Jaren or with dread at what awaited her cousin. Sage had been so upset she hadn't even gotten out of bed that day, though she managed to get up for her Watcher duty the day after.

Still, Sage refused to leave Leelo's side, insisting that they walk everywhere together, even to see Isola. Leelo felt like

a traitor for wanting an hour or two to herself so she could
sneak away, but she was worried sick for Jaren. He might be
able to fill up his waterskins, but what was he going to eat?
She told herself he was nearly a man, that he could take care
of himself for a few days in her absence. But knowing that
even if he was all right physically, he would think she'd abandoned him, made her throat ache with unshed tears. Because
there was nothing she wanted more than to be with him.

On the afternoon of the third day, when Leelo thought she
might actually explode if she didn't get away from Sage and
the house, she told her family she was going to visit Isola. And
by some miracle, Sage didn't offer to go with her.

Leelo raised a questioning brow. "Are you sure you'll be
all right here?" she asked, afraid to get her hopes up in case
Sage changed her mind.

"Will I be all right?" Sage scoffed. "Believe it or not, I can
take care of myself, Leelo."

There was a strange relief in Sage's gruff response. If she
was well enough to be snarky, then she was at least a little
better than she'd been the past two days. Leelo couldn't get
Sage to talk about Hollis. Saints knew she'd tried. But she
also knew she would never make Sage talk about something
she didn't want to, and Leelo was worried that she was making things worse by bringing it up all the time. Sage had six
months before the wedding; maybe she just preferred not to
think about it till then.

Before leaving for Isola's, Leelo went to check on her
mother. She was out in the yard, weeding the little vege-
table garden she tended in the summer. It had gotten rather
unruly this year, considering how little Mama had felt up to

the work, but today she looked healthier than Leelo had seen her in months.

"Heading to see Isola?" she asked as Leelo approached her. She tested a plump tomato in her fingers for ripeness, then plucked it from its vine and handed it to Leelo. "Wait just a few minutes, and I'll put together a basket for her family."

Leelo eyed the growing pile at her mother's feet. Fiona was the kind of neighbor who never showed up at someone's house empty-handed. She enjoyed giving people gifts, and as she always reminded Leelo, you never knew when you would be the one in need.

In this case, however, it was more than just neighborly kindness. Rosalie raised chickens, and her eggs were usually in high demand. But with the community shunning them, she likely had far too many eggs on her hands and not nearly enough of everything else.

When her mother was finished, Leelo hefted the basket, kissed her cheek, and went out, torn between going straight to the cottage and heading for Isola's first. The responsible thing would be to visit Isola so she had a witness in case anyone asked after her. And while Fiona had meant the basket as a gift, not a trade, Leelo decided she would ask Rosalie for a few eggs. They were likely to go to waste otherwise, and she knew someone who could use the additional protein. Jaren was growing thinner by the day, and he needed to keep up his strength for his escape.

The thought of Jaren leaving made Leelo's stomach churn again, but she tried to focus instead on seeing him. She didn't have the excuse of wine to kiss him today, but she doubted she needed it. Jaren had clearly enjoyed kissing her. She wondered if he'd been thinking about it for the past three days the way she had. Maybe she could get enough of him in whatever time they had left that she could live off the memories for the rest of her life.

But she knew full well that was impossible. She would never get enough of Jaren Kask.

Leelo knocked on Isola's door and waited. It took several minutes for Rosalie to answer, and she looked a bit harried as she wiped her hands on her apron.

"Leelo, what brings you here, dear?"

"I came to walk with Isola," Leelo said, even though she would have thought that was obvious. "And I was hoping I could offer you some of my mother's vegetables in exchange for a few eggs."

Rosalie nodded and stepped outside, closing the door behind her. "That's generous of your mother. I was baking and haven't had a chance to gather the eggs yet. It will just take a few minutes."

Leelo tried not to let her frustration show on her face. Every minute she wasted here was a minute she could be with Jaren.

Rosalie ducked into the low chicken coop in the yard and emerged a few moments later with a half dozen eggs in her apron pocket. "I can give you three, if that's all right. One of our chickens was killed by a fox last week, so we're a little shorter than usual."

"Three is perfect." Leelo held out the basket. "Help yourself."

Rosalie hemmed and hawed over the assortment, finally settling on two tomatoes, a bunch of carrots, and some lettuce. By then, Leelo thought she might leap out of her skin with frustration.

"Would you mind getting Isola for me?" Leelo asked. "I can't be gone too long."

"Oh, silly me. I forgot to mention that she left about an hour ago."

Leelo blinked in confusion. "Left?"

"She went walking. Said she needed some fresh air."

"Alone?"

Rosalie smiled. "I know. I was as surprised as you are. I think our girl is finally coming back to us. I'll tell her you stopped by."

Leelo nodded and stared at Rosalie's back as she went inside and closed the door behind her. She had seen Isola yesterday, and the girl had seemed no more like her old self than she had a month ago. Was it possible she'd made a complete turnaround overnight?

Leelo wrapped the eggs in a tea towel and started toward the hideaway. Not only did she no longer have Isola as an excuse to go walking, but she genuinely couldn't fathom where Isola would go on her own. Every walk Leelo had taken her on had been like pulling teeth. Where could she possibly want to spend time by herself?

Fear washed over Leelo like snowmelt. The cottage. She ran, her breathing ragged as she sprinted down the path, no longer caring if she broke the eggs. If Isola discovered Jaren, if she told anyone about him...

Her mind raced with all the possible outcomes. Would Jaren tell her who had been helping him? Was it foolish for Leelo to go to him now, in case Isola was still there? She would know instantly who had been hiding Jaren, if she didn't already.

She told herself to stay calm. It was entirely possible that Isola hadn't found Jaren, and if she had, that she wouldn't betray them. After all, she had done the exact same thing herself. But she might also be furious with Leelo for using her cottage, for putting all of them at risk if anyone else were to discover their secret. Isola had made it clear to Leelo how precarious her situation was, and Leelo had done exactly what Isola warned her against.

She was nearly in tears by the time she broke into the clearing by the cottage. There was no sign of Isola. It was late afternoon, and sunset was still a way off with the solstice having just passed. But evening always came to the cottage early, due to the height and density of the trees surrounding it. The windows were dark, the door closed. Most likely Jaren was inside waiting for her, maybe even angry with her for taking so long.

She crossed the clearing as quietly as she could and raised her hand to knock, when she heard someone clear her throat behind her.

Leelo spun to find Isola watching her, arms folded, her lips pressed into a flat line.

"Isola. I can explain," Leelo blurted. She heard the door open behind her and felt a surge of protectiveness over Jaren, causing her to back up, as if she could shield his body somehow.

"It's all right," he said gently. "She already knows everything."

Leelo turned. "Everything?" she hissed.

"Well, almost everything," he whispered. "I figured out pretty quickly that she was the girl you told me about, the one who kept an incantu here."

She turned back to Isola. "I'm so sorry. I know how this must look—"

"He didn't rat you out, if it's any consolation," Isola said. "I put two and two together on my own. Come on. Let's go inside and talk. It will be dark soon, and our mothers—and your cousin—will wonder where we've gone to."

Leelo tried to control her breathing. Things could be worse. Sage could have been the one to find Jaren.

They ducked into the little cabin and sat on the floor, pressed so tightly together that their knees touched. Leelo's eyes darted shyly to Jaren, and it did nothing to slow her rapid heartbeat. His hair was damp, recently washed, by the look of things, with a wave sweeping over his forehead that practically begged Leelo to push it back. He smelled like the lavender soap she'd given him. She wanted to bury her face in his chest and tell him everything she'd been feeling since the night of the festival.

Instead, she clenched her fists in her lap and willed herself to calm down. She could feel his eyes on her, though, and she wished desperately that she'd gotten here first, that she'd had him to herself for just a little longer. Because reality was sinking in. This was no longer their secret. They couldn't pretend there weren't consequences to their relationship anymore.

Not when one of those consequences was sitting right here, watching them.

Isola pushed her hair behind her ears. "Jaren explained to me how he ended up in the boat and washed up on shore.

He said you found him in the woods, injured, and told him he could hide here."

Leelo felt one of the hundred knots in her stomach slowly loosen. He hadn't told Isola that she'd helped pull the boat in, at least. "It was meant to be temporary, Isola. Just until we could find a way to get him safely off the island."

Isola nodded, but Leelo could tell she didn't fully believe her. "When did you realize he would be stuck here till winter?"

Leelo's eyes darted to Jaren's. "What? He isn't—"

"You can't possibly think you'll get him across the lake otherwise," Isola said. "Even if you could find the boat, how would you get it to the water without someone seeing?"

"We hadn't exactly worked out all the details yet. But we have to try. The longer he stays here, the higher the odds of him being discovered." She gestured to Isola. "Case in point."

"And what makes you think he shouldn't be discovered?" Isola asked, but her voice wasn't cruel, like Sage's could be. She was conflicted, and Leelo couldn't blame her for that. Saints knew she had been. "This is not the same as Pieter. He's an outsider, Leelo."

"Believe me, I know."

Jaren raised his hand hesitantly. "If I may. Isola, I mean no harm to you or anyone else on Endla. Or to Endla itself. As I said, it was an accident that I ended up here in the first place, and I would do anything to get home." He paused, and though Leelo avoided his eyes, she could feel his on her. "If this stays between the three of us, then no one else ever needs to know I was here."

Isola sighed. "I won't tell. Not yet, anyway. But if you give me any reason to doubt you…"

"I won't," Jaren said. "I promise."

Isola nodded and rose. "I should get home. Mother will be worried about me. Come find me tomorrow, Leelo. We have more to discuss."

Leelo glanced at Jaren, then rose and followed Isola outside. "Thank you, for not telling. I'm sorry I wasn't honest with you. I didn't know what to do."

Isola's demeanor changed once they were out of Jaren's hearing. "This was why you asked me about the cottage and the boat, wasn't it? I can't believe you, especially after seeing what happened to Pieter. Not to mention my family. Why would you ever endanger your mother over a stranger?"

Leelo sighed, dragging her hands down her face. "I know how irrational it all must seem. But I didn't plan any of it. When it came down to it, I couldn't kill a person, even if he was an outsider."

Isola softened a bit. "I can see that. You don't even like killing rabbits."

"Exactly."

Isola shook her head, and in that moment she seemed so much older, like she'd lived a decade in the past few months. "This is dangerous, Leelo. More than you can possibly understand. You could have spared yourself a lot of trouble if you'd just killed him to begin with." She glanced over at the cottage. "I hope he's worth it."

Leelo swallowed the lump of apprehension in her throat. "Was Pieter?"

Isola inhaled sharply, then released her breath with deliberate slowness. "Ask me that in another six months, Leelo."

"Why did you come here today?"

Isola had large brown eyes, and they seemed even larger when they were filled with tears. "I just wanted to feel close to him again. The blanket smells like him." She narrowed her eyes a little, but she didn't seem angry. "Well, it used to."

"I'm sorry. I know it was your place. I just didn't know where else to take him."

Isola stared at Leelo for a moment. "You don't know, do you?"

"Know what?"

But Isola only shook her head slightly. "Come find me when you have time to talk. I really do need to get back."

Leelo swallowed and waved goodbye as Isola disappeared among the trees. She returned to the cottage, shutting the door behind her.

Chapter Thirty-Seven

"Leelo, I—"

"Jaren—"

They both laughed nervously. She wasn't sure why things should be awkward between them, but they had been tipsy when they'd kissed, and now they were both completely sober, with Isola's presence still hanging in the air like clouds after a storm.

"I'm sorry I was away for so long," she said, taking a seat on the floor next to him and raising her eyes to his for the first time since she'd arrived. She was afraid of what she might find there: anger that she'd abandoned him; hurt that she hadn't come when she'd said she would; fear that Isola wouldn't keep their secret.

But all she saw there was longing. Sweet, desperate longing. For her.

Leelo raised onto her knees and took his face in her hands. He had a few light freckles across his nose that she'd never noticed before. "I'm so sorry. There were a dozen reasons why I couldn't come, but it doesn't matter. I should have found a way."

He blinked slowly, his lips curling in a soft smile. "I'm just glad you're here now."

"I can't believe Isola found you," she whispered. "I was so scared."

He rubbed his hands absently up and down her bare arms, sending a shiver up her spine. "It's all right. I'm all right."

Her lip trembled when she thought of how close she'd come to losing him. She'd known how tenuous this was, how fragile. But today had shaken her more than she would have thought possible. "Jaren."

"I know," he said, leaning forward to kiss her, his voice low with understanding.

They eventually ended up lying beside each other on the blanket, though Leelo had been so absorbed in kissing Jaren that she didn't actually remember how. He had been the one to pull back, though she could see it hadn't been easy for him.

He sighed and tucked a strand of hair behind her ear. "You probably need to get home, don't you?"

She pretended to sit up. "Well, if you want me to go…"

He laughed and pulled her back down next to him, tucking her into the soft nook where his chest met his shoulder. "Stay. Stay as long as you want."

Now it was her turn to sigh. "I wish I could. But I should get home." She explained about Sage's engagement to Hollis, how her cousin had needed her the past few days.

A look of guilt washed over Jaren's features, but she smoothed the wrinkles away from his brow with her fingertips. "It's all right. She has my aunt, and she seemed better today. I can stay a little longer."

"Do you think the boat has been repaired?" he asked after a few quiet minutes, each breath filled with equal measures of bliss and fear.

"I don't know. I'll try to check tomorrow."

"A part of me wishes it would never be fixed."

"I know."

"But I have to get back."

It took her a moment to find her voice. "I know." She rolled to face him and gently traced the line of his jaw. She wondered what he would look like in ten years, if he would wear a beard or cut his hair short. She understood now what her mother had meant when she said she wanted to freeze time. Leelo wished she could live in this moment, just for an hour or two, so she could memorize his face.

"Do you remember how I told you I felt like I'd always been searching for something?" he asked.

She nodded.

"Would it be strange if I said I feel like I've finally found it?"

A bloom of warmth spread in Leelo's chest. She sat up a little and he did the same. "Why would that be strange?"

"We've only known each other for a short time." He flushed and dropped his gaze. "I don't want to say anything that might upset you or frighten you."

She placed a finger under his chin and tipped it up so he would look at her. "I'm not frightened."

"I feel like I know you, Leelo. Like I've always known you."

"So do I."

"And that doesn't scare you? Not even a little?"

One side of her mouth curled in a grin. "Why? Are you scared of me?"

He laughed softly. "Terrified."

She placed her hand in the center of his chest. "Your heart *is* beating very fast." She traced his lips with the fingers of her other hand. "Hmm…even faster, now." She leaned forward, feeling bold, and kissed him exactly where her fingers had been. "It's really racing. Perhaps you need to—"

He cut her off with a playful growl, pulling her toward him to kiss her firmly. When he placed a tentative hand over her heart, she bit back a gasp.

"Is this okay?" he asked softly.

She nodded, and his touch became less hesitant. In just a short time, they were learning to read each other. She wondered what it must be like to have a lifetime with someone, if eventually you didn't even need to speak to communicate. Or maybe, she thought, it had nothing to do with time. Maybe with the right person, you just knew.

In the distance, a bird called, and Leelo forced her mind back to reality. She pulled away from him and took a deep breath. "I could get lost in you," she whispered, and for a moment, she *was* afraid. She remembered what her mother had said, that it wasn't the falling that killed you. Leelo was undeniably falling for Jaren, and while in the moment it was wonderful to experience all these new feelings, she knew it wouldn't last.

The fall would end, and what would be left of her then? A broken heart amid a pile of shattered bones?

"That's funny," Jaren said, twirling a strand of her hair around his finger. "I feel like I'm finally found."

And for the moment, Leelo forgot to be afraid.

Chapter Thirty-Eight

The next few days passed in relative peace for Leelo's household, although on the inside she felt as though she were scrambled up, every part of her vibrating and alive in a way she didn't recognize. She wasn't sure how no one else in her family noticed. It was a wonder she didn't come apart at the seams, sending all those jumbled-up feelings exploding out of her like a flock of startled birds.

Sage was back to her grumpy old self, but at least she wasn't lying in bed all day or clinging to Leelo. She had recovered some of her focus, which meant she was taking Watcher duty seriously again. Every now and then, doubt or worry would flicker over Sage's face, but Leelo could see the wheels turn in her cousin's head, how she brought herself back to the present moment by shutting everything out other than what they were doing. It made her particularly critical of Leelo, but Sage must have assumed that she was thinking about Tate, because she never questioned her.

Miraculously, Fiona seemed to be growing stronger by the day, and Ketty was more cheerful than Leelo could ever remember her being. Of course, she had everything she had ever wanted. Tate was gone, and Sage was engaged to a boy who would provide them with the kind of security they'd been lacking since Kellan and Hugo died. The Hardings were helping sheer the sheep this year, a task that was almost impossible for Ketty to accomplish without Fiona.

Leelo had been hoping to visit Jaren this afternoon, since they'd been on early Watcher duty and she had only been able to see him briefly the past few days, but, to everyone's surprise, Ketty had proposed a picnic. The weather was perfect, and they were caught up on all the housework for the first time in memory. Leelo hadn't realized how much they'd all taken on to account for Fiona's illness. Before, she'd only been able to knit in bed or by the fire, which did help the family financially. But now she was also gardening and cleaning, which gave Leelo and Sage a little more time to themselves.

But as much as she wanted to see Jaren—her thoughts had been on little else since their last meeting, and she found herself flushing at memories in the middle of meals or Watcher duty—she had to admit it was nice that Fiona and Ketty were getting along so well. Fiona was sitting back on her elbows, her face turned up to the sun, looking at peace for once, with no strained lines around her eyes and mouth from the constant pain.

As Ketty laid out their lunch, Sage went to fetch some water from a nearby stream. Leelo was sitting next to her mother, braiding wild daisies into a chain and trying not to remember bathing with Jaren, when Ketty poked her in the arm.

"Now that your cousin is engaged to Hollis, it's time for you to start thinking about your prospects."

Leelo blinked and turned her attention to her aunt, hoping she would attribute the color in her cheeks to the sun.

"You can't be surprised. You'll be eighteen soon, and you know how badly we need help around the house."

"But surely with the Hardings…" She looked at her mother imploringly.

"There's no rush," Mama assured her. "Although of course we'd all like to see you happily settled someday." She tucked a wayward daisy behind Leelo's ear and smiled. "That's what I want more than anything, my love."

"I'm not saying she needs to get married right away," Ketty said, handing her sister some bread and cheese. "But if she doesn't even have someone in mind…"

Fiona grinned. "What makes you so sure she doesn't?"

Leelo's stomach, which had been full of butterflies only a moment ago, twisted in fear. Of course, her mother didn't know whom she liked, just that she liked someone. She had been reminding Leelo of it lately, always fixing her hair or clothing before Leelo went out, even for Watcher duty. She'd made Leelo a new dress to wear for *someone special*, as she'd put it, with Leelo's first corseted bodice and soft pink lace that had been carefully hand dyed.

Leelo had laughed at the implication, not wanting to deny her feelings too much; that would only make Mama more suspicious. But she'd never told her mother explicitly not to say anything to her aunt.

Ketty glanced meaningfully at Leelo. "I see. Is there something you want to tell me?"

"I—"

"About what?" Sage returned and dropped the full water-skins on the picnic blanket next to Leelo, oblivious to the tension radiating off her. She plunked down so close that she bumped Leelo's thigh and reached for a strawberry, twirling it by the stem.

"Leelo has a secret romance," Ketty said, her voice tinged with that tiny hint of suspicion she always had when it came to Leelo.

Sage laughed around the strawberry. "No, she doesn't."

Leelo glanced at her mother, who was averting her gaze, having realized her mistake too late. If Leelo hadn't told Sage about the boy she liked, then Leelo was clearly trying to keep this a secret, and Fiona had just outed her.

Leelo wasn't sure what to do. If she denied it, either Mama would appear to be a liar or Leelo would. But if she told them the truth, she would arouse Sage's curiosity, and that would make it even harder to get time to herself.

"It's Matias," she blurted, choosing the name of a boy roughly their age out of thin air. "Matias Johnson. I haven't told anyone about it because he doesn't know I exist." That part, at least, was true. Matias was another Watcher, but he lived on the far side of the island. Leelo knew nothing about him, other than that he had two older brothers and that his mother was a potter. She instantly wished she'd chosen another name, someone more credible, but it was too late now.

Sage screwed up her nose in disbelief. "What?"

Leelo blushed under her family's scrutiny. "I know, it's a little unexpected. But I think he's nice and attractive. We danced at the summer solstice festival." Lies, lies, and more lies. Leelo hadn't danced with anyone that night, and she didn't think Matias was attractive. He wasn't *un*attractive; Leelo simply had never thought of him that way.

Fiona was watching Leelo from the corner of her eye, clearly not persuaded by her fabrication. She couldn't have chosen a blander way to describe a boy she supposedly liked.

Ketty glanced away finally. "I hate to be the bearer of bad news, but Matias is as good as engaged himself. His mother told me at the most recent council meeting. He and Reddy Wells have been promised to each other for ages now. I'm surprised you didn't know."

Leelo flushed further, which at least seemed like an appropriate reaction to the news that her love interest was spoken for. "Oh."

Ketty nodded smugly. "If you liked him, you should have made yourself known a long time ago."

"It's new," Leelo said. "I didn't know about Reddy." She glanced at her mother and Sage, who were watching this exchange with completely different expressions that both said the same thing: they didn't believe Leelo in the slightest.

Fortunately, Fiona was willing to accept the lie from her daughter. She tucked Leelo under her arm and kissed the top of her head. "I'm so sorry, my dear. But not to worry. There are other boys on the island. I'm sure we'll find someone for you."

Leelo allowed herself to be comforted, but on the way home, Sage was still staring at her with those narrowed, suspicious eyes.

"So. Matias," she said when their mothers had fallen behind. "It's funny. I don't think I've ever heard you mention him before."

"Really? I'm sure I have." Inside, Leelo was cringing at her own terrible lie. She wished she'd mentioned someone else, but she'd panicked. She should have known this would come up eventually, especially now that Sage was engaged. But she'd been so focused on Jaren that she hadn't thought to come up with *another* lie.

"He's a strange choice for you."

"He is?"

"His father is a butcher."

Leelo's stomach twisted as she suddenly remembered that Matias often had bloodstains on his clothing from helping his father work. "Oh, that's right. I'd forgotten."

"Well, I suppose it's for the best that he's marrying Reddy. Otherwise you'd have to learn how to butcher meat, and I'm not sure you'd be able to stomach it."

Leelo managed a watery smile. "Probably not."

"Don't worry, Lo. I'll find someone for you. We'll have you engaged by the end of the year, too." She slung her arm over Leelo's shoulder, gripping her a little too tight.

Whether Sage thought Leelo was lying about the boy or about liking someone at all, one thing was clear: Leelo hadn't fooled her cousin for one second.

Leelo had a secret, and Sage wasn't going to rest until she discovered what it was.

Chapter Thirty-Nine

Jaren was sound asleep when he heard a tap on the door of the cottage. He opened his eyes, blinking in the darkness. He had waited for Leelo all day, knowing she had the afternoon free, and had fallen asleep thinking of her. For a moment, he was convinced he was having a lucid dream. Saints knew he'd imagined Leelo's presence enough times lately. But then he felt a pain in his hip from sleeping on the hard ground, and he blinked fully awake, worried it was Isola. Or worse, someone else.

The door creaked open, but it was Leelo's familiar silhouette in the moonlight, and the tension in Jaren's muscles was replaced with a different kind of anticipation.

She crept in quietly and crawled over to where he was lying, and without really thinking about it, he closed his eyes again and pretended to be asleep.

There was a long silence, and then he felt a slight tug on the blanket as she lay next to him, curling her slender body around his carefully so as not to wake him. It was a warm night and he was sleeping shirtless, the blanket down around his waist, and every nerve in his body came alive when she slipped her arm over his torso.

He inhaled and rolled toward her a little. "Leelo."

"I'm sorry I woke you," she whispered, placing a small kiss on his shoulder. "I just needed to see you."

"Is everything all right?"

She shook her head and closed her eyes, and he could see tears slip down her cheeks in the moonlight.

"What's wrong?" he asked, his heart breaking at the sight of her crying. She always seemed so strong and confident. He didn't know what to do with her like this, raw and vulnerable as an open wound.

"It's nothing," she said, but he could hear her struggling not to sob. "I just... I don't want you to go, but I also know you can't stay."

He rolled over all the way, and she buried her face in his chest, her tears cool against his bare skin. "Did something happen?" he asked gently.

"Not yet. But I'm terrified it will. And I couldn't live with myself if something happened to you."

"It's okay. Everything is going to be okay." He wrapped her in his arms, realizing for the first time how little she was. She was like an egg in his palm; he could crush her, if he wanted to. And while some small, selfish part of him wanted that, wanted to hold on to her so tightly she could never leave him, the vast majority of him wanted to cradle her like some precious, delicate thing, to make all the hurt go away, to shelter her from the world and everyone in it.

Eventually, her tears subsided amidst his soothing words and tender touches, and then something shifted. She kissed him once, hesitant at first, as though she was confused by how her sorrow could have transformed so quickly to something else. But Jaren understood. He was sad and frightened, too, but he needed her. Out there, in the real world, he might have listened to the conventions of society that said they should wait until they were older. But he knew there could be no waiting. They would never have anything other than this moment, and if it was greedy to want her, then he was greedy. If it was selfish to need her, then he was the most selfish person in the world. How could he let her go, when he'd only just found her? Why shouldn't he consume all the happiness he could, when it was such a fleeting, elusive thing?

Jaren had never asked for much out of life. He'd only wanted the security of his family. He had no big dreams of seeing the world or aspirations to make a name for himself. He hoped his sisters would find happy marriages, that his father would find solace in his new life in Bricklebury, perhaps even a new wife of his own so he wouldn't have to be alone when the children left. And yes, Jaren knew he wanted to start a family of his own one day, but he had never dared to imagine this kind of joy. In truth, he hadn't even known it existed.

He had meant what he said before, about feeling found. The furious, constant spinning in his head quieted when he was with Leelo. That terrible longing he'd been trying to fill his whole life was sated in her presence, and the only longing he felt now was the sweet, sharp craving of wanting more of something wonderful. Of wanting, and knowing that she wanted him, too.

He opened his eyes to find her looking at him, and they both stopped for a moment, their bodies pressed closer with each breath. She sat up and raised her arms above her head, waiting for him to help with her dress. As he set it aside, she reached for the blanket to wrap around herself, then seemed to realize there was only one.

"Are you cold?" he asked her gently.

She shook her head.

He took the blanket from her and smoothed it on the floor, where they lay down beside each other. In the moonlight, her hair and skin were luminous, as if her entire body had been dipped in liquid silver. Her kiss-swollen lower lip was caught in her teeth, and it felt like the entire universe was there in that tiny gap between them.

The feeling in his chest was almost overwhelming. How could one person change his entire sense of purpose just by looking at him? How could a single touch make him forget everything he'd ever known? Could he even really fall in love in a matter of days?

As she lowered her mouth to his, he decided that he could, because he knew without even the slightest doubt that he had.

Chapter Forty

Leelo woke to the twittering of birds in the trees, realizing with a start that she was not home in her bed. She'd fallen asleep in Jaren's arms.

She sat up abruptly, rousing him. "What's wrong?" he asked, his voice thick with sleep.

"We fell asleep!" Leelo pulled her dress over her head and tied on her boots as quickly as she could. "I'm supposed to be Watching this morning."

Jaren blinked blearily. "What time is it?"

"Nearly dawn. I have to go." She glanced back at him, his cheek swollen and lined from where it had pressed against her in the night, his hair tousled from her fingers. She felt that swelling in her chest again, a feeling she knew now was love. She bent down to kiss his cheek. "I'll be back as soon as I can."

He grabbed onto her wrist, but it was a gentle tug. He knew she couldn't stay. "I'll miss you."

She smiled down at him. "Me, too."

Outside, the cool morning air helped clear her head. She started jogging toward home, telling herself that it would still be all right. She could sneak inside and change before Sage noticed she'd been gone. She could always lie and say she'd slept in Tate's bed.

As she ran, she couldn't help remembering last night. Jaren had been so gentle with her, like she was a girl made of glass, as Sage said. She'd had to be the one to take charge, to assure him that she would not break at his touch. She'd never asked him if he'd been with a girl before, and he had never asked her about her experience. She suspected they were both new at this, which had been comforting, in a way. There had been no pressure, only mutual wonder and desire. And even though she knew that she had just allowed herself to fall even farther toward some inevitable end, she had no regrets or doubts about her decision. In another world, she would have spent forever in his arms.

But here, in the real world, she was going to be late.

When she slipped through the front door, the house was quiet, the sun not yet risen. She breathed as quietly as she could, tiptoeing up the stairs to her bedroom. She was nearly there when she heard a creak from downstairs. She turned to find Ketty sitting in one of the armchairs, watching her.

"Aunt Ketty," Leelo said, her blood turning to ice. "What are you doing up so early?"

Ketty didn't say a word. She was waiting for Leelo to come back down. Reluctantly, Leelo descended the stairs, her still-racing heart stuttering for a different reason now. "I'm sorry. I was just—"

"Don't lie to me, girl." Ketty was in her nightgown and

robe, her long auburn braid hanging over her shoulder. But she looked like she'd been awake for hours, waiting in the dark for Leelo to return.

Leelo's eyes dropped to the floor. She bit her lip to keep from attempting another excuse. There was too great a chance she'd inadvertently give something away. Better to wait for her punishment in silence.

"Who were you with?" Ketty asked. "I know it wasn't Matias, so choose your words carefully."

Who could she name without implicating someone innocent? There was no one, and she would sooner die than give up Jaren.

Ketty waited with growing impatience, her nostrils flaring. "You're not going to answer me?"

Leelo gave an almost imperceptible shake of her head. "No."

Ketty released her breath through her nose. "Very well. Don't tell me. But until you do, you are not to leave this house for any reason other than Watcher duty, and you won't go anywhere without Sage. Do you understand me? We have rules for a reason, Leelo. I don't know what you think you're doing, but if you end up pregnant before you're even married—"

Leelo's eyes shot up to her aunt's. "That is none of your concern."

"Oh, isn't it? Who do you think would care for a baby? You're certainly not capable. You can't even take care of yourself."

"I'm not your responsibility," Leelo ground out.

Ketty laughed dryly. "No? Whose, then? Don't forget that without me, there would be no food on the table. Without your cousin's marriage prospects and with no men around to help out, we could all be starving by next winter."

Perhaps it was the lack of sleep that made Leelo reckless. "There would be men around here if it weren't for you."

"I know you aren't referring to Tate. Even you aren't so foolish as to blame me for that."

Leelo wasn't sure who she meant. Hugo and Kellan had died in an accident. But Leelo couldn't help remembering what her mother had said, how Ketty had sacrificed everything for the family. And then Isola, with her strange reaction about the cottage. There were secrets in this house, all right. But they weren't all hers.

Leelo let her gaze fall again. Arguing with Ketty wasn't going to get her anywhere. And as long as she was under her aunt's watchful eye, she'd never be able to see Jaren. The thought made her feel hollow inside. "I'm sorry," she mumbled. "I didn't mean that."

Ketty snickered. "Of course you did. You're as naive as my sister, and twice as ungrateful. I suppose I can't blame you. You are your parents' daughter." She strode forward, stopping when her toes were nearly touching Leelo's. Gripping her chin between her fingers, she tilted Leelo's face from side to side roughly.

"Whoever he is, I hope he's worth it," she said, dropping Leelo's head and pushing past her. "Get dressed. Your Watcher duty starts in half an hour."

Chapter Forty-One

Jaren had decided it was time to act. He'd allowed himself to grow weak and pale in the hovel, counting on Leelo to provide for him and keep him safe. But he was never going to be able to get off the island in his current state. Day by day, he ventured a little farther from the cottage, strengthening his legs and learning the geography of the island in the process. Inside, he did crunches and push-ups to get some muscle back into his arms and torso. He made sure to bathe every other day because he found it gave him a schedule, something to look forward to even if Leelo couldn't come.

As the days began to get shorter, Jaren's plans took on a new urgency. He'd been gone for weeks now, and he could only imagine what his family was thinking. Surviving, and then being with Leelo, had been overwhelming at the beginning. But now, in the afterglow, he could think more clearly. He had to get back to the mainland.

And he was going to take Leelo with him.

He hadn't mentioned this new plan to her yet. He knew there was a very good chance she wouldn't want to go, which was why he'd spent the past few days telling her about how wonderful life on the mainland could be. Leelo loved to listen to his stories, her head on his chest, her fingers drawing circles on his skin. She wanted to know everything about his sisters, what it was like to travel from Tindervale to Bricklebury, and she was fascinated by the idea of a forest that didn't require anything from its inhabitants but respect for nature.

"If you didn't have to give half your kills to the Forest, wouldn't your lives be easier?" he asked her, genuinely curious. It was several days since she'd come to see him in the middle of the night, and their visit had to be kept short, since Leelo's family was now suspicious of where she'd been disappearing to. Jaren felt terrible that she'd been caught sneaking back into the house and wished they hadn't fallen asleep, but he wouldn't change anything else about it. That night had been the best of his entire life.

"Not really," Leelo said. "Because the Forest provides more for us than a normal forest could."

Jaren wasn't sure that was true, but it was clear Leelo believed it. "And the other Wandering Forests? Why does this one stay in one place, while the others didn't?"

"Because they didn't have us, I suppose."

Jaren glanced out the window toward the trees. From what he'd seen of the island, it didn't have more game or resources than any other wood he'd been in. But he had noticed that the Forest changed in odd ways from one day to the next. A fallen tree would be on its side one day, covered with moss as though it had been that way for ages, only to be upright a day later. At first Jaren just thought he was getting himself lost, but he'd taken to leaving markers for himself, and the Forest was definitely changing.

Once, when Jaren was whittling with a little knife Leelo had given him so he could skin his own game, should he actually catch anything, he'd clumsily nicked himself attempting to make a...well, it was supposed to be a squirrel, but it was turning out more like a beaver. Blood had poured from the wound into the ground by the little stump where he sat.

Before he could staunch the bleeding with his tunic, he'd watched in horror as the earth itself began to churn, consuming the blood within seconds of it falling.

Jaren didn't want to tell Leelo all the things he thought were wrong with her home. If he did that, he knew she'd be hurt and angry, and she would never agree to leave with him. So he was gentle, listening with genuine interest when she spoke, and never pushing back when she defended something about Endla.

He kissed the top of her head, breathing in her warm lavender scent. If she wouldn't agree to escape with him, he wasn't sure what he would do. He knew he had to get home, but the thought of losing her was unbearable. "When is your next day off?" he asked her. "I was thinking we should go to the boat, make sure it has been repaired."

She sat up and looked down at him. "We?"

"I know you're worried. But I think it's important that I know where it is, in case I need to get to it without you."

"But you'd never be able to move it on your own."

"I know. But what if we had to meet there?"

She looked skeptical, but she settled back into the crook of his arm, where she fit perfectly, like a piece of a puzzle he hadn't known he'd been missing. "I have a day off in three days. But I don't know how I'll get away from Sage and Ketty. They've been watching me like hawks lately. I was only able to get away today because Sage had to go visit the Hardings with my aunt."

"How is she feeling about her engagement, by the way? Any better?"

Leelo shrugged. "I don't know. She won't speak about Hollis. But she didn't seem terribly upset about going to see him today, so perhaps she's accepted it."

"I feel sorry for her," Jaren said, twining his fingers through Leelo's silky hair. "No one deserves to end up in a marriage they didn't choose."

Leelo sighed, releasing a soft puff of air onto Jaren's bare chest, and his heart clenched at the sweetness of her. "No, they don't."

"You mentioned that your aunt's marriage wasn't a happy one, either."

"No. And sometimes I wonder if my mother's was happy after all."

"Really?"

She was quiet for a minute. "She was talking to me about love recently, and she seemed so happy and moony. Then I mentioned my father, and her entire demeanor changed. Isola said something strange to me the other day, and Sage is clearly keeping secrets from me. I know they're all trying to protect me, but I don't need protection. I need the truth."

Her words made Jaren tense up. She wanted the truth. He wasn't deceiving her, necessarily, but he also wasn't being entirely honest. "Leelo, I need to ask you something."

She rolled onto her belly, still pressed up against his side, and propped her chin in her hands. "What?"

When he sat up and motioned for her to join him, a little furrow appeared between her pale brows. "I have to go back soon. I don't want to leave you, but I can't put it off any longer."

"That's not a question," she said.

He glanced down at his hands, then forced himself to meet her eyes. "Will you come with me?"

Leelo blinked in surprise. "What?"

"I know Endla is your home. It's all you've ever known. Your entire life is here. But I can't help thinking that if you stay here, you'll end up marrying someone you don't love to appease your family. Or you'll end up alone because you refuse to settle for a life like that, and you deserve to share your heart with someone, if that's what you want. Which is not to say I think you love *me*, of course." He started to ramble, his thoughts tangling up like string, when she stopped him with a hand on his.

"Jaren, I…"

"I know. Your family. But your mother could come with us. Sage and Ketty wouldn't want to, but you said yourself that your mother isn't like the other Endlans."

"She isn't well. And she would never leave her sister."

"Even if it meant reuniting with Tate?" He almost hated to bring the boy up, dangling him like bait before Leelo, but he knew how much her little brother meant to her. "I can't promise we'll find him, but I promise we'll spend every day trying."

Her eyes flickered with pain at the mention of Tate. "We would be a danger to him out there. That's why he had to leave. Because Endlan magic could hurt him. Because *my* magic could."

"You would never hurt him, Leelo."

She tensed. "You haven't seen a drowning. You don't know what this Forest is capable of."

"I know *you*."

Leelo softened at his words, but there was doubt in her voice. "We've known each other for such a short time, Jaren."

"I've spent more time with you than I've spent with anyone outside my immediate family in my entire life. Please don't diminish what we have because you're afraid. I'm afraid, too."

She sighed in frustration. "You're asking me to go against everything I've ever known."

"That's not what I'm doing."

She shook her head. "I'm starting to wonder if you really understand what I've been telling you. Endla protects us, but it also protects *you*. Do you think my people would have spent generations on a small island if we had a choice in the matter?"

"Leelo, up until a few months ago, I'd never even *heard* of Endla. If your people were so dangerous, the news would have traveled to Tindervale. You have so little experience—"

She leaped to her feet, nearly smacking her head on the ceiling. "So that's what you think about me? That I'm some sheltered, gullible child?"

"No. That's not what I mean at all." Jaren attempted to run his fingers through his hair, but they snagged painfully on the knotted strands. "This wasn't how this was supposed to go."

Leelo crossed her arms over her chest, staring down at him with suspicion. "How *what* was supposed to go?"

He raised up onto his knees slowly, afraid one wrong move would send her running. "Don't you think it's at least possible that the world has changed in the years since your ancestors came here? I'm not saying you don't have reason to be afraid. I'm only saying that staying here will be difficult, too." He sighed, wishing he could find the perfect words to convince her that he wanted what was best for her, that this wasn't just a selfish request. "I'm sorry. I know it's foolish. I just don't want to lose you."

She took a deep breath, sinking down next to him on the floor. After a moment, she managed a small smile and cupped his face in her hands. "I don't want to lose you, either." She kissed him gently. "And I do love you. Very, very much."

"You do?"

She nodded. "Of course."

His fear and sadness faded in the wake of her words. He smiled and keeled over as if he had fainted with happiness, and it was only somewhat exaggerated.

She laughed and poked him in the ribs. "What about me?"

"Eh, you're all right."

Her mouth dropped open and she was about to punch him playfully, but he caught her hand and pulled her close, smoothing her hair from her face. "I love you beyond measure, Leelo…" He thought for a moment. "I don't think you ever told me your last name."

"Hart," she said softly. "Like a stag."

He pressed a kiss to her forehead, then the tip of her nose. "As I said, Leelo Hart. Beyond measure."

Chapter Forty-Two

Leelo cut her way through the Forest, hoping to get back to her house before dark. Jaren's question—would she go back to the mainland with him—played over and over again in her mind. Her initial reaction had of course been to say no. It was a ludicrous suggestion; she could never leave Endla, not just because she'd spent her entire life believing the outside world was wicked, but because she couldn't leave her family.

But then she thought of Fiona, how weak she'd been lately. Sage was moving out soon anyhow, and Leelo had secretly hoped Ketty might go with her. It wasn't that Leelo wouldn't miss her cousin, but she didn't think Ketty's presence was good for Fiona. If she only had the two of them to provide for, Leelo was certain she could do it all on her own. She would learn to weave and take over for Mama. Without Watcher duty, she would have plenty of time to get it all done.

And then there was her brother. Mama, Leelo, and Tate could all live together out there. And wasn't that everything she wanted? That, and to stay with Jaren?

But leaving Endla would mean she would never be able to sing again, and that thought was perhaps the most painful of all. She touched her throat, trying to imagine never letting her songs pour out of it. Maybe she'd eventually stop feeling the desire. Maybe, but she couldn't count on it. And that would endanger everyone around her, including Jaren.

Up ahead, Leelo heard the sound of someone tromping through the woods. From behind, she recognized Isola's short brown hair, and she trotted to catch her. She was about to call out to her friend when she noticed that Isola wasn't alone.

She covered her mouth with her hand to stifle her gasp. Sage was in front of Isola, standing on her tiptoes to peer over the rim of Isola's basket. "Gathering, you say? A little late for berries. A little early for mushrooms."

Isola glanced around the Forest like she'd rather be anywhere than here. "I'm gathering herbs, if you must know."

Sage grinned. "I see. Would you like some company?"

Isola studied her for a moment. To her credit, she smiled back. "Absolutely."

"Please, lead the way."

Leelo breathed a sigh of relief as Isola led Sage away from the cottage. She followed from a distance, straining to overhear their conversation.

"What are you doing out here?" Isola asked. "You're not on duty, are you?"

"Leelo has been sneaking off a lot lately. My mother wanted me to find out where she's been going. You don't know anything about that, do you?"

Saints, Sage had been following her. Leelo's back broke out

in a cold sweat as she dashed behind a tree just before Sage turned to look in her direction.

"Why would you think I know anything about it?" Isola asked.

"You and Leelo are friends, aren't you? Leelo is your *only* friend, after what you did with Pieter."

Leelo knew exactly what her cousin was doing: trying to get under Isola's skin, to see if she would slip up. But Isola was tougher than Sage had ever given her credit for.

"Leelo has been extremely kind and patient with me. I am fortunate to call her a friend. But if she's been sneaking off, I haven't noticed. She and I take walks without you, so it's entirely likely that I'm who she's been seeing."

"I suppose Leelo is helping to fill the hole that Pieter left behind?"

Now Isola stopped and turned to Sage. "What are you implying?"

"Nothing at all. No one needs to tell me how special Leelo is. It would be perfectly understandable if you fell for her."

Leelo swore under her breath as Isola's face turned beet red. "Yes, it would be. But that is not what is happening between Leelo and me. She's just a good friend, something you clearly don't understand. If you love your cousin so much, why don't you ask her yourself where she's been going, instead of sneaking around trying to catch her in a lie?" She lifted her chin. "Perhaps it's because you know she wouldn't tell you, that she doesn't trust you at all."

Sage's lips thinned. Even from here, Leelo could see she was struggling to keep control of her temper. "You don't know anything about my relationship with Leelo. You can't possibly. But believe me when I say that I will do whatever it takes to protect my cousin, even if that means discovering a secret she wants to keep hidden. Leelo doesn't know what's best for her. She made that perfectly clear when she chose to be friends with you."

Isola flashed a small, condescending smile. "That's right. She *chose* me. The poor thing got stuck with you." And with that, she turned on her heel and disappeared into the Forest.

Sage stood in silence for a few minutes, her face white beneath her freckles, her hands clenched into fists. A part of Leelo wanted to run and comfort her because she could see that while Sage had been trying to land a blow, it was Isola who had hit Sage where it hurt most.

But if Sage knew Leelo had witnessed the encounter, she would only grow defensive. Even now, she was straightening her spine, flexing her fingers and swiping the tears from her face before they could fall.

Besides, Leelo wasn't feeling particularly warm toward her cousin right now. Not when she knew she'd been spying on her. She wasn't sure what she would have done if Sage had simply asked her for the truth, rather than trying to flush it out like an ambush predator. But Sage had never respected her enough to ask.

Leelo waited until Sage had turned and headed back toward home before releasing her breath and running in the direction Isola had gone.

"Isola," she hissed when she'd nearly caught up.

The girl whirled around, her eyes wide. "Saints, it's you, Leelo. You startled me."

"I'm sorry. I didn't mean to."

"Sage was just here."

"I heard you talking. Thank you for not telling her about Jaren."

Isola snorted. "Sage is the last person I would tell, Leelo. I know she's your cousin, but she's as cunning as a fox and twice as devious."

"I know. It's a miracle she didn't..." Leelo paused, suddenly realizing how odd it was for Isola to be all the way out here, alone. "Oh, Isola," she breathed in horror. "Please don't tell me you went to the cottage."

Isola shook her head. "No. At least, I hadn't yet. I was going to take some food to Jaren, since I wasn't sure when you'd see him again. I'm sorry. I should have been more careful. But I led Sage away from there."

Leelo's heart was in her throat now. "You know how she is. She's suspicious of everyone and everything. If she finds him..."

"She won't. Even if she knew what to look for, the cottage is not easy to find."

"*I* found it!" Leelo began to pace in a small circle. "Saints, what am I going to do? She'll tell Ketty, and Ketty will tell the council. They'll kill him, Isola! Just like they killed Pieter."

Isola's eyes filled with tears. "I'm sorry. I'm so, so sorry."

Leelo forced herself to take a breath. It wasn't right of her to bring Pieter into this, and none of this was Isola's fault. "It's okay. We don't know that she found him. I'll think of something." She considered going back to check on Jaren, but Sage had headed toward home, not the shack. If Leelo ran, she might be able to beat Sage home and avoid any more questions. "I should get back. Please don't go to the cottage tomorrow. I'll go, as soon as I can."

Isola took Leelo's hand, gripping it tightly. "If you need

help, I hope you'll ask me. I couldn't save Pieter. I should have, but I didn't. I won't let that happen again."

Leelo embraced Isola, who folded her arms briefly around Leelo before stepping back.

"Look, I didn't want to tell you this, but I think you should know now, with everything that's been going on."

Leelo's eyes searched Isola's. "Tell me what?"

"Your mother…she… I think she was the one who built that cottage."

Leelo laughed uncertainly. "My mother doesn't know how to build a house."

"Okay, she didn't build it herself. But I think she had help. And I think she kept an outsider there."

Leelo felt as if everything had gone still around her, and all she could hear was her own heartbeat in her ears. "What are you talking about? When?"

Isola looked pained when she said, "I think about nine months before your brother was born."

Leelo's eyes widened as she realized what Isola was implying. "You think my mother hid an outsider and had a child with him? Isola, that's impossible. My father would have known. My mother would have told me. And Ketty…" She trailed off. There was clearly a secret in their family, one so huge that it had forever changed Ketty and Fiona's relationship. It would explain why Tate looked nothing like the rest of the family and why Ketty despised him so much.

She shook her head. It was impossible. Fiona was too loyal to do something like this.

Isola went on, trying to fill the uncomfortable silence. "I

found something in the cottage when I first discovered it. A book of mainland poetry."

"I've seen it," Leelo said. "What does that have to do with anything?"

"There was an inscription on one of the pages, and a pressed flower. It said…" Isola swallowed. "It said, 'To my dearest love, Fiona. Yours forever, Nigel.'"

Leelo's vision began to tunnel as the blood drained from her head. "I need to sit down." She collapsed where she stood and Isola crouched down next to her. "There has to be some mistake. My mother loved my father. I know she did. She wouldn't have done this. She couldn't have." She let her head fall into her hands.

Isola placed a tentative hand on Leelo's shoulder. "I'm sure your mother did love your father. This doesn't change that."

Leelo's eyes shot up. "Doesn't change that? How?"

Isola shook her head helplessly. "I'm sorry."

Leelo forced herself to take a deep breath. She was angry, but a part of her knew Isola was right. She'd seen it when her mother spoke of the different kinds of love. Fiona had cared deeply for Leelo's father. She remembered her mother's grief when he died. But was it the kind of love Leelo felt for Jaren? Or was it a love that had grown later, slowly, over their years together?

Isola waited a few minutes before helping Leelo to her feet. "I'm sorry you had to find out this way. But you might want to consider telling Fiona the truth about Jaren. If she really did help an outsider get off this island, she could be your only hope for saving him."

Chapter Forty-Three

When Leelo was gone, Jaren lay on his blanket, staring up at the ceiling and seeing only Leelo's face. He wanted to memorize it because he knew there would never be another one so lovely.

It was growing dark outside when he finally forced himself to get up. He could still go to the pools for a bath tonight; the cold water would help clear his head. Even if he couldn't fathom leaving Leelo, he liked having a plan. And besides, there was still a chance he could convince her to join him.

He stripped down and lowered himself into the water until it was over his head. The pool was small but deep enough for him to submerge completely, and he liked the feeling of weightlessness. It was quiet under the water, peaceful.

When he was finished washing, he reached for his clothing, only to find his tunic was not where he'd left it.

He ducked back down, scanning the woods, and noticed his tunic was just a few feet away. Still here, fortunately, but definitely not where he'd left it. It had to have been the wind, he told himself, or a curious animal. But everything was quiet and still, and he had the distinct feeling he was being watched.

He climbed out of the pool and dressed as quickly as he could with his skin still damp. Just as he was tying the laces on his boots, he saw something move in the bushes.

There. A face. Pale skin and freckles, yellow-green eyes that could have belonged to a wildcat as easily as a girl. She disappeared a moment later, silently. And Jaren knew that whoever she was, she had wanted him to know she was watching.

Chapter Forty-Four

When Leelo stepped into the house, she was relieved to see Sage peeling vegetables at the sink while Ketty cooked. Fiona had fallen asleep in an armchair.

"Where have you been?" Ketty demanded. "You've been gone for hours. I thought I made myself clear."

"I was with Isola," Leelo said, her eyes darting to Sage. But her cousin didn't look at her.

She went to her mother and knelt down, pressing the back of her hand to her forehead. She didn't have a fever, but her skin was sallow and dull. It didn't make sense. She had been fine last week. What could have changed since then to make her so ill?

Fiona's eyes fluttered open. "Oh, Leelo. How are you, dear one?"

Leelo sat on the arm of the chair, careful not to bump her mother. "I'm fine, Mama. Are you all right? You don't look well."

"It's just another bad spell. It will pass, as it always does."

"You're not singing enough," Ketty said over her shoulder. "You always get sicker when you don't sing."

Fiona ignored her sister and stroked Leelo's cheek with the back of her hand. "You look so beautiful, so grown."

Leelo smothered a shy smile. She *felt* different, but she couldn't imagine she looked like anything other than her old self. "I don't know about that."

"Well, I do." Fiona gestured that she wanted to get up, and Leelo helped steady her. "Come upstairs with me. I have something I want to show you."

In classic Sage fashion, she chose that moment to chime in. "Dinner will be ready soon."

"We won't be long," Fiona said. "Help me up the stairs, darling."

Leelo couldn't remember the last time she'd been in her mother's room. Once, it had been Fiona and Kellan's, and she had distant memories of sitting in the corner rocking chair with her father, of her mother brushing her hair at the vanity. But now there were two small beds, one for Fiona and one for Ketty. There were no bright felted ornaments in here, just lace curtains yellowed with age and a charcoal sketch of Leelo and Sage as girls.

"What did you want to show me?" Leelo asked as her mother sat on her bed.

"It's in the wardrobe. There's a box at the top. Fetch it for me?"

Leelo nodded and opened the doors of the wardrobe. Inside, it smelled like cedar and lavender. All of Mama's sweaters were folded neatly on shelves next to her few skirts and single dress. Though she delighted in making clothing for Leelo, she was a creature of habit, wearing the same plain blouses and skirts most of the time.

Leelo reached up to the top, feeling among the knitted blankets and linens, until her hand closed on a small wooden box. She pulled it down, her fingers running over the carving of two swans, their necks bowed toward each other, forming a heart.

"Where did you get this?" Leelo asked as she handed it to her mother.

"Your father made it for me. He was quite a skilled carver, you know."

Kellan had been a carpenter—he'd made most of the furniture in their home—but Leelo had never known he could craft something so delicate. "It's beautiful."

"It was my wedding gift. He said the swans are a symbol of fidelity, since they mate for life."

"How did he know that?"

"I think he heard it from his father, who heard it from his father. He was among the group of people who settled Endla, though he was just a child at the time."

"I wish I could see that. Two swans, swimming together." Leelo traced the curves of the swans' necks with her finger. She'd only ever seen birds drown, thanks to the poison in the lake, but once upon a time, that hadn't been the case. At least according to the stories. "Do you really believe the Forest made the lake poisonous to protect us?"

Fiona's brow was furrowed, her mouth curved in a frown, but after a moment she swallowed down whatever she had been planning to say. "Your father always said that stories are like wood, bending and warping with the passage of time. But I believe there is some truth to the legend, yes."

Leelo's heart began to pound as she realized what she was going to ask her mother. "Mama—"

Fiona lifted the lid of the box before Leelo could finish. Inside was a little green velvet pillow, topped with two gold rings tied with a satin ribbon. "Your father's and my wedding rings. I stopped wearing mine when he passed away. It felt wrong to wear it when his was no longer on his hand, and the thought of burying him with it was too painful. So I've kept them here, in this box, ever since."

"Why are you showing me this?" Leelo asked.

"Because when the time comes, I want you and your partner to have them."

Leelo's eyes met her mother's. They were the same color as Ketty's and Sage's, but the hazel was softer, more green than yellow, and there was none of the guile Leelo always saw in their gazes. "Mama, I don't plan on marrying. Not yet, anyway."

"I know. But someday. It's clear to me you're in love. I don't know why you won't tell me about them. I hope you know I would support you in whatever partner you chose."

Leelo flushed at the shame of lying to her mother, who truly wanted what was best for her daughter. "I want to tell you about him. It's just…"

Fiona lowered her voice. "You can trust me, darling. I won't tell Ketty and Sage."

"I know you wouldn't. Not unless you felt like you had to. And I'm afraid when I tell you who it is, you'll think you have to tell them."

She took Leelo's hand. "Why?"

"Because he's not…" Saints, was she really going to do this? There would be no turning back from here. But she had crossed the point of no return a long time ago, the moment she pulled Jaren to shore.

"I know about Nigel," Leelo blurted, then threw her hand over her mouth. She hadn't meant to say it. She was going to tell her mother about Jaren.

Fiona gasped, her own hand flying up to cover her open mouth. "How?"

Above her fingers, Fiona's eyes were wide and shining with tears. Leelo couldn't tell if it was fear or shame, maybe both. This was a secret Fiona had spent all of Leelo's life burying, and now Leelo was deliberately bringing it out into the light, where it sat between them as naked and vulnerable as a baby bird.

She hated doing this to her mother, but she needed her to know that she would love her no matter what secrets she kept. Just as she hoped her mother could still love her once she knew about Jaren.

"I found the cottage, and the book of poetry," Leelo said, and before she knew it, everything was pouring out of her in a rush. "I won't be angry, Mama. Just tell me the truth. Was Nigel Tate's father?"

Fiona's face had gone pale and shiny with sweat, as if she were about to be ill. "Leelo," she breathed.

Leelo went down to her knees before her. She took her mother's hands, trying not to notice how they were smaller than her own. "It won't change the way I feel about you. Or him. He will always be my brother. But is that who you sent him to? Is Tate with his father?"

"Oh, child, this wasn't how I wanted you to find out. It all happened so long ago."

"Please, Mama. I need to know the truth."

Fiona swallowed thickly and dabbed at her eyes with the edge of her sleeve. "I know. It's…difficult."

Leelo lowered her head to her mother's lap. "It's all right, Mama. I'm almost a grown woman. I can handle more than you think I can."

"It's not just that, love. It's difficult for me to remember that time." She began to comb her fingers through Leelo's hair as she spoke, the way she had when Leelo was a child.

After a moment, Fiona inhaled deeply and released her breath in a slow stream that cooled Leelo's cheek. "It was more than a decade ago, now. We had a harsh winter that year. The entire lake froze for the first time in living memory. It was so bitterly cold that the Watchers refused to stand their shifts after multiple people lost fingertips or toes to frostbite. But an outsider hunting a man-eating wolf that had been terrorizing a village crossed the ice, not realizing where he was in the snowstorm. He fell into a ravine and injured himself badly. He sent his dog away when he saw a figure approaching the next morning, assuming the person would kill them both."

Leelo lifted her head a little. "It was you?"

Mama sighed. "It was. The outsider was nearly unconscious and half-frozen already. I considered leaving him to die. But when I got closer, I could see that he was a young man, only a little older than me. Then he opened his eyes and looked at me, really looked at me… I can't explain it, but I couldn't just abandon him, darling. I helped him out of the ravine, and we managed to get to a part of the island I thought no one would go, especially during such a brutal winter. At first, it was little more than a lean-to made from fallen boughs. But over the following weeks, I managed to pilfer supplies from your father's workshop, and as Nigel healed, he built the little cottage."

Fiona was quiet for a moment, and Leelo was afraid she wouldn't tell her the rest, the part she needed to hear most of all. "And you fell in love?" she prompted.

Leelo felt her mother's legs trembling beneath her, and she sat up to find her weeping. "It's all right," Leelo said, sitting on the bed beside her and wrapping her mother's thin frame in her arms. "It's all right, Mama."

After a few minutes, her tears subsided. "I'm sorry. I know this must be a lot for you to take in."

"Will you tell me about him?" Leelo asked.

"About Nigel? Are you sure?"

She nodded. "He was Tate's father. Of course I want to know about him."

"Well, he was tall. He had dark hair and eyes, like your brother."

Leelo smiled to herself. So much for those traits being inherited from their grandfather.

"It's hard to remember much, to be honest. I just have those stolen moments together over one brief winter. In the end, I suppose it didn't amount to very much time. But it felt momentous."

"I understand," Leelo whispered.

"He was kind," Mama said finally. "That's what I remember most. He wasn't at all like I'd been told about outsiders."

Hot tears seeped from the corners of Leelo's eyes. "Is Tate with him?"

"I hope so, my darling. I hope so."

Leelo believed that her mother hadn't meant to hurt anyone by her affair, but she wasn't sure she could understand betraying Kellan. By all accounts, he had been a good husband and father. "Can I ask you something?"

"Anything."

"Did you really love my father?"

"I did. Very much."

Leelo released her breath. "But differently than Nigel?"

"Yes."

"Why didn't you tell me? Were you ashamed?"

Fiona was quiet for a long time. "Was I ashamed of my infidelity? Yes, of course. I made a vow to your father, and I broke that vow. Shame is a very powerful emotion. It eats at you like poison, killing you slowly from the inside out. But if you're asking me if I regret it, then the answer is no. Nigel gave me Tate, and he showed me a different kind of love, the kind we choose rather than the kind we are given. I did love your father, but I don't know how much he ever really loved me. He stood by me, even when he knew what I'd done. But sometimes I wonder if *not* standing by me would have meant he truly cared."

Leelo tried to imagine marrying someone she loved as a friend. She knew that marriage provided security and companionship, but after being with Jaren, to marry for convenience would feel like a betrayal of her own heart. She realized now that she had taken it for granted that her parents had always been in love, the way most children probably did. But she didn't actually know anything about their relationship, other than the little bit she could remember.

"You never told me how you and Father knew each other."

"To understand that I have to first tell you about Aunt Ketty and Hugo. His father was the island's only blacksmith, so their family always had steady business. Their house was larger than almost any on the island, in part to accommodate so many children. Hugo had six brothers, and they were all big, strapping boys, their mother's pride and joy. She was a diminutive woman, standing no taller than her sons' chests, and everyone marveled at how she'd managed to produce such massive offspring.

"As the youngest of seven, Hugo was the baby of the family, and his mother was always packing his lunch before Watcher duty, sometimes bringing it to him during his shift if he left it at home. Ketty and I would giggle about this. There was certainly no one at home packing *our* lunches. And Hugo, believing that everyone adored him as much as his mother, seemed to think Ketty's giggling meant she liked him, because he started singling her out at every gathering, bringing her gifts, and generally making his intentions clear.

"At first, Ketty seemed indifferent to Hugo's clumsy advances. But as our parents began hinting that an affiliation with Hugo's family would be very good for everyone involved, she had begun to take him more seriously. Hugo was a perfectly decent suitor, but I had always seen my sister as a wild thing, carefree and independent, not someone who would willingly be tied down."

Leelo couldn't help thinking of Sage then, of what her mother had done by betrothing her to Hollis.

"As Ketty and Hugo started to spend more time together, I was often dragged along against my will as a chaperone. That was how I met Hugo's quiet, fair-haired best friend, Kellan. He somehow seemed younger than the rest of us, and shy, but then, so was I. Ketty liked the idea of the four of us marrying together, in one grand ceremony. And I loved Ketty. The idea of marrying best friends was comforting. We would always be close. And it wasn't so scary to think of marriage and children when my sister would be going through it with me.

"We were all married two years later, in that grand ceremony Ketty dreamed of. It wasn't until a few years after that that Hugo started drinking too much and his cruelty emerged. By then, we were both pregnant, and even your father couldn't calm Uncle Hugo when he'd had too much drink."

Leelo felt a stab of pity for her aunt. Things might have been different if she'd married someone else. Different for Ketty *and* for Mama.

"Was there a part of you that wanted to go with Nigel when he left?" she asked.

Mama wrapped her arms tighter around Leelo, like she was trying to keep her from leaving. "Yes, of course. But I knew that I couldn't."

"What did Ketty do when she found out about him?" Leelo asked.

Fiona was silent for a long moment. "She found a way to punish me for it. Ketty always does."

They both startled at a creak on the stairs, and then Sage's head appeared in the doorway. "Dinner is ready," she said, flashing a smile that seemed far too innocent to be genuine. *How long has she been standing there?* Leelo wondered. *How much does she already know?*

"We'll be right down," Fiona said, then waited till they heard Sage descend the stairs before turning back to Leelo. "Now tell me, quickly. Who is this young man you've fallen for?"

"You don't know him," she said, unable to meet her mother's eyes.

"No?"

Leelo stared at the carved swans, thinking of the cygnet she and Tate had recovered from the lake. Somewhere in the world, swans swam together on safe waters, bonded for their entire lives. Leelo would always love Endla, because it was her home, but Isola was right. If Mama had helped get Tate's father off the island, then she might know how to help Jaren. And if Leelo knew her cousin, she wasn't going to rest until she figured out Leelo's secret. They had to get him away from here, as soon as possible.

She looked up, meeting her mother's soft gaze, and swallowed. "I am in love, Mama. His name is Jaren. And he is an outsider."

Chapter Forty-Five

As they sat around the table eating their dinner in silence, Leelo did her best to appear calm, but she was rattled to her core. It seemed impossible that she and her mother could both have rescued outsiders and then fallen in love with them. She wondered if there was some strange curse on her family or if she was being tested by the Forest to see if she would follow in the footsteps of her traitorous mother. If that was the case, she had failed miserably.

"Leelo, can you please pass me the potatoes?"

She looked up to find Sage watching her, that too-keen look in her eyes. Not knowing how much her cousin had overheard was only making her more uneasy. Sage obviously knew more than Leelo had, but how much, exactly?

After dinner, Leelo and Sage washed the dishes side by side. Fiona was darning a pair of Sage's torn stockings, and Ketty was checking on the sheep.

"Is everything all right?" Sage asked.

"I'm just tired, I think."

"Mother and I are going to visit the Hardings tomorrow. Why don't you come with us? You love their garden."

Leelo toweled off the bowl she was holding and handed it to Sage to put in the cupboard. "I would, but I promised Mama I'd help her with the sewing." This was a lie. She had promised Jaren she would visit him, and she had no desire to see Hollis. But it seemed like a good sign that Sage wasn't complaining about the visit. "Are you feeling better about your engagement?"

"How would you feel about it, if you were me?" Sage asked, her voice curiously devoid of venom.

"What?"

"I mean it. If you were me and you had to marry Hollis Harding, how would you feel about it?"

"I don't know. I suppose I never really considered it before. I liked Hollis, when we were younger. But he's a bit…"

"Dense?" Sage asked.

"I was going to say imposing, but no, he's not the sharpest tool in the shed."

Sage snorted. "No, he's not."

"So don't marry him, Sage. You can wait for something better. You can wait until you fall in love."

Sage crossed her arms over her chest and leaned back against the sink. "Like you, you mean?"

Leelo wasn't sure if Ketty had told Sage about the night she snuck out. She had no idea how much her cousin knew, and her stomach sank as she realized all the possible pitfalls ahead. The more she said, the more likely she was to plummet. "I didn't say I was in love."

She arched a brow. "So you're not, then?"

"I'm just saying you can marry someone else, Sage. That's all."

She went back to washing, hoping Sage would drop the subject, but her cousin was still watching her. "What were you and Aunt Fiona talking about earlier? It looked like she was crying."

Of course she wouldn't drop it. This was Sage, the most stubborn person she'd ever known. "She was talking about Tate." Not a lie, but definitely not the whole truth.

"What about him?"

"How much she misses him. We both do."

Sage watched her for a minute from under her furrowed brows. "I heard her say something about Nigel."

Leelo set the dish she was washing in the sink and turned toward Sage. She didn't want to play these games anymore. "You know who Tate's birth father is, don't you?"

Sage pretended to inspect her fingernails.

"I assume your mother knows, too. And she's probably held it over Mama ever since. But it doesn't change anything. He's still my brother."

Sage scoffed and grabbed Leelo's arm, dragging her toward the door.

"Where are we going?"

"Outside, where your mother can't hear."

Leelo followed reluctantly. Sage sat on the porch step that looked out over their garden, waiting for Leelo to join her.

"What?" she asked when she sat down.

"I don't understand you. How can you say it doesn't change

anything? Tate wasn't just incantu." She spat it out like a curse. "He was outsider spawn."

Leelo started to rise. "I'm not going to listen to—"

"I'm not finished," Sage said, grabbing Leelo's arm and dragging her back down. She hadn't realized how much stronger Sage was until that moment. "Your mother was a traitor. Your father was a fool. And Tate—"

"Tate is my *brother*," Leelo growled.

"He was an outsider," she finished. "He belonged with other outsiders."

Leelo shook her arm free of Sage's grip. "You're so entrenched in your own prejudice you don't realize how vile you sound. At least, I hope you don't. Because the alternative is that you truly are that vile."

"And you're so ignorant you don't even realize how dangerous your ignorance is."

It took all of Leelo's resolve not to walk away then. But she needed to know how much Sage was hiding from her. "You're so convinced you know more than me. That if I knew what you know, I'd break. Well, try me. Let's see how fragile I really am."

Sage snickered, but she looked away.

"Go on. Tell me what I'm so ignorant about," Leelo demanded. The truth might be painful, but the lies were as corrosive as rust, and now that she could see the damage they'd wrought, it was a wonder that any of them remained standing.

Sage shrugged, but she watched Leelo from beneath hooded lids, refusing to give anything away.

"How long have you known about Tate's father?"

"A year."

Leelo raised her eyebrows. "A year?"

"I overheard our mothers fighting. Mama was angry with Tate for failing to do some chore, and Aunt Fiona was defending him. I heard my mother say, 'You know that boy is incantu, and you know he has to go. He's not even Endlan!' Your mother started crying." She paused. "You know how I feel about crying."

Leelo snorted in disgust. Of course. Other people's tears made Sage uncomfortable. She would have left immediately.

"I asked my mother about it later that night. That's when she told me about Nigel Thorn."

Despite her anger, Leelo whispered the name, just to hear how it felt on her lips.

"It was a mistake not telling you. I know that now."

Leelo turned to look at her cousin. "Why?"

"Because you would have known to be careful."

"Of what?"

"Of men. Especially ones from outside."

Leelo's blood ran cold. Sage hadn't said that Leelo *would know* to be careful in the future. She had said it in the past tense. She steeled her voice the best she could, trying to keep her expression vague. "I've been told my entire life how dangerous outsiders are. Why would you think I'd trust one?"

Sage studied her for a long, uncomfortable minute, and Leelo couldn't tell if her cousin truly knew about Jaren. But it was enough that she suspected. She had to get him off the island, before it was too late.

If it wasn't too late already.

Chapter Forty-Six

In the day and a half since the girl had seen him at the watering hole, Jaren hadn't slept or eaten. He'd contemplated attempting his own escape, not relishing the idea of spending his last hours as vulnerable as a plucked chicken. But he knew he couldn't leave without seeing Leelo one last time.

When the door to the cottage finally creaked open in the afternoon of the second day, he glanced up but was too weary to stand. His breath left him in a rush when he saw that it was Leelo. She hurried over to him, and he pulled her into his arms.

"Thank goodness it's you," he breathed into her hair.

"Of course it's me," she said, leaning back to look into his eyes. There were shadows beneath hers, as if she hadn't slept.

"There was a girl in the woods, the last time you came. I went to bathe after you left, and while I was underwater, she snuck up on me."

Leelo's breath caught, and she closed her eyes, but she didn't seem surprised. "Not Isola, I take it?"

He shook his head. "She had auburn hair and freckles. She was watching me from the bushes. I think she wanted me to see her."

"It was Sage. I thought she might have seen you. I came as soon as I could, I swear. I don't think she's told anyone about you. Not yet, anyway." She laid her cheek against his chest. "I'm so sorry. You must have been so scared."

"I was worried about *you*." She'd told him the consequences if anyone discovered she'd helped him, and as much as he wished she would come with him, he knew how devastating banishment would be. He set his chin on the crown of her head, relishing this closeness. Saints, all he wanted to do was kiss her. They'd only had the one night together, and he would have done anything for one more. But he was grateful they'd had that much, at least. One perfect night was surely more than most people got.

She squeezed him tighter. "It's only a matter of time before she talks, Jaren. We have to get you out of here. Tonight."

He'd been anticipating this, but the words still stung. She wasn't coming with him, after all. "I already packed."

"My mother and Isola will meet us at the cave. We have to hurry. Sage told me she was going to visit Hollis today, but I don't know how long she'll be gone."

He hesitated. He had to ask one last time so that twenty years from now when he was still missing her, he'd know he tried his best. "Leelo…"

"I can't go with you," she whispered, her voice cracking. "I'm so sorry."

"Are you sure?" he asked gently.

Her voice broke when she said, "No."

They held each other for a minute, all the time they could spare, and then he wiped her tears away while she did the same for him.

She waited outside while he disappeared into the cottage. He emerged a moment later with his few belongings: a waterskin she'd given him, the clothes on his back, and in his left hand, the little songbook.

He smiled, looking a bit sheepish. "Is it all right if I keep this? I won't tell anyone about it ever, I promise."

"Of course."

"There's one other thing." He pulled another book out from his back pocket. "The poetry book."

"I thought you hated that thing," she said with a smile.

"I do, but what can I say? I had a lot of time to kill. Anyhow, I found an inscription in it. I know this sounds strange, but I think it's to your mother."

Leelo took the book from his hands. "It is," she said. "I'll explain as we walk. Come on, it's a hike to the cave, and we don't have much time."

The sun was hot on their heads and shoulders, and Jaren was quickly drenched in sweat from the exertion of hiking after weeks spent cooped up in the cabin. They had to move slower than Leelo could alone to avoid being seen, since Jaren wasn't nearly as quiet as she was.

As they walked, Leelo recounted her conversation with Fiona from the previous night. No wonder she hadn't slept, Jaren thought. She'd had her entire world upended in one day.

"After I told her about you," Leelo went on, her tone changing, "she confessed something about the lake. Something I wasn't supposed to know until my year as Watcher was over."

Jaren remembered how he'd asked Lupin about Lake Luma, but she hadn't known the answer. "Is it about the poison?"

Leelo stopped, dropping her voice to a whisper. "You remember I said there's a pond in the grotto? I saw water lilies growing there. They're part of the spring ceremony, but I didn't give them any thought beyond that."

"That's what you all were releasing into the water that day, when I saw you by the shore?"

"Yes. They're supposed to represent the new Watchers. That was all I knew. But my mother said that during the end of our year as Watchers, there's a different ceremony, a secret one. A council member brings a cage with her, containing a mouse or a chipmunk, whatever they can find." She swallowed, clearly disturbed by what she was about to say. "Then the council member drops the poor creature into the pond. Mama said it was reduced instantly to bones, then nothing."

"So the lilies have something to do with the poison."

Leelo's blue eyes filled with tears. "Yes."

"But you put the lilies into the lake every spring."

She blinked and the tears spilled over her lashes, streaking down her pale face. "Yes."

It was fortunate neither of them knew what to say, because in the ensuing silence they heard something coming through the underbrush. Leelo grabbed Jaren's hand, dragging him down behind a rock. It was a man in a cart pulled by a shaggy pony. Fortunately, he didn't hear their breathing over the sound of the cart, and he disappeared into the trees a few moments later.

Leelo stayed kneeling where she was, swiping her tears away with the back of her hand. He wanted to comfort her, but she was trying her best to compose herself. "I already knew that Lake Luma wasn't full of poison when my ancestors came. That was how they made it across in the first place. But the poison doesn't come from the Forest, like we were told. It comes from *us*."

"Saints," Jaren breathed. "How?"

"They were brought from the mainland by one of our people, a botanist. She planted and cultivated the lilies in the cave, then moved them to the lake every subsequent spring. And we've continued it every year since."

Leelo's voice was laced with disgust, and Jaren could understand why. She had just learned that something she had perceived as special was part of an elaborate lie, one only revealed to her when it was too late. "And this was all to protect your people from outsiders."

She nodded.

"But it also kept you…"

"Trapped," Leelo finished, her voiced ragged.

Jaren helped Leelo to her feet and pulled her into his arms finally. "I'm sorry, Leelo. That must have been so difficult to hear."

She sighed deeply against him. "I think I understand why they did it. I just don't understand all the lies. Instead of honoring our ancestors' traumatic pasts with the truth, they've wrapped everything in flowers and ribbons, until my entire generation forgot why we're here."

"They make rules to protect us," Jaren said, thinking of all the times his parents had warned him not to wander. "They just don't realize we'd be far more apt to listen if we knew what they were protecting us from."

Leelo tilted her face up to him. "Would we, though?" She smiled, the light returning to her eyes. "Even if my mother had told me about Nigel before, I'd have saved you. I'd save you every time, Jaren Kask."

To Jaren's relief, Fiona and Isola were already waiting when they arrived. They wouldn't move the boat until dusk, to give themselves the added advantage of darkness, but they would still have to go carefully. There were Watchers on duty, and it was entirely possible they'd be patrolling the beach Jaren needed to launch from. Leelo had spoken with Isola that morning, and she had agreed to provide a distraction, if it came to that.

He studied Leelo's mother surreptitiously, trying to find some trace of her daughter in her, but they were as different as spring and autumn. Fiona was not old by any means, but she looked so faded and brittle compared to Leelo. Once again, he had the feeling that Leelo was special, even here. Maybe it was simply because he loved her, but in the slanting late-afternoon light, she looked ethereal.

"Is everything all right?" Leelo asked her mother when she reached her. "Are you sure you're up to this?"

Fiona nodded. "Of course I am." She looked past her daughter to Jaren, who was hanging back a bit, unsure.

"You must be Jaren," she said, holding out her hand. "It's very nice to meet you."

Jaren stepped forward and took her hand. "It's nice to meet you, too. Thank you, for helping me."

When she smiled, Jaren saw Leelo in the small gap between her teeth, in the genuine warmth in her eyes. "You're very lucky, you know. Most Endlans would have killed you on sight. It's a miracle you found Leelo."

Jaren blushed and looked at his feet. "I sort of think of it as fate."

Fiona studied him for a moment, and Jaren forced himself to meet her gaze, hoping his eyes could convey how much he loved Leelo. That he was good enough to deserve her love, too.

Finally, Fiona nodded. Jaren glanced at Leelo and was somewhat relieved to see she was blushing, too.

The boat, fortunately, was repaired and already loaded into the pulley system that would take it to the surface, as Leelo knew it would be from her reconnaissance mission in the middle of the night. She'd found new oars propped against the cave wall and lashed them to the inside of the boat.

"Just remember," Fiona said as they took up their positions. "We treat the boat with a special sap that is immune to the poison, but it usually has months to cure, and it's only been a few weeks since the last application."

By the time they started moving, night had settled over Endla like a stifling blanket. Leelo didn't seem to be suffering from the same looming dread Jaren felt. She had taken charge the moment they arrived, directing Jaren and Fiona to the same end of the boat, since he was the strongest and she was the weakest. He tried not to let his fear show on his face as he strained under the weight, supporting it as much as he could to spare Fiona.

It took them nearly an hour to get the boat to the beach. Several times they froze at some sound in the woods, and Jaren could feel the trees around them listening, a phantom breeze ruffling the leaves as they communicated with each other. He would be allowed to leave, he told himself. He was an outsider, and frankly it was a miracle the Forest hadn't already tried to harm him in some way.

When they finally reached the shore, they set the boat down, the girls collapsing in exhaustion while Jaren tied the end of the rope around a rock. The wind had picked up, buffeting all of them. There was no time to lose, but as Jaren helped Leelo to her feet, he was unable to hide his despair.

Isola must have seen the look in his eyes, because she said a quick farewell before stepping away. "Thank you for helping us," he said to her.

When he turned to Fiona, she smiled in a way that told him she wished things could be different. He smiled back, and for a moment, her expression faltered.

"What's wrong?" he asked.

"It's nothing. You just seem so familiar to me." She cocked her head, studying him.

Leelo laughed a little, embarrassed, and took Jaren's hand. "Mama, you don't know him. I promise. Can you give us one minute?"

Fiona and Isola stepped into the Forest while Leelo and Jaren pushed the boat toward the water, choppy from the wind coming off the mainland. Perhaps the Forest was still afraid one of its daughters would try to escape, Jaren thought as his skin erupted in goose bumps.

As he turned to Leelo, knowing what he was about to do, he told himself not to think about the Forest or the island or the lake. He was going home finally, to hug his family and sleep in his own bed and eat something other than stale bread or bitter berries.

But now, as he took Leelo's hands, so small yet so capable,

he almost couldn't remember why he'd ever wanted to leave at all. He wished he'd taken the time to prepare his goodbyes, because now he found himself at a loss for words. Then again, what could possibly encompass everything he felt for her? How could he say goodbye to this girl who meant so much to him, to the girl who had somehow *become* his home?

Leelo's velvet-blue eyes were shining with tears, and wordlessly, Jaren leaned down to kiss her, breathing in her scent one last time. "I'm so sorry," she whispered as she tilted her face up to his. When their lips met, he could taste her salty tears, and he felt his shattered heart break a little more.

"You have nothing to be sorry for," he said. "You have done so much for me, Leelo. I'm the one who should be sorry. It was selfish of me to ask you to leave Endla."

She sobbed and fell into his arms, and he hugged her tightly, telling her that he loved her and that he always would. Finally, he released her and turned to the boat.

They both froze when they heard a rustle in the nearby bushes, their tears already drying on their cheeks in the wind that now whipped around them in a fury.

"What was that?" Leelo whispered.

Before he could respond, a woman with hazel eyes that seemed to glow with anger stepped out from the trees. On the surface, she wasn't a threat. She was unarmed and wore a dress and slippers. She wasn't a Watcher.

But Jaren knew in his bones that whoever she was, they had waited too long. This woman had no intention of letting Jaren go.

Chapter Forty-Seven

Leelo gasped as her aunt burst onto the beach, with Sage right on her heels. She must have followed them to the grotto and gone back to get Ketty. Leelo pushed Jaren behind her. "What are you doing, Sage?"

Her cousin's face was twisted in a triumphant grin as she glanced between Ketty and Leelo. "I'm saving you," she said.

Something that was half sob, half laugh burst out of Leelo. "From what?"

Ketty pointed at Jaren as though he were some disease-ridden creature. "From *that*. Sage told me he was trying to seduce you and lure you away from Endla." She turned to where Isola and Fiona stood, holding each other and crying. "It all made sense, finally. I just had no idea my own sister was trying to help him."

"Leave them alone," Fiona said, but Ketty had already taken a step toward Leelo.

"I should have known. The apple doesn't fall far from the tree."

Leelo pressed her back to Jaren's chest, as if she could somehow save him with her body. "Let him go. He hasn't done anything. This was all a misunderstanding." She looked at Sage imploringly. "Please, you have to know he didn't mean any harm. He just wants to go home to his family."

"I might have believed that," Sage said. "If I hadn't heard what you said to him in that pathetic hovel."

Leelo's stomach sank at the thought of her cousin watching them, of her listening to their private conversation. "You were spying on us?"

"Someone had to! I heard how uncertain you were when he tried to coerce you into leaving. I knew there was still a chance you would fall under his spell. *Someone* had to be strong. You're too soft, Leelo. You always have been."

Leelo wanted to scream at the way Sage repeated everything her mother said, like a starling. Instead, she made a final, desperate appeal to whatever loyalty she still felt for Leelo. "I told him no, Sage. I wasn't leaving with him."

"We couldn't take that chance," Ketty said. "Not with Endla at stake."

Through the trees, Leelo could see the glow of torchlight moving toward them. Ketty must have alerted the council. "Just don't hurt him," she pleaded. "He hasn't done anything wrong. He's leaving now. He doesn't know anything. Just let him go."

"You know we can't do that," Ketty said. "Give him to me. The council will decide his fate."

"No!" Leelo pulled her knife out of her waistband. The

tiny blade glinted in the moonlight, and as Leelo bared her teeth, one arm still held out protectively toward Jaren, Sage actually took a step back.

But Ketty was not easily cowed. She strode forward and knocked the knife from Leelo's hand, shoving her aside as she reached for Jaren.

He backed up toward the lake, his heels only feet from where the water lapped against the shore. Isola was crying great, heaving sobs, clearly traumatized from what she'd gone through with Pieter.

Fiona was trying to console her, but she, too, was crying. "Let the boy go, Ketty. He hasn't done anything."

"How could you be so foolish, sister?"

"I only just learned of his existence."

"And then what?" Ketty spat. "Decided to let him take your only daughter?"

Jaren shook his head. "I would never do that. It was always Leelo's choice. And she chose you!"

Ketty ignored him. "You already let one outsider tear our family apart," she said to Fiona. "Do you really want to do it again?"

"*You* tore our family apart," Fiona growled, the anger in her voice startling Leelo. "You could have let things be. You could have let me have one thing of my own."

"You had responsibilities," Ketty spat. "And you abandoned them for some stranger!"

"I didn't abandon anyone. Kellan knew. He knew, and he forgave me. If it hadn't been for your involvement, if Hugo had never found out…"

Leelo was more confused than ever. She was torn between

pushing Jaren into the boat to save him before it was too late and trying to find some way out of this nightmare they hadn't considered yet.

"Mother," Sage warned. The other council members were nearly upon them.

Ketty turned away from Fiona toward Jaren, who had inched closer to the boat. If he jumped in, the movement might be enough to push the boat those last couple feet into the water. Leelo rushed to his side.

But it was too late. The other council members arrived, all nine of them, including several large men. They would kill Jaren, and they would make Leelo watch.

Suddenly, Isola broke into a sprint. She picked up the knife Leelo had dropped and dove for the rope.

"Go!" Mama screamed at Leelo, and everything slowed down as she turned and reached for Jaren's hand, hauling him toward the boat. Isola slashed repeatedly at the rope, trying to free it, and Fiona, finding some strength Leelo had never witnessed before, was there at the stern, pushing with all her might.

Sage hurled herself at Isola, knocking the girl down. The rope was frayed but still holding on by a thread. Jaren was in the boat, taking up the oars and using them to push away from the shore. Sage screamed when she realized that Leelo was in the boat with him.

"Leelo!" Sage was at the stern, her boots perilously close to the water's edge as she pulled with all her might in one last desperate attempt to stop her cousin from escaping. "Don't leave me!" she screamed.

And then the others were there, pulling next to her. Sage

collapsed in relief, sobbing like a baby, as Jaren and Leelo were hauled out of the boat—Leelo kicking and screaming like a wild animal, Jaren silent and resigned to his fate.

And as Leelo was torn away from the people she loved, she saw that Sage was smiling in relief, even as holes formed in her boots where they'd been splashed in the commotion. Sage didn't care about the pain she caused anyone, not even herself, Leelo realized.

Just as long as Endla was sated.

Chapter Forty-Eight

Jaren stood at the center of the pine grove, trussed up like a turkey, surrounded by the Endlan council members. There had been an argument about what to do with Leelo, her mother insisting that she be taken home to avoid any further trauma, while Ketty insisted she stay and watch what her selfish actions had wrought.

Ketty, unsurprisingly, had won.

Leelo sat next to her mother on a log just outside the circle of council members. Her cousin was there, too, attempting to speak to her, but Leelo just stared dead-eyed at the ground in front of her. Her braid had unraveled in the chaos and her hair hung around her in soft waves. Jaren wanted nothing more than to hold her and promise her everything would be all right, to apologize for involving her in this awful mess, to tell her he loved her again and again.

"The punishment is clear," one of the council members

said. He was a large man, one of the ones who had hauled him out of the boat. "The Forest, or the lake."

"That may be true under normal circumstances," Ketty said. "But this boy has done far worse than the average criminal. Not only did he use our own vessel to deliberately cross to the island, nearly destroying our one boat in the process, but he seduced one of Endla's daughters and tried to lure her away."

Jaren wanted to point out that was not entirely true, but with a gag in his mouth, the most he could do was gurgle in protest.

"Shut up," Ketty said, poking him with a stick in between his ribs, which were already bruised from being dragged through the Forest by several burly men.

"And what would you have us do with him?" another council member asked. "Kill him ourselves?"

Ketty began to nod, but someone else spoke. She was an elderly woman with a kindly look about her, and Jaren began to feel a small spark of hope that someone might defend him. "What about a Hunt?" she said in a honey-sweet voice.

There was a murmur of excitement among the council members, and Jaren realized with growing dread that the little old lady was not defending him at all.

"What's a Hunt?" Sage asked, a little too gleefully.

"We let the boy go on the far side of the island, and then we sing the hunting song," Ketty explained. "Whoever catches him gets the honor of sacrificing him to the Forest."

Jaren's eyes met Leelo's, and he knew the terror he saw there was reflected in his own.

"Let's put it to a vote," Ketty said, but Jaren stopped listening then. He already knew what the answer would be.

It could have been several minutes or several hours later

when Jaren was hauled to his feet (he'd collapsed to his knees at some point, it seemed) and dragged through the Forest.

He lost sight of Leelo and her mother, and maybe that was for the best. He couldn't stand to see the anguish on Leelo's face anymore. He hoped for her sake that she wouldn't have to participate in the Hunt, that she would be well clear of the pine grove when they slit his throat. He hoped Ketty wouldn't be the one to catch him.

Around him, the Forest was silent. It had to be the middle of the night by now. Would they do it tonight, he wondered, or would they wait till morning? Either way, he was so exhausted he knew he wouldn't last long. He decided he hoped they'd do it tonight. He wanted to get this over with.

Finally he was pulled up a walkway to a large cottage. The big man who had spoken first at the council meeting yanked him through the doorway. "You'll stay here tonight," he told Jaren, which was the first information he'd received all night, and he was strangely grateful for it. "The Hunt begins tomorrow night at sundown. You'll be fed before then, though not much. And if you cause any trouble, I'll slit your throat myself."

Jaren nodded. He was pushed into a bedroom, brusquely untied and ungagged, and locked inside.

He collapsed on the bed and curled onto his side, too tired to even check his body for damage. What did it matter, when he was going to die tomorrow anyway? His stomach turned sour at the realization that he'd been so close to freedom, of escaping not just on his own but with Leelo, and now he was going to die. He didn't even hate Sage and Ketty or the other Endlans. They were doing what they thought was necessary. He just wished he could prove to them that he would never hurt Endla, or any of the people on the island.

At some point he fell asleep, and he woke to sunlight streaming through the windows. For a moment, all he could think about was how nice it had been to sleep on a real bed. He stretched out and rolled onto his side, and that was when he remembered where he was and why. His mouth felt fuzzy, his wrists were raw where they'd tied him with rope, and his injured leg was acting up again. But he was still alive.

A few minutes later, there was a knock on the door. A man—not the same one from last night, but one similar in stature—brought in a tray of food and set it on the night-stand without looking at Jaren. As if he was afraid Jaren and his outsider ways might rub off on him somehow.

Jaren hadn't had a hot meal since he came to Endla, and he quickly gobbled down the porridge, scalding his mouth in the process. For jailers, they were being awfully considerate. There had been cream and honey in the porridge, though Jaren had eaten it so fast he'd hardly tasted it. He wondered if it would be considered rude to ask for more, then decided it probably would be.

Later, the same man came back and told Jaren to follow him. In the daylight, he could make out the size and quality of the house better. Whoever this family was, they must be powerful in some way, because this cottage was far grander than any of the others he'd seen on Endla. Once they were back among the trees, Jaren realized with disappointment that they were returning to the pine grove. He didn't like that place. It smelled of old blood and had an eerie, watchful feel about it.

The rest of the council was already there when they arrived.

"Did he try anything last night?" Ketty asked the man who was escorting Jaren.

"No. He was quiet as a mouse."

"Good." Ketty glared at Jaren and took her place with the rest of the council. "Everyone has been alerted of tonight's Hunt," she said. "One member from each family will be permitted to take part. Except for the Hart family," she added. "My sister and niece will be kept at home, in case they get any ideas about helping the outsider."

Jaren was glad that Leelo wouldn't have to see this, but knowing he would not see her even one more time made his chest feel hollow.

"Weapons?" one of the council members asked.

"Bows, knives, and spears will be allowed. No traps or snares, though if the fool should run into one that's already been set up, that's his own problem. The first Endlan to draw blood will have the honor of sacrificing the prisoner."

It was almost impossible to fathom that they were talking about him. He'd never taken part in a hunt before, though his father had, and he could imagine their conversations were very similar to this one. Stepan was a decent hunter considering he'd grown up in a city, but he'd never taken down anything larger than a turkey. Jaren had so many things working against him, he might as well be a slow, injured, flightless bird. At least a turkey could flap into a tree. He doubted the Forest would even grant him access to one.

When they were finished speaking, he was tied to one of the pines, given a waterskin and a chunk of bread, and told they would return at sunset. Exhausted and afraid, Jaren sat down on the Forest floor and waited for his time to die.

Chapter Forty-Nine

Leelo hadn't slept at all the night before, which had fortunately allowed her to sleep for most of today. She had woken up in the late afternoon, her eyes red, her throat still hoarse from screaming. Fiona tried to get her to eat something, but all Leelo could stomach was a few sips of water. She couldn't believe how close they'd come to escaping, only to have it snatched away from them by her own family.

Leelo and Fiona had shared Leelo's room for the night, and she assumed Sage had stayed with her mother in her bedroom. She would never forgive her cousin. Never. She couldn't even look at her.

And Sage, of course, wouldn't look at Leelo. She had been tasked with guarding them tonight while Ketty participated in the Hunt. Sage had actually argued that she should be the one to go, since she had found Jaren, but Ketty had said it was too dangerous, that there was too great of a risk of being injured by another Hunter.

Leelo wasn't sure if Ketty was still traumatized by her husband's death, or if it really was going to be that dangerous. She knew what the hunting song sounded like, after all, how bloodthirsty Endlans could become. She thought of poor Jaren, alone and defenseless, and her eyes filled with tears again. She didn't think she'd ever run out.

"Can I do anything for you?" Fiona asked gently, stroking Leelo's hair. She'd been so kind to Leelo through all of this, never once blaming her for getting their family involved. Leelo knew it was partly because she herself had fallen in love with an outsider, but it was more than that. Mama would have accepted Jaren anyway; that was just the kind of person she was.

"I want to go out there," Leelo whispered. Sage was standing by the door with her bow and arrow. "I want to help him."

"You can't, darling. I told you about those men who came to Endla, the ones your father and uncle found?"

She nodded.

"They were… Hunted. And it was a terrible, bloody business. You don't want any part of it. Trust me."

"But this time it isn't three strangers. It's the boy I love being Hunted, Mama. How can I abandon him now?"

"You're not abandoning him. He would want you to be safe."

Leelo rested her cheek on her folded arms, the cool tears rolling over her skin and onto the table. "I don't know how to go on after this. What am I supposed to do now?"

Fiona laid her head down next to Leelo's, their eyes meeting. "You will grieve, child. You will grieve for the rest of your life. But you *will* go on. For Jaren. For Tate. For yourself."

"And for you," Leelo whispered.

In the distance, they heard a loud cry, followed by the hum of Endlan voices scattered all around the island. The Hunt had begun.

Chapter Fifty

By the time evening began to fall, Jaren was so uncomfortable from being tied to the tree that he was actually looking forward to the Hunt. Anything to put him out of his misery. He had one plan and one plan only: get to the boat, assuming no one had moved it. That was his only chance off the island, and he would get to it or die trying.

When the council members returned, Jaren was dismayed to see them heavily armed and dressed to Hunt. He was wearing the same ratty tunic and breeches he'd been wearing since he arrived, and though he'd tried to stay healthy, he was still far weaker than he'd been before he came. He'd had nothing but the porridge and bread to eat today, and the summer heat had been stifling.

"I'm going to untie you," one of the men said. "You'll have a head start."

"How long?" Jaren asked, rubbing at the places where the rope had chafed him.

"When the sun sets, once the singing begins, the Hunt is on."

Jaren stared at the man, who nodded, and with that, Jaren took off for the shore. He stumbled over roots that appeared out of nowhere, tripped over rocks he didn't see. Branches that should have cleared his head smacked him in the face as he ran in what he hoped was the direction of the beach. He could hear the singing now, eerie and yet hauntingly beautiful. It didn't lure him in, however. It just made him aware of how many people out there were trying to kill him.

He thought of his family: his gentle, loving father, his sisters, each so different and yet all just as loving as Stepan. He thought, too, of his mother, how he had always secretly believed that he was her favorite, though she would never admit it out loud. And he thought of Leelo. He wished he could spare her from all the pain he'd caused her, but he would never regret loving her. Whether it was fate, bad luck, or simply a hungry wolf that had brought him to Endla, it was all worth it to have fallen in love with her.

There, through the trees. He could just make out the glint of moonlight on water. He was almost there. A few more yards, and he would be on the beach.

Suddenly, a shadow stepped out of the trees, blocking his path. He couldn't make out much in the darkness, though he was relieved it wasn't one of the burly men who had held him prisoner. He skidded to a stop, wishing he had some weapon—any weapon—to defend himself.

The person stepped forward, and as the moonlight slanted across her face, he felt his breath leave him in a rush.

"I knew you would come straight here, coward that you are," Sage said. "And now I get to be the one who kills you."

Chapter Fifty-One

Leelo sat with her hands over her ears, trying to drown out the sound of the Hunters by humming a lullaby to herself. Her mother had fallen asleep beside her, but she woke with a sudden start, wincing in pain.

"Mama?" Leelo peered into her mother's face. "What's the matter? Are you ill again?"

Fiona took a sip of the water Leelo offered her and shook her head. "I've been ill for a long time, darling."

Leelo tried to ignore the distant singing, but it was almost impossible. Worst of all, her own throat ached to join in. She reached for the cup of tea Ketty had prepared for Fiona before she left to soothe the pain.

"No!" Fiona's hand shot out so fast it knocked the cup over, sloshing liquid all over the table.

For a moment, they both sat staring at each other, catching their breath.

"Saints, Mama. What was that about?" Leelo rose to fetch

a towel and began to blot up the tea, but as she leaned closer, she was hit with a scent that was unfamiliar until yesterday. The same scent that filled the cave where the boat was kept. Where the lilies were grown.

Her eyes darted to Fiona's. "Mama? What's in this tea?"

Fiona must have seen the realization on Leelo's face, because she only closed her eyes and breathed a deep sigh.

"Answer me. Why does your tea smell like the lilies?"

When Fiona opened her eyes, they were wet with tears. "It's my medicine."

Leelo was trying to understand what her mother was saying, but she was too distracted by the distant singing to make sense of it. "What medicine?"

Fiona leaned back in her chair. "You know that poisonous plants can have medicinal uses as well as fatal ones."

Leelo nodded. "We use autumn crocus to treat gout. And the foxglove leaves for your heart troubles. What does that have to do with anything."

"After your father died, I became ill. I couldn't sleep. I wouldn't eat. Your aunt nursed me back to health. The lilies, if highly diluted in water, can treat several ailments, including depression.

"After a time, I began to heal. But I refused to sing again, not even at the funeral. It wasn't like not eating. That was a choice. But singing was different. I simply couldn't do the thing that had once brought me so much joy. Not after what I'd done."

Leelo wasn't sure if singing had ever brought her joy. It had simply been a part of her, like the breath in her lungs and the blood in her veins. Giving it up didn't feel like an option.

"Ketty used to chide me at every festival. 'Sing, or you'll get ill again. Sing, or you're going to die.' But the more I refused, the angrier she got. And then I took a turn for the worse."

"Did you know she was making you sick?" Leelo asked, her fury rising.

"No. Not at first. I believed her when she said it was because I wouldn't sing. But then one day I saw her making my tea. And I knew then she was using too much of the extract of lily. Enough to cross the line from medicine to poison."

Mama was the one who had warned Leelo of that very thing. Every time she prepared a tea or a tincture, Leelo had to check her calculations three times. "Then why did you keep drinking it?" Leelo demanded. "How could you do that to yourself? To Tate, and to me?"

"Because she threatened to tell you what I'd done. She threatened to tell everyone. And I suppose it was because some part of me believed I deserved it. I thought it was the punishment I had earned by betraying my family, and Endla."

Hot tears pricked at the corners of Leelo's eyes. "That's nonsense. Not helping Nigel would have been the true betrayal, because you would have been betraying yourself." There had never been a choice, for either of them, because when it came down to it, they were good people. They wouldn't willingly allow anyone to suffer. Unlike Ketty, who for years had been killing her only sister.

"I know that now," Fiona said softly. "I'm sorry. I should have fought harder, for your sake."

Leelo shook her head and rose. "I forgive you, Mama. But I have a choice. I have to fight for Jaren."

Her mother tried to grab her arm as she walked to the door. "You can't! Sage is out there!"

But Leelo was already standing in the open doorway, and there was no sign of her cousin. "She must have gone to join the Hunt," she murmured, feeling more betrayed than ever. Like her mother, Sage was loyal to the island even more than her own family. Like Ketty, Sage probably thought she was doing Leelo a favor.

"Maybe he's safe," she said. "If the singing didn't work before, perhaps it won't now, either."

"What did you say?" Fiona asked.

Leelo glanced at her mother over her shoulder. "I said maybe the magic won't work on him."

Fiona took a step forward and stumbled, clutching her head in her hands. "Saints," she breathed as Leelo rushed to her side.

"Mama? Are you all right?"

Fiona shook her head, trying to clear it. "I don't know how I didn't see it before."

"See what? What's wrong?"

"I knew he looked familiar, but I couldn't believe... I should have known."

Leelo gripped her mother's shoulders, forcing her to look up. "What are you talking about?"

"Nadia. She was a Watcher the same year I was. We weren't close, but she didn't make it a secret how she felt about Endla's rules. She scowled through the entire ceremony and came to none of the festivals after. None of us were truly surprised the winter she tried to escape across the lake with her newborn son."

"What?"

Fiona's eyes had glazed over. "A little sooner, and she might have made it. But the ice gave way beneath her, drowning both of them. Unless…"

Leelo had stopped breathing. "What are you saying, Mama?"

Finally, Fiona stopped rambling, her hazel eyes focusing on Leelo's. "I'm saying, what if the baby survived?"

Chapter Fifty-Two

Jaren and Sage stared at each other for a long while, trying to gauge who would be the first to move. Unsurprisingly, it was Sage. She ran toward him with her knife outstretched and missed him by mere inches when he dodged at the last second, sprinting for the lake.

But Sage, with her righteous fury and full belly, was faster than Jaren. She leaped onto him from behind, tackling him to the ground. He barely managed to get a hold of her knife-wielding hand, pinning it by her side. But whereas Jaren had spent most of his days daydreaming, Sage had clearly been preparing for a moment like this. She kneed him in the crotch, waiting until he curled up in pain before rolling on top of him and pressing the knife to his throat.

"You had to know it would end this way," she said, her eyes glinting in the darkness.

"It doesn't," he choked out.

"I don't know why you came here, and I don't particularly

care. You should have died in the crossing, but you didn't. And my cousin wouldn't let a fly suffer, let alone a human. But she was never yours to have, and I was never going to let you take her from me."

For the first time, Jaren realized how much Leelo meant to Sage, and he couldn't blame her for that. "I know she isn't mine," he said. "But she isn't yours, either. She should be free to make her own decisions."

"And you're so sure she would have chosen you over me? She may have fallen prey to your outsider tricks, but Leelo loves this island and her family. She would never have abandoned us."

He could understand how much it must hurt to feel cast aside for a near stranger, though of course, it hadn't been that way at all. "I know. Not unless she felt like she had to," he said.

Her eyes narrowed. "Is this what you do? Agree with everything Leelo says? No wonder she liked having you around." She ground her knee farther into his stomach. The singing, which had been a distant hum up until now, seemed to be growing closer. "You're my kill," she said, and with that, she slowly drew the knife across his throat. Just deep enough to draw blood. Just deep enough to let him know that next time, she would cut to kill.

Chapter Fifty-Three

"Mama, wait!" Leelo screamed as she ran after her mother through the Forest. She'd never known Fiona could move so quickly, especially given how ill she'd seemed just moments earlier, but she was driven now, not trying to save her strength for later.

"We have to tell Ketty," Fiona rasped. "She can't kill him if she knows he's an Endlan."

"Are you sure?" Leelo wanted so desperately to believe her mother was right. And her theory made sense. Jaren had never reacted to Endlan singing the way an outsider should. And his voice, though untrained and unpracticed, was as sweet as any Endlan's. *Saints, let Mama be right.*

"I'm sure," Fiona said, pausing just long enough to take Leelo's hand and pull her along down the trail.

The singing was everywhere, and Leelo wished she could block it out somehow. She'd always hated this song, punctuated by shrill shrieks and guttural cries, but she loathed it now. A family of raccoons hurried across the trail; she wasn't sure if they were running toward the singers or fleeing. The Endlans wouldn't kill any animals tonight. That wasn't the goal of their Hunt.

Finally, they reached the pine grove, but only a few elderly Endlans were there, sitting on log benches, waiting for the main event to start. Leelo glared at them.

"What are you doing out?" an old man asked. "You're supposed to be under guard at your house."

"Our guard left," Leelo spat. "Where is Ketty?"

"Hunting, of course," the old man said. "And based on the way things are quieting down, I'd say he's been caught. It won't be long now."

He was right. Only a few minutes later, which Leelo spent pacing, her hands pressed against her ears, the Endlans began returning to the pine grove. "Who caught him?" someone asked. A few people shook their heads.

And then Sage entered the clearing, and they had their answer.

Leelo gasped at the sight of blood running from a wound in Jaren's neck onto his tunic. Sage had her knife to his back, her intent clear. Leelo pushed her way through the crowd until she reached him.

"Leelo?" he breathed.

"I'm so sorry," she said, a moment before she was ripped away by several Endlans.

Ketty materialized out of the crowd with her burning gaze fixed on her daughter. "What are you doing here? You're supposed to be at the house."

"I was the one who discovered him," Sage said. Her knife

was still inches from Jaren's spine, but he didn't appear to be in any shape to try to escape. "I deserve this kill."

"She's right," a few people said. "She caught him. She deserves the kill."

Leelo thought she might be sick. "She wasn't even a part of the Hunt!"

Some of the Endlans seemed to side with Leelo, but there was so much commotion it was impossible to know which side was winning.

Fiona had found her way to Leelo, and they stood clutching each other. "Mama, say something," Leelo urged.

"Ketty," Fiona said, but her voice was too weak to be heard above the excited chatter of the crowd, which was growing more animated by the second.

"Ketty!" Leelo screamed. "You can't kill him!"

"Why not?" Sage asked. "Because you think you love him?" Anyone else might only have seen the sheer loathing Sage felt for Jaren, but Leelo could tell that beneath her sneer of derision was a hint of sorrow and regret. *Choose me*, her eyes said. But it was a choice Jaren would never have forced her to make.

Leelo turned to the crowd. "Because he's an Endlan," she said, her voice ringing out over the clearing. "And he has as much of a right to be here as the rest of us."

Sage lowered the knife a fraction of an inch. "What are you talking about?"

Ketty was gripping Jaren's arm now, and it was clear that their battle lines had been drawn. "Lies," Ketty said. "We know all Endlans. This boy is a clear outsider."

Fiona shook her head. "Look again, sister."

A flicker of doubt crossed Ketty's face.

"That's Nadia Gregorson's child. The child she died trying to save."

A murmur of disbelief went up amongst the Endlans. "It can't be," someone said.

"We saw her drown," another added.

"Haven't you noticed that your songs didn't work on him?" Leelo asked Sage. "He was trying to escape, wasn't he? He didn't come to you of his own will. If he was an outsider, he would have run toward you, not away."

Sage's vicious scowl started to give way to doubt. "You're wrong. He can't be Endlan."

Leelo stared into Jaren's gray eyes, letting the rest of the world, his bleeding neck, her cousin's fury, fade away. She stepped toward him, and this time, no one stopped her. "He is."

"Is it true?" he asked, taking her hands.

"It's the only explanation. Does it make any sense, with what you know of your parents? Would they have taken in an abandoned child, even if they knew he was Endlan?"

Jaren's eyes filled with tears. "Yes."

"I'm so sorry," she whispered against his chest. "I wish I could have told you some other way." She leaned back, cupping his cheek in her palm. "Come on. Let's take you home."

Ketty, who had seemed speechless just a moment before, managed to find her voice then. "Home? You just said this boy *is* home. If he's Endlan, then he is exactly where he belongs."

"He has a family," Fiona said. "He needs to return to them."

"And let me guess. You intend to go with him. Your loyalty was always to *them*, never to us."

Fiona shot her sister a warning glance. If *them* was Nigel and Tate, as Leelo suspected, then she likely didn't want the rest of the island to know. "My loyalty is to my family, yes. It always has been."

"What are you implying, sister? That mine hasn't been?"

Fiona lowered her voice. "Let's discuss this at the house, Ketty."

"No. I think it's high time these people know the truth about what you did. That you're no better than your traitor daughter."

Again, the crowd buzzed with speculation. "What is she talking about, Fiona?" someone asked.

"We deserve the truth."

Leelo took Jaren's hand and started to push through the crowd. "Come on, Mama," she said.

But Ketty and Fiona stood their ground.

"The truth," Ketty said, "is that my sister had a bastard. An incantu bastard, with an outsider father."

There was a collective gasp from the Endlans. "What outsider?" a woman shouted. "When?"

"Twelve years ago," Sage said. "Isn't it obvious?"

There were more demands for the truth, and Fiona finally turned to face the crowd. "My sister speaks true. There was an outsider who crossed the ice twelve winters ago. He was injured, and I helped him. And I fell in love with him. My boy, Tate, was the result of our relationship." She turned to Ketty and leveled her with a gaze that could melt iron. "And Kellan knew."

Ketty's eyebrows rose in shock. Apparently she hadn't expected Fiona to admit as much in public.

"Why don't you tell them the rest of the story?" Fiona said. "Tell them about the accident."

Leelo's eyes darted between her aunt and mother. "What are you talking about?" she asked quietly.

Fiona continued when she realized her sister wasn't going to stop her, seeming to gather strength as she spoke. "There was no accident, was there, Ketty? There was only you and your desire to always know the truth. And worse, to share it, no matter who you hurt in the process. And when you told Hugo the truth of Tate's origin, he threatened to tell everyone on the island so that I would be turned out with my illegitimate offspring."

Ketty stepped toward Fiona. "Be quiet," she hissed. "Stop this."

"And then," Fiona went on, "when Hugo confronted my husband about it, threatening to tell the truth if he wouldn't, they argued. Hugo shot Kellan, by accident, perhaps, but he watched while my husband bled to death."

"That's enough!" Ketty shouted.

"And you saw the whole thing, didn't you? You decided that this secret would destroy us if it got out, so you did the only thing you could think of, the thing you'd secretly been wanting to do for a very long time."

Ketty began to tremble. "Stop. Please."

Fiona's face softened just a fraction. "I know you thought you were protecting this family, sister. I know you thought you were fixing it. But you destroyed us instead."

"What is she saying, Mother?" Sage stared at Ketty as if she was seeing her for the first time. "Did you do something to Father?"

Ketty didn't need to answer. Sage had already gleaned the truth, and now so had the rest of the island. Leelo felt as if the world was spinning out from underneath her. Her uncle had killed her father, and her aunt had killed her uncle. There was never an accident. It had been murder, and Fiona was right. It had destroyed them all.

The silence of all the listening Endlans erupted into shouts and cries, but Leelo couldn't hear them. All she could see was her broken aunt, who had fallen to her knees; her shattered cousin, who didn't seem to know where to look; and her mother, who clearly took no delight in what she'd done. How long had Fiona known it wasn't an accident? Had her loyalty to Aunt Ketty ever been real, or was it simply to prevent Ketty from revealing Fiona's secrets? So many lies, and all they had wrought were years of fear and resentment.

Leelo turned to her cousin. The anger had washed out of her, and she looked small and vulnerable without it. All this time, Sage had believed Leelo would be the one to shatter if she knew the truth. But Leelo was the one looking at a broken girl.

"Sage," she began, but there was nothing more to say.

Sage's face collapsed before she turned and ran.

Chapter Fifty-Four

"Leelo."

She blinked and shook her head. Jaren was standing behind her.

"Do you want to go after her?" he asked.

The other Endlans present were caught up in their own arguments. The large men who had held Jaren captive were the loudest of all. Hugo's brothers, Leelo realized, though she had never met them before. After her uncle died, Ketty had cut herself off from her husband's family. And now it was clear why.

"Where's Aunt Ketty?" Leelo asked her mother.

Fiona shook her head. "I imagine she slipped away amid the commotion." She pressed her fingers to her temples. "Saints, what have I done?"

"What you had to do," Leelo said. "Come on, let's get you home."

"No. We need to get Jaren out of here before it's too late."

A sudden wind had picked up, Leelo realized. Another storm was brewing, and Jaren would be caught in it if they didn't move.

"Hurry," Fiona said, urging them toward the boat. Above the canopy, the tips of the tall pines were swaying back and forth in the wind. Sharp raindrops began to pelt Leelo's face.

"What's happening?"

"It's the Forest," Fiona whispered. "I had hoped that it wouldn't notice…"

"What are you talking about?"

"Just get in the boat. Quickly, before it's too late."

Realization washed over Leelo, as cold and unwelcome as the rain. "You're not talking about the storm, are you?"

Fiona's face was streaked with rain or tears or both. "It isn't just the lake that keeps us here, Leelo. We can't leave Endla. The Forest won't let us. This may have been an ordinary Wandering Forest at some point, but it's far stronger than the others now, grown fat and monstrous on Endlan blood. That's why I couldn't leave to be with Nigel, even if I took you with me. Especially if I took you with me. We raise you to believe that we need this Forest to protect us, but it's the other way around."

They say Endla grows roots around your feet so you can't leave, even if you want to. How many times had Leelo heard that phrase, smiling at the nonsense of it because of course no one would want to leave? Now her stomach churned with growing horror. If they left, would the Forest retaliate and harm the other islanders? She couldn't do that to them.

She turned to Jaren. "You have to go. This may be your only chance."

"I'm not leaving without you. Besides, if what your mother says is true, I won't be allowed to leave, either." He squeezed her hands in his, wincing when her skin brushed his raw wrists. "Maybe that's why the wolf brought me to Endla. Because it somehow knew I belonged here."

Their eyes met, and for a moment the world faded away around them. She'd come so close to losing him it was almost impossible to believe he was still here with her. She rose on her tiptoes, pressing a gentle kiss to his lips, just to make sure he was real.

When she lowered herself back down, she let her eyes travel to the Forest. Once, she had believed that nothing mattered more than this place. She had allowed her brother to be sent away for it; she had nearly lost Jaren to it, too. But the power those lies had held over her for seventeen years was gone, replaced by a new understanding.

She had come to realize that the only thing that mattered—the only true magic—was to love and be loved. And she was not willing to live in a world where something was controlling that magic. The original Endlans might have foregone their freedom for safety, but they hadn't given their descendants a choice. No one should have to say goodbye to a beloved child. No one should have to choose between their freedom and their life.

"I love you, and I don't want to lose you. But you *don't* belong here, Jaren. You belong with your father and your sisters."

He stared at her, bewildered. "And what about you?"

"I belong with Mama," she whispered. "I belong with Tate. And with *you*."

Before he could ask what she meant, she took his hand,

leading him to where the rest of the gathered Endlans were still bickering among themselves about what to do with Ketty and what to make of the knowledge that an Endlan had not only managed to escape the Forest but later returned.

Leelo climbed onto a fallen log, using Jaren's hand for balance. Finally, someone noticed her presence, and then a hush fell over the crowd as everyone turned toward her. She saw familiar, friendly faces, but also angry ones. She cleared her throat.

"I know some of you may think of me as a traitor, but we all, every one of us, share something in common—Endla has taken too much from us." She pointed to Isola's parents, who stood near the front of the crowd. "Isola lost the boy she loved. Rosalie and Gant, you lost your community." She turned to Pieter's parents. "You lost your son, first to the outsiders, and then to the lake. And you lost your eldest daughter," she added, looking at Vance's parents.

"I lost my brother. My mother lost her only son. And we've borne it because we never felt like we had a choice. But now we've seen living proof that an Endlan can safely reside among outsiders without coming to harm or harming others. We continue to feed this Forest with our own blood, and for what? We know how to hunt, how to build shelter, how to care for each other. We can survive without the Forest."

Even though there hadn't been a sacrifice in weeks, Leelo could still smell the blood, the greedy closeness of the pines. They would never be sated, no matter how much the Endlans sacrificed. "The truth is, the Forest can't survive without *us*."

A rustling started in the branches above them, like children whispering to one another. She could have sworn the gaps

between the trees' crowns had grown smaller, that the space
between them was shrinking. The wind picked up, howling,
surrounding them with the sound of creaking limbs.

"What are you saying?" someone shouted from the crowd.

"I'm saying it's time to take care of ourselves, for a change.
To allow people who want to leave—or even people who
want to return—to make that choice."

"The Forest won't allow it," a woman called.

Murmurs of agreement rose up, but to Leelo's surprise, Rosalie held her knife aloft. "I will help you, Leelo." Her husband stepped up next to her, hefting his axe. "We both will."

Vance's parents exchanged a glance, and then they, too,
stepped forward.

Leelo looked to Pieter's parents. "Will you help us?"

For a long moment, she was sure they would say no. And
then they nodded as well. "We will help."

A few other Endlans who had been listening nearby joined
them. But as Leelo's plan began to disseminate among the islanders, shouts of anger went up as well.

"You can't do this!"

"The Forest will kill us all!"

"Endla is our home!"

She waited for the adults on her side to do something, but
they stood watching her, frozen with indecision, and she knew
she would have to strike the first blow.

She took the axe from Gant, who released it willingly, and
turned to her family's pine.

She'd never liked the grove, or this tree. A patron saint was
supposed to bring blessings and good fortune, but all it had
ever brought her was suffering. Still, when she raised the axe

over her head and swung it at the trunk, it felt like she was striking down an old acquaintance.

The blade struck the bark so hard that it buried itself, and Leelo remembered the stories Ketty had told, of the bloodred sap and the screaming trees. But all she could hear was the sound of her own breathing. Even those who opposed her had fallen silent, as if waiting to see how the Forest would retaliate.

She pulled the axe free and struck again. It would take her hours to cut such a massive tree down on her own, but a moment later, Jaren joined her, wielding an axe he'd taken from another Endlan. Pieter's father joined as well. Within a few minutes, the tree began to groan under its own weight, sounding as lonely and ancient as the wind itself. They stepped back as the massive pine crashed to the earth, taking a smaller tree with it.

Leelo turned to the next tree. A few Endlans stood before it, their weapons raised. "Don't do this," a man said. "You don't know what the consequences will be."

"No. But I do know the consequences of letting things continue as they have been. I'm willing to take the risk."

To her surprise, the people stepped aside. As she and Jaren swung their axes, first one, then the other, it struck a primal beat that Leelo could feel in the soles of her feet. She felt that desperate choking sensation in her throat, that insatiable need to sing.

"Are you all right?" Jaren asked her.

She nodded, but she felt like she was suffocating. She clamped her mouth shut, and with one final swing, she struck the death blow. The sound of branches snapping and the trunk splintering was ear-shattering.

This tree fell against its neighbor, taking it down with it. Many Endlans had gone home, but some stood watching, still waiting to see if there would be any consequences for what Leelo and the others were doing. Within twenty minutes, they had taken down all the pines, save the tallest. Leelo and Jaren were preparing to strike when a sudden bolt of lightning flashed overhead, followed instantly by a clap of thunder so loud Leelo screamed.

"Look out!" Jaren shouted, knocking Leelo to the ground. Just inches from where she'd been standing, a massive branch crashed to the Forest floor.

Leelo scrambled to her feet with Jaren's help. She told herself it was a coincidence, that this had nothing to do with the Forest. But then the ground beneath her began to tremble. Suddenly, a sinkhole opened up nearby, swallowing the man who had warned Leelo to stop.

"Leelo!" Jaren screamed. She followed his gaze to the top of the pine, where flames blazed against the night sky. The lightning had started a fire.

She searched frantically for her mother as the wind roared and the other Endlans fled.

"I'm here," Fiona said, taking Leelo's other hand. "Quickly. We have to get you to the shore."

Leelo's mind was racing, trying to process what was happening. Somehow, they had succeeded in destroying the pine grove, but she had never accounted for lightning. She could only hope the rain would put out the flames before the fire spread.

They ran, dodging falling branches and fissures that opened in the Forest floor without warning. Leelo could hear people screaming in the distance, and a sob caught in her throat. What had she done?

They didn't make it far before a mob of Endlans, still carrying their weapons, materialized from the trees. "Stop this madness, Fiona," one of the men said, stepping forward. "Rein in your wayward daughter before she kills us all."

Behind them, Leelo could hear the roar of flames growing louder.

Fiona pushed her wet hair out of her eyes. "My daughter was the only one here brave enough to call for an end to this Forest's cruelty. For decades we have lived the lie our ancestors passed down to us. We told it to our own children. We sent our babies away!"

Several of the Endlans exchanged glances. They knew deep down that what they'd done to scores of innocent children was wrong, and they'd justified it by telling themselves it was for their own good.

"The Forest has already killed several of us tonight," someone shouted from the crowd. "Even if Leelo is right, it's not worth the cost."

"The Forest protects us," a woman cried. "Without it, we'll be slaughtered."

"You won't," Jaren shouted. "The outsiders aren't what you imagine them to be. My family is kind and loving." He glanced at Leelo, as though he were seeking some kind of confirmation.

She nodded.

"They took me in," he continued. "They found me by the lake. They must have known what I was, but they brought

me into their home and raised me as one of their own." His
voice broke, and Leelo squeezed his hand tighter.

"Just leave," an old woman said. "Let those of us who wish
to stay remain. Take the boat and be gone. The Forest will
forgive the rest of us."

Leelo had lost some of the islanders who'd been helping
her amid the chaos, but she turned to Rosalie and Gant. "I'm
sorry. I failed to destroy the Forest, and now all I've brought
is destruction to our people."

Rosalie stepped forward. "You tried, Leelo. You were the
only one who would visit us after our entire community
shunned us. You brought Isola back to us. You're a good person. You should go, now. While you still can."

"But what about you? Mama said the boat can only make
the trip once."

"We'll be all right," Rosalie said. "We can't leave without Isola."

Leelo looked up into the trees. The flames were spreading, though the rain seemed to be preventing the fire from
growing into a conflagration. "The Forest…"

"Go," Rosalie insisted.

Jaren squeezed Leelo's hand, and she nodded. The mob
parted, allowing them to pass, reforming behind them as
they walked.

When they reached the shore, Leelo was relieved to see
the boat was still there. But the storm wasn't just affecting the
Forest. The surface of the lake churned with foam, and large
waves crashed on the rocks, bigger than any she'd ever seen.
She glanced back at the mob, who stood with their weapons

brandished. The crossing would be perilous, but they didn't have any other choice.

"Get in," Leelo shouted to Fiona above the wind. "Jaren and I will push the boat into the water."

Jaren stepped forward, prepared to help Fiona into the boat. But to Leelo's horror, she stepped away from them.

"Mama? What are you doing?"

Fiona was shaking her head, her eyes wide and shining. "I'm sorry, my darling. I can't."

Leelo wanted to scream in frustration. "What are you talking about? Of course you can. They *want* you to leave," she said, nodding toward the mob.

"The lake is too choppy. That boat wasn't built for three adults. If I upset the balance, we could capsize. I can't take that risk. Not with you."

"We're not going without you," Leelo cried. "We'll wait until the storm passes."

"I'm not sure they'll let you," she said. She lowered her voice and pulled Leelo into her arms. "The only thing that matters to me is your safety."

"But the boat. You said it can only make one crossing. We won't be able to send it back for you."

Fiona released Leelo. "You'll come back for me one day, after you've found Tate."

"No," Leelo sobbed. Now that they were here, now that they were really going, she couldn't leave without her mother. There would be no one left to take care of her.

"I am going to get better," Fiona said. "I promise."

"Leelo…" Jaren was staring above the heads of the crowd,

where the Forest glowed a brilliant orange. "The fire is getting worse. We need to go."

"Please, Mama. Just come with us," she pleaded, but Fiona was pushing her back toward the boat.

Someone screamed in the distance. "The fire! It's reached the cottages!"

The mob surged forward, intent on driving them from the island. Jaren had a hold of Leelo's arm and was pulling her toward the boat. "I'm not leaving you!" Leelo screamed at her mother, just as her feet hit the hull.

"And I'm not letting you stay." Fiona shoved Leelo backward, digging her heels into the dirt and using all of her strength to push the boat into the water before Leelo could get her bearings.

"Mama!" she screamed. The boat rocked perilously as soon as they reached open water, and Leelo found herself scrambling for an oar. There was a strong wind coming off the mainland, blowing toward Endla, and there were still shouts and screams coming from the Forest.

"I love you!" Fiona shouted, but her voice was lost to the wind. It was too late to go back, Leelo realized. Too late to save Mama.

"Pull!" Jaren screamed. Tears coursed down Leelo's face as she rowed, her arms burning with every stroke, the tendons in her neck straining to the breaking point. Just when she felt as though they were gaining ground, another strong gust of wind blew them back toward the island. Endla was refusing to let them go.

Leelo couldn't help thinking of all the people she was leaving behind. Selfishly, she wanted to be free of Endla, to never sacrifice for it again. But if the cost was her mother, her friends, even her aunt and cousin, then it was too high. It would be easier to give up and return to Endla. It would be easier to let the boat capsize.

She glanced at Jaren through her wet hair and the slashing rain. He was rowing with all his might, but it wasn't enough. They were just two people against an entire Wandering Forest, strong enough to bend the wind itself to its will. Who were they to think they could defeat it?

From here, it seemed as though the entire island was on fire. What if their cottage was already burned to the ground? Where would Mama go? Panic began to descend on Leelo. What had she been thinking? What had she done?

The music was so soft she didn't hear it at first over the crashing waves, but then she realized Jaren was singing.

It was the prayer for lost things, the one that had brought them together, that had brought Jaren back to Endla. He had found himself in Leelo, he said, and she had found her answers in him: things *didn't* have to be the way they'd always been. They didn't have to accept the world they'd inherited from their ancestors. They might have bowed under the pressure of their rules and expectations, but they were strong enough not to break, resilient enough to bend.

For the first time, Leelo didn't feel like she had to sing.

She *wanted* to.

The song spilled out of both of them, their voices joining in perfect harmony, and when Jaren looked at her, she knew he felt it, too.

Magic.

She'd never told Jaren the rest of the song, but as she

sang, his voice rose to meet hers. When they finished, Leelo watched in wonder as the waves began to calm.

"Leelo, look," Jaren breathed.

Her eyes followed his gaze to Endla. The rain had stopped. The fire had gone out. Just as the old woman had predicted.

She'd never seen her home from afar before, and she understood for the first time that Jaren was right. It was unsettling to realize how small her world had been.

She was setting out for a different world now, one that she had always believed was full of unimaginable evils. But how could that be true, when it had brought her Jaren? Her only regret was that she had not vanquished the evil she'd grown up with.

Without thinking, she closed her eyes, and a song she'd never sung before poured out of her. It was an Endlan song, wordless and haunting, and though her voice rang out alone, she could tell it was full of magic. It didn't matter that she hadn't sung it before, or even heard it. Leelo knew in her bones what it was.

A farewell song.

It came from a time before Endla and the Wandering Forest. A time when her people passed only stories on to their children instead of lies. A time of peace and prosperity that required nothing more than the sacrifice of hard work and patience, rather than blood and innocence.

The Forest's reign had come to an end.

When at last she finished singing and opened her eyes again, the Wandering Forest was gone.

Chapter Fifty-Five

By some miracle, Leelo and Jaren made it to the mainland unscathed. The boat's hull, however, was cracked in several places, and Jaren knew Fiona had been right. It wouldn't make it back for another voyage, and a new boat was useless without the sap to protect it from the poison. In the distance, Endla sat small and smoking, the pine grove gone from the horizon. For a few minutes, they lay side by side on the narrow beach, their chests heaving as they struggled to catch their breath.

"What now?" Jaren asked. He knew what he wanted more than anything: to see his family. But from here, it was impossible to tell what had happened on Endla when the Forest vanished, and he knew Leelo must be desperate to learn what had become of her mother.

Leelo sat up, staring out over the black water. "I know we can't go back now. I just wish I knew if she was all right."

Jaren helped her to her feet. They were both exhausted, but staying here for what remained of the night was unimaginable. They began to walk, and while Jaren had once believed it was Endla calling to him, he knew now it had been Leelo all along.

By the time they made it to his house, daylight was just beginning to creep among the tightly curled ferns and damp undergrowth. Leelo's mouth was open in awe for most of the journey. Every now and then, she would pause to pluck a berry from a bush or a flower from the ground, and she would pause, listening and waiting, to see if the forest would retaliate. And every time it didn't, she smiled at Jaren like she was witnessing a little miracle. Those smiles kept him going, though every muscle in his body ached and he was unable to stop his mind from spinning, knowing he was about to confront the truth he had just learned, that he was not who he had always believed he was.

Klaus's rented cottage had never really felt like home to Jaren, but seeing it now, quiet and nestled among a small copse of birch and elm, he felt the relief he'd been longing for since he landed on Endla. Having Leelo with him, his missing puzzle piece, made it even more profound.

They paused at the door, Leelo looking at Jaren expectantly. Should he knock first? Walk in and surprise them? He knew that for his family, his appearance would be like he was coming back from the dead. He didn't want to scare them. But the thought of waiting even one more minute to see them was unbearable. Hesitantly, he knocked.

It took several moments for the door to creak open. It was Stepan, his beard several inches longer than Jaren remembered. He rubbed at his eyes as if waking from a dream.

"Hello, Father," Jaren said, before he was engulfed in an enormous bear hug and the air was squeezed from his lungs.

"Girls!" Stepan shouted, and a moment later three familiar faces were at the door behind him, their eyes bright and shining with tears. They surrounded Jaren, exclaiming and squealing like a trio of elated squirrels.

"You're home! I can't believe you're really home!"

"Saints, we've missed you."

Someone pinched Jaren on the arm, hard, and his eyes shot to Tadpole's.

"What was that for?" he demanded.

"Just making sure this isn't a dream," she chirped and went back to jumping in delight.

"That's not how it works!" he shouted, but he was laughing, too.

Finally, when they had all affirmed that he was indeed alive and well, they stepped back and noticed for the first time that Jaren was not alone.

"Hello," Leelo said shyly, and Jaren's heart threatened to explode in his chest from happiness.

He pulled her against his side. "Father, Summer, Story, Tadpole—"

"My name isn't Tadpole," Sofia hissed.

Jaren ignored her. "Everyone, this is Leelo Hart. She came from Endla. She's going to be staying with us for a while."

Jaren's family made a valiant effort not to react in a way that would offend Leelo, but he couldn't help noticing the way Summer shrank back a little and Tadpole gasped in wonder.

"Like, a *real* Endlan?" she asked. "Not like Tate."

Jaren was about to admonish his sister for being rude, but Leelo's face broke out in a radiant smile.

"You know my brother?"

"Of course we do. He's staying with Lupin."

Now it was Jaren's turn to gasp, but Tadpole had already grabbed Leelo's hand and pulled her into the house.

"It's too early to go there now," Stepan said, following his family inside like this was how things had always been.

Jaren smiled as he closed the door behind him, marveling at how this too-small house suddenly didn't feel crowded at all.

After stuffing Leelo and Jaren full of food, his sisters took Leelo into their bedroom to find her some clean clothing, and, he felt certain, to marvel over her hair and argue over who would get to brush it.

Jaren and Stepan tidied up and sat down on their little couch, which easily fit all three girls but was a tight squeeze for two grown men.

"I'm so sorry," Jaren started, at the same time his father said, "We missed you terribly."

"It was foolish," Jaren went on. "I kept going back to Lake Luma after that first night, when I camped near it. I thought it was just curiosity at first, but it was something more than that that made me go back. Something more powerful than me."

His father stroked his beard like it was a new nervous habit, and his brow was creased with worry. "What happened out there, son?"

"I got lost. And then I found Leelo," Jaren said. And then, in a softer voice, "I found home."

Stepan turned his head so Jaren wouldn't see his face begin to crumple.

"It's true, isn't it? I was born on Endla?"

Stepan swallowed and wiped his palms on his thighs. Jaren had never seen him so discomfited. "Jaren, you are my child as much as your sisters are. I have loved you since the day you came to us as a tiny wee babe."

Jaren knew his father believed what he was saying, but the fact was that he was different from the rest of them. He always had been. "And Story?"

"She is not your twin, no."

Jaren had suspected as much, but hearing his father say the words out loud hit him like a blow to the chest. She was his twin. They had shared a womb. They had grown up in lockstep, sometimes leapfrogging each other in height but going through all their milestones together. They lost their first tooth on the same day. Of all his siblings, Jaren felt a connection with Story that was special. And it wasn't because he was the only boy. It was in spite of it.

"Don't cry," Stepan said, gently wiping a tear away from Jaren's cheek with the calloused edge of his thumb.

He wasn't sure why he was so sad. He didn't love Story or any of his other family members any less because of this revelation. But he felt a loss just the same.

"How?" Jaren managed finally.

Stepan sat back a little. "Klaus's wife found you, near the lake. It was wintertime. At first she thought you were just another stone by the water's edge. But then she heard a cry. You were wrapped in a beautiful knit blanket, but it was covered by the snow. She wasn't sure how long you'd been out there. You were so small and barely breathing. She could tell that you were just a few days old, at most."

He rose and walked to the cedar chest in the corner, the one where they kept all of Sylvie's good linens. Jaren waited for his father to rifle around in the chest for a few minutes before he came back and handed him a blanket he'd seen before but never thought much of. Now, though, he wondered how he hadn't noticed it before.

The blanket was woven of soft wool in bright stripes that had been carefully hand dyed. It was quite clearly Endlan handiwork. There was even a chance that someone he knew had made it.

Stepan looked at his son. "Shall I go on?"

Jaren nodded.

"Understandably, Klaus and his wife, Ana, were distraught at the idea of an abandoned infant, but they didn't know if you'd been left on purpose. There was a hole in the ice, a couple meters from the shore. It looked like someone had fallen in."

"Leelo's mother thinks my birth mother drowned trying to save me."

"Ana believed as much. She was sure that the person had shoved you across the ice to safety when they went in."

Jaren didn't know why his birth mother had been leaving Endla, although after everything he'd witnessed, he could guess. And if it had happened once, maybe it had happened again. There could be others like him, Endlans living among outsiders with no idea who they really were.

"Ana and Klaus cared for you as best they could, but they already had five children of their own to look after. Klaus knew we had one daughter, Summer, and a brand-new baby girl, Story. Her delivery was a difficult one, and your mother wasn't sure if she'd be able to have more children. But we had always wanted a son. So Klaus came to Tindervale with you and asked if we would adopt you. Your mother was nursing you alongside Story before I could even respond."

Jaren smiled at that. They may not have shared a womb, but they were still twins. Nothing would change that.

"Did you know about Lake Luma, about the Endlans?" he asked. "Did you suspect that I could have magic?" For the first time, he didn't trip over the word. How could he deny it anymore when he'd *felt* it? When he and Leelo sang together, they were no longer separate entities. They were one. He'd never felt so whole and right. He only wished his happiness hadn't come at Leelo's expense. He knew she wanted to be with him, but she had never planned to leave her mother behind.

"We assumed you were one of their voiceless children, the incantu. Why else would your parents be taking you away?"

He'd been an infant. It would have been far too soon to tell if he was incantu. But his father couldn't have known that. "They didn't want me to grow up on Endla. That's all we can know for certain."

Stepan nodded slowly. "I suppose you must be right. I'm so sorry. If I'd known, I never would have moved here." He hung his head, looking so sad Jaren thought his own heart might break.

"It doesn't change anything," Jaren said finally. "I'm still your son. My sisters are still my sisters. And my birth parents were right: I didn't belong on Endla."

"But what about the girl, Leelo?"

"She didn't belong there, either. I don't think anyone truly does."

A moment later, the girls emerged from the bedroom. Leelo was clad in a russet dress of Sofia's, who was shorter than Leelo but nearly the same size. Her hair was loose with a few scattered braids throughout. Tadpole's doing, no doubt.

Leelo's beauty took his breath away, as it always did, and once again he had the feeling that she was not of this world. Even in the morning dimness of their house, she drew the light to her. It shined off her fair hair and translucent skin. She wasn't meant for Endla, perhaps, but he wasn't sure she was meant for Bricklebury, either. A fae kingdom, perhaps.

She blushed, and he realized he'd been staring. "You look beautiful," he said, even though he knew his sisters were watching and judging.

"Thank you," she said softly. "So do you."

Jaren ignored Summer's blush, Story's wide eyes, and Tadpole's snort of laughter. "Come on," he said, taking Leelo's hand. "Let's go find your brother."

Chapter Fifty-Six

Leelo's heartbeat quickened when they came over a rise to find a lush green meadow spread before them. A blonde girl and a smaller, dark-haired figure were tending to a row of beehives. The girl waved and turned to help the smaller figure remove the netting covering his head.

Story had explained how Tate came to be with Lupin's family on the walk over. "I was out searching for Jaren one day when three incantu children materialized from the forest," she'd said. Tate, Violet, and Bizhan. She'd gone to Lupin for help, not knowing who else to ask, and together they had found temporary homes for the other two children. Meanwhile, Lupin and Tate had bonded, so her parents had agreed to take him in.

When Tate looked up and saw Leelo, he came running across the field at full speed, nearly knocking her over with the force of his embrace. She covered Tate's head and face in kisses until he'd finally had enough and gently pushed her away.

"What are you doing here?" he asked, his expression wavering between joy and fear. He had grown in just the short time since he left, she thought. Or maybe distance was helping her to see him as he'd always been.

"It's a very long story."

"Where's Mama?" He looked at the gathered people, as if expecting to see her face among them.

"She couldn't make it, Tate. I'm so sorry." She almost added that she was safe, but the truth was, she didn't know that. And she couldn't lie to her brother again.

"Why don't we go to the house to talk?" Lupin said after a moment. "Honey on warm bread makes everything a little easier."

Leelo studied her, trying to decide if she recognized her face at all. She could be Vance's older sister, she thought, or any one of the incantu who had left over the course of Leelo's life. So many broken families, and yet, for the people like Lupin who found new families, perhaps life on the mainland was not the worst thing that could happen to someone.

"Thank you for taking care of him," Leelo said as they walked toward the house. She still couldn't believe that she was no longer on Endla, that she was on the mainland among outsiders. "I'm so grateful that he's safe and healthy."

"We're happy to do it," Lupin said, ruffling Tate's hair.

Leelo pointed to the bundle of netting in Tate's arms. "You don't wear one of those when you tend to the bees?"

Lupin shook her head. "I don't need it."

"She sings to the bees," Tate explained as Lupin drifted ahead to catch up with Story.

"What do you mean?" Leelo asked. "She's incantu."

"She says she doesn't have Endlan magic, but I've watched

her. The bees go into some kind of trance when she sings. They land on her, but they never sting her."

Leelo thought on this as they made their way up to a neat log cabin with red geraniums in the windows, just like Leelo's house. She wondered if she'd misunderstood magic this entire time, if maybe Endlan magic, as she thought of it, wasn't Endlan at all. Maybe everyone had a little magic in them, if you knew where to look.

Lupin's mother, Marta, welcomed the group into the house, serving up fresh bread and honey that melted in Leelo's mouth. As the two families caught up with each other and Jaren explained what had happened to him, she shook her head at how wrong she'd been about outsiders.

"Is Mr. Rebane home?" Stepan asked Marta when they finished eating.

"He should be back any minute," she said, then turned to Tate. "If we're lucky, your father will be with him."

Leelo nearly choked on her last bite of bread. "What?"

"He moved away from Bricklebury a few years ago," Marta explained. "After Tate told us about him, my husband went to see if he could find him. That was four days ago now, so I expect he'll be returning soon."

Tate, who only moments before had been scarfing down his own slice of bread and honey, glanced at Leelo. She couldn't tell what his expression meant, if he was ashamed of discovering that he had a different father or perhaps worried that Leelo would be ashamed of him.

"It's okay," she said, covering Tate's hand with hers. "I know about Nigel. Nothing has changed. You'll always be my brother."

While they waited for Oskar to return, Lupin and Story filled in the holes of what had happened while Jaren was gone. Story had had adventures of her own while searching for Jaren, including meeting a group of incantu who lived in an underground den near Lake Luma. Leelo and Jaren couldn't help noticing the way Story blushed every time she mentioned their leader, Grimm.

In less than a day, Leelo's world had grown in scope to an almost overwhelming degree. But every time she started to feel like it was all too much to take in, Jaren took her hand under the table and squeezed it, and she remembered that she was not alone.

After they finished eating, the front door opened, admitting two men. The first was clearly Mr. Rebane. He went to his wife and daughter, embracing them, then gave Tate's hair a warm ruffle. A narrow figure stood behind him in the shadows.

Marta cleared her throat and nodded at the man, and Oskar turned to look behind him. "Goodness, I nearly forgot! Everyone, I'd like you to meet Nigel Thorn."

A man with shoulder-length raven hair parted down the middle stepped forward. He was fair, like Tate, with the same nearly black eyes. *Is that what Tate will look like when he grows up?* Leelo wondered, trying to come to terms with the fact that this man had fallen in love with her mother once. That her mother had loved him.

"You must be Tate," Nigel said, approaching the boy who looked like a miniature version of himself.

Tate nodded and stepped closer so he could shake Nigel's outstretched hand. "It's nice to meet you, Mr. Thorn."

Nigel smiled down at him. "It's nice to meet you, too. A

little strange, considering that up until two days ago, I had no idea you existed."

Tate ducked his head. "I know what you mean."

"Well, then, I suppose we're both new at this." He crouched down so that he was eye to eye with Tate. "How is your mother?"

Tate glanced at Leelo, looking a little desperate. "She…"

Leelo rose and went to stand beside her brother. "She's as well as she can be," she said gently, for Tate's sake. "I'm Leelo. Fiona's daughter."

Now Nigel was the one to look a bit helpless. "Leelo? Saints. You were just a little girl…" He seemed to catch himself and glanced around at the other people in the room. He straightened and turned to Mr. Rebane. "I clearly have some catching up to do. I don't think I'll make it back to the farm tonight. Is there an inn I can stay at? One that allows dogs?"

For the first time, Leelo noticed an enormous animal with shaggy gray fur who had snuck in behind Nigel and made himself at home on the sofa. For a second, she thought it was a wolf, and she nearly leaped into Jaren's arms.

But Jaren didn't seem afraid. "Is this your dog?" he asked Nigel.

"Wolfhound, yes." He whistled, and the dog placed his front legs on the floor, pausing to stretch before trotting over to Nigel. "This is Percy." He turned to Tate with a wink. "Your little brother."

At that, the massive creature jumped up and placed his paws on Tate's shoulders, nearly knocking him over.

"Sir Percival!" Nigel grabbed the dog by his leather collar

and pulled him off Tate. He smiled sheepishly. "Apologies, Tate. He gets a little excited when he meets new people."

Leelo was still reeling from the fact that this man had referred to the dog as Tate's brother. As in, they were both Nigel's sons. She didn't know what she'd expected, but she certainly hadn't expected him to accept Tate quite so readily.

"Tate," Lupin said. "Why don't we go and get some blankets? Mr. Thorn can sleep in your room. You can sleep on the floor of mine, if you like."

Tate looked to Leelo. She took his hand and followed Lupin to the hall cupboard, where the linens were kept.

"You look a little worried," Lupin said softly to Tate. "Are you nervous?"

He took the blankets from her. "A bit."

"He seems like a nice man, but I understand if you need more time."

"But what about your parents?"

"My parents will let you stay here as long as I say. All right?" She must have seen Leelo's expression, because she cleared her throat. "Both of you are welcome, of course."

"Oh, I think I'll be staying at Jaren's house for now. But Tate can choose." She turned to her little brother and managed a smile. "Don't worry, Tate. Things are a little confusing right now, but we'll get it sorted out."

Lupin smirked. "Besides, how dangerous can a man who names his dog *Sir Percival* be?"

To Leelo's relief, Tate came back with her to Jaren's house that night. Leelo and Tate were given Jaren's loft to sleep in, while he slept on the sofa downstairs. Nigel was spending the night at the Rebanes, and they had all agreed to meet up at the market in the morning.

Leelo and Tate were curled up together just like they had in his little room under the stairs. She could almost convince herself they were back there if she closed her eyes tight enough. But this house didn't smell the same, and she knew Mama was not here with them. Every time Leelo thought of her, guilt and sorrow threatened to drag her under.

"Tate? Are you awake?" she whispered in the dark.

"Mmm-hmm."

"How are you feeling about everything?"

"I don't know," he admitted. "It's a lot."

"It is. You've been very brave, little brother. I'm proud of you. Mama would be proud of you, too."

"Is she all right?" he asked. "Really?"

"She's ill," Leelo said. "But I think she's getting better."

He nodded. "When will we go back for her?"

"When the ice freezes. I promise."

"That's a long time from now."

"I know. I wish we could go sooner." She chewed her lip for a moment. "Tate, when did you find out about Nigel?"

"Mama told me, not long before I left Endla."

"That must have been difficult for both of you."

He shrugged, and Leelo had to remind herself that Tate didn't remember Kellan. He had never known any father, really. "She said that there was someone here who wanted me. And that if I was with him, she wouldn't have to worry about me. I didn't really know what to think. Especially when I was such a burden to Aunt Ketty, and she's known me my entire life."

Even free of Endla, Leelo felt bitter resentment toward her

aunt for what she'd done to their family. "Ketty was wrestling with her own demons," she said. "It didn't give her any right to treat you the way she did. But it was never about you. It was never about any of us."

"I feel sorry for her," he whispered, and before Leelo could reply, he fell asleep.

In the morning, Tate seemed nervous as they dressed and headed out to meet the Rebanes and Nigel. Leelo wasn't sure when she and Jaren would be able to talk about everything they'd been through, although for now, maybe that was better. They hadn't had time to process anything yet.

Nigel Thorn hadn't been back in Bricklebury for a few years, but he still had plenty of friends, judging by all the people who came over to talk to him as they passed through town. Percy trotted next to him, a gentle giant, they had come to realize.

"Why did you leave Bricklebury?" Leelo asked him.

He glanced down at her with dark, kind eyes. "I raise wolf-hounds now, in the countryside. There's more room for the hounds to run. Besides, the hunting here wasn't good anymore. The forest was changing."

She raised her eyebrows. "What do you mean?"

"It wasn't like Endla," he said quickly. "I don't mean that. It just…it didn't feel safe anymore."

"Do you have a family?" It was probably none of her business, but she wanted to know if he still cared for her mother the way Fiona clearly did for him. If maybe her mother still had the chance for a happy ending after all these years.

"No," he said. "I never married." Leelo had the sense he

wanted to say something about Fiona, but he must have been feeling shy as well, because he didn't speak anymore.

At the market, Leelo walked with Jaren, one eye on all the goods for sale and the other on Nigel. She knew her mother had trusted him, but she'd only known him for a few months, and that had been years ago. She would let Tate make his own decisions, but not before she'd had a chance to study him.

After he'd finished catching up with the townspeople, Nigel bought three sandwiches and invited Tate and Leelo to have lunch with him while the Rebanes and Kasks did their shopping.

"Do you want me to come with you?" Jaren asked, his arm still wound tightly through Leelo's.

"It's okay," she said, kissing him on the cheek. "I think this is something we need to do alone."

They walked to the bank of a small creek and settled on the grass, where Nigel passed out the sandwiches. "So tell me, Tate, how are you liking life on the mainland?"

"It's all right," Tate mumbled around his food. Leelo was tempted to tell him to be more polite, but Nigel wasn't her father, and they would have to find their own footing together.

"Are you enjoying beekeeping?"

"I didn't like the bees at first. But I'm used to them now. I got stung a few times at the beginning, but once I learned how to be still around them, they stopped."

Nigel nodded. "That's a little like me with the dogs. At first, they were big and intimidating. But once you get used to them, you realize they would never hurt you on purpose."

Leelo glanced at Nigel. She suspected he was talking about more than just wolfhounds.

"It must have been difficult," Nigel continued. "Leaving

the only home you've ever known. And it must have broken your mother's heart to let you go."

Tate glanced at Leelo. She didn't want to interfere in their relationship, but she could see that her brother was uncomfortable with these kinds of questions. If she was ever going to get to know him, she needed to talk to Nigel alone.

"Tate, why don't you go and get us some of that fresh lemonade I saw on sale," Leelo said, handing him a few coins that Jaren had given her. "Take your time."

He nodded, looking relieved, and hurried away.

"I'm sorry," Nigel said almost immediately after he was gone. "I shouldn't have brought up your mother."

Leelo tossed some of the crust of her sandwich to a pair of ducks swimming in the creek. "It's all right. I haven't told Tate everything yet. There are things I'm not sure he's ready to know." Things she wasn't ready to talk about.

"Does your father know?" he asked after a long silence.

Saints, he thought Kellan was still alive. Why wouldn't he? The last thing he knew, Fiona was married with one young daughter. "My father died," Leelo said. "When Tate was just a baby."

All the color drained from Nigel's face. "How? When?"

Leelo explained about her father and Uncle Hugo, stressing again that Tate didn't know any of this and she wasn't ready to tell him. He had been through enough already.

When she was finished, Nigel blinked and cleared his throat. "I'm so sorry. I had no idea. Your poor mother. She must have had a very difficult time after your father passed, raising two children on her own."

"She did. She's had a hard life."

"I hate to think I made it harder."

Leelo swallowed down the lump rising in her throat. "She misses you."

Nigel looked up at her in surprise. "She spoke about me?"

Leelo nodded. "Yes. Just before I left."

He inhaled a deep breath and released it slowly. "This is a lot to take in."

"I know."

"It seems as though you have friends here in Bricklebury. And I know we've only just met. But I want you to know that if you and Tate would like to live with me, you have a home. Always. Sir Percival and I would love to have you."

Leelo ran her fingers through the grass, avoiding his gaze. "Thank you. That's very generous." She was grateful for the offer, though she couldn't imagine going to live with Nigel now. "You know, Tate was just his nickname," she said, desperate for a change in subject.

"Oh?"

"Our aunt came up with Tate. His real name is Ilu."

"Ilu. What does that mean?"

"Precious one."

He smiled. "That's a lovely name."

"It is," Leelo said, glancing up to see her brother walking toward them, struggling to hold three jars of lemonade. She rose to help him, thinking of all the things that she'd once held dear—a lace-trimmed dress, a striped feather, a wooden box engraved with swans—and knew in her soul that nothing was more precious than this.

Chapter Fifty-Seven

Over the next few months, the Rebanes, the Kasks, and Nigel helped build a small cottage for Leelo and Tate, close to the Kasks'. It was hardly bigger than the shack Jaren had stayed in on Endla, but it was far sturdier, and more importantly, it was theirs. Leelo hadn't been ready to move to Nigel's house, to be so far away from Jaren and, if she was being honest, Fiona. She was always in Leelo's thoughts, helping to guide her when she felt lost and afraid, which happened more than she wanted to admit now. Before, she'd known her place in the world, even if she hadn't always agreed with it. She didn't feel prepared to run her own household, to make all the decisions for herself and Tate. Still, Nigel was a part of their lives now, and Leelo was grateful for it.

Tate helped Lupin with the bees and often spent time at her house with the Rebanes, who still thought of him as their foster son. Leelo had gotten to know Lupin a little—as much as she could, anyway. There was something that separated them, probably the fact that Leelo had chosen to leave Endla, where Lupin had been forced to. Leelo and Jaren were the first Endlans ever to leave by choice and survive, as far as she could tell. And she was the only one who knew the songs.

But she had soon discovered that she didn't have to sing. Or, if she wanted to, she could sing the sorts of songs that Jaren taught her. Sometimes they sang together, and the harmony of their voices would remind her of being home, and she would feel an ache in her chest that she knew was homesickness, even if she didn't want to admit to missing Endla. Here, when she ran her fingers through the grass, there was no answering vibration. When the trees rustled overhead, they weren't speaking to each other. There was no hum of magic in the air, and though she knew that the Forest's magic had been evil in many ways, she missed it.

She missed helping Sage with the lambs and gathering berries and herbs in the Forest. She missed swimming in the spring-fed pools. She even missed Watcher duty sometimes, sitting on the shore as the sun rose across the water, hearing the wild swans trumpet in the sky, praying that they would land somewhere else. She missed the festivals, the way Endlan voices would join together so perfectly that it was almost as if they were one voice, the voice of Endla itself, releasing its cry into the universe. She missed feeling like she was a part of something.

It was strange, to be a stranger. To feel the eyes of every villager following her when she went into town. No one was ever cruel to her, and over time they began to speak to her—and eventually accept her, when they knew she wasn't going to lure away their children with one of her wicked songs or seduce their partners in the night. She was just a girl, they would come to realize. A girl wanting to be accepted, a girl who had never wanted to harm anything.

But there was Jaren, and his very existence helped on even the hardest days. His sisters had warmed to her, especially Sofia, who followed Leelo around like she was some kind of mythical creature.

You still have magic, even if you don't sing, Jaren had said to Leelo one time as she lay in his arms, winding his fingers through her hair gently. It reminded her of what Sage had told her, and she reached into her pocket to touch the crude swan carving her cousin had made.

She still missed Sage sometimes, and even, every now and then, Aunt Ketty. Leelo couldn't help feeling that if she'd known the truth all along, things could have been different. Ketty had killed Uncle Hugo, but she'd done it to protect her sister, and that altered Leelo's perspective of everything. It was such a Ketty thing to do, to defend one thing at the complete expense of another. To be so afraid of what the truth could do that she would literally bury it. Sage had been fed a different poison than Fiona, but it was no less bitter, no less destructive.

Mostly, though, she missed her mother. Knowing that she was so close yet so far away kept her up at night. Tate still cried for Fiona in his sleep, and while Leelo did her best to comfort him, she often wished there was someone there to comfort her.

One November night, she, Tate, Jaren, and Nigel were sitting on the porch of Leelo's cottage, wrapped in blankets and scarves against the cold.

"The lake will be frozen soon," Nigel said. "Two more months, at most."

As badly as Leelo wanted to get her mother, a part of her was afraid of what they would find when they went. What if Mama didn't want to come with them? Worse still, what if she hadn't survived? At least from here Leelo could convince herself that things on Endla were as they'd always been.

Leelo had told Nigel about Ketty poisoning her mother, but she'd kept that and many other things from Tate. She knew one day she'd have to tell him everything, but she didn't want to add to his heartache. Hers was profound enough for both of them.

"Yes," Leelo said. "We'll go as soon as it's safe to cross."

Nigel smiled and Sir Percival sighed, tucking his long nose under the edge of Nigel's blanket.

"What about Story's friends?" Tate offered. "The other incantu. I bet they miss their families, too."

Nigel and Leelo shared a glance. Tate was right. If anyone had an interest in uncovering the truth, it was the exiled children of Endla, the ones who had lost everything because of the Wandering Forest.

"I bet Story would be happy to pay Grimm a visit," Jaren said, and their laughter echoed in the dying light.

They waited two months before they made the journey back to Endla. January was the coldest month, when they could be sure the ice was as solid as possible. Leelo believed the others would be safe from any singing, now that the Forest was gone, but they wore wool in their ears, just in case.

Grimm, the leader of the incantu, had managed to gather

up more than twenty to join them. They were children who
had been forcibly taken from their parents and thrust into the
world alone. As Tate had guessed, they wanted a chance to re-
unite with their families. And many of them wanted answers.

It had taken a lot of convincing to keep Tate at home with
Lupin and Jaren's sisters, where he would be safe. But Oskar,
Stepan, and several other villagers had agreed to come. Leelo
stood among them now, gripping Jaren's hand and praying
that whatever they found, Mama was safe.

They crossed the ice silently. Leelo was half-sure the ice
would give way beneath them, but they were spread out, and
it was a particularly ferocious winter, like the year Nigel had
accidentally gone to Endla. The ice held.

As they drew closer, Leelo couldn't help but notice how
desolate the island looked. There were a few remaining trees,
some bushes and shrubs, but what stood out starkly against
the snow were the cottages. Miraculously, they hadn't all
burned. She could see candles glowing in several windows,
and the familiar scent of woodsmoke pluming from the chim-
neys gave her hope.

But though she was relieved to see that at least some Endlans had survived the fire, this place that she had once loved
no longer felt like home. It felt sinister and dead, not like the
living, thriving Forest she'd once known. There were no animals rustling in the brush, no leaves whispering overhead.
It was winter, and the Forest was always quiet at this time of
year. But it was a different kind of silence that lay over the
island like a blanket, and, for a moment, Leelo was hit by a
wave of fear, that perhaps no one had survived, that it was
ghosts who lit those candles and sat by those fires.

As they approached the pine grove, a shape materialized just feet in front of them. Leelo gasped. Wildcat eyes and fiery hair blazed out of the white and black of the winter landscape.

"Sage," Leelo breathed. Despite everything, despite the hurt and betrayal, Leelo still cared about her. She wasn't sure if she could call it love. But loyalty was a difficult thing to quell, and Leelo wanted to believe that Sage would have made different choices in another world.

"You came back." Sage's voice was so quiet it was almost a whisper. She took a step toward Leelo. "Or am I dreaming again?"

"It's not a dream," Leelo said, her voice cracking.

Sage looked at Jaren, her jaw clenched. "I didn't think I'd ever see you again. It's been so quiet here."

"Where is Aunt Ketty?" Leelo asked, half expecting her to appear at the sound of her name, like a demon summoned.

Sage shook her head. "Gone. She disappeared the night of the fire, when the Forest vanished. I'm not sure if she died or if…"

"If what?" Leelo asked.

"If the Forest took her with it."

Leelo felt her stomach twist with horror. She didn't know what fate Ketty deserved, but surely it wasn't this, to be taken by the very thing she had sacrificed everything for.

"Grimm?"

They all turned to see a man in his fifties emerge from a cottage, his weathered face wet with tears. "Grimm, is that you?"

"Uncle?"

"It really is you," the man said.

Leelo and Jaren stepped back as the two embraced and more Endlans began to come out of what Leelo now realized was hiding. They must have seen them approaching and taken shelter. And something about that, about her once proud people hiding in the face of danger, made her heart ache.

Slowly, one by one, Endlans began to search among the incantu for their lost loved ones. After that, there was a lot of crying, some joyful, some pained, as families learned of the fate of their sons or daughters, sisters or brothers. But slowly, one by one, the twenty incantu who had come with them dispersed among the crowd.

Through all of this, Sage had stayed close to Leelo, but she hadn't spoken.

"Where's Mama?" Leelo finally asked. She'd been waiting for her to join them like so many of the other Endlans, but she hadn't, and Leelo was beginning to fear the worst.

"Come on," Sage said. "I'll take you to her."

Sage was dressed in furs and leather, a large knife strapped to her thigh, Leelo's old bow across her shoulder. She looked like she had prepared for battle. But as Leelo gazed deep into her cousin's eyes for the first time that day, she saw that all of the fight had gone out of her.

As they approached the cottage that had been Leelo's home for so long, she noticed that there was no smoke coming from the chimney. When she opened the front door, the bells, which were frozen under a layer of ice, didn't ring their cheerful welcome. The house was so cold and still that Leelo was convinced her cousin had brought her to her mother's grave.

And then she heard a familiar creak on the stairs, and Leelo collapsed in relief.

"Is it really you?" Mama descended the stairs slowly, but though she was thin and pale, she wasn't clinging to the banister for support. She knelt down next to Leelo and gathered her into her arms, and now it was Leelo's turn to cling to something, to be held like a child and comforted by her mother.

"Are you all right?" Leelo managed between sobs.

"I'm fine. A little cold, but I'm getting stronger by the day." Of course. With Ketty gone, she wasn't being poisoned anymore.

"I'm sorry I let the fire go out," Sage said, and Leelo whipped around to face her, having forgotten she was still there.

"I was lighting it when I sensed something was out there."

"You're still living together?" Leelo asked Mama. "After everything she did? What happened to the Hardings?" She turned to Sage, unable to keep the venom out of her voice. "Did they abandon you, too?"

Sage gave a tight shake of her head. "I told them I wouldn't marry Hollis."

Fiona pulled Leelo's face back to her. "Sage is still family. The only family I had left."

Leelo rose and helped Fiona to her feet, then turned to her cousin. "Thank you for looking after her," she managed.

Sage lowered her gaze. "It's the least I could do." After a minute, she cleared her throat. "What happens now, Lo?"

Leelo nearly scoffed. Was it possible that all this time, Sage had been waiting for someone to tell her what to do? Leelo supposed that without Watching, without Ketty's orders or a family to care for, Sage must be feeling lost. She'd never wanted anything other than to be a good Endlan. "That's up to you, I suppose."

Sage grabbed Leelo's hands. "I'm so sorry. I'm sorry I didn't trust you. I thought I was doing what was best for our family. I thought I was keeping you safe. I *love* you, Leelo."

Leelo swallowed back tears. It was like her mother said: too much of anything could be a poison. Even love. "I know that's what you believe, Sage. But I don't know if I can forgive you for the way you treated Tate. You tried to *kill* Jaren. You only stopped when you learned he was Endlan. Out there, in the world, most people don't have magic. At least not the kind you and I are used to. If you can't accept that those people deserve to live and be happy just as much as any Endlan, then I don't think you should leave here."

Sage blinked back tears, her eyes darting between Leelo and Fiona. "But my mother is gone. I'd be all alone."

Leelo didn't answer.

"What would I do if I stayed?" she asked, her voice high and thin.

A part of Leelo—the part of her that had spent hours exploring in the Forest with Sage, that had been spared from so much blood and death by her cousin, that had depended on Sage to be strong when she believed she was weak—wanted to embrace her. But that part of Leelo had grown farther away in the past year, a year that had been half Watching, half unlearning the lies she'd been fed all her life. Sage would have to unlearn those lies for herself. Leelo couldn't do that for her; no one could.

"Are you leaving?" Sage asked finally, when she realized Leelo wasn't going to ask her to come.

Leelo stepped over the threshold and into the clearing surrounding their cottage. She looked out over the few skeletal trees and snow-covered ground, thinking how strange it was to see this place that had once been as familiar as her own reflection without the presence of the Forest. Against the snow, a winter fox appeared, picking its way silently across the clearing.

A sad smile spread across Leelo's face. Maybe Sage had been right when she'd compared herself to a fox. Foxes were, above all, survivors. She turned back to Sage, to ask if she had seen it, too.

But Sage was gone.

Many of the Endlans dispersed in the coming days and weeks, abandoning their homes to resettle out in the world. Some incantu children reunited with their families, like Bizhan and his two mothers. Other relationships were too damaged to repair. Violet remained with her adopted family, and the rest of the Hardings moved elsewhere. Isola and her family moved to Bricklebury, however, and Leelo saw them frequently. She even helped them build their new henhouse, which they took great pains to ensure was entirely fox-proof.

Fiona came to live in the little cottage that Tate and Leelo shared, and though she was recovering, it was obvious that she was permanently weakened by the years of poisoning. Leelo hoped that fresh air, healthy food, and never having to work again would help restore her to some semblance of her former self, but she wouldn't count on it. In the meantime, Leelo began to knit the beautiful clothing her mother taught her to make and brought it to the market, where people came from miles around to buy her goods.

Sage had not followed them off the island, though Leelo

didn't know if she had stayed in the end. She could find Leelo someday, if she wanted to. Leelo was just grateful to have her mother and Tate so close, in their own little home where they made all the rules. Where love was found in abundance, and no one was ever scolded for burning a pie or spilling the sugar.

Spring was coming to the mountain, and Summer, who was now engaged to her carpenter, smiled at them all knowingly as they walked to market one day. "Spring came early this year," she said, gazing up at her fiancé.

Tadpole smirked and muttered under her breath, "No one likes a know-it-all," and Story elbowed her in the ribs.

Nigel and Fiona walked side by side, but they were shy around each other, as Leelo and Jaren had once been. Still, it was obvious there was love between them, and there was no reason to rush that love. That was one of the greatest gifts leaving Endla had granted them all: time.

Perhaps it shouldn't have surprised them when the Forest did what its name had foretold all along: wandered. Once it realized that it was no longer needed or wanted, it had disappeared and traveled somewhere new, where Leelo supposed some other unsuspecting group of people would either accept it or drive it away. And though a part of her wished they had destroyed it, there was another small part of her that was glad it had survived. Just like all of them, it only wanted to live.

Percy bounded ahead of them now, and Leelo rested her head on Jaren's shoulder, drinking in the beauty of the moment. She was beginning to appreciate things as they were, not as they had been or how she wished them to be.

"What are you thinking about?" Jaren asked her, swinging their hands between them.

"Just that I'm happy," she said.

"You look awfully concerned for someone who claims to be happy." He placed his finger on the furrow between her brows, trying to rub it away, then gave up when it was clear it wasn't going to budge.

"I'm not concerned," she said. And for right now, it was true. She wasn't going to worry about the future or try to make sense of the past. She was going to accept things as they were and be grateful. "The sun is just in my eyes."

That moment, a shadow passed overhead, and Leelo and Jaren looked up at the same time to see a pair of wild swans high above them. "I wonder where they're headed," Jaren said.

But Leelo already knew. They were going to Lake Luma, which was once again a safe place to land. She felt a fleeting sadness at the thought of the treeless landscape and abandoned cottages, until Jaren squeezed her hand and kissed her cheek, and she returned to the preciousness of *now*.

If Leelo had gone back, she would have seen that the cottages weren't abandoned at all. The animals that had been driven from their homes when the Forest vanished found shelter between the wooden walls of houses, nestled their families among the sofas and settees. They roosted in chimney tops and raided the pantries. Those wild swans would build their nest on Endla that year, and their offspring would return for generations to come.

Though the roots of the Wandering Forest had been deep, they had not been able to snuff out every little seed blown across the lake by the wind or dropped by a passing bird. Grass would grow next spring, and saplings would begin their long lives on the island. The land would restore itself, as it always had.

And somewhere, on another mountain in another kingdom, a Forest would appear as if by magic. And it would be very hungry.

★ ★ ★ ★ ★

Acknowledgments

I wrote *The Poison Season* during lockdown in Serbia, while homeschooling my kids and spending most of my time in our small guest room turned office. So perhaps it isn't surprising that I wrote about a girl in a very insular world for a change, rather than one who goes on grand adventures. The pandemic has brought so many challenges, but it has also been a time of reflection and soul-searching, and this novel is a direct result of that. Of course, I haven't handled it with nearly as much grace as Leelo does, but then again, she didn't have to listen to the same YouTube meme compilations on repeat while attempting to write a novel.

As always, I couldn't have written this book without the help of my amazing team.

Thank you to everyone at Inkyard Press, especially my editor, Connolly Bottum, without whom this book (and its title) wouldn't exist. Huge thanks to Bess Braswell, Brittany Mitchell, Laura Gianino, and Kathleen Ortiz.

A special thank-you to Charlie Bowater for creating the cover of my dreams. I am so honored that the first thing people will see when they pick up this book is your beautiful artwork.

Thank you to Uwe Stender and the rest of the gang at Triada US.

Big hugs to the Belgrade Embassy community, especially

Erin Hagengruber. Honorable mention goes to Tate Preston for believing people would donate money for a character name in one of my books for a good cause; you didn't win, but you earned your spot! Robin and Zamira won with their son's name, Bizhan. Thank you both for supporting our community.

Thank you to the amazing TPS Street Team, who have helped celebrate every step of this book's progress. Henry and I are so grateful for your encouragement and support!

I wouldn't be where I am today without my writing community, especially Elly Blake, Nikki Roberti Miller, Kristin Dwyer, Autumn Krause, and Helena Hoayun.

A warm shout-out to my family: Mom, Dad, Aaron, Elizabeth, Amy, Jennifer, Patti, and the kiddos. I love and miss you all so much.

Special thanks, as always, to Sarah, for being the person who always gets me, even when I'm at my worst.

Most importantly, to my husband, John, and our sons, Jack and Will, for the laughter, love, and chaos that make up our beautiful life. Home is wherever I'm with you.

And finally, thank you to the readers. Your messages, posts, photos, and reviews are a treasured connection to this wonderful bookish community, no matter where in the world I happen to wander.